MORE RAVES FOR CLAUDIA DAIN!

A KISS TO DIE FOR
RITA Award Finalist

"Dain is a fresh, potent voice in the genre, always striving to make the usual unique, and she succeeds with a book that holds your attention from page one."

—Romantic Times

"A fast-paced, fun read that was hard to put down."
—Old Book Barn Gazette

"Readers will relish this charming story."
—Midwest Book Review

"Dain provides lots of suspense and a nice twist in this nice and creepy tale."

—Booklist

THE WILLING WIFE
Romantic Times Award Finalist

"Excellent character development makes this a memorable story."
—Romantic Times

"Readers will deign this author as one of the subgenre's aristocracy."

—The Best Reviews

TO BURN

"With its wealth of rapid-fire repartee and smoldering sex scenes, Claudia Dain's *To Burn* lives up to its title, spinning a red-hot, medieval-era romance. A seductive romance by one of the genre's fastest rising stars, Dain's newest brims with beguiling characters and historical richness."

CLAUDIA DAIN

The Fall

LEISURE BOOKS NEW YORK CITY

*For my children, who have to live with a writer,
and for my husband, who has to sleep with one.*

A LEISURE BOOK®

September 2004

Published by

Dorchester Publishing Co., Inc.
200 Madison Avenue
New York, NY 10016

ISBN 0-8439-5221-0

Printed in the United States of America.

Visit us on the web at www.dorchesterpub.com.

The Fall

The Tale

And so it was that she was married in good time.

She had completed her fourteenth year and was as soft and warm and golden as the day itself, her hair of burnished and shimmering gold and her eyes as blue as summer. She took her place by her husband's right hand and waited upon his pleasure.

The priest in that darkened chamber of stone murmured his prayers, then turned his eyes from heaven to look upon the bride. He urged her to do rightly by her father and her lord, bringing honor to both their houses by proving the fertility of her loins.

As she was called upon to do, she submitted her will and her life in perfect piety. Her head was bowed and her eyes clear of guile as she promised to do all that a woman should do in this earthly life.

Her father, that strong knight of fame, grunted his own

admonition, which she received in all humility and good heart. The priest blessed her and blessed her new-made husband, he whose name for fighting and for wenching had settled upon him like a warm cloak of comfort. For is a man not made for such doings and such a name? And was he not a man to make a father proud and cause a daughter's heart to tremble in delighted fear at a contract so well made?

Aye, it was so and more. 'Twas a match to make all glad.

The ceremony concluded, both father and priest departed, leaving husband and bride and one more within the cold stone walls of an early spring. One more to watch and witness and wait. One more, a woman of her father's house, to see that what was done was as it must be done. To tell the tale of what befell in that conjugal chamber. To tell what she did see befall between a husband and his virgin bride.

'Twas the second night of their bond, and, by the bride's own telling, there was much to see.

Or rather, by her word, there was much not to be seen.

With a look to the lady of her father's house, the bride bared her breasts to the man who had claimed her. White and round they were and gleamed like alabaster in the soft light of fire as it teased shadow and stone. She cupped her breasts in her hands, holding them for her husband's approval and finding it in his eyes.

The lady of her father's house urged her to keep on, to tempt the man who stood before her, to bring him to fullness, to bring him to need. And so the bride walked across the boards to her husband, her breasts soft and warm, and when she reached him, she stretched out her hand and took him within her grasp.

All this was watched and approved by the lady of her father's name.

And yet he failed to rise.

So yet the lady chided the bride and told her to warm her chill hands by the fire's heat, bringing warmth to them both with a loving grasp gone hot. And so she did, this submissive maid, performing all as she was instructed, her very heart determined to be all that a wife should be to a man.

She knelt by the fire, her breasts a beacon of desire for any man, and held out her hands to the flames. Her hair tumbled down her back and across her shoulders, a shimmering fall of shining gold and amber. A rare maid and beautiful. God had not cheated her of that which men hold dear in their women. Yet her husband's desire was slow to rise, which surely is against God's design and plan.

Her hands warmed, she turned and knelt with the fire at her back, facing her husband, her blue eyes soft and yearning, her manner docile and submissive; in all ways she was a wife to please a man.

At the lady's urging, the man came forth, his member lit by fire as he drew near his wife. With gentle touch, she stroked him, murmuring words of love and duty, willing in this and in all ways to be his wife. With a smile, she stroked him, pressed him, teased him. With a furrowed brow, he watched her, listening to her words, listening to her promises.

Yet still, he did not rise.

And so it was that the lady saw all was as the bride had told it. He could not rise. He could not consummate. The marriage was null. The bride was a maiden still and would a maiden remain.

And so it was that Juliane of Stanora lost the husband arranged for her and became known as Juliane le Gel, for though she was rich in beauty, it was the beauty of winter frost, and men lost their heated passions when she cast her eye upon them.

And so it was that from that day all saw that her eyes were the blue of winter ice, her hair the gold of frost-burned autumn grass, her skin as smoothly cold as white alabaster.

Still, men came to her, drawn to her beauty and her wealth, eager to test themselves against her ice, and yet not a one of them could rise high and hard when she smiled upon them.

And so it was that the legend of Juliane le Gel was born.

Chapter One

"You cannot say that you have not heard of her."

Ulrich shrugged and smiled. "I cannot? Then I will not."

"But what do you think of her?" Roger asked.

"I think she is a lady much spoke of," Ulrich said with a grin. "That is what I think."

"You have gone hard in your age, Ulrich. There was once more of jest and laughter in you. And more of heart."

Ulrich ignored the jibe, ignored the truth of it, ignored the cause of that truth. That was for no ears beyond those of his confessor. He had confessed, been forgiven, set a penance; he was free of it now. If only memory would release him.

But those thoughts were not for now. Now was for joy and laughter. It was a brilliant summer's day, his oldest friend was riding at his side, and joy was for the taking. All he had to do was reach out his hand for it.

"Now answer me, Roger, for I have a question of my own."

"Ask it, then," Roger said easily.

"Has Juliane le Gel not heard of me? Does she tremble, do you think, knowing I am come into her domain? Does she fear the loss of her icy power and her frosty name?" Ulrich said, laughing by the end of his inquiry, his mount tossing his head in what seemed shared humor.

Roger rode at Ulrich's side into the rising heat of a midsummer day. The fields about them were heavy with seed, and high above them flew a hawk in swooping circles against a white-blue sky. It was not often that they found themselves together, and perhaps their friendship was the sweeter for the little time they had to share. A bond of men it was, of men who fought and were paid for fighting in a world of never-ending fights. The world had need of such men, and so they found their way in it, sometimes together, more often apart. Yet friends in all, distance and silence no barrier to their bond.

"You want her to fear you, Ulrich?" Roger said, looking askance at his sometime companion. "Never have I heard it said that fear was what you desired in a woman. Verily, your heart has gone hard as mortar to even jest in such a fashion and against such a lady as Juliane of Stanora."

"You judge me hard, brother," Ulrich said. "Do I not have a legend of my own to protect? Shall I toss years of courtly battles into the mist for this lady of frost? Perhaps she should and does fear me, for you know better than any that I am not afeared of her, no matter the tale told of her and her strange powers over a man's manhood."

"Perhaps you would do well to fear her," Roger said, baiting his friend in arms. "She is formidable by every tale told of her. There is none who can best her in this game of seduction. And many upon many have tried."

Ulrich grinned, seeing clearly where this would lead. "You claim to know me, and yet you charge me with fear of a comely damsel? You know me little, it seems."

"I know you well enough," Roger said, looking back at the horizon. "I know you care less now for the trials of courtly love than you did even three summers past."

"Once a game is mastered, the joys diminish," Ulrich said easily, watching the hawk as it was beset by two sparrows. The hawk seemed unconcerned by the small and noisy warriors diving above her.

"Yet is this not a game that must be mastered with each new lady? To master the game is not to master the woman."

"To master the game is to master all women," Ulrich said. "This I knew even as a man newly made. How that you do not know this most simple truth, Roger?"

"I know enough to know that Juliane is not as any woman you have ever known. Would she have found a place for herself in every troubadour's song from here to Jerusalem if she were not above the mark?"

"She might, if her beauty were great enough."

"And so they sing," Roger said with a chuckle.

"If her father were powerful enough."

"The second stanza, if I remember aright."

"If her resistance to the lure of men and the sweet call

of adoration were as strong as the gates of Fontrevault," Ulrich continued, grinning, enjoying the battle.

"The fourth verse. I remember it well."

"Methinks you are well enamored of this lady, Roger," Ulrich said. "Have at her, if it please you."

Roger bowed his head to Ulrich in mock submission. "Yet she is not yours to bestow, Ulrich. Never yours, nor any man's. And so her legend stands, with nary a scuffle to mar it. You are more changed than I knew," Roger said softly and somewhat sadly. And very deliberately.

"And you are as subtle as a battering ram, which is no change at all," Ulrich said, laughing. "Come, what is your wager?"

Roger grinned, and all pretense of sadness fell from him like a dropped cloak. "Win her," he said. "Be the man to win past Juliane's frost. Melt her, if you can."

"She is a virgin and a lady," Ulrich said, turning from his friend to look upon the horizon. "I will not wager on such a thing."

"She has been married and set loose. Many upon many women wear that cloak, and Juliane is of their number."

"A virgin still," Ulrich said. "I will not sweetly steal from her what can never be replaced. That is a game I will not play."

"Let her a virgin stay, if your honor will have it so," Roger said.

"Trust in that," Ulrich said, looking hard at Roger. "Her virginity is beyond my reach and will remain so. I will not wager on her blood."

"But will you wager on her heart?" Roger said, returning the look and lightening it. "Can you win her heart?"

Of course he could. He was a master at this game of

hearts and smiles and furtive embraces. Of stolen kisses. Of lying promises that lived with as much beauty as the primrose and died just as quick. At the game of courtly love, Ulrich had achieved much renown, yet games wore thin with passing years and he had little to show for his achievement, little more than a string of names only half remembered.

"Come, what else to entertain us? Times are hard and uneasy now with Thomas of London fled to France, a traitor to the king. Let us find our joys where we may take them. What harm in this?" Roger said with more seriousness than mirth.

Aye, that was so. At the birthing of King Henry's rule all the world had seemed to glow with promise. Now, ten years past his coronation, Thomas, the king's friend and chancellor and archbishop of Canterbury, had betrayed the king's trust and expectation and fled to Henry's abiding enemy, King Louis of France. Times were uneasy, in truth.

Yet this game of winning hearts beneath the haze of heated whispers stolen in the corners of vast halls did not suit Ulrich as it once had. He gained nothing by it but the increase of his legend, and for his legend he had come to care little.

"You put much weight upon the foundation of the tale of Juliane. If she is as all say, then I will fail before I have begun," Ulrich said, looking at his friend, trying to ease himself free of a wager he had no heart for.

"Yet is this not a wager to test the truth of tales?" Roger countered.

Ulrich grinned and shook his head in mock disgust.

"What say you, William?" Ulrich called to the rear. "Shall I take this wager?"

William, a boy of eight and Ulrich's squire, ran to his mount's side. "My lord, I think it will amuse."

"Amuse you, or amuse me?" Ulrich asked, grinning and reaching down to take William upon his horse. The boy was tiring.

"Amusements are not so particular," Roger said. "It will simply amuse, and what harm in that?"

"Well, if it will amuse all here for me to battle frost and ice and the legend of Juliane, then can I say nay? The wager is struck," Ulrich said, decided. If she was as stalwart as her legend, then this challenge would come to naught and none would be harmed by the attempt. "When her heart and her passions are mine, then I will have won."

"And what shall be the mark of this winning?" Roger asked.

"You shall see it in her eyes, my brother. And you shall see it in her melting. Can ice withstand the heat of summer?" Ulrich grinned. "Summer comes to England, and Ulrich with it."

"His name is known to you?" Avice said.

"His name is known to me," Juliane answered.

Avice looked at her older sister over the chessboard and then averted her eyes as she moved her pawn.

"They say he is a man to make a maid dream, a man blue of eye and strong of arm," Avice said. "A man whose tongue is smooth and sweet and whose smile is sweeter still."

"And so it is said of many men, most often by men themselves. Of themselves," Juliane said with a wry grin. "I listen not. Why talk of such tales now?"

"Because he comes," Avice said, sliding her queen forward on the board.

Juliane did not look up. She kept her eyes upon the board and moved her knight to distantly flank her sister's queen.

"When?" Juliane asked.

"Soon," Avice said. "I heard it from Marguerite. Christine came close to swooning."

"She would. Christine swoons at the lightest cause," Juliane said, looking up at her sister. Avice was composed, her curiosity well masked. "What will she do when Ulrich of the Sweet Mouth comes? She will fall into the dust at his first look and stay there till he passes out of Stanora, missing all."

Avice laughed softly and fingered her bishop. "You will not fall though, will you?"

"Nay. I shall not fall."

She never did. Surely Ulrich knew that. He must have heard the tales of her. Of course he had. And, like a man, he had come to test his fire against her ice.

Juliane smiled as she watched her sister deliberate over her next move. Let Ulrich come, she welcomed him. The play of fire and ice was ever fine. This was a game in which she excelled and of which she could never tire.

"Where will you be found when he comes?" Avice asked, abandoning her bishop and moving her queen instead.

"It is more a matter of where I will not be found," Juliane answered. "I will not be found standing in the outer ward like a cygnet flapping for his *maman*. I will not be in the hall standing in a shaft of sunlight, glowing like a beacon to draw him to me. I will not," she said, smiling, planning, "be found in the garden, kneeling amongst the flowers of summer, summoning him with fragrance. I will, instead, let him find me when he has given up all hope of finding me. That will be a fine beginning to this game."

Avice grinned and shook her head in delighted censure. "Your name will be made if you can withstand Ulrich."

"Oh, I can withstand him, and I shall mortar my name into the flow of time by not only withstanding him, but by defeating him. It shall be done, Sister, and it shall be done beautifully. Checkmate."

"Checkmate?" Avice looked down at the board. Her king was exposed and trapped by Juliane's queen. "Did you cheat?" she playfully accused.

"Nay, Avice, it is only that I have won," Juliane said. "I do not need to cheat to win."

"You speak of Ulrich again," Avice teased.

Juliane grinned. "For some little time to come, all will be of Ulrich. I hope he is flattered by the hours I shall give him."

"From what they say of him, I think he will expect *you* to be flattered."

"Then he has many surprises coming to him, does he not?"

"I think our father will not be pleased," Avice said. "It could be said that you have carried this game of yours too far, too often."

Juliane moved the heavy chess pieces around on the board in a random pattern. "Can I do aught as to that? I did not create this game, I only find myself a player in it. And when I play, I play to win. If our father cares not for the game, then let him only forbid the players entrance into his hall. All games would cease then."

"You know he will not," Avice said.

"Nay, he will not," Juliane said easily. "Can he deny his wish to see me wed?"

"He only wants what all fathers want: to see his daughters set well within a good betrothal and a profitable marriage," Avice said, laying a light hand on Juliane's arm.

"I had my betrothal," Juliane answered, standing. "And my marriage. I did my duty as a daughter. Once. It will not happen again."

"You heard?" Lunete said as she ran into the hall. She was ruddy from running up the stairs to the tower. The pink in her cheeks was lovely against the cool, pale blond of her tumbling hair and the light gray of her eyes.

"Do not say it! Let me tell it!" Christine said, bursting in behind ten-year-old Lunete. Christine was all of fourteen and should have had more dignity, though there was no one in the hall of Stanora who would rebuke her for her outburst.

"I am certain it is known. There is no need to shout," Marguerite said, coming into the hall last. Of the three girls fostered at Stanora, it was Marguerite who claimed dignity and solemnity as her mantle, when she could remember it. At thirteen, determinations were fleeting things.

"Did you tell her, Avice?" Christine asked.

They stood, the five of them, in the high-ceiled hall of Stanora. The fire was soft and slow, heating stones that had not felt the cold of winter for months and yet were still cool to the touch. Much like Juliane, always cool, ever impenetrable.

"Aye, I told her," Avice said. "I could not wait for you to regain consciousness; the news was too wonderful to wait."

"Swooning is a sign of high birth," Christine said in her own defense.

"Then you are daily proven to be highborn," Avice said, laughing.

"What do you think of Ulrich's coming?" Marguerite asked.

"I think that," Juliane said slowly, pausing for effect, "he comes to Stanora with a name for prowess in the games of courtly love, and that he will leave Stanora with a new name altogether."

Christine laughed, as did Avice. Marguerite only smiled with polite dignity.

"Yet of all the men who have come against you," Avice said, "he is the most fearsome in games of love."

"Then it follows that he will fall the farthest," Juliane said.

The fire flickered as if in shared laughter as the light and playful voices of the women stirred the air. Even the stones of Stanora seemed to warm themselves in the easy confidence they exuded.

Juliane had been many times tested and as many times declared the victor in this oft-played battle of love. Could any man stand against the power of Juliane? Nay, none could. None had. Yet . . . Ulrich was a man with a legend of his own, and it was not for defeat in matters of love. Of all men, this one might challenge the legend of Juliane le Gel.

What a fall that would be.

Chapter Two

"No matter what man is brought against her, she tumbles not," Philip said.

"You do not truly want her to tumble," Father Matthew said.

They stood in the open sunlight of summer, the wind pressing at their backs and through their hair upon the heights of the battlements. It was quiet and they were alone and it was a place that brought his heart more ease than the solemn shadow of the rood of Christ, though it might be sin to confess it. Philip would not confess it. Had not God made the sun? 'Twas no sin to stand in the light when his thoughts were so heavy and dark.

Juliane must marry.

He could find no man to marry her. With this chain of legend wrapped about her, no man would try. No man wanted to be the next man linked in legend with her, not when his part in it would be only of his falling against her cold regard.

He had not foreseen that.

And he would not leave this earth with Juliane unmarried. He would not leave her defenseless against the devices of Conor.

"Nay, perhaps not," Philip said, looking at the distant treetops as they swayed in the wind. "But it would not hurt her to be tempted."

"Lord Philip, you cannot want your child to be tempted into sin. She is a woman and weak; temptation would bring her too close to a fall. Pray not for such."

Philip made a noise of dissent. "Juliane is not weak, woman though she is. No man can topple her; that is becoming certain. Many have tried. The ranks grow thin and weak. I do not know what man will come to her now. Hugh of Normandy was my best hope, and he ran from here a month past, his confidence shattered against my daughter." Philip sighed and looked down at his hands upon the stone battlements. "Conor would have her wed Nicholas of Nottingham, but I would not have Conor make a betrothal for my eldest child again. The first marriage he arranged for her was not to my liking and had no good end. Yet Juliane must wed, and I can find no man to stand against the chill of her legend. I cannot find my way out of this maze."

"With God, there is ever a way out," Matthew said. "There are women who do not marry. Send her into seclusion, into a life of productive prayer. A worthy life for a woman, a life which meets her skills most well."

Philip looked askance at his priest. They were of an age and had been almost friends for twenty years. Almost, for a priest's devotion was set upon his vows, and Philip's mind was of the world and its ways. Yet there was much common ground between them and many shared years.

"Her skills?" Philip said with a wry grin. "You know her not if you say Juliane would be content to spend her life on her knees, her eyes cast heavenward. She is all of the earth, that one, though she chills every man who touches her."

"Then find a man who is hot enough to withstand her

chill," Matthew said. "For everything under God's eye, there is a match. Find the man hot enough to warm her. That is the answer to the riddle of Juliane."

"You speak my very thoughts, yet where dwells such a man?" Philip said. "Not within the bounds of England. Who has not passed through my gates? What man of merit and of means has not felt the ice of Juliane's regard?"

"Henry's domain is larger than England," the priest said. "Though perhaps not as large as he would like."

Philip only chuckled. "All kings want more, as do all men. There is no fault to be found in wanting."

"My lord!" came a cry from below.

Philip looked down at the porter, who pointed toward the river, and there he saw them. A small host of men were trotting toward Stanora, their mounts commendable, their armor in good state; more men come to Stanora. It was well, and well timed, God be praised. Philip squinted against the sun, taking their measure, counting them out. A knight, nay, two, and a bundle. Nay, no bundle, but a boy, he saw as they came closer, crossing the golden plain that stood between his tower and the river.

"God is quick in answering a righteous prayer," Philip said with a grin. "I can only pray that these knights are well suited and well matched to Juliane. I would see her married well and married soon."

"'Tis too soon to talk of marriage," Father Matthew said with a smile, "when they are half a league from your gates and you do not know their merit or even their names."

"I know they are men," Philip said with a shrug and an unrepentant grin. "That is enough to know for a start."

And as they watched from the heights of the battlements, another rider came sprinting from out of the bordering wood. A cry was loosed, and all riders rode hard for the gates of Stanora. It seemed a rout from this vantage point, though there was nothing of fear in it, even from this distance. Nay, they rode hard yet they rode joyously too.

The pack of men and horses slid to a dusty stop just shy of Stanora's outer gate. Aye, they were laughing. There was naught prompting their charge but manly play and manly wagers of superiority. A good beginning, if any one of them would stand and face Juliane. Without a goodly dose of proper male superiority, no man stood a chance of standing true and hard when facing his daughter.

"My lord?" the porter called. "Shall I admit?"

"Your names and places?" Philip called down from the battlements. "I will admit no rough men into my domain."

A lie. He would admit any man of sound health and bulging arm.

"Ulrich of Caen," said a knight, calling up his name and place to the hazy sky. A tall man, by the measure of his stirrup, broad in the shoulder, long in the arm. His gear was fresh and polished, his cloak of finely woven azure wool. Well turned out and free of mud. He would do.

"Roger of Lincoln," said Ulrich's knight companion. Thicker, broader, and more ruddy than Ulrich of Caen, Roger wore a cloak of nut-brown wool with a band of crimson at the hem. His mount was breathing lightly from their charging race, as was the man. A good judge of horses was Roger, or fortunate. A man would need to be fortunate to meet well with Juliane. He would do.

"Edward of Exeter," said the man who had begun the race from his run out of the wood. Tall and fair, riding a horse of pale gray, Edward laughed up into the sky, his humor still running high. A jovial man, then, if only with his knight brethren. He would do.

"My squire, William," Ulrich offered, gesturing to the boy at his back, his voice a trumpet against the stone of Stanora. "We are here at the king's direction. May we enter? Will Stanora welcome the men of King Henry?"

"Aye, and that is the question," Roger murmured, the wind snatching his words and lifting them to the lord of Stanora and Stanora's priest. He might as well have whispered into a funnel, the words rose so clear and sharp. "Will Stanora, that oft-sung Juliane, welcome this man of Henry's?"

"Lay coin upon it, if you doubt," Ulrich answered. "I could use some extra coin and would spend your money most well upon a cloak of scarlet."

Roger laughed and said, "The deal is struck, brother. I will not add nor subtract from our bargaining."

"Losing heart so soon?" Ulrich said as he looked up at the battlements, awaiting entry. "My lord?" he said loudly. "We are of Henry, king of England. Will you admit us?"

"Open the gates," Philip called down to the porter.

As the knights urged their mounts into the dark stone portal of Stanora, Philip heard, "It is not *my* heart which must be lost, Ulrich, but the lady's."

"And so it shall be," Philip heard in answer.

Aye, Ulrich of Caen would do most well.

"He is come!" Christine cried, rushing into the hall. For all her propensity to faint, Christine was an able runner.

Juliane looked up from her sewing. "Who is come?"

She knew who was come. They had spoken of nothing but Ulrich since his name had first been mentioned. Long hours they had been, too. *He is come, he is come.* So they all came, fell, and left. 'Twas a game that was beginning to bore, except that winning was still so sweet. And Ulrich of Caen would be a victory most treasured.

Could she topple him?

Of course she could. Any man might be toppled. In fact, she had yet to meet a man who was not the better for it.

"Ulrich!" Christine said on a huff. "He has not come alone, either. Two knights are with him, and his small squire."

"Will you manage them all, Juliane?" Avice asked. "Four is a mighty number of men, even for you."

"I will leave the squire to you, Avice," Juliane retorted with a grin as she set down her sewing. It was a new pelisse of soft green; it would look well on her, if she could but finish it.

"Nay, I will take the squire," Lunete said. "He is of my size."

"And weight," Christine said. "You could best him, pound for pound."

"What talk is this?" Maud said, coming into the room behind Lunete. "Ladies do not speak of such."

"And not within the hearing of men," Avice said softly to her sister.

"We have guests and must greet them," Maud said, casting a suspicious eye upon Avice. "Philip will expect no less of his daughters."

"Which is to the good as he will get little more," Juliane whispered back to Avice with a wicked grin.

"Come, come," Maud said, clapping her hands and

shooing the girls in front of her. "Fresh faces, clean gowns, smiles, and soft greetings; come now. We go to welcome guests to Stanora. 'Tis your function and your place."

" 'Tis not my function," Juliane said with a half smile. "And I will not be found by Ulrich in any place he thinks to find me. Even the finding of me will not come easily to him. And so the game begins," she said to Avice.

"And so the game is won," Avice said as Juliane ignored their aunt's direction, not joining them as they made their fluttering way down the stairs from the hall to the tower gate and the mighty door that protected them. Ulrich would see the ladies of Stanora, yet he would not see the one lady he most desired to see.

Avice had seen this game played time upon time and each time Juliane the victor. What would it be like if Juliane should lose? Would she then be given in marriage, the spell of her frost broken? If any man were made for the breaking of a woman's heart, that man was Ulrich of Caen. If tales spoke true.

Did tales not ever and always speak true?

If Juliane were the measure, then, aye, they did.

And so Ulrich was a man worth watching.

"Come, come, let us be about our calling," Maud said from the front of their skirted troop.

"I am come," Avice said. In truth, she was all eagerness to lay eyes upon Ulrich. Let the tales of him be tested against the Frost of Stanora. 'Twould be worthy play, if naught else.

Maud allowed Juliane to disappear into the mural gallery on the upper floor of the tower. Juliane had known that she would. It was not in the game for Juliane to be so easily found. Let Ulrich and his cohorts work for their first glimpse of her; it only made the first sighting sweeter when frustration melted into frantic desperation and starving impatience.

Juliane smiled as she trailed a hand along the uppermost wooden rail that protected against a fall onto the wooden roof of the tower below. She could hear the ladies of Stanora chattering and laughing at the prospect of facing Ulrich of Caen for the first time. He was a man, it was said, to make a lady blush with pleasure. It might even be true. Yet not so with her. No man had the heat to make her blush, not even Ulrich.

Though . . .

The tales of him were strong and sweet, of winged words, of sparkling adoration, of eyes of deepest blue that shone with humor and wit, of hands that stroked a lady's vanity as well as moving gently upon her skin. Within all tales, all tunes, and all times he was spoken of most well. And so had been since she was a girl. He had been out in the world, finding his way, making his name, and leaving his mark upon damsel and battlefield.

Yet when was any damsel not a battlefield? Aye, they were the same. A man must leave his mark upon the earth, and he did it in what ways he could. Damsels did not fall to words, not easily, not softly. Nay, they fell from breathy battering and whispered entreaty when they fell at all.

By the tales, Ulrich knew how to make a lady fall into the spell of him.

And by the tales, Juliane robbed men of breath and will

and heat so that they lay spent and cold, all thoughts of winning beaten from them by her very look.

Would it be so with Ulrich?

A breeze snaked down from the battlements above her to slide across the rooftop, stroking a gentle hand against her face, moving fragile fingers across her unbound hair—an invisible caress of air, warm and summer sweet and full of birdsong from the fields surrounding Stanora. The wind was her companion when all the others had flown off to giggle and twitch before the men eyeing them.

Had it always been so? Had Eve paraded her beauty and her charm to Adam in the garden? Had she enticed him when it was just the two of them on the whole great Earth? And had Adam spoken words of love to his woman amidst the golden sphere of earthly perfection, or had he spoken words of power?

Was there a woman in Henry's kingdom who would lay a wager on the question?

Juliane chuckled under her breath and ran a hand over her cheek, brushing the wind from her skin, standing alone, untouched. Nay, there was no woman who would take that wager. Men lived to wield their power, in whatever ways they could, against whomever they could.

And so she lived to stand against that sword of power, wielding a power of her own.

It was with thoughts of power in her mind that Juliane decided where she would allow Ulrich to find her.

Ulrich and his band rode into the wide bailey of Stanora wearing smiles of greeting and goodwill. As he smiled, he looked about him. The tower of Stanora was large and low, wider than tall, two stories above the undercroft, crowned with a thick ridge of battlements. A most unusual tower, of recent construction and in a fashion he had but heard of before now; 'twas a tower that strove to be a dwelling. A tower that was more than defense, it was an embrace to all who dwelt within.

A tower difficult to defend?

Ulrich looked again, his smile constant and his gaze mild. A thick curtain wall with an earthen rampart, a wide and clean-swept bailey with outbuildings of stone, a battlement like a crown against the sky; nay, Stanora would not fall easily, though she wore the look of welcome.

Would the same be said of Juliane? It was most like.

In all his years of wandering, he had yet to meet a maid, damsel, or queen who did not have a smile for him. Juliane had built her name upon other hearts than his, and it was upon his name that she would fall. A gentle falling with no ill intent, that was sure, but a falling all the same. Did she know yet that he had even now breached the outer defenses of Stanora? Did she know that he had come to take the chill from her name and bring to her the heat of love?

Aye, she knew. By the look of the ladies just now descending the outer stair, she knew and was come to face the man whose name carried the weight of a legend that was older and more secure than hers. Yet which of these ladies was the woman of frost?

"She comes to you at a run, brother," Roger said on a chuckle of delight. "My wager is lost before it has begun."

"Wager?" Edward asked. "What wager and what stakes? I have a skill for winning, as you will attest."

"Tighten your lips over your tongue," Ulrich said with a stiff-lipped growl. "We are newly entered here. Hold all until we are well within the gates. It is by such talk that wagers are blown to mist. I would not have her forewarned."

"Ah," said Edward, "of course. A wager of women against your wiles."

"Aye," Roger said, grinning. "A wager Ulrich fears to lose, as it is against the lady of this place, one Juliane le Gel."

"By Saint Ambrose, can you not keep still?" Ulrich said in an undertone. "My lord?" he said more loudly as the lord of Stanora came across the bailey from the stone stairway to the battlements, his priest at his back. "Your hospitality is most generous."

"To those who travel in the name of the king, any man would be generous," Lord Philip replied softly.

"Then shall both the king of England and the lord of Stanora be thanked," Ulrich said with a smile.

"All are well thanked, then," Edward said. "My lord, we met at Winchester a summer past, and you offered me the warmth of your hearth if ever I was in the region. I thank you individually for a place by your fire."

"Yea, I remember you," Philip said. "My fire is still lit, and you shall have your place by it, but what brings you all to Stanora, or are you on some other mission which calls you elsewhere and only seek a night's repose upon my hearth?"

"For myself," Edward said, dismounting and handing the reins to a groom, who waited expectantly for the other knights to dismount, "I am come at the bidding of the archbishop of York, a mere messenger of God and His servant, the bishop. Yet it is not to you, my lord, that this message is writ, but to your priest, Father Matthew."

"A rare message that it could not be carried by a less exalted messenger than a helmed knight," Philip said easily.

"Be it otherwise said," Father Matthew said pleasantly, "that the archbishop, as the exalted servant of God, is a careful man and chooses his messengers with a rare hand."

"A flurry of words most courteous for so simple a thing as a message writ on vellum," Philip said. "I would talk of other things than bishops. Tell me, Ulrich, for I have heard of you, what brings you to the gates of Stanora?"

There were many answers he could have given, many things he could have said. Ulrich chose the path of cordiality and humor, leaving darker paths untrod, hoping that the lord of Stanora and, aye, even his brother knights, would look no deeper for his true purpose in riding hard for the gates of Stanora.

"You need only look behind you, my lord, to see my purpose," Ulrich said with a grin. "The ladies of Stanora are well spoke of, my lord. Your daughter Juliane is the subject of much verse. Could any man resist the temptation of Juliane le Gel?"

Philip smiled and shook his head slightly. As his hair flowed in that gentle breeze, Ulrich saw that the lord of Stanora was minus an ear. A war wound, by the look, and his left ear. A strong right-hand stroke had made clean work of it. The wound was old and white and seemed to trouble Philip little. Ulrich had seen worse in his day.

"There is hardly an answer I could give which would serve my Juliane well," Philip said with a slight smile. "Would any father admit that his daughter tempts a man?

Would any man admit that his daughter has indeed doused temptation in most men?"

"Most men?" Ulrich asked with a grin. That was not the tale as it was being told, and both men knew it.

Philip shrugged and said nothing.

"Will you welcome me into your holding, my lord?" Ulrich asked. "I come to test myself against the tale of Juliane, yet I would not dishonor her on any point. Her virtue is safe, it is only her legend I come to best."

"You are not the first," Philip said. "Yet," he said on a rising laugh, "I can see in your eyes that you mean to be the last. Well enough. Try your hand with her, and welcome. But is it only the one who will throw himself against the chill of my elder daughter? Will none of the rest of you try your hand at wooing?"

"My lord," said Roger with a slight bow, "in the field of courtly love, Ulrich has no equal. We stand as witnesses only to see the beginning of a new legend, the legend of the fall of Juliane, if it is in your will."

"It is in my will for you to try," Philip said. "Who shall be the winner in this contest will make good wagering."

"If we could meet the lady?" Edward said with a wry grin. "I would not wager blind, even knowing Ulrich."

Philip glanced behind him at the ladies curved around the base of the tower stair. "I have a daughter there, but not the one you seek. Juliane has flown, guessing your purpose here, if I know her. You must needs seek her out, Ulrich of Caen. She will be found when it suits her to be found."

If the ladies fluttered to be so dismissed by the lord of Stanora, none of the men appeared to make mark of it. Yet flutter they did, and Avice most especially.

* * *

The sound of fluttering marked Juliane's quiet entrance
into the falcon mews. The air was dark and still and soft
with the sound of feathers and the feel of bright, unblinking eyes upon her face. The ground was thick with feathers and down and casting, and her thick leather shoes sank
deep. The grooms had been slack.

Juliane's eyes adjusted quickly to the dark, and she
went directly to her falcon, a dainty merlin with brilliant
eyes of deepest brown.

"Come, Morgause, let us away from these walls and
find our quarry," Juliane said, moving the varvels, those
small rings of silver that adorned her bird, to clear the
leather jesses from beneath the talons. "Though I would
not doubt that Ulrich of the Sweet Mouth would name me
his quarry. We shall instruct him better, shall we not?"

"Lady?" came a soft voice from without the sheltered
quiet of the mews.

"Aye, Baldric," Juliane answered softly.

"You take her out today?"

"Aye. Have a horse saddled and brought round for me. I
hunt today," she said with a smile, laying gentle fingers
over the breast of her bird of prey.

"The black, lady?" he asked.

The black was a mare, gentle and old and perfect for
hawking. She did not want the black. The black lacked
speed and fire. Today, for Ulrich, she would need fire
trapped in ice, a mount to thrill and dazzle: the gray.

"Nay, bring me instead the gray. I hunt far afield today,
Baldric. The gray will do for me."

"Mist? He is too big for hawking, lady. Lord Philip has

so declared it and would have my skin if you took him out and were thrown by him."

"The gray," Juliane said again, unmoved. "Be quick, Baldric. I have an appointment and I must not be tardy."

"Lady?"

"The gray," she said again on a grin as Morgause felt the air with her wings, seeming to taste it and devour it. A most wise and beautiful hawk was Morgause. "And have a care in bringing Mist to me. I would not alert my quarry that I am about to fly high above him. Have a care, Baldric."

"Aye, lady," he said, shaking his head with a rueful grin.

Juliane smiled at his retreating back and stroked her bird, laying firm hold on the jesses and fastening the leash. Baldric would ride with her, that she knew; he was her most able companion in these jousts of hers. He did not approve, but what man did? If a man wilted, was the frost to be blamed? Let him only hold his own heat and no frost could touch him. She had yet to meet a man who could not be bitten by her ice.

Baldric returned softly, even the metal trappings of the horses muffled.

"All awaits, lady," he said. "The field is yours."

Juliane came out of the mews, Morgause flapping her wings in eagerness and restless delight.

"You saw them?"

No need to elaborate; all knew who had just come into Stanora, as well as how welcome they would be made to feel by Stanora's lord.

"Aye, a most well-favored company this time, lady. Eager and fit."

"And confident?" she asked, handing Morgause off to him while she mounted. Mist was as restless as her bird. It promised to be a fine outing.

"Aye, as they always are when first they come upon Stanora."

"And what of Ulrich? Did you mark him? Is he all that is sung of him?"

Baldric ducked his brown head and shook it in mild disclaim. Dust came drifting down out of his hair to powder his rough boots.

"He is a man like any other, or so these eyes see him. It may be that a lady would see him with different eyes. You will judge soon enough."

"So I will," she said with a cold smile. "Then away with us, Baldric. Let this hunt begin in earnest."

They rode away from the mews at a brisk walk, staying well back from the tower where the guests of Stanora huddled beneath her stony shadow.

It was a fine beginning to the game.

Chapter Three

The sound of horses. That was first, and then the knowing, the deep knowing that she was near. Ulrich turned, as did they all, to see her, Juliane le Gel, the lady of frost who ruled all men's hearts, and lower parts, with an icy fist of cold intent.

She did not leave by the main gate but rode her gray gelding out of the small gate in the western wall. The sun, bright and blazing, lit her hair to molten gold and her skin to polished, palest amber. Her hair trailed down her back, loose and almost straight but for a whisper of curl. A merlin was upon her arm, the varvels glinting silver-white in the sunlight, the narrow jesses hanging down, twining upon Juliane's arm like an embrace.

This was the lady. There was no doubt. His heart beat the truth of that. He needed no word, no explanation, and he sought none. Nor did his companions. Ulrich forced himself to turn from her, a mighty act of will and strength which stunned him, and gazed upon his fellow knights. All were caught by the sight of her, all eyes black with instant desire, all mouths loose and panting for the touch of her, nay, even the scent. She called to them, to each of them, and they stood struck. Numb with longing. Hungry. Ready.

What, then, of the lady of frost? How that they all, if he could judge, stood ready to do her service? What of her legend?

What of her father?

Ulrich turned to look at Lord Philip and was instead snared again by the sight of Juliane riding through the narrow western gate into the fields beyond. When she was shadowed for a moment by the high stone portal, she turned, giving him hardly more than a profile. She turned and briefly looked him in the eye. A smile. And then her groom blocked all sight of her and she was gone.

It was a call, and he wanted nothing more than to answer her with all his heart and strength.

"My daughter Juliane," Lord Philip said into the silence that surrounded both her appearance and her departure.

Edward had already grasped back the reins of his horse

and was half ready to remount. Roger was snapping his fingers for a groom to bring him a horse, any horse. Ulrich swallowed hard, blinking away the sight of her, and turned to face the lord of Stanora.

"She is a daughter to weary any father, my lord," Ulrich said with a strained smile. "I would have known that this is the lady I seek even if you had denied it."

Philip nodded and smiled. "Deny her I never would."

"Nay," said Edward. "No man would."

"But away with you," Philip said with a grin. "Is this game not begun? Test your skill against her, Ulrich of Caen. You have a name which must be guarded. Guard it well."

"Aye, I will," Ulrich said as he mounted, his grin a banner of delight.

"Aye, a horse," Roger cried to the air. "I will ride with you."

"You? A player in this game?" Philip asked. "Did you not decry just moments ago?"

"A misstep, my lord," Roger said.

"Aye, a misstep for us all," Edward said. "You will not run to this field alone, brother."

"Yet did you not have a message for my priest?" Philip said. "And is it not still in your saddlebags?"

Edward lowered himself slowly to the ground with a muffled groan. "Aye. 'Tis true. Do not tell the archbishop of my folly. I shall stand unmanned."

Father Matthew came forward and tucked his hands into the folds of his long sleeves. "Come and do your function, and not a word shall leave Stanora of your temporary distraction. You have my vow on that. You are not the first to fall to her face, and you shall not be condemned for it."

"My thanks, Father," Edward said.

"I am away, then," Ulrich said, "and you will follow or not at your will, Roger, but expect no mercy from me. My will is all upon the lady."

"And so she does expect," a feminine voice said from across the bailey. "Run to her, my lord. She awaits you in this game she has begun."

Ulrich turned and faced the voice, soft and light and full of play. So light and sweet that almost the barb within the words were hid. Almost. She who owned the voice was dark of hair and blue of eye, her skin pale as cream, her beauty soft and sweet and strong in the midday summer sun.

"My daughter," Philip said. "Avice is her name and betrothed to Arthur of Clairvaux," he finished, either setting Avice completely out of the game or else completely in it, depending on the man and his honor. "My sister, Maud," he said, gesturing to a comely lady of fair hair and blue eyes, a mature woman of fine features grown sharp with time and age. "And with her are Christine"—a lovely lady of brown hair and eyes and delicate, fetching features— "Marguerite"—a lady somewhat younger with black hair and eyes, skin of whitest alabaster and a mien of dignity—"and Lunete, the youngest of the ladies of Stanora. They are betrothed all," Philip finished. Lunete was perhaps just ten with soft blond hair and cautious gray eyes. A lovely quartet of ladies to orbit Juliane. Lovely, yet none could compare to the hot allure of the lady of legend, the lady of ice.

"Ladies." Ulrich bowed, as did his brother knights. Even small William, not much smaller than Lunete, made his practiced bow. Lunete looked at Ulrich's squire and smiled. William did not smile back; he stared. Lunete was petite perfection.

"Will you fly to her, my lord Ulrich?" Avice asked, holding his gaze. "She awaits just such a coming."

"Lady Avice," he said. "I fly willingly and most eagerly to any lady who awaits my coming." He smiled. "It is the very foundation of my name to be so willing. To do less would be to disappoint, and I never disappoint a lady."

"Then fly," she answered with a shallow smile. "No jesses hold you."

Lord Philip looked on and listened, his manner easy at the courtly jousting taking place within his bailey. Avice was betrothed, her future set and secured against his death; what she did with her time before she was sent to her husband was her own concern, providing only that she remain pure. Beyond the matter of her purity, let her play at love; it was an honorable pastime and much hungered after by the ladies of noble houses.

Were Ulrich and his cohort true? It remained to be seen. They would be watched most carefully until their mettle had been fired and found sound. He would not allow these ladies in his keeping to be fouled by an untoward touch or a wayward word.

"Lady," Ulrich said softly, looking down at Avice, "you hold yourself too cheap if you do not see the unseen jesses that hold me here."

Avice glowed a delicate pink, her cheeks stained by flattery and praise. A lovely girl was his Avice, Philip thought, most like her mother.

Philip sighed and buried the sound. Juliane strove to fly beyond his aid, yet perhaps Ulrich would stand against her chilly legend. A prayer or two at Vespers would not be amiss, though of this prayer God seemed hardened to deafness.

"Come," Philip said, turning his thoughts with his words; "come into my hall, any of you who are free to enter," he said, looking briefly at Ulrich. Would he be turned from the fight for Juliane so quickly? Was his fire to sputter at a wisp of wind? "You are welcome to Stanora, to the bounty of the hall. Come, those who are free of jessed entanglements."

"My lord, I enter most glad of heart," Roger said. "I would not escape this entrapment of skirts for my weight in gold."

"Nor would I," Ulrich said, bowing to Avice and then to the younger ladies. "I stay and will stand upon the counsel of Avice of Stanora, for who knows a sister better than a sister? If Avice counsels me to stand, then fly I shall not. Let Juliane find her own pleasure in the wait; this quarry shall not be flushed."

Avice cast a nervous eye upon her father, as well she should for so disrupting this most important game, and said, "Lord Ulrich, I spoke without thought. Fly to your quarry, sir, for in this game of hunts it will be Juliane who is the hunted, not Ulrich."

"You are so certain, then?" Ulrich asked as the others—the priest, his brother knights, the small ladies of Stanora under the watchful smile of Stanora's lord and the stern mien of Maud—moved into the shadow of Stanora's tower.

"Can there be any doubt?" she answered, ducking her

dark head against his stare in a most beguiling maneuver of blatant femininity, sliding her gaze to where Edward stood in solemn silence.

"Lady," Ulrich said softly, "there is always doubt when the battle is between a man and a woman. It is the very meat of the game."

"Is your quarry, then, the Lady Avice?" Roger called from the bottom of the stone stair that led into the darkness of Stanora tower. "I will find my way to the Lady Juliane, brother, if you have lost your way."

"To lose one's way with this lady is simple indeed," Ulrich called back, winking at the lady, enjoying her flush at his words.

"I can see it is so," Roger said. "She is as tempting as the dark moon, while her sister is the sun. What man among the fallen does not yearn to linger in the dark?"

"I am betwixt two enchanters," Avice said, looking again at Edward, silently scolding him for his silence. Edward returned her look with a scowl. Ulrich watched and smiled. He understood this game. She bantered with Roger, but the game was all for Edward. "I stand not a chance of surviving such an onslaught of words," she said.

"Lady," Roger said, coming across the bailey to offer her his arm, "I think you stronger than any onslaught, be it words, sticks, stones, or spears."

Avice jerked on his arm and stared up into his light brown eyes while Ulrich laughed.

"Brother, you have lost her," he said with a bark of mirth. "Will you shoot spears at the lady to test her mettle? Nay, lady, have no fear. He will not harm you, unless it be by a wayward word in this joust of flattery."

"Go, brother," Roger encouraged with a lopsided grin. "I can find my way without you."

"Find your way, aye," Avice said. "The tower is before you, its shadow slight and thin in the midday heat. All light, it is. Surely you can find your way into the very heart of Stanora."

"Words of encouragement indeed," Roger said with a chuckle. "Find my way I shall. I take it for a promise, Lady Avice. You will not betray?"

"I make no promises, my lord," she said. "The way will not be easy for you."

"In that you prophesy," Ulrich said with a grin as he turned to gather the reins for his mount. "In all the ways of women, the way is never easy for Roger of Lincoln."

"Be gone, brother," Roger snarled cheerfully. "Have you not game enough of your own?"

Aye, he did, and he only hoped he had kept her waiting a sufficient time to ruffle her. In this hunt and by her sister's words, he thought that Juliane le Gel had played by her own rules long enough. It was time to play by his.

"By the saints, where is the man?" Juliane growled softly at the clouds. Baldric smiled in response, but he was not such a fool as to smile in such a way that Juliane would see it. "Can he not come when and where he is bidden? I called to him most well, did I not, Baldric?"

"Most well, lady," he answered softly. "Perhaps he is short of sight?"

She only grumbled at that. 'Twas not possible for a knight to be poorly sighted and still make his way among the living. Short of sight indeed. He was not that, no matter what other shortcomings he might possess. Tardiness was surely one. Perhaps obstinacy? Almost certainly.

Would he best her?

Resolutely not.

"How fares Morgause?" she asked Baldric, who held her merlin upon the block.

"Restive, lady," he answered. As were they both, and small wonder. "She yearns to hunt."

Juliane could not possibly have been more sympathetic. "Then let her fly," she instructed. "Let at least one of us enjoy the hunt today."

"Aye, lady, but I think he will come. In time."

"In time? In his own wretched time, I will vow," she said, adjusting her gloves.

They were gloves for hawking, aye, but they were also of lambskin dyed a most pleasing shade of red. She would have worn her oldest gloves if she had thought to hunt alone. Certainly, Baldric did not care which gloves she wore. As to Ulrich, he would not be the man they sang of if he spent more than a moment noticing the fineness of her gloves. Nay, by all tales, his eyes would be elsewhere.

Yet by the tales, he should be here, by her side, striving against her chill courtesy even now.

Tales were wretchedly unreliable things.

Baldric loosed the leash that tied Morgause to the block and set her free. The merlin set straightaway to ring up, her sails glistening black in the sun as she climbed in circles high into the summer sky. It was a beauteous thing to see. On she flew, upward and ever upward until she hovered at the top of her pitch, waiting on for her master to spring the game for her eager beak and talons. 'Twas the nature of a hawk, this joy in the hunt and in the blood of the kill. This joy at being unstoppable and unbested; this joy in beauty and power and skill; this joy in taking quarry in a stoop of speed past measuring: aye, Juliane could not possibly have been more sympathetic. She understood Morgause to perfection and shared her joy in the hunt and in the kill.

Of course, her own path was far less bloodthirsty. She killed no man and wanted no man dead, but still, she did hunt after a fashion, and in this battle of seductions there was only one victor. And that victor was she. Ever it had been so and ever it would be.

Even if her present quarry, one Ulrich of Caen, hid himself within the sedge of summer, she would find him and take him and defeat him. If he would only appear so that the game could begin.

"She waits on, lady," Baldric said.

"Aye," said Juliane, her eyes focused high above the earth upon a small black dot circling in the heavens, ever patient, ever sure that she would be served and that she would know the thrill of the stoop that led to the kill. "Aye, she waits on, yet will not for long. 'Tis not in her nature to wait. Serve her, Baldric. Drive out the grouse which I know huddle in the turf. This is fair ground. There is good game here for Morgause."

And so Baldric beat the ground, a long stick he had taken up working well for a bludgeon. In time, the grouse sprang loose from the grass and took flight. In an instant, Morgause stooped, dropping like the very hammer of God down, down, down to earth, without hesitation, without slowing, without caution. She was the master of this game, and she would take the grouse in beak and talon and cold, unblinking stare.

The grouse could find no place to shelter, and to take to the air would have meant only death more quick, yet take to the air it did, hungry for life, desperate for escape. If the grouse escaped this first stoop, its chances for survival would rise dramatically. Like a bow shot, the grouse flew across the meadow, bouncing, trying to find cover and finding none. Upon her horse, Juliane raced to outrun the grouse, eager to be there for the kill. In the next instant, the merlin flew into the grouse, a small and dainty hunter, outsized yet not outmatched, making the kill, tearing into the flesh, claiming her prey.

Juliane let her merlin devour what would have made a respectable showing upon Stanora's table; grouse was good eating. Yet she would not steal away Morgause's victory. She understood this sweetness, this satisfaction too well to rob it from another.

"A fine stoop," Baldric said, coming up behind her. "She grows in strength and in ferocity."

"That she does," Juliane said softly as Baldric swung the lure to call Morgause back to the block.

The grouse was only feathers and bone and a smear of blood upon the long grass of summer. Morgause came to the lure, sat upon her block, and preened. As well she should.

And so it would be with Ulrich, his name for winning hearts only a smear of broken pride upon the grass of Stanora. If only he would be flushed from his protective cover so that the game might truly begin. What bludgeon could she use to drive him out? What means beyond the glimpse of her profile and the beckoning curve of her back and breasts? What words to make him flush with pleasure and then with shame as his manhood lay shrunken and small and soft against his thigh?

She had no beak and no talons and she did not thirst for blood. Nay, not blood. Yet she had her weapons and her skills and the will to use them. Let Ulrich only show himself.

It was with that thought that Ulrich came.

Chapter Four

Her hawk was blooded and stood upon her block, watching him with glistening eyes of black. A more distant match for her mistress Ulrich could not imagine. The merlin was all black and white and sharp talon and beak. Juliane was white and gold and soft blue eyes, a curving line of gentle womanhood, her mouth bowed in a gentle smile of pale rose lips and white teeth. All welcome. A haven of beauty in a hot summer day. A woman to make a man dream of love.

And then she grinned and tilted her head at him, and with the change he understood her better: This was a woman adept at the game. All to the good, for he would not play against a woman who was not his equal in these amorous wars. Not again. With this woman, with Juliane, he would not need to tread softly. Nay, she could take whate'er he gave her. A match of equals. A jousting of like hearts in the ruthless games of courtly love. This was a woman to conquer.

Ulrich smiled. At conquering women he was well adept, and what was love but a weapon? Upon the point of that weapon he would defeat her, this woman who glowed with sensual beauty like a summer sunset, hot and shimmering and golden. Upon that point, aye, upon that point . . . and with that thought, he sprang up, hot and ready.

"Good morrow," she said softly, her voice pitched low.

"Good morrow, lady," he answered with some hesitation. When was it ever that a woman spoke directly to a man unless bidden to do so? His point did not fail him, yet his blood thinned and cooled by the barest measure. By what rules did she play?

"You found your way," she said, smiling in tepid amusement. "Finally."

So all Avice had said was true. Juliane had swung the lure and he had followed. Well, there were worse charges to make against a man, and she was a worthy lure.

"Do not all ways and all paths within the bounds of Stanora lead to Juliane? So I have found you. Finally," he said, matching her tepid smile.

They were both horsed, as was her groom, the bird well upon the block and watching him with bright eyes. Juliane looked as if she were ready to run. Would she? Would she run from him again, luring him to follow? Or would she match him point for point? He watched her carefully for her next move in this pleasant parrying.

"Only within the bounds of Stanora?" she queried, smoothing the leather reins against her gloved hands. Her gloves were red, like drying blood, and covered her arms to the elbow joint; costly gloves and most fine. "Did you only seek me then once you had found your way into

Stanora? Did not the name of Juliane find you in your sleep and call to you, my lord Ulrich? Did not you cross the very breadth of this isle in search of me?"

The smile was gone from her lips, yet her eyes glowed still in amusement. Was she laughing at him? This woman-girl who had no man to warm her bed and no children to give her life form?

Yet . . . yet how had she known his name if not for the strength of his own legend? Ulrich smiled. Aye, she knew him and, if she be wise, she feared him. He would not fall to her, and in that standing, her name would fall into defeat. No other wound would he inflict, but this woman, this golden, gleaming woman, would not laugh at him again. She had not met his like before; it only remained for him to show her that truth.

With his knees he urged his mount forward, closing the gap between them, setting himself between Juliane and her groom. The groom gave way without hesitation. Juliane eyed him coldly and with grim amusement, and it was then that he saw her eyes were like Avice's, of the same icy blue bound by rims of deepest lapis. The same large almond shape, the same arching brow. Yet not the same, for Avice's eyes were soft and tender with all the aching need of women, while Juliane's eyes offered the hard, cold stare of a man confronted, his pride pricked, his honor challenged.

Juliane had not the soft look of a woman.

His point slipped and faltered, and Juliane smiled.

"Come, answer, lord knight," she commanded, holding his gaze. "How far did you come in search of me, and how quickly did you think to defeat my name? Was I to last even the hour?"

"Lady," he said softly, holding her gaze, holding her icy look within his own, claiming her, controlling her if only in this. "Lady, I came far, but it was not your pride I longed to build; nay, it was only your ardor."

"And your own name?" she asked, taking his look and devouring it, drinking it, possessing it. He would not cow her with a look; she was a mightier foe than that. "Was that not also something you wished to build?"

"Between us, Lady Frost," he whispered, "there can be only fire, the fire that burns body, bones, and even names into dust. What I bring to build the flame is the flame-bringer's art. Do not look too deep into that fire or you will lose yourself . . . in me."

She kneed her horse a step away from him and then laughed in pure delight. A worthy foe she was. All his fears for her vulnerability faded into mist. She needed no protection from him; she could well protect herself. The tight band of caution loosed itself from his chest, and he breathed freely for the first time since this unsought wager had been set.

"You are truly Ulrich of the Sweet Mouth. I have named you well," she said with a laugh.

"If you have named me Ulrich of the Sweet Mouth, you have indeed named me very well. Lady, you have the gift of prophecy. In God's time, I will prove it upon you."

"In God's time?" she said with a grin of soft joy. "I may have mistook you, my lord, for I would have wagered that all things done were to be done in Ulrich's time and not the Lord of Hosts'. You enchant me, my lord, with your modesty and your piety."

"That I enchant is enough. As to my piety, if you find it

fits, you may rename me Ulrich the Pious. If the name comes from Juliane of the Flame."

"As to naming, let us leave that in God's good time," she said. "This game has taken a quick turn, even for you, Lord Ulrich."

"I am well matched," he said, nodding his head in a courtly bow.

"And I would be well sought, my lord," she said, urging her mount, a splendid gray gelding that was no true lady's mount, into a canter and then a full gallop. Her groom, sensing her intent, was right behind her, the hawk on his fist, yet he found the means to look back at Ulrich and grin, shaking his head in male commiseration.

Ulrich, knowing she expected him to dig in his heels and pursue her, sat his horse and watched her go. She flew straight over the meadow grass, the flowers of summer bowing to tease the earth with their nearness, yet holding themselves aloof. Aye, he understood her now. She wanted the joy of an ardent wooing, certain in her cold defense. She would not only be well sought, she would be well won, and it was to his lure that she would come, not he to hers.

He did not follow her lure. She had known he would not. The rules of this game they played were now well set, each having taken the full measure of the other. Well, mayhap not the full measure, but enough for her to know that this was a man who would play long and play well. He was well deserving of his reputation. He was a man to make a maid swoon for pleasure, but she had expected nothing less. Names were not built on empty air, but on the sound footing of experience and of knowledge.

Of experience and knowledge of women, Ulrich clearly had much.

That he was certain of success was also clear. Juliane smiled into the wind; let him be certain. 'Twas part of the charm of this game, this prideful certainty that men cloaked themselves in, the sweet charm they tossed to the women of their momentary choosing, certain of the humble gratitude and shy pleasure their attentions would bestir in female breasts and on feminine lips. So certain, so confident, so casually arrogant.

So destined to fail.

Aye, a most pleasing game was this to play upon a man's pride, and she knew it would be no less lovely with Ulrich of Caen. He was a man made to fall and fall far, from a very great height. It would be a great thing to behold.

"Does he watch?" she called back to Baldric, keeping her own eyes firmly forward upon the horizon.

"Aye, he watches most hard, though he smiles, lady. He said it true; you are well matched, I think," Baldric answered.

"I think so as well," she said, letting the wind carry her words to her following groom.

Well matched? Ulrich had the hard beauty of a man who finds his pleasure in women easily and often. He had the countenance and the manner of a knight, sinew and muscle and stamina, yet within his piercing blue eyes there had been humor and expectant joy. He was a man who looked for laughter in his life and then made certain that it was found. A man both hard with living and tender with laughing, he seemed to her. An odd sort of man, but then, they were all odd in some way or other.

Well matched? Perhaps in the techniques of courtly love, but within her was a determined will which would outmatch him easily, as the merlin could outfly the raven.

With just such assurances ringing through her head, Juliane rode confidently back to the gates of Stanora, Baldric and Morgause following docilely behind her.

"He shall hardly find her docile."

"I hardly think he expects to."

The two eyed each other over the soft flames of the center fire in Stanora's magnificent hall. Roger looked on and grinned; it seemed that no matter where one turned in this holding, there were battles aplenty to entertain a knight weary of blood. That these two had been destined to clash he had seen from the start. All her words had been for him and for Ulrich, already snared by the power of Juliane, yet it was to Edward that Avice looked when jousting with other men. It was Edward's eyes she wanted upon her. As they were upon her now.

With a curt wave of one finger, Avice indicated that the young squire should refill Edward's cup with watered wine. The boy obeyed. Edward bit off half his smirk, leaving the other half tilted upon his face.

"You have known him long?" Avice said from beyond her fire barrier. They circled each other like two wolves, the fire between them, lighting their faces and their animosity to a rare glow.

"Long enough," Edward answered.

"I have, no doubt, known her longer. She is my sister, after all."

"Yet you are very young, lady, and the years have had

no time to creep over your bones. I may have known him for more years than you have been on this earth."

"May have? Do you not know, then, how long you have known Ulrich of Caen?"

"He has known *me* for fifteen years, and I do not know whether to count myself blessed or cursed," Roger cheerfully interjected. No one was speaking to him, but he did not think that any cause for him to remain silent. It had never stopped him before.

"Why do you care, Lady Avice?" Edward asked just before he drained his cup.

"Have I not said it? She is my sister," Avice answered.

"I care, and she is not my sister," Christine said with a quick look at Roger. Roger winked in conspiratorial good humor; it was best to just leap into a conversation one was not a party to. That was his practice and it had not served him ill. Too often.

"Of course you do," Avice said. "We all care. Now," she said, turning her eyes again upon Edward, "how will Juliane find Ulrich? Tender? Bold?"

Edward smiled. "How did *you* find him, lady? Let that answer you. He is not a man to change his cloak upon the hour to match his mood. Ulrich is a man who knows himself and understands others. I ask again. How did you find him, lady?"

"If anyone should care what I think," Roger said, shrugging at Christine, Marguerite, and small Lunete, which caused them each to giggle, "I think I would not mind having so many cloaks that I could change them upon the hour. What say you to that, Lady Marguerite?"

"I say," she said thoughtfully, "that anyone with that

many cloaks should, in good charity, give them to the poor."

"You are piety itself, lady," Roger said with a small bow.

"I think that there is nothing amiss with having many cloaks, particularly if they are all different colors," Christine said. "If I had two brown cloaks, then I would, of course, give one to the poor."

"Does Ulrich give cloaks to the poor?" Lunete asked.

Edward smiled and answered her. "I have seen it, aye, and it was a rich green cloak without a single tear. He is most generous, most tender," he said, glancing across the fire at Avice.

"I would say it is rather bold to be giving good cloaks to the poor when he has no land of his own," Avice said. "That is not generous; it is foolish."

"If any man be foolish in his charity, surely God will make up the lack?" Edward said.

"I am more than willing for God to prove such upon me," Roger said. "I have so little in this life that any generosity which pours out from God's provision would be noted by me without delay and I would sing His praise upon the hour, proving the example that God blesses those who bless Him."

Avice grinned and ducked her head to hide it. She was engaged in tender warfare with Edward and did not want to so easily be turned from it. Ulrich was not the only man among them who understood women.

"I am quite sure, having listened well to all that Father Matthew has to say on the nature of God, that it is required of God's creatures to bless Him no matter what the gifts He has bestowed. I do not think our blessing of Him is to be in the nature of a bribe," Avice said, scolding playfully.

"I do not believe that God can be bribed," Lunete said.

"Of course He cannot," Marguerite said.

"Then by that fact, which is most certainly true, we know that Ulrich's charity in the giving of his cloak was a gift rooted in piety and greatness of heart, and not in vain bribery to pry from God's bounty that which God has prized to keep," Edward said with a nod to Roger.

"If I listen to you long enough, I will be persuaded not to keep up my prayers for a new cloak," Roger replied.

"Keep still then, brother; I want that cloak."

"Did you not bargain in good faith for one?" Edward said with a sly grin.

"A bargain?" Avice said, moving around the fire, the younger maids trailing in her skirted wake. "You have struck a wager . . . about Juliane?"

"You strike well, lady," Edward said, "even striking blind."

"Oh, 'tis not a blind strike, not when it concerns Juliane," Lunete said, coming to stand near Roger and give him a firm looking over.

"Then there has been a wager?" Avice asked again, this time looking at Roger.

"There is always a wager between men, Lady Avice," Roger said. "Let it not dishearten you. No insult to your sister was intended."

"Disheartened?" she said. "Nay, I am not disheartened. Tell me only, what was this wager . . . and may I lay my own wager on Juliane's success in the defeat of Ulrich?"

Roger looked down into the lovely blue eyes of Lady Avice. She appeared to be in earnest. Roger then looked into the stunned hazel gaze of Edward. Edward appeared as blindsided as Roger felt. Edward looked at Roger. Roger looked back at Edward. They blinked almost in unison and then turned to Avice of Stanora.

"You would wager? On your sister?" Edward asked.

"I would hardly wager against her," Avice said with a small smile.

"Is it . . . that is," Roger said haltingly, "is it quite proper for a lady to wager on such a thing?"

"On such a thing as a seduction?" Avice said cheerily. "I will not counter by asking if it is the stuff of knightly honor for *men* to wager on such a thing as a seduction. I will instead point out that I am not wagering on Juliane being seduced, but on Ulrich failing in his . . . rising to the occasion of a successful seduction."

"Lady Avice!" Edward said sharply. "This is beyond the bounds of courteous discourse."

"Yet not beyond the bounds of knightly wagering?" she countered, unbowed.

"Lady Avice," Roger said slowly, "you astound me."

"I think, my lord, that there is little in this life which astounds you," she said with a half grin. "In the matter of Ulrich, I think that nothing would surprise you."

"Nothing but his defeat in this . . . matter."

"Then," she said slowly, encouragingly, "we have a wager?"

"You are confident," Roger said, stroking his chin.

"I have good cause to be. Is not the weight of legend behind Juliane le Gel?"

"And what of Ulrich of Caen? He bears the weight of legend as well, and one that is older than your sister's."

"Older and perhaps weaker? Enfeebled by time, or

falsely inflated by the passage of years?" she countered with mock solemnity. "I believe with all my heart that Juliane can bear the weight of Ulrich and his legend very well."

"It is upon the bearing of weight that this wager hinges," Roger said.

"You are too forward, my lord," Avice said stiffly. "My sister will not be taken, her honor and her chastity are her own, and she guards herself very well."

"My pardon, lady," Roger said in all sincerity. "I did outstep all bounds. My tongue would rule me, if I would let it."

"And you have not?" she said.

Christine giggled softly and ducked her head.

"More than I will admit to," Roger said with a smile.

"I will ask you to admit to nothing, my lord. Your sins are your own," Avice said with an answering grin.

"And I will bear the weight of them?" Roger countered, laughing.

"The words are yours, my lord," she said, her grin widening.

"Another weight I am made to bear," he said on a sigh.

"You stand straight enough under so many weights," Marguerite offered.

"Come, enough," Edward said to them all and turning to Avice said, "What would you wager on your sister's victory, and how shall it be measured?"

"What is your wager with Ulrich?" she countered, lifting her chin and abandoning her smile.

"I will not speak of it before this crowd of women," Edward said.

"Yet you will make the wager about a woman's honor," Avice said tartly.

"I wager nothing on a lady's honor," Edward said hotly. "It is only upon her legend that this wager rests."

"And the wager is?" Avice prompted, raising her brows until they stood as high as the arches upon the church door.

"There is no sport in laying the same wager," Roger said, easing the tension between the two. "Let us devise a new wager. 'Twill keep me more interested, and that is always to be desired."

Avice nodded and relaxed her stance, though she eyed Edward with cool skepticism. "Then allow me to propose . . . that Ulrich will . . ."

"Not be able . . ." continued Marguerite.

"To lay a kiss upon . . ." said Christine.

"Juliane's . . ." said Lunete slowly. "Juliane's . . . throat."

"Her throat?" Edward asked. "That is not much of a wager."

"Is it not?" Lunete asked sweetly.

"For Ulrich?" Roger said. "Nay, I would say it is not. He may even have kissed her upon her throat even now."

"Oh, I do not think he has," Lunete said with simple confidence.

"Shall the wager also include that this kiss must be done with other eyes to witness it?" Roger asked.

Avice shrugged. "If you cannot trust your comrade to tell you the truth—"

"No witnesses, then," Edward said abruptly.

"No witnesses," Avice echoed, holding Edward's gaze.

"And the loser in this wager shall pay . . . ?" Roger said.

"I would rather decide what the winner shall receive, since we are sure to win," Avice said.

"You are confident, ladies," Roger said with a cheerful grin. "I like that in a wager. Makes for more fun."

"Especially when we win," Avice said.

"Then the loser shall pay the winner a single kiss upon the brow," Roger said.

Christine giggled.

"How is that winning?" Avice said, sliding her gaze once again to Edward.

"Aye? How?" Edward agreed, looking hard at Avice.

"Oh, come, 'tis a wager among friends," Roger said. "Shall we instead wager an exchange of blows? The reward is in the winning, not in the prize."

"Not in this prize, surely," Avice said with a tight little smile.

"Then we are agreed?" Roger asked them all, his hands outspread. The fire played lightly upon all their faces, casting light and shadow over their eager expressions.

"Aye," answered the women.

"Aye," responded Edward.

"My lord?" a voice said from the huge, arched doorway to the hall. "Father Matthew awaits."

"Your pardon," Edward said courteously to the group and then melted away into the outer shadows of the hall, disappearing through the arch.

The ladies began to disperse with Edward's departure, up and away to the great stair that led to the upper floors. Roger, in two large steps, caught up with tiny Lunete and said softly to her as she walked at the rear of the ladies,

"You are certain that Ulrich has not even now kissed the Lady Juliane?"

"Oh, yea," Lunete said with a delighted smile, "I am very certain."

Roger stopped and let her go, let them all go. He watched them as they floated up on the stone stairs, their hair and their skirts moving softly behind them, like waving sea grass upon the shore. Watched and pondered and chewed his lip with his teeth.

She did indeed seem very certain.

"You are certain?" Father Matthew said.

"You know me well enough to know that I am," Philip answered.

They stood in the doorway to the chapel, leaning against the stone, seeking shade from a day gone hot and white with massed cloud.

"You know so little of him, nothing beyond his name," Matthew said.

"I will know more before I am done," Philip said. "I can see no other course. Conor hounds me, and I must have it settled. Time runs from me, Father. I fear this gnawing pain in my breast. I cannot wait."

Father Matthew sighed and looked down at the dirt beneath their feet. It had not rained for a fortnight, and the smallest touch set the earth up into the air as powder. The crops were in danger of burning on the stalk.

"When will you begin?"

"Now," answered Philip. "I dare not wait."

"I will pray that he is the man you hope for."

Philip looked at his priest and grinned. "Yea, pray for that. That prayer must not go amiss, and your prayers are likely heard with closer attendance than mine shall ever be."

"Father?" Edward said, interrupting them. "I am here at your summons."

"And I leave you to each other," Philip said, straightening from the stone and nodding both greeting and farewell to Edward as he strode across the bailey to his tower.

"I did not interrupt?" Edward asked as he faced the priest.

"Nay, we had said all that was needful," Father Matthew said. "I have read the missive from the archbishop. You know its content?"

"Nay," Edward said. "I am a messenger, no more."

Father Matthew smiled and scratched his head. "I think you are more than messenger, Edward of Exeter."

"Unlooked-for praise," Edward said easily, "and welcome."

Father Matthew looked into the eyes of this reserved knight; hazel eyes more green than gray and a hard, straight stare that did not turn away from hard study. He was tall and supple of form, hard with muscle and with purpose, reserved of speech, or so he seemed at first meeting. A quiet, hard man who was in sometime service to the archbishop of York. No fool, then, this Edward. Matthew had heard some small things of him, but nothing to sink his teeth into.

"Did the archbishop give you any word for me, beyond the bounds of his written message?" Matthew asked.

Edward held the priest's stare within his own, swallowing it whole. "He sent no message beyond the one I gave you, my lord. Did it not suffice?" he added with wry humor.

Taking a leap of deadly faith, Matthew said, "It was not the message I was praying for."

There was a silence between them that stretched out languorously, like a cat stretching after a sleep in the sun. Stretched as they studied each other, priest and knight.

"Keep praying, Father," Edward said softly. "All prayers are heard, in time."

They held still, the two of them, reading secrets in each other's faces, and then Father Matthew smiled.

"I shall. Prayer is my function and my art."

"Good day then, Father," Edward said in easy parting. "Until Vespers."

"Until Vespers," Matthew repeated, watching Edward cross the bailey until he was lost to sight in the jostling bustle of a rich man's holding.

She rode through the gates of her father's holding, the sun lowering toward the treetops, casting her shadow forward in a long, thin, disembodied line. Ulrich was safely behind her, beyond sight, but not beyond knowing. She could feel him at her back, out there, trying to find the path to her, sure of himself and of her. And knowing all that, she rode in an easy canter with an easy smile upon her lips into the home that embraced her.

She knew who she was and was safe in the knowing.

Juliane rode to the stable and dismounted with the aid of a groom. Baldric, coming upon her, asked, "Shall I put the merlin back upon her perch in the mews? She is still full of fire."

She knew well the feeling.

"Nay, give her to me," Juliane said. "I will take her into the hall. She shall sit beside me while I eat."

"A good barrier to Lord Ulrich," Baldric said, nodding his head.

"A barrier? I need no barriers. Let us call Morgause a stumbling block, a tiny caltrops thrown into his way."

"A caltrops? Would you lame him, then?"

"If he cannot manage to avoid stepping onto a caltrops, and one in plain sight . . ." Juliane shrugged. "He is not worthy of his name if he cannot manage one small bird."

"There is no such thing as a small hawk," Baldric said on a laugh.

"You are too familiar, I think," she scolded mildly, taking the bird upon her gloved wrist.

"I think so, too," Baldric agreed cheerfully, his brown eyes dancing with good humor, "yet you have ruined me for any other service, lady. I shall never clean the cesspit with the same goodwill again, now that I have served you and stood as witness to the men who have dashed their hopes against your name."

"If I think on that long enough, Baldric, I am sure I will find that I have been insulted," she said with a smile.

"Nay, lady, I would never—" he began.

"And as to their hopes, I have no interest and no concern," she finished, grinning. And with those words, she turned with Morgause on her wrist, her arm held high, and walked across the bailey, ignoring all, thinking only of Ulrich and the many ways to ruin his meal.

Chapter Five

"Tell me that you kissed her," Roger demanded.

Ulrich handed his cloak to William, who was very careful not to let it touch the floor before he hung it on a peg set into the stone wall. It was a very high reach for the boy. Ulrich watched as he managed it on his own.

"I did not kiss her," Ulrich said. "I only spoke to her. Would you have her think me a baseborn lout?"

"I would have her think herself well kissed. And on the throat," Roger said, throwing himself down upon the wide bed in the chamber they were all to share. Edward sat upon a stool near the brazier and tipped back against the wall, a delicate balancing act as the stool was three-legged and none too new.

"You have made another wager," Ulrich said flatly. Flatly unsurprised. "What is it now, and with whom have you struck it?"

Roger said nothing, only threw an arm over his eyes and sighed.

Ulrich looked at William. William shrugged and shook his head, pouring water into the basin for Ulrich to bathe his face and hands.

Ulrich looked then at Edward. Edward grinned tightly and said in a strangled tone, "Her sister."

Ulrich turned to Roger and kicked him on the leg. Roger only sighed again.

"You did not."

"I did not do it alone," Roger said, moving his arm and looking up at the wooden ceiling. Ulrich looked up as well. It was painted blue, with the signs of the zodiac done in red. The sign of Aries was flaking. "And it was not my idea."

"Whose, then?" Ulrich asked just before he dipped his head into the water and scrubbed his jaw and neck. It had been a hot day and the insects had been fierce, almost as fierce as Juliane le Gel.

"Hers," Edward said as Ulrich rose from the water. "Avice's."

"She wanted to wager? On her sister?" Ulrich said.

"Well, she would hardly want to wager *against* her," Roger said.

"Strange women come from Philip's loins," Edward said.

"Beautiful, though," Roger said.

Edward shrugged and tipped his stool back farther. It squeaked, but held. Edward's silence told a tale that Ulrich could read right well; his was not to be the only battle of hearts played upon the fields of Stanora.

"What is the wager?" Ulrich said.

"A kiss upon the throat," Edward answered.

"A kiss upon the throat?" Ulrich asked, sitting down on the bed next to Roger. William hung back against the door and watched, saying nothing.

"Aye, a kiss upon the throat. Can you do it?" Roger said.

Ulrich laughed and got up from the bed and strode to the wind hole. It was a fine southern exposure, the sun sliding warm and golden across the land as it disappeared in the rolling hills to the west. Far off stood a wood tinged red in the sunlight, blowing green in the wind. Stanora stood high upon a rocky hill, dominating all that walked or flew for miles around. The wood had been pushed back again and again since the time of the Romans until rocky Stanora stood high and alone, her feet girded by stone and grass and bulwark, her head lifted to the sky. A well-defended spot of earth.

"Can I kiss her?" Ulrich asked the wind. Could he kiss the maid who pushed all from her with hot looks and cold words? Could he find his way past her defenses to the damsel who surely yearned for a man's touch and a man's might? Could he find the woman beneath the legend? "Can I win this wager for you?" Turning back into the room, facing all eyes, he said, "You know I can."

"That is well," said Roger into the general rushing away of tension that Ulrich's proclamation had generated, "for then I can claim a kiss from Christine."

"Christine?" asked Edward. "Is she the one who has turned your eye? All she does is giggle."

"Aye, and I would be the one to turn that giggle into a sigh," Roger said, grinning.

Edward grunted and straightened up his stool, running a hand through his hair. "You are welcome to her."

"Oh, I know," Roger said. "You prefer them snarling and suspicious."

"I do not," Edward said, standing.

"Who?" Ulrich asked Roger, though he knew the answer. They had been at this before, once in Caen, twice in York, and once again in London. 'Twas an old game between them, started when they were knights newly made and on their own in the world, making a way for themselves where no way had been made for them. They knew each other well and, for all their puppy snarling, were as close as brothers and as true.

Edward kept himself aloof from ladies, knowing he had no hope of winning one to wife without land or place or name beyond the city where he was born. He did not allow himself to want that which he could not have except by God's miraculous grace. Yet what man could control his every thought? Some stray desires crept through the best defenses, even of a man as careful as Edward.

"The sister Avice, of course," Roger said. "She is more like her sister than first appears, by the way. There is more bite to her than purring. At least with Edward."

"Avice?" Ulrich said, brows raised.

Roger of Lincoln as the oldest of them had been the longest in the world and knew its harsh ways and careless indifference, yet he was the most good-natured and joyous of them all. A man who smiled at snow and laughed at storm. Ulrich saw him rarely, as they served their king in differing lands and battles. For all Roger's laughter, he lived a solitary life, yet found no cause to complain of it.

"I think she is pretty," William said from his spot by the door.

"Do you?" asked Ulrich, turning to his squire.

"Her eyes are very blue," William said in explanation.

"They share the same eyes, those two," Ulrich said. "I saw it when I saw her. The same chill blue surrounded by the darker band."

"Very chill," said Edward in an undertone.

"Then warm her, if you will," said Ulrich. "Or do not. Since no net of wager has been cast around *you*, you are not constrained to act in any way but that which meets your will."

"Is this fear I hear?" Roger said, sitting up and grinning. "Do not say I will lose my wager. I need all the kisses and cloaks that may fall into my hand."

"What falls into your hand is the province of your own will, brother. I cannot meet all your needs; you must sometimes, in some ways, meet your own."

"If I must," Roger said, shrugging lightly. "If you must fail me, then I must."

"Leave off," Edward said. "He will not fail, either you or himself. How can he? Is he not Ulrich?"

"And has the lady not already christened me Ulrich of the Sweet Mouth?" Ulrich said, leaning against the wall next to William.

Roger laughed and said, "Has she? Then the game is almost won. By the saint who protects me, how this will soar your name to the ends of Aquitaine. This is quick even for you, brother."

Ulrich smiled and said nothing. Quick? Nay, it would not be quick. Not with her. But it would be done, and he would find much joy in the doing, for this was a woman who could see to her own defenses. He need not wear gloves of gentleness with her. Nay, not with her.

The meal was ready. The hall was half shadow, half light in the hour before Vespers. Dark was hours away yet, but the sun was low on the horizon and the light it sent forth was long and low, skimming the treetops, gilding the hills, turning the stones of Stanora to molten gold. Lighting the Lady of Frost to sparkling ice and frozen fire.

All were within the bustle of the hall, all finding a place at the tables spread out around the central fire; squires, kitchen serfs, men-at-arms, serving girls, gentlefolk, all finding a place, be it at work or at rest, in the vast hall. All except Juliane. She stood in the doorway that housed the stone stair, her hawk upon her red-gloved hand, watching them all. Waiting. Smiling.

She saw him and did nothing. She did not blush. She did not turn. She did not hide her face or drop her eyes or seek the company of the other women of her house.

Nay, such acts were not in her.

She watched him watch her, and she smiled a cold, hard smile. Predatory, he might have said, if such a thing were said of a woman. Perhaps it was the merlin upon her wrist which made him think it.

But it was not.

She watched him, taking his look as easily into herself as sand takes the sword, and with as little effect.

This was what she did to men; he understood it now. She took all that a man was and did not shy or turn away or behave in any way that a man expected of a woman, and so the men were turned upon themselves and awkward shy with her, losing all the heat and passion and power that a man brought to a woman who was knitted together in the proper way of things. A submissive woman. An obedient woman. A woman under a man's will and hand.

This woman was under no man's hand.

This woman taunted them all.

Yet in her strength, he rested easily. In her strength, he could relax and find his way with her as he would. By her very weapon, he would defeat her, taking her down as softly as he could. Yet she would fall.

Ulrich smiled and kept watching her, wanting her to see him smile. Wanting her to know that his fire was not dimmed, that his power had not turned, that he was not cold with dread of her. He rather liked the icy fire of her, this Juliane who turned hard men soft with a look, a word, a touch. Let her look, let her speak, let her touch; he would not be turned. He would not fall soft. Her strength fed him.

"She looks for you, brother," Roger said quietly.

They walked through the hall, past the tables set and steaming with food. He had been invited to sit at the high table as an honored guest, though Ulrich could not think why. He was a simple knight, owning nothing to give him worth in the eyes of the lord of Stanora; a place with the men-at-arms would have better suited his station. Yet who would complain of the honor of the high table? Not even he, though he did wonder at it.

"And she has found me," Ulrich said, smiling at her again before he looked away. He could look away from her. Let her know that and ponder it.

"By the saints, she is a beauty," Roger whispered. "How can you turn from her? 'Twould be like turning from a treasure chest heaped and gleaming with gold and jewels."

"This jewel cannot be mine," Ulrich said. "How else but to turn away? Yet I will show her that I am the man who will remain a man with her. Let her see that and wonder if her power fades."

But he could feel her pull, despite the noise, the smoke,

the smells, the bodies twisting in the twitching light of setting sun and fire and candle. He could feel her. He had never known such desire. It pulled at him like the surf, dragging him out of himself and under, to be lost.

Yet he must not be lost and he must not lose. There was too much loss in losing for Ulrich of Caen. He could not lose one thing more.

Edward and Roger sat quickly at a table, William at their backs, ready to do service. Ulrich made his slow way to the high table, sure to be there before Juliane began her march across the long length of the hall.

And so it was.

"She comes," Edward said as William lifted the wine for pouring.

Across the floor she came, like a queen, like a goddess from far-off ancient Rome, that fabled empire of dreams and swords. Her merlin sat easy on her arm, its black and staring eyes searching the hall for prey and finding none, yet searching all the same. As did Juliane. But she had found her prey in Ulrich, or so she thought, if he could read the look behind her eyes.

He read her well enough.

She was wearing gold. Her bliaut was of honeyed white and her pelisse was gleaming goldenrod. She shimmered. Her hair hung down in feathered whispers that caressed her breasts and curved around her back to lie in tatters on her hips. Upon her hips lay a girdle of golden circlets lit with lapis lazuli. Upon her breast was a brooch of silver chased with amber and topaz and shaped like a bird in flight.

It suited her.

She suited him.

Ulrich shook the words from him. She would suit any man who saw her, such was the power of her sensual beauty. Yet when the man drew close, her talons would strike, bleeding from him all that he prized in himself. All power, all heat, all control.

Still, she suited him.

Still, he would master her.

"Come, Juliane," Lord Philip called, his hand outstretched in welcome. "Your place is at my side."

And next to Ulrich. Ulrich looked at the lord of Stanora, who whispered loudly, "I only mean to help you, boy, to win your wager."

Juliane sat down, the merlin set between them. The hawk turned cold eyes upon Ulrich and considered him; Ulrich returned the look.

"A wager? About me?" she asked, looking at her father first and then at Ulrich. "What a first for me. Who shall win, do you think?" she asked sweetly, her talons gleaming as boldly as her jewels.

"I shall win," Ulrich said, staring into her pale blue eyes.

"You sound very sure," she said.

"I am very sure," he said in his turn.

Father Matthew rose to offer the blessing on the meal, ending their battle for the moment. If his prayer seemed overlong, there was none there who would remark upon it. Perhaps because it seemed the quiet before the battle trumpets.

The prayer of thanks and supplication ended. The battle began.

She took a delicate bite of fish and followed it with a twist of bread and a swallow of wine. He watched her eat.

She was thorough, dainty, methodical. If she was hungry, her manner did not show it.

"If you think that by watching me you will understand me, you have taken a wrong turning in your reasoning, my lord," she said, looking full at her plate and with no glance for him. "Other men have tried that course and failed."

"All men have failed with you, Juliane," he said.

"Yea, they have," she said, glancing at him as she dipped her bread in fish sauce.

"And so will I?" he asked with a half grin.

She laughed softly and said in mock seriousness, "Have you read that in my eyes, my lord? Let me give you something better and surer: the words of my mouth. Yea, you will fail with me. I will not fall to you."

Ulrich laughed with her and said softly, "And I, sweet Juliane, will not fall to you."

"Will you wager on it?" she said. "Oh, I have forgot. You already have."

"There is too much talk of wagers in this hall," he said. "I would not waste such talk on you, lady. Let us do more with our time than talk of wagers and of falling. Shall we not rise up together, at least in the speaking of it? That is more to my liking."

"What is to your liking does not interest me, my lord," she said, giving her full attention once more to her plate. "Rising and falling, those are the concerns of a man. I am a woman. My interests take a different course."

"Let me run that course with you and you will find that rising and falling will be a part of all."

"Are you so sure?" she asked.

He noted that she still avoided his gaze. She was keeping to herself what she could, her eyes and the thoughts behind them. A woman's game she played, after all.

"I would not injure you with a careless word, my lady, I would only remind you that you are a woman of compelling beauty. Nay, more than beauty. Fire. Heat. Passion burning low and dim, but burning still. You glow, Lady Juliane, you glow, and my eyes burn with desire at the sight of you."

"Then turn your eyes, my lord of legend; I would not burn you for the world," she said simply, unmoved, eating her fish with precise bites.

Philip sighed into his wine and looked at Ulrich over his cup in disappointment.

"What course would you have me run, lady? Command me," he said.

"I do not want you, my lord, neither your service nor yourself," she said. "I have all the devotion I can suffer."

He was failing. He could feel it, though he had never felt the like before this moment. She was beyond the reach of his words. Of his charm and his seduction, his ribaldry, his play, his look, his manner, his very self; she was beyond his grasp. The hardness of his cock, which rose and stood whene'er he looked or even thought upon her, failed him. He sank. He fell.

How was it so? He could not fail, not from mere rejection. Yet when had he ever been so boldly and so publicly rejected?

Hard, hot anger rose in him that she dared defeat him with dismissal.

"Shall I tell you what the wager was and is?" he asked, turning upon the bench to face her as best he could. Their knees bumped and pressed. He did not pull back from her.

If he bruised her, let her wear that mark of Ulrich upon her, if no other. "There are two. One is that I will stand before your chill, lady. The wager is that I will not fall. No harm to you, no seduction of your body, no ripping of your maidenhead, no blood, no wounds, unless they be upon your cold and stony heart."

The hall had gone still.

"The second wager was struck just after None. Your sister and your fosterlings and my brother knights, albeit against their own counsel, wagered that I would tender a kiss upon your tender throat. That is all. A kiss. A single kiss."

Juliane had stopped eating. She sat looking at her food, her head bowed, the merlin upon the edge of the table fluttering in agitation. Her pulse was racing in her throat, a sign of emotion in a taut, still neck. Her skin was the color of ripening wheat, her hair a tangled web of golden strands that sheathed her neck and breast with all the comfort of a cloak. That pulse, it rushed, it pumped, pressing against her skin, calling to him of blood and heat and life, of passion's very heart. Calling to him, beating for him, pulsing, pressing, calling, calling.

And he would answer it.

"A wager I would win, lady," he growled with a nod of apology to her watching father, "if I shall win no other."

Ulrich reached out and took her head hard in his hands and forced her back upon the bench against his arm, her neck exposed, lifted up for him, her pulse leaping beneath the thin, white skin. He held her by her jaw and by her golden hair; he held her for his mouth to take and lowered himself onto her with a buried growl of sudden, hot hunger.

There was no sound in all that vast hall. The only sound was the pulsebeat in Juliane's throat and the answering roar of his heart. She made no cry, no protest. She did not fight.

With a snarl, he laid his mouth upon that line of hidden blood and mouthed her, tasting her, learning the scent of her, the salt tang above the hot sweetness of her skin. His lips opened into a hungry kiss, his tongue licked out, testing her heat, the lick before the bite. The bite of the kiss. A kiss of hunger and of need and of blind lust. She was hot under his mouth, hot and sweet and soft. A kiss, a hot kiss with his open mouth upon her skin. A kiss to mark her, as no other had done. A kiss to bruise, if he could.

In that moment, she was his and he would mark her so.

She mewled a cry deep in her throat, and then her merlin struck. A beat of wings and then a clawing on his throat. With a single hand, he pushed the merlin from him, his mouth still upon her. No hawk would drive him off. No wound would kill his lust. Not in a lifetime of wounding would his hunger for her be met.

Fool thought. She was just a woman, and the world was full of women.

With a single hand, she pushed him from her throat, her hand going to the spot where he had been, wiping him away. Wiping his touch from her.

"Too late, Lady Frost," he said so low that none could hear, save her. "You have my mark, as I have yours."

He lifted his hair from off his neck and showed her the mark her merlin had made upon him. A stripe of blood flowed down his throat. 'Twas not deep, 'twas not long, yet it was a mark he would have for all his life. Let her know it. If this was to be the only bond they shared, then let them share it to the full.

"The second wager has been won," he called out to the hall.

Into the silence of that pronouncement, all eyes turned to Lord Philip. What would he do? His daughter had been treated most foul; no chivalrous knight would act so bold with a daughter of the house and in the public gaze.

"The second wager has been won," Philip repeated. "In the sight of all," he added.

Ulrich nodded his thanks at such benevolent mercy, and then Roger said with a laugh, "By all the saints that love me, Ulrich. I never meant for you to eat the girl!"

And all was laughter after that. Save from Juliane and, more strangely, Avice.

The second wager had been won and she was supposed to sit and be the source of merriment? Nay, she would not.

Her father had supported Ulrich and his stolen kiss. 'Twas hardly surprising. Her father had a sudden need to see her wed, and for Juliane to be lawfully wed, a man must keep his cock up and crowing. It mattered to no one that the only cock she cared to see was dead and roasted and served up on a platter. Whatever good was a man-cock? It could not be eaten and was as ugly as a runt piglet.

"I never thought to lose that wager," Avice whispered upon her left, beyond Philip and his useless ear.

"It was ill-advised of you to wager upon your sister, Avice," Maud said. Hopeless counsel now when all was done.

"I only wager when I think to win," Avice said. "I ask

your pardon, Juliane," she said softly, leaning to look behind her father's back. "I did not think it in him to act so. He was almost wild. The tales of him speak of no such thing."

That was true. That was most true. That told something.

Juliane smiled. She was winning. Oh, he had stolen a kiss from her, and made the blood leap in her throat, but he had leapt upon her in anger. Because he was losing. Because he feared he could not manage her, or his floppy cock.

"Did he hurt you?" Avice asked, keeping her voice below the sounds of the hall, beyond Ulrich's hearing.

"Nay," Juliane answered loudly, "he did not hurt me. That blunt assault? That mistimed, ill-bethought seduction? Am I to fall from such rough handling? Nay, he did nothing more than reveal his desperation. Make any wager you wish, Avice; I will stand and he will fall. This game is playing out as do they all."

"Truly?" Avice asked, eyeing her sister with a soft gaze. "His kiss upon your throat did nothing?"

"Nothing but annoy," Juliane said, and if Ulrich heard, all the better, "and lose me my bird. Baldric?" she called, beckoning him with a hand. Baldric came at a trot, knowing her mind.

"She has flown, lady. I cannot find her in the hall."

Morgause, worth more to her than any man, had flown, her jesses trailing in the murky light of the hall. The sun still shone beyond the stone; she must be found before night fell or she would not be found at all.

"Then we are away," Juliane said, rising to her feet. "I go in search of Morgause, who, after rough handling, has flown. Your pardon, Father?" she asked, not asking at all but merely informing.

"Aye, your pardon, my lord?" Ulrich said, standing at her side, taking her arm in his hand. She pried him off with a stiff grin on her lips.

"You are not needed," she said.

"All hands are needed in this," he said.

"You have hardly made her easy in your company," she said, walking from the table.

"I could as well say that she has hardly made me easy in hers."

"Say it, then. 'Tis nothing but the truth," she said. Baldric and Ulrich, soon joined by his small squire William, were on her heels.

"I would only help you, lady," Ulrich said softly from behind.

"Then leave me, my lord," she said stiffly. "I need no help from your hand. I want none."

"Need and want, they are not the same, lady," he said. "Let me only give you what I may. All else is in God's hands."

She was turning to set him down again, once and for all, when the boy spoke.

"He is very good with hawks, lady," William said, his gray eyes clear and earnest.

"We could use a good hand with hawks in this, lady," Baldric offered. "Morgause was in high feather. She will not come easily."

"Come, say yea to me," Ulrich urged, smiling, his blue eyes sparkling with good intent and latent humor. "I shall even swing the lure."

Aye, he was good at luring. She could feel his mouth upon her even now. The place upon her neck where he had taken her tingled and throbbed still, the feel of him fresh and hot.

"Very well," she said against every bit of common sense, "but if I know my merlin, you shall *be* the lure. Beware your eyes, my lord."

"Lady, in your company 'tis my heart I must guard," he said.

He said it with such overblown sentiment, with such sad eyes and mournful mouth, that she could not help laughing. It was to his credit that he laughed with her, making mock of all courtly ritual and the terms of courtly love. Which was only right.

"That went well," Philip said, watching them leave his hall.

"It did," Father Matthew agreed. "He is not afraid of her, that is plain. Is he still the one you would have her take?"

"If all is as it should be," Philip said. "Let us see how he fares by Vespers tomorrow. I shall know enough by then."

"You know he has no land," the priest said.

"I know that few men do. If he can bed her, making the marriage lawful and unbreakable, then that is enough. It might be that I can find land for the man who can find his way with Juliane."

"You could still give her to the church."

"She will not go to the church," Philip said, shaking his head with a smile.

"And you think she will go to him? To any man?" Father Matthew said.

"Do I think she will go to any man? Nay, it is more than certain she will not. Do I think she will go to Ulrich?" Philip shrugged and rubbed his nub of an ear. "I think she might. What is more likely is that I think he has it in him to take her. She is a woman who must be taken; she will not give herself. That was proved when he took the kiss just now."

"She spurns a life lived in the power of the flesh. By your every word, she sounds destined for the abbey."

"Then you are not hearing me," Philip said with the smallest edge to his voice. "She will be wed. It is not in her to be praying away the hours of her life; she was not made for that. I will not send her to that."

"Yet if she wants it?" Father Matthew pressed.

"She will have what I want for her," Philip said, ending it. "But if you need your mind eased, ask her yourself. She will answer you straight; no other way is in her."

"That I know full well," Matthew said, smiling, easing the sudden strain in the conversation.

"But enough of this. What was in your packet from the archbishop of York? Any tidings?"

"Nothing but the province of the church," Matthew answered, swirling the liquid in his cup. He drank his wine well watered; he would not lose his head to drink.

"Then let that be your concern alone," Philip said easily, letting the conversation slide away.

Father Matthew let it slide and did not call it back.

"She laughs with him even now, her anger sliding from her like ice in August," Christine said. "That kiss did not bruise, not her heart nor her temper."

"She has a forgiving heart," Marguerite said. "She

should be more wary. He has proved himself a man who will take what will not be given."

"A forgiving heart?" Christine said, laughing. "Nay, not that. It is that he did not move her at all. What man ever does? I had more hopes for him than for any other who has come here; I will confess to being disappointed."

"I think it is too soon to be disappointed," Lunete said. "It has only been a day."

They sat at one of the lower tables, away from the drama of the high table but with an excellent view of it all. A most lovely situation. They could observe, speculate, and analyze amongst themselves with no worry of being overheard.

Yet Roger and Edward did overhear them.

"Not even a day," Roger said, sliding next to Lunete and throwing a brotherly arm over her ten-year-old shoulders.

Lunete looked at his hand upon her shoulder, and then looked up at him until, with a small cough, he removed his arm. She had not fostered with Juliane for nothing. Did it matter to her that Roger was three times her age? It did not.

"What of our wager? We have won it. Ulrich took his kiss," Roger said.

"He *took* it; you say it well," Marguerite said. "There was little of soft seduction in it."

"A kiss upon the throat was the wager," Roger said. "Will you cry off now that you have lost?"

Marguerite did not answer. Nor did any of the ladies. With an exasperated sigh, Marguerite leaned across the table and kissed Edward upon the brow. Edward was hardly expecting it.

"There," Marguerite said. "The terms are met."

"Those are not the terms I would have called!" Roger said in humorous outrage. "I had that kiss in mind for me."

"The terms are met," Marguerite said again with demure dignity.

"Will you argue the terms now?" Christine said.

"Nay, he will not," Edward said.

"Easily said," Roger mumbled. "I am the one who has lost a kiss."

"And of kisses, you expected Ulrich to be farther in his pursuit of Juliane . . . or not so far?" Marguerite asked. "We could have told you that he will not win."

"How can you say he will not win when you do not know the wager?" Edward said, leaning forward, his elbows on the rough table. No cloths were spared for the lower tables; they were reserved for the high table.

"It is always the same wager," Christine said softly. "It is always the same result."

"Which is?" Edward asked.

"You know the tale," Marguerite said. "Why call us to repeat it? If not for the tale of her, would Ulrich even be in Stanora?"

Roger shrugged and said, "She is a known beauty. Men will travel far to see such."

"There was one," Lunete said, "who traveled from Navarre. Is any woman as beautiful as all that?" When Roger looked surprised and amused, she added, "Not that Juliane is not beautiful."

"Of course," Roger said, grinning.

"I think she is very beautiful," Lunete said again.

"I believe you," Roger said, nodding, smiling. Disbelieving.

Lunete sighed in heavy exasperation and kept her silence.

"You are so certain that her legend will stand?" Edward asked them all.

The ladies said nothing, they only looked amongst themselves; a look passed from brown eyes, to black, to gray, a shared look that excluded men.

"What do you know that we do not?" Roger asked, his light brown eyes suddenly hot with intensity. "What secret skill does Juliane possess that gives her this power? Or is it a potion?"

At their dead silence, Edward added, "Or is it an incantation?"

"Ask her," came a voice. Avice.

Edward turned; she was at his back, her dark hair hanging down to tangle with her silver girdle. Her bliaut was blue, a light, clear blue, and her pelisse was the deep green of the wood. She looked a wood nymph, haughty and elusive. Her pale blue eyes seemed almost light green in the changing light of the setting sun. He stood to face her.

"She is not here," Edward said. "You are."

"Go and find her," Avice said, looking up at him.

"Ulrich has her," he said softly, only for her ears, though Roger chuckled.

Avice said only, "Has he?"

"No man has her," Lunete said. "Or will. She is Juliane le Gel, the Lady of Frost. It is who she will remain."

"Those are just tales," Roger countered.

"Are they?" Lunete said. It was not a question, and all at that table knew it.

Chapter Six

"You are not angry?" Ulrich asked.

"Should I be?" Juliane answered.

They were out beyond the curtain wall, beyond the ramparts, beyond the stone that held up Stanora to the sky. They stood on the plain, the four of them, Ulrich swinging the lure of blood and feather, as he had promised, while Baldric called to the skies for Morgause to return.

"I was hard upon you," Ulrich said, swinging the lure around his head in easy loops.

"You were," she said, sitting her horse. "Yet mayhap not so hard as you meant to be."

He turned to look at her then, uncertain if she was aware of the double meaning in her words. He looked. She returned the look.

She knew. She knew he had fallen, if but for a moment. A single moment that would not be repeated.

"Lady," he said, grinning, "I will not break upon you."

"My lord, any breaking that will be done between us, will be done by you."

He burst out laughing. He could not stop himself and had no will to try. She was a rare one, this lady of ice, rare and wonderful. In all his jousts against skirts, never had he met a woman who played the game by the same rules as governed a man. She was bold. She was proud. She was arrogant.

Wonderful rare.

"You are not frightened of me at all, are you?" he asked, swinging the lure with a harder, faster hand.

"Nay, I am not, but do not take it hard, my lord. I am frightened of no man."

"I would not have you frightened. 'Twas never my intent."

"Nay? Shall we wager on that?" she asked, the smile in her voice ringing out against the sky.

"A wager? Against your fear? 'Twould be most strange," he said easily. "Why would I want your fear?"

"Why does any man want a woman to fear him? How else to control her will and manage her heart? Yet 'tis not uncommon strange. What is uncommon is that I fear no man and will not."

"And why do you not?" he asked, looking up at the sky. Was that not a speck of black against the distant clouds?

"Why, my lord," she answered, following his look, searching clouds gone pink in a twilight sky, "because there is nothing to fear."

"There *is* nothing to fear with Ulrich," William said as he stood at Baldric's back, his small head tilted back to face the sky.

Juliane smiled and said softly to Ulrich, pointing to William, "He is your best and greatest champion, my lord. I hope you know it."

"I do," he mouthed to her, smiling fully.

"I sense an unfair advantage," she said quietly. "Your two to my one."

"I am a warrior, my lady. I take whate'er advantage I can, when I can."

She laughed silently, holding his gaze with her own. "Fair enough," she said.

Fair enough, she said. And she was.

She pushed old fears and dark whisperings out of his thoughts, banishing all to dust in the heat of her smile and the brilliance of her beauty. She was unlike any woman he had known—her strength, her warrior's heart, a meal to be savored with raw and wolfish bites in a world of cold broth. She called forth an ease in him that he'd thought long lost, while at the same instant, she made his blood run hot and fast.

They called her cold, but she was not. It was only that she was as hard and firm as a shield when every man she met wanted only to thrust against her like a sword seeking blood.

Not cold, then, but hard. And did any man want a woman to be hard?

Aye. He did.

"She comes!" Baldric called out, breaking the moment, clearing his head. Ulrich looked hard into the sky and saw the black dot of the merlin swinging down from her pride of place, the highest point of her upward flight. "Keep up with the lure, my lord," Baldric said.

He did, his arm swinging tirelessly in a circle over his head, calling down the merlin with the scent of blood and flesh. Juliane made ready with her handful of fresh pigeon, raw and bloody, to reward the hawk for returning to her mistress and her home.

Down she came in an effortless stoop of speed and grace. Down until they could see her feathers shining in the upthrusting rays of the submerging sun. Down until her beak and talons gleamed black against the pink-gold sky. Down until she was a merlin clear to their eyes, a merlin trailing jesses in the wind and looking to feast on pigeon meat.

She broke her stoop and circled once, then came down to land at Baldric's feet. He took her on his arm, taking hold of her jesses, and then walked slowly, murmuring words of encouragement and praise, to where Juliane sat with the flesh in her hand. With the warmth of a lover, she took the bird upon her wrist, cloaked in worn, brown leather gloves this time, and smiled her welcome. She gave the flesh to the hawk freely and without restraint. Her hawk was home again.

Ulrich slowed the lure and let it drop, watching the Lady of Frost. There was warmth in her, and welcome. If a bird of prey could find its way with the lady, then surely a man could. Ulrich smiled as he wound the string that tethered the tassel of feather and flesh. The hawk would teach him, one hunter to another.

He was wearing an odd sort of smile. She did not like it. When a man smiled that way it was because he thought he knew something no one else knew. Men often thought that, though they were seldom correct.

Still, Ulrich was not quite the same as other men. That was something she was coming to know.

That kiss. That kiss upon her throat. That full, hot kiss that had been all of power and anger and hunger still throbbed upon her skin and in her blood and in her memory. Unwelcome memory. Why should one man's kiss make a mark upon her memory when no other man's had?

She had been kissed before and had done her own kissing in her turn, but never with this effect, never with this throb, this ache, this . . . heat. She was the frost; there was no heat in her and could be none in him.

Why this kiss and why this man? It could not be that the tales of him were more truth than lie. She knew enough about tales to know that they were little beyond pretty words strung together by hungry troubadours thinking more of dinner than of chivalry. She knew better than any the truth about tales, for was her own tale, the legend of Juliane, not extraordinary?

Of course it was. It had served her well and would serve her still.

"She seems little the worse for it," Baldric said. "I am surprised she came to the lure; I would have thought that, with her freedom, she would hunt."

"I think she did," Juliane said, stroking her breast feathers, "yet she returned to the lure."

"When the lure is strong enough, even hunger is not necessary. Only desire," Ulrich said.

"Desire?" Juliane asked. She had known that his smile boded no good.

"To return," Ulrich said in explanation, his look mild. Too mild. "To the hand that strokes and pets. To succor. To pleasure," he said, adding innuendo upon innuendo.

"Aye, I take your meaning," she said sharply, cutting him off. "You seem to know the mind of my bird very well."

"I have a hawk of my own," he said lightly, coming to stand at her side. "I understand what desire will drive a hawk to do."

"To hunt," she said. "Hawks live to hunt."

"So they do," he said, laying a hand upon her foot.

"Ulrich's hawk is a goshawk," William said. "A most fine hawk and well mannered."

"I am certain she is," Juliane said. "A female?"

"Of course," Ulrich said. "I would have the most ferocious of the pair, and is not the female the better hunter?"

Juliane turned her foot within the stirrup and scraped mud on Ulrich's unwelcome hand.

"Always, I would say," she said with a cold smile. "Where is your hawk now?"

"In good keeping, some ways south and west of Stanora, in Greneforde."

"I have heard of it and its lord. How do you know him? His name is great within Henry's domain."

She knew he had heard her insult, for though he was stupidly bold, Ulrich was not stupid. Yet he only smiled and knelt in the grass, wiping the mud from his hand.

"I was his squire," he said.

He could have said more, of that she was certain. William le Brouillard was a name that attracted legends like grass gathered dew; that Ulrich was intimate with him was a surprise. Yet, perhaps not. Had not Ulrich a legend of his own?

Baldric came and took Morgause from her hand and put her on the block, tying the jesses, muddy and wet, carefully. William, at a look from Ulrich, was at Baldric's side, helping with the bird, admiring her. Morgause looked well pleased with herself. She had defended her lady, flown free for a private hunt, returned to the lure, and could now look forward to a quiet sleep in the mews.

Ulrich looked at his squire and smiled.

"He loves birds of the hunt," he said, standing again at

her side, his hand on the bridle this time, well away from her stirrup. "He misses Ela."

"Your goshawk?"

"Aye," Ulrich said, motioning for William to help Baldric in any way he could. "We trained her together from an eyas. He has a gentle hand."

"Did William of Greneforde train you with such ... care?" she asked softly. She had almost wanted to say "affection" but had found a different, better word. A more impersonal word.

Ulrich looked away from his squire and up at her. The light was all but gone, the hour of Compline long past. In the dim light of distant stars and sinking sun, Ulrich's eyes were as dark as sapphires. And as beautiful.

"He did," Ulrich said. "And so will I do with my own squire, and pray daily that young William will be a better man than Ulrich was and is."

"You are a good man," she said without thought. Yet was it not the truth?

"I would be good. For you," he said softly, holding her gaze, and then, breaking the moment, he chuckled and said, "Can this be Juliane le Gel, Lady of Frost, who speaks such wondrous kind words to me? Nay, it must be a lady of the wood and glade, a nymph from the old days who speaks so to me by the light of stars and sun commingled. With such enchantment in the very air, what hope have I?" he finished, all laughter gone from him.

They stared at each other for a few moments more. The sun departed altogether, leaving them in starlight and in the shallow, white light of a rising moon. The green of the woods turned black and the night air was full of the thrum of insects. And in the darkness, they stared upon each other and stiffened themselves against a fall.

"Black as pitch," Baldric said, breaking the enchantment. " 'Twill be God's good grace if we don't break both legs and lose this bird again in finding our way back to Stanora."

Juliane looked away from the shadow that marked Ulrich and, turning her horse, said, "I could find my way to Stanora in a blinding snow."

"What care I for snow? Can you find it in the dark, that is what I ask," Baldric grumbled.

Ulrich, mounted, said to her, "He is very familiar, is he not?"

"He is," Juliane answered stiffly, looking over her shoulder at the lump that was Baldric. It was too dark for him to see her censure, which was a pity.

"He has served you long?" Ulrich asked, checking behind him where William sat upon his small horse at his place behind Ulrich. He would likely have preferred to be behind Baldric, keeping an eye upon Morgause, but that was not his place. A very well-trained squire, by the look of things.

"Very long," Juliane said, "though that could change at any time," she said loudly.

Baldric said, "Get me to Stanora without wolf bites on my neck and you shall see me satisfied. What you do to me after that will only count as blessing, lady."

"You see what I deal with," she said, shrugging.

"I do not hear any wolves," William said, urging his horse closer to Ulrich's.

"Nor do I," Ulrich said comfortably. The track they followed was narrow, wide enough for two to ride abreast but not three. If William could have slid between the two of them, Juliane was certain he would have. "'Tis too early for wolves to hunt. They wait for full dark and moonlight."

"Oh, aye," the boy said, easing his mount back.

"You are very kind to him," Juliane said in a voice just above a whisper. "Is it not strange that your life has been surrounded by Williams? First the knight of your fostering and now your squire."

Ulrich took a deep and easy breath and said, "I found it strange at first, but no longer. Now I do not find it strange at all."

They returned without mishap and with no wolf tales. William, once they were safe inside the walls of Stanora, seemed almost disappointed. They had missed Vespers and Compline, which did not disappoint him at all. To be at his prayers was not William's most favored activity.

Morgause was set safely within the mews, her night to be constrained with enforced quiet. She hardly seemed to mind; her day had been full, even for a hawk, and her belly more full yet. What she had caught while free and on the hunt they would never know, but to judge by the angle of her close-feathered head and the glint in her eyes, she was well content.

As was Ulrich. He was content to let the night pass in quiet peace. His amorous battle with Juliane must wait until the rising of the sun to continue; she had been greeted sweetly by the women of Stanora and hurried off to her chamber, there to certainly tell the tale of her reclaiming of Morgause . . . and her defeat of Ulrich's art.

Let her tell her tales. He was not defeated. Nay, he had come to see some kindred heart in her, some spark of tenderness in her eyes as the sun had set and the moon had risen; in that half-light, that shadow land between the day and the night, he had seen something in her, some soft, quiet thing. A melting.

A small thing, yet . . . something. And in this battle with the frost, even small things were victories. He had won a victory with her, and it warmed him.

The fire in the center of the great hall danced before his eyes, the smoke lifted upward by invisible currents of heat. Invisible currents of heat, yea, it would be just so between them. Drop by drop he would melt her down, finding the woman beneath the legend of ice, finding Juliane.

She was a woman worth the finding.

"Did you kiss her again?" Roger asked, coming from behind him.

"Not all victories are measured by kisses," Ulrich said.

Roger turned and said to Edward, "He did not kiss her again."

Edward came to stand next to them, making a half-moon of the three. William had been sent up to the chamber they would all share, to see that fresh water was ready and that the fire was hot. They were almost alone in the great hall of Stanora. Only a few men-at-arms played at dice upon an upturned and polished stump in the corner beneath a torch, their wagering consuming both ears and eyes.

"I did not kiss her again," Ulrich said with a small smile, shaking his head.

Roger shook his head, too. "And why did you not? She did not take her dagger to you when you stole that first, raw kiss; it could only mean that she was open to more kisses."

"Is this my wager or yours?" Ulrich asked. "Is it my legend for wooing which is to be tested or yours for crashing?"

"I do not crash," Roger said, crossing his arms over his chest. "I am only bold. Many women prefer boldness."

"Not this one," Edward said, rolling a pebble in his hand, moving it from hand to hand.

"She took that kiss to the throat well enough," Roger said.

"She would take anything well enough. Anything that did not touch her," Ulrich said.

"She was not touched?" Edward asked.

"She looked well touched to me," Roger said, brushing his dark hair off his brow.

"Did she?" Ulrich asked.

In truth, he was not certain. He had been all heat, all white anger, all passion when he had taken her by the throat, her pulse beneath his lips. Her body soft and vulnerable under his hands. Of what she had felt, he could not know. He had been lost in his own fire and had known only the desire to touch her and to lay his mouth upon her. Never had he lost so much of himself in the net of a woman.

Never had he been so vulnerable.

He shook free of the memory and lifted his eyes from the fire. The hall of Stanora was whitewashed, the floor stoneflagged, the stones lichen gray and tawny white and set close upon each other. A clean, white hall was Stanora, with little of the dark, smoky shadows that haunted other halls in other holdings. Wooden shutters bleached pale gray by time and weather were closed against the wind holes at night, keeping out the night birds and the night air which they rode upon. A welcoming hall, a wide-open, sunlit hall, yet shuttered, walled, and stony nonetheless.

"Enough of Juliane," Ulrich said. "We are in this place for more than wagering against a most compelling legend, though she serves our cause well enough."

Roger and Edward nodded and stepped back from the fire, finding what shadows they could in Stanora's hall.

Chapter Seven

"Did he kiss you again?"

They stood all round her, Christine, Lunete, Marguerite, and Avice. Her aunt Maud was to bed an hour or more past, once she had seen that Juliane was safe returned; for the hawk, she had not spared a care. Hawking was not to Maud's taste and she could not see how it could possibly be to anyone else's.

They stood in the chamber that Juliane shared with Avice. Marguerite, Lunete, and Christine slept in a smaller chamber with a yet smaller bed just to the south of her own. A great gallery, overlooking the hall below, was the passageway that bound all the chambers together. Her father slept in the lord's solar, just beyond the small chapel on the corner. Maud, her father's sister, slept in the lady's solar, which had the advantage in winter of a center fire, and the disadvantage in summer of a center fire; in either condition, there was room for only a very small bed tucked against the cold stone wall. Maud did not complain. She had little cause and little enough recourse. If not for Stanora and Stanora's lord, she would have been bundled off to an abbey long since, and abbey beds were not known for their comfort.

"Did he?" Christine asked again.

"Would he have dared?" Juliane answered, not answering.

"Then he did not?" Marguerite asked. "He is more cautious than the tales of him, then."

"Or perhaps only more patient," Avice said with a smile and a shrug. "You are not quit of him yet, Juliane, if I read men right."

"Not too difficult a task," Juliane said with a smirk, "as they trumpet every thought like the blast before the joust."

"Then what thought did you read in him while you were out hunting Morgause?" Marguerite asked, sitting herself down on the high bed in Juliane's chamber. It was a much softer mattress than her own and the linens finer.

What had she read? Too much. Far too much.

He was not dissuaded, this man from Caen, and by this point in her amorous joustings, all others had been. He was more confident, then, or simply more arrogant. But nay. He came bringing more than arrogance to this game of love. He brought laughter and lightness of heart, and that was welcome indeed. More, he seemed to be unafraid of her.

It was even possible that he liked her.

What place for friendship in the rituals of courtly love? No place at all. 'Twas a game of power, an exercise in dominance, a game she played very well, even if she played it with little true joy. But with Ulrich she had found, for a moment, a measure of joy, of joviality, of pure play, and it had tasted very sweet.

By such confections a woman could fall, she knew that very well. She would not fall to him, losing her heart, her name, her pride of place in the skies of legend. Not for him. Not for any man. Not even once.

She had not conceived this game, but, thrust within it, she would surmount it. Victory was all that mattered, and no cost was too high to own it.

"Juliane?" Lunete asked, calling her back from her thoughts.

"He may not have kissed her, but he did *something* to her," Avice said with a chuckle intended for all to share. All did share in her chuckle, but their eyes were worried. All except Avice's.

"What did I read in him?" Juliane said, shaking thoughts of Ulrich and his too blue eyes from her mind. "I read in him a man who plots to win even when the sword has pierced his heart. A man who laughs when trodden upon. A man who smiled when, by purest chance, I used his hand to wipe the mud from my boot."

"You did?" Lunete said.

"You did not!" Christine exclaimed.

"I did!" she said, laughing.

And it had felt glorious, as had his wry smile at her bold affront. Strange man to be so mild when so vilely insulted. He played with more heart than most she had encountered in her years at this game.

"Did you mind his kiss upon your throat so very much, then, that you would take such a revenge against his bold claim?" Avice asked. The brazier was behind her, her features hidden in shadow. The rest of them were on the bed. Avice stood alone, heating herself by the flames. She was ever cold and always sought the fire.

"We should not have made that wager," Marguerite said somberly. "We pushed him to it."

"You did not push him to anything, and do I look harmed to you?" Juliane said. "He lost his temper, a simple thing for a man to do, and he won his wager by force and not by skill, which tells me something of the nature of the man in this game we play. As to revenge, there was and is no need. He stirs nothing but my increased desire to win. This game will play most well."

"Are you certain you are not angry? We did not think it would go so far," Christine said. "Though it was a kiss of passion, was it not?"

"If fury is passion, then yea, it was," Juliane said.

"And you felt nothing?" Avice asked, lifting out her skirts to capture the heat. It had been warm all through the day, yet the stones held the chill of December even in July.

Had she felt nothing? Nay, she had. Something. Something dark and burning and buried. Something, some fiery pulse, some . . . exhilaration. He opened doors in her that must stay closed, stirring passions that ought not dwell in her, unleashing heat when all must stay cool and distant, cold and unreachable.

But there was nothing as to that. She would master herself. He would ne'er take a kiss from her again, nay, nor a touch.

"You looked . . . frightened," Lunete said.

"Upon all the saints, I was not frightened," Juliane answered, thankful that here was a question she could answer in all truth. She had not been frightened by that violent, stolen kiss upon her throat.

She had been aroused.

"Now, speak to me of that kiss."

Ulrich knelt before the lord of Stanora, his head bowed. They were in the quiet solitude of the lord's solar. Alone. The day was behind them and the night stretched forth, the dawn a dream of tomorrow.

"I ask your pardon and your forgiveness, lord," Ulrich said, not lifting his head. "I make no excuse. Your mercy is all I may rest upon, and I will rest easily in whatever judgment you choose to make."

Silence greeted this abject apology. Dark and heavy silence which was, in time, broken by a chuckle of laughter.

Ulrich kept his head bowed, but he felt the beginnings of a smile twitching at his lips.

"The tales of you are true, then," Philip said. "You are most fluent of speech, your manner most smooth. Tell me, and lift up your head; I shall not smite you, though I have the right. Tell me, Ulrich, what wager have you made concerning Juliane?"

Ulrich lifted his head, his smile flown. 'Twas one thing to make a wager, 'twas another to tell the lady's father of it.

"I spoke of the wager in the hall, my lord." At Philip's lifted brow of diminishing patience, Ulrich elaborated, " 'Twas wagered that I could . . . stand," he said, choosing that particular word with care, "in the face of Juliane's legendary frost. That is all, my lord. By no touch and no word will I compromise her virtue. She will be as chaste when I ride from here as she was when I arrived. 'Tis only that I will—"

"Stand," Philip interrupted. "Yea, I take your meaning. Yet I think there must be more to this wager than that. Is there nothing in it of the melting of the frost? Is there no . . . response required of Juliane?"

Ulrich swallowed and kept his silence. This part of the wager could see him killed, and none would question the justice of it.

"Tell me," Philip commanded. "If you be man enough to make the wager, be man enough to stand by it, in all the ways that word implies."

Ulrich stood, his hand upon his sword hilt, and faced Juliane's father. He might just slit Roger's throat when he saw him again. If he saw him again.

"I will stand, that is half the wager. The other half," he said, looking into Philip's unflinching gaze, "is that I will make Juliane le Gel melt for me, her legend running from her like snow on sea sand."

"And leave her chaste?" Philip asked.

"And leave her chaste," Ulrich stated.

"And can you do this thing?"

Ulrich was caught unprepared by that question, and he tilted his head in surprise, blinking hard.

"Well," Philip said, crossing his arms over his chest, "can you?"

"Yea," Ulrich said with a wry smile, "I can."

"There is no doubt?"

"Nay," Ulrich said, shaking his head, "no doubt at all."

Philip made a noise of approval mixed with skepticism and then turned to the wind hole that faced the distant woods to the south. The first stars were out, large and bright in their dominance of the sky, a summer sky, warm and mild and clear. A quiet sky.

"Then you are alone in that, for I have grave doubts. What of that kiss?" Philip asked. "Was there not a falling there, Ulrich of Caen? Did not your standard flag and fall with my daughter under your hand and mouth?"

"Nay, there was no falling," Ulrich said, "and she was unharmed. Never would I use my power against a woman. Never would I tease from her what she has no will to give."

"Yet if you tease her will to give you what you want—how then, Ulrich? How will my daughter fare against such wagering as that? I am a man as well as you; I know the course a man will travel to achieve his ends with a woman."

"I will not lie," Ulrich said. "I have done so in my life, yet I have sworn to scorn that path. Your daughter is safe with me. Though I may say that she is safe enough in her own care. A stalwart and fierce maid you have in her, my lord. She can well see to her own defense."

"Do you think so?" Philip asked, stroking his missing ear. "She will be glad to know it, for Juliane prizes fierceness as tenderly as any knight. Yet to me, she is a daughter, and her protection is all my concern."

"Have I your pardon, my lord, for that display against your authority over the daughter of your loins and of your house?"

"A moment and one question more," Philip said, avoiding a direct answer. "You did not fall, and, one man to another, I will believe it. But what of her? Was there a softening? Did she begin to melt, Ulrich?"

How to answer this? Aye, as man to man, 'twas one thing, but this man was a father, and fathers did not speak of their daughters' melting. Unless the man was Philip, in charge of a daughter who would not melt for any man. Philip must take a different course with a daughter who would not and could not be wed.

There was Ulrich's answer.

"My lord," he said, blue eyes meeting blue in that bright-lit chamber, "she did."

"Did she?" Philip asked, measuring the confidence in Ulrich's eyes, a scouring Ulrich could feel like a brush against chain mail in a close fight. And so this was.

Ulrich only nodded, content to let Philip take this where it would go.

"Then," Philip said, "keep on with your wager, Ulrich of Caen, and tomorrow, if this wager plays out the way you predict, I will sweeten the pot, adding wager upon wager. Are you game?"

"My lord," Ulrich said with a slow grin, "I am always game for a good wager."

The hall of Stanora was quiet, empty of all but sleepers and their sleeping noises, the favored dogs upon the hearth the moon high now in the sky and white as new teeth in a hungry wolf pup.

He went by corners when he could, keeping to the shadows, and then tripped softly down the wide, straight stair that led out of the hall and into the stone forework of the tower gate. All was still, serene, the night slipping past like water in a stream, quiet and full. The dogs shifted in their sleep, one lifting his head and gazing with blinking eyes as he left the stony confines of Stanora tower. With a huff of sleepy air, the dog lay down again, rearranging his head upon his paws, content, drifting back into dreams before the man had even left the tower gate.

No one had seen him.

The main chapel, the one that served all Stanora, was on the eastern wall and close by the main gateway into the holding. The men-at-arms upon the wall and posted at the gate looked outward for any sign of danger, not seeing any within. Not knowing there was any within.

He made for the chapel, and, though he might have been seen, what was there to note? A man on his way to church? A man in sudden need of prayer? What harm in that? None, and so he could claim if stopped. But he was not stopped.

He entered the chapel by an open door and knelt in piety. A figure stood under the rood of Christ, his head cowled and his shoulders cloaked. This man stood and waited, saying nothing, yet expectant for all his silence.

"Father," the other man said.

Father Matthew stepped out from beneath the shadow of the cross and said, "What can you tell me?"

How they both came to be at the line of garderobes just before the hour of Matins, neither could have said. They had come silently, each from separate chambers on opposite sides of the spiral stair. There were three garderobes in a line, stone slabs with holes cut in, dumping what was put into that hole into the cesspit below.

They stood staring at each other in the dark, the only light coming but faintly from the arrow slit high above them. The moon was low now, brushed by distant tree-tops.

She was not going to use the garderobe with him so near, even if she was standing with her legs crossed, trying not to put her hand between and hold it in.

Even in the dark his eyes looked light. Strange eyes, so gray and light that they almost showed silver against his glossy black hair. He wore his hair long, longer than the priests liked, longer than outward piety demanded, yet it seemed to suit him. She liked it, though she supposed she should not.

"Go to," she said. "Go first."

"You go first," he said. "You live here."

"You are the guest. Besides, is it not easier for you?"

"What?" William asked.

Lunete sighed and squeezed her legs tighter. "Just . . . go to. Be quick."

He shrugged and faced the garderobe, not caring that she watched. She sighed again and turned to face the dark and the gallery rail.

She could hear it, of course. A long fall of water, thin and oddly musical. It was easier for boys. Everyone knew that.

"Your turn," he said, dropping the fabric of his tunic and turning to face her.

"You have to leave," she said, not able to resist the need to press her hand against her urge, an urge that grew stronger as relief came close.

"Oh," he said, obviously perplexed. "Yea. Yea, I shall leave."

"Leave, then!" she snapped, lifting her shift even as he stood there, staring at her.

He shuffled down the short passage until he escaped it, his body blocking her view of the gallery rail, and then he was gone. She threw herself upon the open hole and quivered with relief. She almost felt like laughing, the release was so sweet.

When she was finished, her skirts pulled down, enjoying a deep and contented breath, she left the passage. He was waiting at the end, his hips leaning back upon his crisscrossed hands.

"Oh," she said. She had not thought he would be waiting. Had he *heard* her?

"I stayed to walk you back," William said.

"Walk me back? My chamber is just there," Lunete said, pointing. Although it did seem rather far in the dark of Matins, past the lord's solar and the chapel and Juliane's chamber. "But since you waited, I thank you," she said, beginning to walk.

"You have been here long?" William asked.

"Three years this month," Lunete answered. "I came at seven."

"You are ten?" William said. "I am only eight."

Only eight. He was very young for a squire.

"You are tall for your age. I would have thought you eleven," she said, though it was not the truth. He looked no older than nine, but why tell him that? "How that you came to be a squire at such tender years? You must be very skilled."

William shook his head, stopped, and then shrugged. A single torch burned in the great hall below, sending uneven light up to them a floor above. He stood mostly in shadow.

"I do not know that I am *very* skilled. What skill I have comes from him. I try to learn what I can."

"As is only right," she said. Was it not the truth for them all? They were fostered out to learn what they could and, with that knowledge gained, to find their place in the world. Her place was set; she was to marry and be the lady of Dunvegan, if the betrothal contracts held. "Where are you fostered?"

"With Ulrich de Caen," he said, looking at her askance.

"I mean, with what lord? What holding?"

"Ulrich is my only lord, and of holdings, he has none. Yet my training with him is all I could wish for. I pray for no other place than to be with him. He is a good knight and a better man."

She had not known that William had so many words in him. She had taken him for a quiet boy. And so he was, unless the talk was of Ulrich.

"So all the tales declare," she said, nodding.

But no matter how many tales were told of him, with no land, a knight's track was rough indeed. With no land, there would be no wife, with no wife, no children, no place to take root or rest on the whole great earth. Still, it was a common enough thing. There were not enough wives for every man who would have taken one.

"Your door," he said, stopping. She would have continued on, talking in the dark, if he had not stopped her. "My lady," he said, dipping his head most courteously and with great maturity.

"Thank you, Squire William," she said, dropping a quick curtsey.

They looked at each other in the heavy shadow cast upward by the distant torch, gray eyes searching gray. Did her eyes look so silvery and lovely as his? Nay, for his were banked by black brows in the shape of wings, while hers were sheathed in ashen blond. His were the more lovely, she was certain.

They stood so, staring, measuring, and then she smiled

at him, a smile of youth and play and pure simple joy. And William returned the smile. Then he turned and was gone, making his way back along the gallery rail, trailing his hand upon the wood, whistling lightly in the dark. In the end, when all sight of him was gone, she could still hear his whistle.

And she smiled.

"Are you awake?"

"Nay," came her voice from beneath her pillow, "I am asleep."

"Then awaken and talk to me," Avice said, lifting the pillow from Juliane's head. Juliane had a death grip on her pillow and held it fast.

"Go to sleep and dream I am talking to you," Juliane said, turning on her side and throwing the blanket to her knees.

Avice reached down and pulled the blanket up to her shoulders, snuggling in as if it were midwinter.

" 'Twould be better conversation than this," Avice said.

"I agree heartily," Juliane said.

There was silence between them for a time. An owl hooted distantly, his call carrying far over the plain where he hunted.

"Are you asleep?" Avice finally asked, her voice hushed.

"Nay," answered Juliane in a whisper, "I am awake."

"Good," Avice said, fussing with the blanket and squirming upon the mattress. "Now tell me truly, how fares it with Ulrich?"

"It would fare better for me if I could sleep."

"Then it goes not well?"

"If I answer 'poorly,' will you lay another wager upon my head?" Juliane quipped.

"I have asked your forgiveness for that," Avice said meekly. "I did not intend that it should turn so foully upon you."

"'Twas nothing, Avice," Juliane said, reaching out to take her sister's hand. They held hands in the dark and let peace gather around them. "I am only tired. You truly would have been better served to speak to me in dreams. I am certain I am more pleasant in dreaming than in waking."

"Not true," Avice said, smiling, squeezing Juliane's hand. "But tell me, was that kiss truly nothing to you? It looked so . . . so . . ." Her voice trailed off into silence.

"How did it look?"

Juliane could feel Avice shrug against her side.

"It looked so full of passion, so relentless, so . . . wild."

Relentless, that was the word for it.

"Have you ever been kissed like that before?" Avice asked.

"Nay," Juliane said slowly, casting the word and the truth of it up into the night air, casting it away from her. "I never have."

"What was it like?" Avice said, turning on her side and propping herself up on her elbow.

"It was . . ." Juliane said, stretching her response out, teasing her sister. "It was . . . passionate . . . and relentless . . . and wild."

Avice laughed in pure delight. "I knew it had to have been! And were you truly not frightened by it? By him?"

"Nay," Juliane answered. "I was not and I will not be. Place another wager if you choose. I will stand against Ulrich, even if he plays false, as he did today."

"I cannot decide if I would enjoy another wager placed against Edward of Exeter's pride or if I do not want even a wager to bind us. He is a most stern man."

"Stern?" Juliane said. "I would not have thought him stern. He is handsome, I did note that, and his eyes are quite green."

"They are not. They are ordinary hazel."

"Ordinary hazel? Is hazel so ordinary, then? I thought you liked hazel eyes, that you thought them very changeable and mysterious," Juliane said, teasing Avice without a drop of mercy.

"There is nothing mysterious about that man. He is irritating and irritable and nothing more."

"He did not seem irritating to me, or perhaps it is that he was not being irritable *toward* me. I found him most agreeable."

"Spend even one hour more with him and you shall discover the truth about his temper," Avice said.

"An hour and I shall know the truth?" Juliane said. "Shall we wager on it?"

Dead silence met her suggestion. It was almost as if Avice had finally fallen asleep; almost but for the stiff tension emanating from her still body.

"What would be the wager?" Avice asked.

"Perhaps it should be that after an hour in his company, I could make him laugh."

"I do not think he *can* laugh," Avice grumbled, tugging at the blanket. Juliane kicked her feet free.

"Then it is a most fair wager. I could well lose it," Juliane said.

"When have you ever lost?"

"Perhaps tomorrow, when I cannot make him laugh?"

"Done," Avice said after the smallest hesitation.

"Done," Juliane said. "And what shall I win?"

"I note you do not ask what you shall lose."

"Win or lose, what are the terms?" Juliane said.

"The terms?" Avice asked slowly. "I am too tired to think of terms now. Tomorrow will be soon enough."

Which Juliane understood to mean that Avice could not now think of terms horrible enough; when she was fresh from sleep, then she would be ferocious enough to think of terms most to Juliane's disliking.

"Tomorrow, then," Juliane said, shifting onto her side. 'Twas only the way of wagering, to make the wager worth the cost. There was no ill will in setting a penalty or a prize.

"What is it like, Juliane?" Avice asked as they slid toward sleep. "The heated wagers and the men come to test themselves against your chill name? What is it like to be bathed in legend?"

Juliane's thoughts tumbled awkwardly, painfully, and she answered her sister with a sigh of weariness. "It is an old game."

"A game you have mastered, winning every pass."

"Aye," she said. "I win."

Of course she won. She had to win. Winning was all that was left to her, but she said none of that to Avice. Avice had slipped down into slumber, finding rest when Juliane could find none.

Chapter Eight

The day dawned bright and hot, the wind hiding behind high-flung cloud, making the sky white and still. The people of Stanora rose for Prime, the first mass of the day and the one designed to set their hearts and minds upon the will and might of God. In practice, some responded better to such guidance than others.

Juliane wore a bliaut of icy blue and a pelisse of startling white. She glowed against the white heat of the day, and she knew it. Her hair she wore unbound, a gleaming net of gold to fall upon her like scattered jewels and careless finery, curling in half-felt embrace about her ribs. Her girdle was silver set with lapis and topaz, hot and glittering against the chill white and blue of her garments.

She was a maid to make a man look. She knew 'twas so, and so was pleased when Ulrich looked and looked again as she came, late, into the church. He looked so long upon her, his jaw slack, that both Edward of Exeter and Roger of Lincoln turned to look as well, which was more than fine. Let them all look. They should look; look and not have, see and not understand. Especially Ulrich.

He, himself, looked most fine today. His dark hair was wet and pushed back from his brow, his skin glowing with the touch of the sun, his blue eyes sharp and bright beneath his lance-straight brows. He had a nose like an arrowhead, straight and slim and smooth, pointing with soft force to a full and generous mouth. A most compelling man, she could admit, if only to herself. She had felt that mouth upon her throat and would not soon forget the soft and urgent heat of him.

He was well deserving of his name, she would grant him that. That and no more. No more kisses, no second touch. No part of him would take any part of her; let that be his lesson for today. His wager was lost. He had only to admit it.

As she let her eyes drift down to the stones beneath her feet, she was the very image of sanctity and piety. The very image of a godly daughter, with only innocence as the chosen companion of her heart; the very daughter any lord would claim with cheer.

Except that her father knew her better and had little cause for cheer,

Avice walked at her side, gowned in shades of green. Her bliaut was the color of the deepest wood and her pelisse the green of March, upon her sleeves were embroidered stems of purple heather, long and lacy and climbing up her arms. Her girdle was of copper bound in silver and set with amethysts that sparkled in the heat. Avice looked beautiful, yet all eyes were upon Juliane, as they ever were in times such as these. These times of wagers and of winning.

As to wagers, Avice had not yet set her terms. That would come after Prime. Juliane was not worried. Did she not even now have Edward's gaze in her possession? How soon would follow his laughter?

As soon as she decreed.

"He cannot stop looking at you," Avice whispered as they knelt side by side.

"I know," Juliane whispered in return, thinking of Edward.

"I think he plans even now to kiss you again," Avice said, thinking of Ulrich.

"Planning is not doing," Juliane said, laying the matter of Ulrich to rest with the dead.

"Proclaiming is not stopping," Avice answered, unburying the dead.

Philip snapped his fingers at them, his brows lowering in stern warning to silence them. But his disapproval did not stop their looking. Nor did it stop the looks they received from the opposite side of the aisle.

Prime seemed to last longer than usual. Perhaps it was the heat. Perhaps it was the stares. Perhaps it was only that Juliane was eager to begin this new game of winning a laugh from quiet Edward. He was a man of Ulrich's age, of Ulrich's generous height, of Ulrich's bearing, yet unlike Ulrich for all that. His hair was light brown, the color of stripped bark in the sun, and his eyes were shining hazel green. His nose was blunted, his mouth less formed, his brows lacking the winged shape of Ulrich of Caen's. Still, a handsome man, steady in his manner, reserved in his speech, a knight of good name and strength. Just the sort of man to find the joy of laughter.

Just the sort of man to fall to her.

"Stop staring at him," Avice whispered.

"I am not staring," she whispered back, keeping her head down in supposed prayer.

"You are! Why else would he be staring at you?"

"He is staring?" Juliane whispered, smiling.

"You know—"

"Lord Philip looks very angry," Lunete said softly, smiling at Lord Philip innocently.

Avice and Juliane stopped talking. Again.

Prime dragged on. The flies were thick and loud as the morning gathered heat. Father Matthew's voice droned on, his Latin perfect and precise, his manner matching. The drone of flies made mock of his Latin, merging and disguising his words, blending with his message and leaving only dreams. All words were lost to buzzing.

"He looks less sour today," Avice said as Father Matthew began his final benediction.

"He looks the same to me," Juliane said.

"I think he looks very handsome," Christine whispered. "The blue tunic suits him most well."

Blue tunic? Edward was wearing the color fawn. 'Twas Ulrich in the blue, a fine, rich blue that mirrored her lapis girdle. As to that, he did look very well in the blue. Yet she had no time for Ulrich; Edward was her goal today.

"Yea, he looks right well," Juliane said casually. " 'Tis a lovely tunic. And look how Edward's hair shines against his soft fawn tunic. Why, he glows like a candle."

"He does not glow," Avice said.

"Glow?" Marguerite said. "Men do not glow, or should not," she said solemnly.

"Is there not such a thing as battle glow?" Lunete asked.

"There is such a thing as penance," Philip said sternly at their backs. The younger girls jumped. Avice and Juliane merely turned to face their father, their faces innocent of wrong, of even the thought of wrong. 'Twould not be far off to say that they came close to wiping the stain of original sin from their expressions.

"Maud!" Philip said, Prime over. "Can you not keep better charge of the ladies of this house? They whispered so that the very flies were deafened by their hissing."

"Brother, I will see to it," Maud said, coming to his side. She had been standing at the end of their row, next to mild Marguerite, who never spoke during the mass. Juliane had chosen her spot well and with much experience.

"Very well," Philip said, and with a look to where Ulrich stood, he left the chapel, his steward close upon his heel.

With a look to where Ulrich stood? What game was this?

In a long stride, Ulrich was before her, Edward, Roger, and William at his back. If he thought to surround her and intimidate her with a force of men, he had misjudged. There was nothing she liked more than a force of men to reckon with.

"Edward," she said, striking first, "that color suits you well. We were all remarking upon it. You truly caught every eye."

"Did I?" Edward asked, bemused.

"Oh, aye," Juliane said, smiling softly. He looked halfway to a grin even now; she really must find out the terms of this wager before it was won altogether and Avice cried off.

"What about his tunic?" Maud asked.

"The color," Juliane said. "It is most fair and suits Edward of Exeter most well."

"Aye, and so it should," Maud said crisply. "A tunic must fit if it is to function, and why not have one in a color which suits? Tell me, Edward, are these the colors of your house?"

"Lady," Edward said solemnly, "I have no house. This tunic is only one which I won from Roger of Lincoln in a wager some months back."

"Does the color suit me as well, Lady Juliane?" Roger asked. "I feared it did not and so I willingly lost it to him," he added in a loud whisper.

"Then your wager was ill-struck, my lord," Juliane said, "for this lovely shade of fawn would suit your dark hair very well indeed."

Edward had no house? No roots to bind him to the earth? That was sad indeed. The world was hard and cold without a house to spring from. She could almost want to win a laugh from gentle Edward for that reason alone.

"A compliment from the Lady Juliane?" Roger said. "I am won at the word."

"The lady is quick to praise and pet," Ulrich said, his voice low and musical. Intimate. "Do not make much of it, Roger, and you will protect your heart."

She would accept no such intimacy from Ulrich, not today. Today was for Edward and the winning of that wager. To put some distance between herself and Ulrich was all to the good. She could still feel that kiss in memory, and memory was too strong.

"And how would you know, my lord Ulrich?" she said. "You never have heard praise from my lips, and certainly I have never petted you."

The girls tittered with cooing laughter and looked at Ulrich, to see what he would do. Would he strike, or would he settle under the slap of her hand? She did not know; she could not read his eyes, though his gaze held her own, a bolt of blue that met hers with unwavering regard.

If he thought to make her cower in girlish disquiet, he did not know the legend of le Gel at all.

"Never petted?" Ulrich said. "Aye, mayhap that is so. But praise? Aye, that you have done, lady. When I took you in my mouth, your skin soft under my teeth, I heard your praise in the moaning cry you let slip past your lips. By my touch, lady, there was praise for me in that."

That kiss again. That stolen, torrid kiss. That kiss that was all of devouring and none of chivalry. That kiss had touched her where she would not be touched, and worse, he seemed to know it.

"If that was praise, you understand little of it, having been praised so seldom in your life," she countered.

"Of this brand of praising," he said without blinking, "I have a great store of knowledge and experience. You are not the first to moan beneath my kiss."

By the saints, this was battle as she had not fought it before. He spoke too hard and too true, all courtly phrases thrown from him like a broken sword. How that she had pushed him to this and so quick? This game was harder to win, yet she would. She always would. The legend of Juliane must stand.

She took a step nearer to Ulrich, accepting his challenge, motioning Maud away with a slight flutter of her hand. Maud would have rescued her from this attack with a look, but the day had long since passed when Juliane le Gel needed rescuing.

"If that is courtly love, then I am not surprised the women of your past have moaned in outrage and in—"

"Fear?" Ulrich said, interrupting her with a hard smile.

"Loathing," she said. "I cannot speak of fear since I

know not the state, and certainly not at the hands of any man."

"Is this the talk of courtly love?" Lunete whispered to the room in general. The words drifted up to the high ceiling of the church, empty now of all but those who battled and those who had wagered on the outcome.

"Nay," Juliane answered, still holding Ulrich's hard, blue gaze with her own. " 'Tis not, Lunete, but this is the game as Ulrich of Caen plays it, and I will not withdraw from any fight."

"I would not fight you, lady," Ulrich said softly, taking a step nearer to her. They were but a handspan apart and he towered over her; she lifted her head and faced him down, her posture easy and defiant. Confident. Arrogant. "I only want"—he dropped his voice to a seductive whisper—"I only want to win you."

"I cannot be won," she said, feeling the heat of him and enclosing herself in chill, sending him the message of her ice. "I play to win what *I* want, my lord. What you want matters not at all."

"Hard words," he said, smiling, unafraid and undeterred.

"Hard meaning," she countered, smiling back at him.

"And so the battle is to make you want what I want."

"It cannot be done."

He leaned down and ran a fingertip over her cheek and whispered for her ears alone, "It shall be done."

A shiver, a shiver of cold chill, ran from where he touched her down her spine and raised the hair upon her arms in foreboding.

Empty, meaningless foreboding. It *could not* be done.

"Is this the same wager as before?" William asked, looking up at Ulrich.

Ulrich smiled once more and then drew back a pace from Juliane; he turned his gaze upon William, standing small and dark in that press of bodies.

"A man does not speak of such in front of ladies, boy," he said to his squire. "The rigors of chivalry do not allow it."

"Nay, not the speaking, only the doing of it," Juliane said, taking a full breath and realizing that it had been many moments since she had. Her breath had all been caught up in her throat.

Ulrich shrugged in easy humor. "I do not make the rules of the world, lady, I only find my way as best I can in the role given me. Of my soul, little else is required."

"Then *is* this the same wager as before?" Lunete asked, looking briefly at William as she spoke.

"I will not speak of wagers when I speak of Juliane," Ulrich said, looking her over with a possessive gaze. Possessive? Where and when had he claimed that right? "Of Juliane there should be only words of love and unending devotion."

"I would rather hear of wagers," Juliane said, interrupting what she was certain was the first note in a speech on her beauty and her worth. "I have some interest in that."

"I find this talk of wagers most unchivalrous," Maud said sternly, making her presence known. "It does your reputation none but ill, my dear, to haggle so with strangers within our walls," she said, tossing a quick and sharp glance toward the men. "Come, the day awaits, and it should be better spent than in this common display of baseborn manners."

And so she had been rescued after all. Indeed, she had been in some small need of it. Worse yet, Ulrich seemed to know that she had just been delivered out of his hand and his will, for he smiled most cheerfully as she followed Maud out of the church.

In all the fuss, she had forgotten about poor Edward and the wager there.

Which had been Ulrich's intent.

"She wants you for some cause," Ulrich said when the men were alone in the church.

"You do not think she could want me for myself?" Edward said.

"'Tis not the time to jest, Edward," Roger said. "There is a new-made bargain on the table."

"So there *is* a new wager? This is not more of the old one?" William asked.

"I think there are many wagers in this place and we are more and more a part of them," Ulrich said.

"I *knew* I liked it here," Roger said, nodding his head in general good cheer.

"She made straight for you, first with her eyes and then with her sweet words of praise for the color of your tunic," Ulrich said.

"It was my tunic first," Roger said.

"But you lost it in a wager," William said. "That is what you said."

"And so I did, but now I wonder if I should have wagered my cloak instead. 'Tis older than the tunic and of not so flattering a color," Roger said.

"I think you put too much upon your tunic," Edward said. "I think it was that the lady was drawn to *me*; she used the tunic only as a lure to draw me into speech with her."

They were tormenting Ulrich without much mercy, though he expected none. They did not want to lose this wager they had struck over the lovely Juliane. They were certainly not going to help him win his wager. Nay, they would strike to draw blood at any turn, finding their fortune where they could. But they would not find it in this. Juliane was on the run, and Edward was both her quarry and her place to put into, a hiding place where Ulrich could not touch her.

But there was no such place.

For herself, she was enough to draw any man to her.

For her legend and the wager that rested upon it, she was enough to keep him near.

For the lure her father dangled before his eyes, she was more again than any woman he had yet to know.

He played hard for her, doing now what he had sworn never to do: win her will to his, so that her heart melted into his desire, her body readied to receive him. Had he not vowed to her father just hours ago that this path he would not take?

Aye, he had, but he would not lose her. His want and his need were too strong to play by the rules in a game he had wearied of long ago. He would not force her, nay, not that. He had not fallen that far.

He would not let her fly from him, and he would not let her cast about for another man to tempt and defeat with her cold beauty. Nay, Juliane was his. He would make her his and then find from her father what the worth of that winning would be.

"Stand before her in cloth of gold and she will still be mine," Ulrich said to them all.

The silence was complete. They looked at him, these brothers in arms, and they did not smile.

"This has gone beyond a simple wager," Edward said.

"Far beyond," Ulrich answered, walking swiftly out of the church.

They followed, William to the rear.

"Has she snared you, then?" Roger asked, brushing his dark brown hair back from his face. The wind was kicking up, odd bolts of unseen power to twirl in a man's cloak and lift his hair.

Had she snared him? Aye, perhaps she had. He had never known a woman like her. Bold. Seductive. Aggressive. Hard and soft at once. Compelling and resisting. Alluring and defiant. She played hard at courtly love, yet so did he. They pushed against the rules and made new boundaries, flying higher than any had gone before. But even so, it was not Juliane who had swung the lure to make him linger and wonder; it was her father.

What was it that Philip was prepared to offer? A man with a daughter who would not marry was a man with an asset wasted. An asset lost.

If Philip offered her in marriage, Ulrich would swear to any terms Philip could name. He would come to that lure. He would be tamed at a word from the lord of Stanora.

To have a wife, a landed wife, was to have power. And Ulrich wanted land power. His only course was to take a wife, but he had nothing to offer in the marriage bargaining, nothing to offer Lord Philip in any negotiations for Juliane. Nothing except his certainty that he would not fall before her cold charm, her hot seduction. And that might be all that was needed to win a woman who felled a man with cold breath and hard looks, who made a legend of her refusal to be seduced.

Was there ever such a perfect pairing as this they made

between the two of them? He, who had vowed to never again press against a woman's virtue, and she, who stood against all threats to the virtue of her virginity?

But he knew nothing yet, and guesswork did not carry a man far. He had his task set before him for today: to prove to Philip and Juliane that of falling he knew naught. Of the hot joy of winning, he knew all.

"Be it said that I would and will snare her," Ulrich answered Roger as they crossed the wide and windy bailey to the tower. Prime was done. It was time to break their fast. It was time to tangle with Juliane yet again.

He had been set to harder tasks in his life, and his proving himself hard was all this task entailed. Did ever a man have more joy in his work? With that thought, he entered the dark portal of Stanora's tower gate.

"What have you said to him?" Juliane asked her father as they sat at table.

Philip shrugged and drank deeply of his wine, his blue eyes avoiding hers.

"You have struck some bargain. I can sense it," she said, staring hard at him. He was her father and lord of all, including her. Most especially her.

"Bargain?" Philip said lightly. "I made no bargain. Am I fallen to the depths of bargaining with a landless knight?"

"I do not know," Juliane said. "Have you fallen that far? To judge by Ulrich's words and way with me, I would say that he has tempted you somehow to fall that far, my lord. But I shall not fall with you."

"There is no falling in this, Juliane, no defeat," he said, throwing off his light mood and matching her dark one. "I would only get for you what you must have. I will see it done, and if bargaining be the price, then the price shall be met," Philip said, turning to face her, his wine forgotten for the moment.

"But not through me," she said stiffly.

Juliane turned from his gaze to look out upon the hall. The light was uncertain, the clouds heavy, the wind gusting hard through the wind holes high above them. And then her eyes turned to the entrance of the hall, to those broad and stately stone steps that led into the heart of Stanora, to the form of Ulrich striding up them, his smile sure and steady, his head high and his eyes bright. He was so very sure of himself of a sudden. This was more than arrogance. This was certainty that the battle was won and all that was left was the catching of his prize in his callused hands.

She was no man's prize.

"Look at him," she whispered, unable to stop watching as he made his way to the high table. His stride was long, his shoulders broad and massive with muscle, his throat a cording of lean tissue and vein; she could not turn away. Could not because in his eyes, in his blue, blue eyes, there was victory. Confident, easy victory.

And she would be no man's victory.

"Look," she said again, turning to face her father. "Do you not see it in his eyes? I know you do. You put something there, some hope, some claiming that is no part of this game between us. What have you offered him, Father? How have I failed you that you would bargain me away to an errant knight with nothing but a name for seduction? Am I to be wagered?"

She struck blind, but hit true. She could see the truth in Philip's eyes before he turned back to his wine.

"I wagered nothing."

"Do not cast me to him," she said softly, grabbing Philip's hand. His hands were gnarled and hard as ancient oak, the tendons rising high and wide beneath turgid veins thick with sluggish blood. "What will become of me if you cast me to him?"

"Juliane," he said, laying his hand over her own. "I do not cast you. I never would. It is only that you must marry, and I must, as your father, find the man to fit the deed."

She pulled her hand from his. "There is no place for me in marriage. Have we not discussed this?"

"Then where will you go?" he whispered harshly. Ulrich and his band had crossed the hall and were nearing the high table. "To the church? Is that the life you seek? Father Matthew would have it so. He wants a nun's life for you and thinks you want it for yourself. Do I know you so little that I told him wrong? I cannot see you fit for a life in the abbey, daughter. You are bred for more freedom than the abbess would allow."

"I do not seek the abbey life," she said, lowering her gaze to her lap. "I do not want the married life."

"There is little in between," he said.

"Aye, there is," she said, looking up at him suddenly. "There is freedom."

"Juliane," he said, shaking his head softly, "there is no freedom in this life. The only freedom is beyond the grave. Why else does the lure of heaven sound so sweet? Why else does death hold no fear?"

"You talk of death too much of late," she said, shaking her head back at him in gentle admonition.

"I am of an age to think of death," he said, smiling at her, their quarrel done.

"When is not the age to think of death?" she countered. "It surrounds us."

"When Juliane speaks of being surrounded," Ulrich said, standing at her back, "I must be named, for I would surround her with praise and sweet companionship until she is enveloped."

"I was speaking of death," she said flatly, refusing to look at him. Let him stand and talk to the top of her head. She would not gift him with a look.

"And when she speaks of death, I would most eagerly be named," he said, and then, leaning down to speak softly in her ear, said, "for who has not heard of the little death that women enjoy at the hands of men? So would I be to Juliane, the bringer of the little death of ecstasy. Let my name be on her lips when she so expires."

Juliane looked askance at her father. He had not heard, for his missing ear was turned to her, yet he did not rebuke this wandering knight for speaking so intimately into his daughter's ear. And all was told by that inaction. So, Ulrich had been given a free hand and a loose rein in this seduction of words. Well, against words she had ample defense.

"I can promise you," she said, turning her head slightly and speaking into his hair, "when I think of death, I shall think of Ulrich. Most heartily so."

"She bats at my intent, wounding me with words, yet she will not look at me," he said, his breath moving the hair near her ear and throat.

"I need not look. I know what I shall see."

"Then look and by looking, prove," he challenged.

She knew she should not. She could feel him, his heat, his scent rising from the wool he wore. A lock of his dark hair hung down just in her sight, and she could see the line of his jaw, the movement of his mouth. His beard beneath his skin was dark, a shadow of masculinity, a brand of manhood; she yearned to touch it, to touch his jaw, to find if his skin was rough, to see if his mouth was soft and warm surrounded as it was by coarse male beard.

"Look at me, Juliane," he breathed. "A single look will not kill. There is no death in that."

And so she looked, telling herself she would not be mocked by him, nor by any man, which was the truth yet only truth in part. She looked because she could not keep herself from looking. He was a temptation to her will, and she gave in to it, in small measure.

He was not smiling. His eyes, so blue, so impossibly blue, stared softly into hers. He did not mock. He did not gloat at his small victory over her; nay, he only looked. And by his look, his victory was increased, for she was now ensnared and could not look away.

What was it in his eyes—some promise, some hope that he was offering her?

Whatever it was, she did not want it. She did not want him.

"And so I have looked," she whispered, aware that all the voices of the hall were sliding into silence. "Now, what have I won for taking up your challenge?"

"Nothing at all, Juliane," he whispered back. " 'Twas nothing more than a look. A look shared. Not everything has a wager behind it," he said, straightening up but still looking down at her.

"Oh, I think in that you are wrong," she said, holding his gaze, refusing to be consumed by it. "Between us, all is of wagers, and of winning."

He smiled, his eyes dancing with humor. "If that is so, then I think I have just won."

"You have won nothing," she scoffed. "No wager was won in this."

"But, Juliane," he said, sitting down at her side, bumping his knee against hers, "I only wanted to look into your eyes and so I have done. I have won. You cannot rob me of it now."

Always he spoke so sweetly, with such careful seduction, trying to win her heart by flattery and worthless praise. That was not the way into her. Man after man had tried that path and found themselves lost in the dark, finding her not at all. He was like all men and walked the same road with her. No matter what her father tried to arrange with Ulrich, no matter how great Ulrich's arrogance, he would fail.

It was only the feel of him wet and hot on her throat, taking from her what she would never give—that was the battle she had to fight. Killing that memory. Banishing the scent of him, the force of him, from her thoughts. That was the only weapon he had brought to this battle, and he had brought it by mistake.

Never had she been taken in such a way. Never had she known such will and hot intent empty of false words, consisting of pure heat and raw need. Never would she know it again.

And that was to the good. It did not serve her and it had no place in her life, as he did not.

"Then keep your memory of it, my lord," she said, turning her eyes from his, moving her legs from his, shutting him out. "It is all you will ever have of me."

She could feel him smile, the arrogance of it hitting her like a hammer.

"Shall we wager on it, Juliane?" he said softly as he ripped into the loaf of bread before him, releasing the tang of yeast.

"Wager on what?" she asked, looking at him from beneath her lids, watching his hands. They were long-fingered, with clean nails, brown with weather and hard with use. The feel of his hands on her jaw, holding her still while he took her throat, the scent of him in her nostrils, the heat of him pulsing through his tunic: all were bound in the memory she would kill.

"This place is rife with wagering," he said, "and the wagering is all to do with us. Should we not gain by it ourselves? Strike a wager with me, Juliane, and let us see who shall win it."

"I shall win it. I win all wagers. I am Juliane le Gel, and any wagering a knight may undertake with me, he is destined to lose. It is foretold."

"Nothing is foretold but that the Lord God will come again. Beyond that, we are free to find our way until He does. Find your way with me, Juliane," he said, running a fingertip across her shoulders.

"You are not afraid of losing?" she asked, holding still under his feathery assault, which was willfully ignored by her father. No bargain indeed. They had struck something between them, that was sure.

Ulrich smiled and leaned closer to her on their shared bench, his mouth hovering near her shoulder, and answered, "I am not afraid of you."

She turned to face him suddenly, his mouth now close to hers, their eyes locking upon each other, and said, "You should be."

The hall was silent now, though all ate and drank, yet

watched the sparring at the high table. And watched Lord
Philip do nothing. And learned the nature of this game,
placing quiet wagers on the outcome. This was battle rare
for Stanora; most knights had run by now, gone before the
laughter died a lingering death. But Ulrich stayed on and
Juliane fought on, and so they wagered on.

"Shall we wager on it?" he asked with raised brows,
holding her gaze, dominating her with his eyes and with
his heat.

"And how shall it be proved that Ulrich is afraid of Juliane le Gel? Such things are not measured, they are felt,
and—your pardon—I would not trust your word on it."

"You ask my pardon while defaming my honor?" he said
on a chuckle. "Such is the language of a lady undefeated."

"You have said it, my lord, and it is so."

"Then other means must prove that I fear you not, lady,
and these shall be the terms. That I can lay another such
kiss upon you as I did yesterday and that, without your falcon to fight for you, you shall not push me off until I release you."

It was then that she felt the first twinge of fear.

Chapter Nine

It was not a wager she wanted to make. He could see that
in her eyes. Wide and wary they were, so light a blue that
they looked like January ice.

He had her. Almost, he had her.

That kiss had done more to shake her chill than she

wanted him to know, mayhap even more than she wanted to know about herself. He had touched her. He had taken her in his grasp and laid his mouth on her when she had not willed it, nor wished it, nor welcomed it.

Yet she had withstood it, and held firm against him even now.

"Come, lady," he said softly, entreating, coaxing, luring. "Will you take the wager?"

"Is this the way Ulrich of Caen wins a kiss he has not won? By wagering for it?" she said.

Ah, she was cool. She would not show him apprehension, though he could feel it ripple out from her like wind-driven waves in a pond.

"Juliane," he said, taking her hand in his. It was cool and dry. He would have preferred her coated in sweat and shaking with nervousness. "I only ask what it is in you to give. A kiss. A single kiss. You are not even required to return it. I shall do all," he said with a grin and a wink.

She smiled at him, shaking her head in wry admonition. "Aye, you shall do all. Grave service. Brave sacrifice," she said. "You have kissed me once, my lord, in just this fashion. Is once not enough for even Ulrich of Caen?"

"Once is barely sufficient for Ulrich of Caen. I would only show you the truth of this." He stared into her eyes, willing that cool blue to warm to him. Willing her to feel the lure of him. Willing her to fall into temptation and desire. "My mouth. Your body. One kiss."

She licked her lips, and her eyes looked out over the hall, escaping him as she could. All eyes returned her look. She and Ulrich were much observed. He could not blame them. With such a woman and such a wager, all eyes should look and keep looking.

"And for all eyes?" she asked.

"Nay, for my eyes only," he said, his voice pitched low. "I would not share you with any other. You will be mine."

" 'Tis only a kiss," she said in reminder.

"You will be mine," he repeated with a half smile, softening the lie he was about to speak, "for the space of one kiss. Is it a bargain?"

She squirmed on the bench, her knee brushing his thigh. He fought the urge to touch her leg and hold her against him, thigh to thigh. What was it about Juliane that beat at his control? Like it, he did not. There was no room for a misstep in this game.

"You like to wager," she said.

"Nay," he said, "it is only that I like to win."

"As do I," she countered.

"Then take this wager, Juliane. At least then one of us will win."

"You think to win," she said, grinning slowly. Her smile lit her face like sunlight on snow.

"I *know* to win," he said, grinning back at her. "But so do you. Let us see which of us is right."

"Where?" she asked, taking a deep breath, stretching her bliaut tight across her breasts.

"In the orchard," he answered, understanding her at once.

"Too many eyes," she countered. "The stables."

"Done," he said, nodding. "When?"

"After Vespers."

"I must wait twelve hours for the taste of you? Nay, that is too long to wait. Terce."

"Terce is but an hour. I will be gone from here in an

hour," she said, looking out over the hall, away from him. "The hour of None."

"Still too long. Sext," he said, enjoying their bargaining.

"After Sext, before the meal."

"After Sext, before the meal," he repeated, considering her. "You will be here? You will not ride off?"

She straightened and faced him, her eyes alight with chilly fury. "I will honor the wager, my lord. Have no fear as to that."

"Then I will have none," he said, touching her hand with a finger. She was warmer now, not so chill, but still not trembling. An able adversary was Juliane of Stanora.

"Where do you go now? How will you spend the hours until the meeting of our wager?" he asked.

She smiled and turned from him, dismissing him, removing her hand from his touch and her eyes from his searching gaze.

"That is not your province, my lord. Do what you will with your hours. Spend them as men will do. I will meet you in the stables at the passing of Sext. Look for me there. You shall find me."

"And have you," he breathed.

She stiffened and swallowed loudly, and then she breathed and smiled away her tension. She stood and turned from him and walked slowly from the hall. At her departure, all eyes turned to him, to see if he would follow.

He would not. Let her think on what the noon hour would bring. Let her wonder where he was, as he would wonder over her. Mystery was part of the game and played upon tension like fingertips on a bowstring; all was nervous pain until the joy of sudden release.

So it ever was. So it would be with her. Though, through it all, he would leave her chaste. That vow had been twice made, both to comrade and to father; he would not break it, no matter the stakes in this gaming. Not again. That price was too high.

But he *would* win.

When it was seen that he would stay, all talk resumed, the sound rising to the rafters to startle the restless birds nested there.

When it was proved that he would stay, Lord Philip turned to him and considered him with a solemn gaze. Ulrich returned the look and kept his silence.

"A most . . . heated wager," Philip said.

"A most certain winning," Ulrich said.

"Oh, aye, it is certain that one of you will win. It is equally certain that each of you is certain who that will be. But how will you pass the hours until Sext?" Philip asked.

Ulrich shrugged in easy confidence and said, "I will hunt."

"The wolves have been most fierce this season. They spend their days in the rocky crags north of here."

"Then I will hunt wolves."

"Until you hunt my daughter at the agreed-upon hour," Philip said without smiling.

"My lord," Ulrich said, turning on his bench to straddle it and face him. "I will do her no ill. I only seek to prove, to her and to you, that I do not fear her, that I will stand, that no woman of this earth can soften me."

"And the proof?" Philip asked.

"The proof I leave to you. But what are the terms of this bargaining? I would know what I wager for."

Philip lifted one shoulder in a heavy shrug. "Stand the test of Sext and we will speak again. For now, tell me of your people and your house."

So this *was* of marriage. For no other reason would Philip inquire as to his house and the merit of his name. And now it came to the time when the talks ever and always ran cold, yet he plunged ahead. The prize was too sweet to deviate or to hesitate.

"I am bastard born," Ulrich said, looking straight and true upon this man who could change the course of his life.

"Your father?"

"Did not claim me."

Philip frowned and said, "Ill fortune. And your mother's people?"

"Did what they could," Ulrich answered, which was true, though what they did was little enough. "I was squire to Lord William le Brouillard of Greneforde. I was knighted after a skirmish in Wales. I have traveled far in the nine years since, as far as Outremer and the white walls of Jerusalem."

"Yet no house, no people, no land."

"Nay," Ulrich said, holding his head high and his eyes steady.

So it always came to pass. Every foray into the hope of a wife and the wealth of marriage turned upon this one point. He had no name and no place beyond what he had carved for himself, and that was little enough by any man's reckoning.

"Well," Philip said, clearing his throat and setting the topic of Ulrich's bastardy aside, "let us see what Sext will bring."

"My lord," Ulrich said over the swelling of emotion. He had not been cast aside out of hand. There was still hope that this wager might turn unto his favor. "My lord, I will not disappoint."

"You have confidence, which is more than any other man had after a day in the cold company of my daughter," Philip said. "We shall see how well it will serve you."

Ulrich stood, William a small, dark shadow at his back, and bowed to Lord Philip. "Until Sext, my lord. I am to the hunt."

"Enjoy your hunt, Ulrich of Caen," Philip said with a grim smile. "I wish you the blood of the kill."

If there was a double meaning in that, Ulrich chose to disregard it. No father would jest so, not even with respect to a woman as formidable as Juliane.

William followed him out of the hall, following the track Juliane had made just moments before. He could almost smell her scent, the heat and glow of her as she had moved over the flagged stones of Stanora's hall.

"Will you ride alone, my lord?" William asked as they ran down the wide steps and through the gloom of the tower gate.

"Nay," Ulrich said, looking over his shoulder at the boy, at the clear gray eyes that shone like moonlight with the hope of an adventure against a wolf pack. "I thought to take my squire. I shall need a strong arm and a cool eye at my back." Ulrich grinned at William's delight and said, "Get the horses. I will find a bow in the armory."

"I can shoot—"

"And one for you as well, though I cannot promise a bow made to your size."

"I am growing," William said, standing tall, a bit taller than usual.

Ulrich looked down and saw that he stood on his toes.

"And growing taller as we speak," Ulrich said, pushing down upon the boy's head until he was flat-footed upon the earth, as God intended boys to be. "Go. Get the horses. Trust me to do right in the matter of the bow."

"I shall, my lord!" William said over his shoulder as he darted off across the bailey to the stables.

The stables. Ulrich ran a hand through his hair and sighed. 'Twas an unusual place for a bout of honor and the winning of a wager, but then, Juliane was unusual. Had he ever found reason to wager a kiss from a damsel? Nay, he had not. A month past he would have scoffed at the insult of the idea. But a month past he had not met Juliane.

The tales of her were true, in part. She was a beauty, that was true. She was a woman to make a man question the unassailable strength of his manhood; that part of the tale was true as well.

In this world, man dominated by the might of his arm, the power of his will, the force of his passion. Man ruled and woman served, as the priests taught. Her body was weak, her soul given to sin, her thinking unreasonable; in this life, a woman needed a man to rule over her and keep her ways straight.

Juliane made mock of such teaching. To look at her, the blood ran hot. To parley with her, the blood ran chill. A frost-rich woman. A woman of hot beauty and cold company. A woman to take and have and hold.

As he had taken her in his mouth.

That kiss had told its own tale, a tale of passion buried

beneath ice and of a will which could be shaken in an instant of unbridled desire. There was fire beneath the ice of her legend. Fire he had touched. Fire he had stoked. Fire he would fan again. He knew now the way, and she had given him the means by agreeing to this wager of stables kisses.

Nay, nay, not kisses piled one upon the other in confusion and disarray; a single kiss upon her skin, a single kiss to mark her. A kiss to cast her into passion's fire, consuming the ice that cloaked her.

He had spoken true to her; he did not fear her. He would not fall. He would win this wager, and if God be kind, Juliane would be his wife. He needed a wife. He needed to make a place in this world, and a landed wife was the path to that goal. And if the wife be Juliane le Gel? Why, he would melt her, as he had wagered with Roger. A single wager to spin so many dreams upon. 'Twas a thing to make a man fear, if it be in him to fear a woman and her ways. 'Twas not a thing he feared. She was a woman. He knew all the ways of women. This game he would win.

He strode across the bailey into the armory, the sounds of all humankind buried by the weight of his plans.

She did not take out Morgause. She did not have the head for hawking; her thoughts were full and heavy with the weight of Ulrich of Caen. Of fear, she had none. He was a man, and she understood men down to the ground. With that knowledge, she would defeat him.

He would not take her, not even in a kiss.

Oh, she would let him lay his mouth upon her, but nothing more. She would not fall to kisses. Of sweet words, he had none to move her. If he thought to make her fear a falling, he was wrong in that, as he was wrong in all.

He thought he knew her. He knew women, she would grant him that in full accord, but of her, he knew nothing.

"Where to, lady?" Baldric asked at her back.

They were striding forcefully and without direction through the bailey. The mews were behind them, the stables before them. The stables. Aye, she had chosen well. The stables were as much a home to her as her sleeping chamber, and there was not a horse in Stanora who did not come to her call. The stables would serve her well in this wager.

"To the hunt," she said. "Get out the hounds. I go for boar," she said with a sharp grin of raw anticipation.

Baldric grunted and mumbled something into his beard.

"If you would say something, then speak out," she said. "Though why I encourage you, I can hardly explain."

"I only said," he said in mock humility, "that I did not think that boar was what you wanted to sink your knife into."

"I do what I can," she said. "Would you have me kill him?"

"I think, lady, that you will do what you will do."

"And so I have always done," she said.

Baldric mumbled something more.

"Yea?" she asked, stopping to look over her shoulder at him.

"I only said that this one, this Ulrich, is a bit . . . more, and that you may have to do a bit more to get from him what you want."

Juliane shrugged and continued walking, the stables

casting a long shadow upon the dirt of Stanora. She paused at the entrance and sighed, feeling at ease hidden within the dark, surrounded by the warm smell of straw and manure.

"I will do what I must," she said. "And it is he who shall pay the price for it."

"I think he will pay whatever price is set, lady," Baldric said softly, distinctly, and without mumbling, "and pay it without hesitation. He wants you that much."

Surely he did. Yet she understood this game, this hunt, and she would surpass him in skill and cunning. She was no untried damsel, and in that lay her confidence. He would not and could not take from her that which all men wanted. Her body. Her blood. Her legend.

She could feel Ulrich's wanting like a brand threatening her: white-hot and hissing, seeking, scorching, but not touching; Baldric was right in that. Ulrich's wanting was a fire that blazed, and she knew enough of men to know that his wanting was for more than her body. He wanted all she possessed, body, heart, and land, and she was going to give up none of it.

"He may want, but he will not have," she said, entering the warm dark of the stables. It was of stone and slate; the horses were a large part of Stanora's wealth and as such were well protected against fire and arrow.

"Lady," Baldric said with a smile, "I believe you. It is only that you must convince him of it."

"Baldric," she said, throwing off the weight of foreboding, "I liked it better when you mumbled."

"I feared you might," he said, mumbling.

Juliane pointed to a black mare, small in size and delicately formed. A groom hurried to saddle the horse for her. To Baldric she said, "I shall need my cloak and gloves. If you will see to it?"

"Lady." He bowed, his eyes alight with humor as he turned to do her bidding.

He left and, to the best of her knowledge, left without mumbling any incautious remark. She appreciated his restraint.

"Come, Onyx," she said as the groom led the black mare out into the bailey. "Let us ride to the hunt and forget all about the murmurings of men and their wayward plans."

"Wayward?" said a voice behind her. A voice she was coming to know well. "My plans are less wayward than forward," Ulrich said, the grin in his voice plainly audible.

Juliane turned slowly and with confident ease. Ulrich stood battle-ready, bristling with bows and quivers packed tight with arrows, his sword hanging upon his hip, his smile ever fixed upon his face. A man for all times. A man underfoot. A man confident of himself and his power.

Why did she feel like grinning just to see him standing before her in all his man-pride? She killed her grin and brought forth bristles; bristles were needed now more than smiles. This one smiled too often. She did not need to learn bad habits from him.

"Your time is forward enough," she answered. "Did we not agree as to the hour? You are before your time, my lord."

"I came not to the stables in search of you, lady," he said. "I came merely for a horse."

"And I thank you that you can make the distinction," she said with a sharp smile.

"I ride to the hunt," he said, smiling at her jab. "And you?"

"I am also to the hunt," she said.

"We have much in common. At least in the stables."

He kept repeating that word, reminding them both of their stables wager. As if she were likely to forget. Or decry. Small chance of that; she would beg off from no wager, no matter how repellent.

"You have a far reach to make that claim of thin kinship. There are many who ride to the hunt and yet few who make the kill."

Let him hear her warning cry in that and run back to the horizon from whence he came.

Ulrich grinned and walked toward her, his sword swinging lazily at the movement of his hips, the gleam of the hilt catching her eye.

"Do you question my skill? I can hunt and I can kill. There is no joy in hunting without the stain of blood to mark it," he said softly.

And she knew he spoke of more than hunting stag or boar or wolf.

"Is it the sight of blood which calls to you, Lord Hunter, or is it the smell?" she asked, standing her ground as he advanced upon her.

Ulrich grinned and leaned close to her face to whisper, "It is the taste, lady. It is purely the taste."

"You are barbaric in your tastes and in your practices," she said, leaning away from him.

"I am," he said unrepentantly. "I hunt for blood and for the kill. To roam through wood and meadow, tilting at yarrow and daisy, is a lady's pleasure. I am a man, Juliane, my needs are more base. My tastes raw."

"With manners to match," she said, turning from him to find her mount.

The groom had led the horse ten paces off, well away from the warfare taking place in the bailey of Stanora and within the dark shadow of the stables. He was no fool.

"My manners do not suit you?" Ulrich said. "Perhaps they will improve by the hour of our wager."

"Scant time," she said.

"Or it may be," he said, with a slow and heated smile, "that I can instruct you in matching your tastes to mine. It has been done."

"A taste for blood?" she said with a smile. "If the blood is yours, then you have good hope of succeeding in that quest, my lord."

Ulrich blinked, his blue eyes wide in sudden shock, and then he laughed. "Well met, lady, and well spoke. This is a wager I would come far to see won. I am sudden glad that I came to Stanora and met Stanora's legend."

And he meant it. She could see that he meant it. Her answering smile was upon her face before she could stop it, and then she gave up all hope of trying.

"Of a sudden," she said, "so am I. At the very least, you have admitted that you have set yourself up against a legend."

"But, lady," he said, laughing, "so have you."

And with a salute to her, he whistled for his squire, mounted, and was gone across the wide bailey and out beneath the tower gate. Gone. For now. Until the hour of their wager.

It was an hour she was growing eager for, more eager by the moment.

Another kiss from Ulrich of Caen. Juliane felt the tumbling lightness in her belly and clenched herself against the rolling of anticipation.

"Looking forward to Sext?" Baldric asked, coming from the tower.

"If I am, it is only because I look forward to winning," she said, licking lips gone dry and swallowing burgeoning eagerness, banishing all thought of Ulrich to the bottom of her cold heart. "As to that, did you see Avice while you were within? I have the rewards of a wager to settle with her before the day is done. Aye, and the sooner the better."

"Awash in wagers, you are," Baldric said.

"Did you see her?" Juliane asked again, clasping the reins of Onyx as she prepared to mount.

"Aye, and still at the table she was, talking, plotting," Baldric said.

"Plotting? Plotting what?"

Baldric grinned at her and shrugged.

"You are becoming more useless by the hour, Baldric," Juliane said. "Your future is looking quite uncertain."

Baldric mounted his own horse and followed Juliane through the gates. Watching her back, he mumbled good-naturedly, "Not if I keep winning these wagers."

"That did not go well," Marguerite said, referring to the display they had all witnessed at the high table.

"Nay? I thought it went very well," Roger said, grinning. "They have made a wager between them. I know the look in Ulrich very well. I wonder what the wager is."

"Do you?" Edward asked, sipping his wine. "Knowing his look as well as you claim to, can you not guess what it is he has wagered with the lovely Juliane?"

Roger sat up and leaned his elbows on the table. "You think you know? What?"

"If he set the wager, which by Juliane's face he did, then it was for something he wanted from her, something she would not give unless forced by the lure of winning a wager against him."

"She would not wager *that!*" Christine whispered, her brown eyes huge and horrified in her delicate face.

Edward laughed and shook his head. "And he would not take his winnings if she did. Nay, this is not so great a wager and harms no one. Look, even her father, who must have heard all, has let it fly, watching to see where it will land."

"A kiss," Lunete said softly. "He has wagered for a kiss."

"Aye," Edward nodded. "But whether he has wagered to get one or give one, that is what I am unsure of."

"At least you have the humility to be unsure of *something,*" Roger said.

"Making another wager?" Avice asked as she came up behind Edward.

Edward stiffened and said, "Wagering seems to be *your* game. I have other ways of marking time."

"You mean besides being discourteous and arrogant?" Avice said with a sweet and deadly smile.

Edward gritted his teeth and said nothing. He did leave the table. He did not look back as he walked across the hall and down the wide steps that led to fresh air and, temporarily, freedom from the female sex.

"Pushing him at your sister?" Roger asked softly. "Or just pushing him away?"

"I would shove him down a well if I could," Avice said, taking Edward's seat.

"If I were going to shove someone into something," Lunete said, "it would be into the garderobe."

"A lady should not shove anyone," Marguerite said loftily, then added, "but if I were going to shove someone, it would be into the moat at Portesdone. It has not been drained for twenty years."

"What of the wager?" Roger said, bewildered by this abrupt shift in conversation. He was mistaken; there had been no shift.

"We are speaking of the wager," Christine said. "Do you think Juliane will just stand there while Ulrich kisses her again? She may well shove him into the ditch that runs the length of Stanora's village. It is running high and wide and stinks of . . . well, you know what it stinks of."

"And do you think that Ulrich will allow himself to be cast into a ditch by a woman?" Roger asked, thinking it was all a jest.

Silence met his words—bored and knowing silence.

It seemed by their look that Juliane le Gel was well adept at shoving.

Chapter Ten

She never had asked what it was he was hunting. No matter. She took the trail that pointed north toward the crags that abutted the marsh and woodland. Boars loved that sparse woodland. Onyx did as well. It was good ground, solid and firm, the rocks clear and easy to avoid. The sun was a distant warmth that flirted with the clouds draping the blue of a summer sky. A good day for a hunt.

A good day for a wager.

But it was always a good day for a wager, especially as she was so skilled at winning.

Theobald, armed and ready to defend her, rode at her side. Baldric walked ahead with the dogs on the leash, searching for tracks in the grass. He had his task before him, and she could let her mind play with the possibilities of the day. She had two wagers before her, Edward and Ulrich. Edward was the easier. She would lure him, laugh with him, and win him. But what was to be her winning? It was just like Avice to avoid the setting of terms.

Had she not done the same with the knight from York, a man of ruddy complexion and riding a gray steed? Aye, Juliane remembered well his horse, a fine animal. Of the man she remembered naught but the wager. And the winning. Of the terms, Avice had been negligent, and since that time, Juliane had been diligent in the setting of them. Except for now. Ulrich had distracted her.

He was a very distracting man.

She did not like what he called forth from her, this treacherous softness, this uneasy joy, this gentle falling into laughter and gaiety and fun. A woman was soon lost if she fell into fun with a man. There was only one sort of fun a man wanted with a woman, and it was not to the woman's advantage.

Even knowing that, she liked him. Liked his company, his look, his laugh.

A most, most dangerous quarry, to seduce the hunter into unwilling admiration and affectionate regard. She would hardly have the will to toss him from her life if he proceeded apace. Yet he would not. Did he not need a wager to worm his way into her presence? She must not fall to that lure again. 'Twas too much to his advantage.

He was very fond of wagering. She liked that about him, understood it. She even understood his confidence that he would win, because she had exactly the same confidence in herself. A fine pair they made in that, though only one of them would win, and it would be she. She would make certain of it.

She always did.

"The dogs have caught a scent," Baldric said, turning to her.

Juliane left her thoughts of Ulrich and their battle in the dust at her feet and looked instead at the pack of dogs clustered around Baldric, their tails high and quivering, their noses to the ground.

"Set them to it," she said, adjusting herself upon her saddle, preparing to set Onyx to a run.

With a baying like a thousand trumpets, the dogs were off, chasing through the wood, their paws setting the leaves of last autumn into the air behind them, turning them to dust. And into that swirling dust rode Juliane and Baldric and Theobald, her favorite man-of-arms, who carried the lance. Theobald was quite good with the lance. They would all enjoy the scent and sight of blood this day, if Theobald held true to his skill.

Through the high shade they ran, the dogs before them running as heralds of the hunt, in their throats the prophecy of blood crying forth to any who stood before their charge. Through the hot air of high summer the horses ran, their withers bunching beneath the gleam of sweat, their breath coming in hard snorts, their hoofs pounding soft upon the damp earth beneath the trees, pressing the leaves of seasons past into dusky mold. Through the mottled light Juliane ran to the blood of a kill, certain that a boar awaited her, certain of victory. Ever and always certain of victory.

It was no boar that awaited her.

Ulrich stood in the deep shadow of a darkened wood, a rough crag of silvered rock rising at his back. Before him was a pack of wolves, snarling, two of their number dead or dying upon the dirt, their coats marled with blood and tissue. Five wolves remained, two at a distance, seeming to want to run into deeper darkness, to flee the dogs rushing toward them. To be outnumbered was not a wolf's desire; a weaker foe was more easily won, and they hunted for food, not sport.

Ulrich hardly noted her coming. His eye was upon the wolves at his feet. His bow was broken. His sword was out. And he was snarling as ferociously as the wolves he faced, his lips lifted to reveal white teeth, his head lowered to match the wolves, stare for growling stare. A match for any wolf.

His squire, the boy William, was upon Ulrich's horse, to judge by the long and mismatched length of stirrup to boy, and he held his small bow with arrow nocked and ready. Yet by his quivering breath and unsteady hand, he looked hardly ready for a wolf attack.

Ulrich did. Of fear he showed none. Of feral anger and blood-lust he showed all. He looked ravenous with the desire to kill and draw blood, tear flesh, break bone. He looked a man to devour a wolf in raw and bloody swipes.

He looked a predator, from skin to bone, a predator. A hunter who sought only to kill. A man who drew blood as easily as he drew breath.

Of the lie of courtly love and chivalric banter, he showed not a trace.

With a sudden swipe of his sword and a lunge, he pierced the lung of a black wolf with a silver-tipped tail. With a squeal, the wolf went down, bleeding fast and hard into the dirt. Ulrich moved back to shield the boy, his sword ready and dripping red, his eyes the merciless blue of fire.

In an instant Juliane saw all. In the next instant, the dogs set the wolves to scattered flight, and arrows sent them scurrying faster past the crag of rising rock and into the deep shade of the wood. In an instant, they were gone, the echo of the crying dogs the only sound to mark their passing. Theobald followed the dogs at a run, nodding to Ulrich as he passed, one man of blood to another, and then he, too, was gone.

Through all the action, Juliane's eyes had not left Ulrich, who stood protectively before the boy who was to serve him.

"Lady," Baldric said, "I would follow Theobald if all is well here."

She could not tear her gaze from Ulrich, from his eyes gleaming blue in the dark green shade of a summer wood, from the movement of his arm as he sheathed his sword, from the tender motion of his hand as he reached to lay a calming touch upon his squire's shaking thigh.

"All is well here," she said, releasing Baldric.

A lie. All was not well. She was shaking to her very heart, the image of Ulrich in his killing feast fresh before her eyes, her eyes dazzled by the rapacious hunger of it.

Baldric left—she knew it by the pounding of his feet against the earth—yet her eyes stayed upon Ulrich. He whispered to the boy, his hand large upon the thigh of his squire, his voice low and sweet, full of gentle mirth and soft encouragement. The wolves lay dead in the dirt, a carcass of silvered fur pierced by a lance of sunlight striking through the trees, the hum of flies already to be heard as they prepared to feast upon the warm flesh of a recent kill. But she could only look upon Ulrich.

Captured by Ulrich.

The sweat, the splattering of blood, the taut muscles of his neck and jaw, the huge fist of his clenched hand upon his sword—all burned into her eyes, scalding memory. A hunter. A killer. A protector. All three together in a single man.

Warrior.

In time, he turned to her, pushing a hand through his hair, walking to her through the lance-light; in that fragmented beam of light his hair shone with sparkles of gold and red, like jewels, like something precious. Like something beautiful.

But he could not be beautiful.

"Lady, you came in good time," he said, leaving the light in a stride, shattering her vision.

"Did I?" she asked, her voice low and soft. "I think not. I think there was nothing here which you could not best."

She meant it. And hated that she meant it. He had killed a wolf or two. What man had not? Yet he had been alone, his squire more hindrance than help, and on foot. The safety of his horse he had given to another, lesser to him in all ways.

Ulrich grinned at her words of praise and came near upon her, stroking a hand down Onyx's muzzle. The horse snuffled against his hand, soothed out of any stray agitation at the smell of wolf so near.

"Including you?" he said, grinning up at her, his hands full of her horse.

Juliane smiled and shook her head at him. "I think I have praised you enough. More than enough."

"*I* do not think so," he said, starting to laugh.

"And why should you?" she countered, pulling her smile into sterner bounds. Aye, he was a warrior, who laughed when he killed and killed with delight. But these thoughts would not help her win their wager, and, like the warrior she faced, she understood that life was all of winning. "But how did you lose a horse? The wolves are fierce now, the summer having been dry, yet I do not think they would have come against two men on horseback, no matter their desperation."

Ulrich smiled and nodded at her choice of words and looked over his shoulder at his squire, who lifted his chin and slipped off Ulrich's mount at her casual notice of his manhood. The small squire swiped a hand across his nose and ran that hand through his hair, a gesture crying loudly of a man who had not a care under heaven.

"And so it would have been," Ulrich said to her in a whisper, "but that my squire had needs which required him to dismount. A whiff of wolf, the horse bolted, and so you find us."

"And so I find you," she said softly in answer, smiling in spite of herself. "A man's needs do ever and always land him in trouble most foul."

"It would have been most foul if he had not attended, lady," Ulrich said. "The air around and beneath him would have been most ripe."

"And the horse would, perforce, have still bolted," she said.

"As you say," he said, laughing silently, careful of his

squire's tender pride even now. "Yet you are here and all is well."

All was not well. He made her laugh too often. He was too beguiling to her senses. He was too aware that he beguiled. He was too close upon the softening of her purpose, urging her to forget her need to win in this wager of theirs. They were too alone, it suddenly came to her. The wood too dark and still. The air too hot and moist. The pounding of her heart too loud and fast.

All was most assuredly not well.

"William," Ulrich said, turning from her, though his hand slid to the bridle, holding her horse, and her, to this spot of heat and stillness and pounding hearts. "Can you find your horse while I stay with Lady Juliane?"

Alone in the wood with Ulrich of Caen? Nay, that would serve her not at all.

"He is afeared," she whispered, leaning down to Ulrich, pulling at the reins and turning Onyx's head from the grip of his hand. His grip stayed firm. He held her fast to this spot of hot earth, and her heart thudded at her entrapment. "Do not ask it of him lest you shame him."

Ulrich looked up at her, his blue eyes vivid against his skin. He measured her, searching for fear in her that he could use. He would find nothing but concern for his squire; there was no weakness in her. Or none that he could see.

"You think of him?" Ulrich whispered in return. "Or is it of yourself?"

"Do *you* think of him?" she countered, holding his gaze, unbowed and undaunted. "Or is it only of yourself?"

He searched her face a moment more, and she let him look his fill. Then he grunted in agreement and nodded.

"Well matched we are," he said. "You have called it aright, lady, though I think I called it well enough. But as you will—alone in the wood we shall not be."

"I can, my lord!" William warbled, his eagerness to prove himself and his reluctance to die by wolf bite warring on level ground within his heart. "I will!"

"Nay," Ulrich said, turning to his squire, releasing her bridle in the doing, "let be. Together we will find your mare, if she is to be found, and protect Lady Juliane between us both. Well bound she will be by two such men as we are."

"Aye, my lord!" William said, grinning and leading Ulrich's horse near.

"Well bound?" Juliane said as Ulrich mounted. "Odd wording to throw upon me."

"Yet not odd intent," Ulrich said, lifting William to sit behind him.

"So you proclaim, yet I own it not."

"Then do not own it," Ulrich said as he turned his mount to follow in the way of Theobald and Baldric and the hounds. And the wolves. "Own me instead."

She twitched the reins between her gloved fingers to hide the sudden quivering that shook her. Own him? He had an odd way of speaking, odd and disturbing. Own him? She had no wish to own him and could not. There was no such thing upon the earth, and well he knew it. A woman did not possess a man. 'Twas against the laws of God and nature.

"I would own no man," she said. "Not even you, though you offer most freely what you could never give."

She spurred Onyx to ride at Ulrich's side, for ride behind him she would not. Onyx compiled rapidly, for she was a horse who would follow none but took the lead in all endeavors. As did Juliane.

William turned his face to look upon the passing trees, giving them the illusion as best he could that their speech was private. He need not have bothered. What she would say, all could hear; aye, she would urge the squire to repeat it. Let all know how Juliane had defeated wild Ulrich.

Ulrich kept his eyes upon the dirt crushed beneath his horse's feet, his hands easy upon the reins, his countenance mild and sweet and undeterred. She was not fooled. He was neither sweet nor mild, and any man could be turned from the scent of a woman if the woman be strong enough to do the turning.

Turn from her he would.

"Nay," he said softly, not looking at her though she looked at him. The sunlight came through the trees in green washes of hazy light, lighting him to tawny brown and gold. He looked a lion of a sudden, on the trail of wolves. "Nay," he said again, "I would give you all of me, my heart and strength, my life and even my death; all given unto Juliane's soft hand. If you would only take me." He looked at her then, his eyes the blue of fire. "Take me, Juliane."

And in that instant, she wanted to. She wanted him. Wanted his strength to cover her, wanted his scent to mark her, his mouth upon her, his body within her.

"I thought this wager was of you taking me," she said over the wash of weakness that coursed through her. When had any man pled for taking when the world was all of men and what they took for themselves?

"This is none of wagers," he said, reaching out to touch her shoulder, brushing back a length of her hair. "I am beyond wagers. All that holds me now is you and what we could make between us."

"What we could make between us?" she said over a forced, hard laugh. "Your speech now is clear to me. Taking and giving, and then making. You speak as all men will, of making a child between us, setting your seed into the future. I will not be bound to you that way, my lord. That way is closed. Best learn that now and for always."

"You turn my words too hard," he said. "I would take nothing from you, and of a child, that is God's will and nothing less."

"Nay, there is my will with which you must contend," she snapped. Had she thought him charming? Amusing? Beautiful? He was as base as the snake, as cunning as the wolf, and as self-serving as she knew men to be. Resistance rose up in her and she sighed in joy at its coming. "I will not fall to you, Ulrich. I will not fall to any man."

"To any man?" he said sharply. "Aye, that is the truth. But to me? Lady, you *will* fall to me."

All charm had been cast from him and he was revealed as a man upon a steed bearing sharpened steel, bearing all the pride and arrogance and blood-thirst that made a man a man. This was the Ulrich she feared, this man of raw intent, his silken words of old cast away. Warm words and sweet smiles she had endured a lifetime; a man blazing high with his intent writ clear upon his face, that was more rare. She stood in momentary shock and felt the surge of feminine weakness steal into her bones. Yet there was no weakness in her. There could not be.

"I will not fall," she said, spurring her horse into a gallop, leaving him to enjoy his arrogance alone.

"Then why do you run?" he called after her.

She did not turn or answer, but kept on, widening the distance between them, letting the trees shield her from his gaze. Of William's mare, she saw none.

Chapter Eleven

"We will settle this now. I would know what I wager for."

Avice kept her eyes and her attention upon the herbs beneath her hands. Juliane had found her within the walled garden, that sheltered place of flower and stalk that was an oasis from harsh winds and cold in the winter months. Juliane was not overfond of the walled garden, especially not in summer when the stone walls pushed the sun's heat out toward them like a fire. Avice loved the walled garden, loved the heavy scent of sun-drenched fragrance, the rosemary, thyme, fennel, and lavender. It was a sweet and sheltered place, a quiet place. Or had been.

"The day passes, Avice," Juliane continued. "I would know what I wager for in urging a laugh from Edward."

"What is it you want?" Avice said, her basket full of fresh-cut lavender. It would look and smell well on the ledge of the chamber wind hole, sweetening the heavy air of summer.

"You leave the laying of the terms to me?" Juliane asked, picking a stalk of lavender from the basket and holding it to her nose. "You must think I have no chance of winning."

"You do have no chance of winning. He is a most foul-tempered man," Avice said.

"So you say, and he well may be. With you," Juliane said, sliding the lavender over her face, teasing her skin with it.

"And so we come again to the wager," Avice said crisply. "To find if he is as foul with Juliane as he is with Avice. I am not afeared. This is one wager I will win."

"It may be so," Juliane said softly, which meant she was not soft at all. Juliane at her most agreeable was most to beware.

"Let the terms be these," Avice said, taking the lavender from her sister and pushing it into the brimming basket. "If you can win a laugh from that black-visaged knight, you may have my red pelisse."

Juliane shrugged in good-natured contempt. "I have a red pelisse."

"Yet not so fine as mine."

"Mine suits me well enough."

So, Juliane wanted something of greater value, or perhaps of greater pain should Avice lose the wager. An impossibility. Avice knew Edward well enough to know that he would not laugh with so mere a thing as a woman.

"And why do you call him black-visaged? His looks are most fair, his eyes a charming hazel, his hair the fairest and tawniest of browns," Juliane said.

"It is his temper which blackens his looks," Avice said. "You know it to be so."

"I do not know it yet," Juliane said. "Hence this wager."

"I told you to name what it is you want," Avice said. "Name it, though my red pelisse would suit you well."

"It is not the red pelisse which I will name," Juliane

said, walking toward the heavy door that sheltered the walled garden, forcing Avice to walk with her, to leave her sanctuary of flowers. "This is what I wager for, Sister. If I win a laugh from Edward—a laugh which you will observe so that there may be no doubt as to the truth of my win—then you shall endure a kiss from him."

If Juliane wanted Avice to be horrified, she was to be disappointed. Avice laughed.

"He will not kiss me, no matter that you have wagered for it."

Juliane took the sprig of lavender that Avice had stolen from her grip and said, "Then you must kiss him, Avice. Kiss him. That is what I bargain for. If I win a laugh from him, he will win a kiss from you."

"He will not see it as a win but as a punishment," Avice said.

"And why should you care if he find punishment in your embrace? Would that not suit you well?"

"Aye, it would," Avice said, taking back the lavender and breaking it in her hands until all was twisted stalk and pummeled flower. "Yet what do I win when you lose? I would name my terms as well."

They left the close heat of the walled garden behind them, closing the heavy oaken door that sheltered it from the dust and bustle of the bailey.

"Name them," Juliane said with ease. She was so confident, Avice thought enviously. So ever and always confident.

It was at that moment that Ulrich rode past the tall gates of Stanora, his squire at his back, bloody wolf pelts dripping from his saddle bow. So, he had returned. Baldric had told Avice of their wolf encounter and of how

Ulrich had nobly defended his small squire. Of Juliane's part in it, he had said naught, yet Juliane had ridden through Stanora's gates with her brow furrowed in angry thought and her smile brittle.

Who else to credit for it but Ulrich?

Ulrich looked at once to where the women stood, their backs against the wall, their hair unbound and shining in the sun, their scent bathed in fresh lavender. Juliane stiffened at the touch of his look, her confidence slipping from her like a wisp of linen, her mouth tightening, her stance stiffening.

Aye, who else to credit but Ulrich of the Sweet Mouth?

Avice smiled in feline pleasure and said softly to her sister, "Then this is what I name. If you cannot win a laugh from Edward, your loss shall be proclaimed thus: You must bestow a kiss upon the mouth of Ulrich of Caen. That is all I ask, Sister. A kiss for a kiss."

"A kiss?"

"Aye," Avice whispered as Ulrich passed them. "I, too, already own a red pelisse."

Juliane looked hard at her, but Avice only smiled. A wager was a wager, after all. Would she cry off? Juliane? It was not in her. And that would be her undoing.

"Upon the mouth? 'Tis too much," Juliane said.

"Only if you lose," Avice prodded. "Did you not say that you could not lose this wager of a laughing Edward?"

"I will not lose," Juliane said hotly. Ulrich had passed them and Juliane was breathing more deeply, the blood hot in her cheeks.

"Then what do you fear?"

"I fear nothing—certainly not Ulrich."

"Nor his kiss," Avice said with a sharp smile.

"Then we are agreed," Juliane said, smiling at her sister with the same sharp smile.

"A kiss for a kiss," Avice said.

"A kiss for a kiss," Juliane agreed, nodding, their wager set.

She watched as Edward came out from the shadow of the stables and took the wolf pelts from the saddle bow of Ulrich's mount. The men spoke in easy sport, their manner smooth, their smiles quick, their eyes turned from the women at the wall. Avice followed Juliane's look and smiled in sharp delight.

"You first," Avice said, indicating Edward with a tilting of her chin.

Lifting her own chin, Juliane left the hot shelter of the wall and made her way across the bailey.

It was a fool's bet. A fool's bet, yet she was not going to lose it. Kiss Ulrich? She would gift neither Ulrich nor Avice with the pleasure.

A kiss for a kiss. 'Twas more like an eye for an eye, this wager of Avice's. But it had always been so between them, this competition that measured itself in wagers and winnings. Until Ulrich, it had been a most amusing way to pass an hour or a day. With Ulrich, it was not as amusing as it was annoying. She did not want to play at any game that involved Ulrich as either pawn, prize, or punishment.

He was too potent for such usage.

She lifted her skirts to avoid a pile of dung and continued on, closing the distance between them. She was for Edward, not Ulrich, her wager against him and his ill humor, yet Ulrich was there, as Ulrich ever and always seemed to be wheree'er she went.

He dismounted and turned to face her in the doing. She ignored him, refusing to meet his eyes. Yet she could feel his eyes upon her, and though she looked at Edward, it was Ulrich who smiled at her coming.

Arrogant man.

This was all of Edward and Avice and the winning of a wager. It was naught of him. Yet he would never believe that. His conceit would prevent any such truth from penetrating. If there were anything needed to make her more determined to win this wager, it was in the gloating pleasure she would get from dismissing Ulrich from her thoughts by turning her will toward Edward.

It was too bad she was not looking at him, because she would have loved to see his face at being so thoroughly dismissed and discounted.

"Lady," Ulrich said, nodding to her.

"Edward," she said in direct non-response to his greeting, smiling into Edward's surprised face.

"Lady," Edward said to her, casting a slightly quizzical look at his friend.

"Oh, do not look to him," she said, laying a hand upon Edward's arm and in the touching of him, drawing his eyes down to hers. "Ulrich wants all eyes upon him at all times. Let us thwart him, just this once."

"There is some wager in this," Ulrich said, throwing his reins to a hovering groom and forcing himself into the narrow net she was drawing around Edward.

"You insult Edward by saying so," she said with a cold smile. "Is he not worth my attention unless there be a wager behind it? You are very arrogant, my lord. Surely such pride is sin most black. Best you get yourself off to confession. Should you die now, your soul would be in peril most deep."

"If I should die now, it would likely be at your hand, lady," Ulrich said with a lopsided grin, winking at Edward.

"Will I argue it?" she said, grinning spitefully. "By my hand, it may be done. And no prayers for your black soul will I utter to hurry you into Paradise."

"You are quick with the hand, then, but slow with the mouth," Ulrich said suggestively.

"Only with you," she said, turning to face Edward again, forcing herself to look away from Ulrich. He turned her head when she had no wish to be turned. "With Edward I may very well be quick with my mouth. Shall we put it to the test?"

With the most sincere and innocent and seductive of expressions, she looked up at Edward charmingly. She knew it was a charming look. She had perfected this look most well.

"Lady, you speak beyond my skill," Edward said with a grin of embarrassment and shy discomfort. "Ulrich is the man for you. You are better matched with him."

"Ulrich is not the man for me until the hour of Sext," she said. "I am available until then," she said sweetly, batting her blue eyes at him.

Edward looked at her, at Ulrich, who itched with an anger she could feel, and back at her again. She winked at him and nodded, a knowing look. A practiced look. A comical look.

Edward, with a cough to mark it, burst out in a choking laugh, his cheeks going red.

At his laugh, Juliane looked over her shoulder to where

Avice still stood with her back to the suppressed heat of the walled garden. She smiled. Avice grimaced. She beckoned. Avice sulked.

Ulrich watched.

"And so the wager is won?" he asked.

Juliane shrugged. "I win all wagers I take," she said, smiling to soften the blow to Edward's pride. There was no need, as it happened.

"Lady, a wager there had to be for you to so bait Ulrich. No woman under Henry's banner would turn from him unless provoked by the lure of gain," Edward said.

"Edward," she said. "You rate yourself too low. This wager was none of Ulrich and all of you. By this wager of laughter, which I was bound to win from you, I have won, and the forfeit must be paid in kisses. A kiss from Avice to you."

His smile fell from him like a falling bird, fast and hard.

"She will win no kiss from me," he said stiffly.

"Nay, good knight," Juliane said, laying a hand upon his arm, "it is her forfeit. She must kiss you. That is how her loss is to be paid. Can you stand, my lord, and let this wager play itself out? And if you cannot," she said when he scowled and started to shake his head, his hazel eyes burning into the slowly advancing form of Avice, "will you then let all wagers die? If this cannot be paid, then no wagers made within Stanora and about Stanora's folk shall be paid."

Edward looked at Ulrich, considering. Ulrich shrugged and smiled, unconcerned. He was either a fool or more arrogant than she had thought, which hardly seemed possible.

"Think on this, Edward," Juliane said, pushing him toward the decision she wanted him to make. "This wounds her. This was her loss, and she had no intention of losing. She called you most foul of heart and mind, most ill-tempered, a laugh from you being as sure a thing as a goose intoning the Lord's Prayer. This will burn her more hotly than it could ever burn you."

Ulrich chuckled and rubbed a hand over his jaw, eyeing her most warmly. She ignored him.

Avice had reached them, her hems dragging, her chin lifted, her blue eyes bright with anger. She had good cause to be angry. She had lost.

"Let it play out, then," Edward growled.

"Spoken like a good sporting man," Juliane said, teasing him. "Come, Avice. Deliver unto me the joy of my winning. Kiss Edward," she brightly commanded.

They eyed each other like two spitting cats, crouched and hissing.

"You saw him laugh," Juliane said, driving home her win against Avice's defeat.

"I saw. You did well," Avice said in good courtesy. "I did not think he had even a smile in his cold, brittle heart."

Edward scowled and might even have growled in the deep darkness of his throat. Two spitting cats? Nay, they were lions seeking blood.

"Will you bend, Edward?" Ulrich said in amusement. "Or must the lady fetch a stool to reach you?"

"She could kiss my hand," Edward said, his sudden smile hard and bright.

"The laying of the kiss is my province," Avice said, suddenly smiling in return, her eyes glittering like glass.

"I choose where to lay my lips, and I choose to meet this bargain with my mouth upon your . . ."

Juliane began to laugh, seeing how Avice was turning this defeat into Edward's shame. All things might be won by a clever woman who was set on winning, no matter the game. No matter the opponent.

"Upon your," Avice continued, playing with him like a cat with a rat, "throat."

Ulrich cleared his throat and sent his young, wide-eyed squire up to the hall. 'Twas rough sport for a small lad to witness. Ulrich tried to spare him the worst of it, which Juliane could not but commend.

"Bare my throat for you?" Edward said in stiff surprise. "Nay, that is no part of this bargain."

"It is now," Avice said softly, her eyes bright shards of pale blue.

"Will you renege?" Juliane asked. "The wager is broken if the terms are not met."

"I did not set these terms," Edward said, looking down at Juliane.

"My lord," Juliane said softly, "I am ever placed in the center of wagers to which I have not set the terms. I play out the game. I understand the rules. Will you say less of yourself?"

If Ulrich looked at her longer and more thoughtfully than she liked, she ignored both him and the knowledge of his look. He was part of this because he was here, other than that, he had no part.

Edward closed his eyes. And with his right hand pulled down his tunic and bared his throat to Avice.

"Bend, that I may find the spot I seek," Avice said in crisp command.

Edward dutifully bent from the waist, his throat extended, his pulse jumping against the golden hue of his skin. The sign of his beard was not strong. His skin looked soft. All this Juliane noted as Avice leaned forward to lay her mouth upon her victim.

The very air seemed to spark, like the scent of the wind before a summer storm, like the howling in the night of a wolf pack on the hunt, like the stoop of the hawk in a cloudless sky; all tension, all expectation, all excitement. Could Avice feel it? Did she know what it was she leaned against?

Juliane looked at her dark-haired sister. Avice's eyes were wide and dilated to a twilight blue, her skin flushed, her lips reddened. She knew. She could feel the power of the man and what it was he called forth from her. Avice was no fool. She knew the trail of this beast and would protect herself against being devoured.

With careful precision, Avice feathered her lips against that beating pulse, her mouth tasting his skin. Her lips counting the beat of his blood against the shame she wrought on him. Sweet tasting, this scent of defeat.

With growing confidence, Avice laid her hands upon his shoulders, holding him to her, reaching into her kiss, letting her teeth press against his flesh. Taking him in her mouth. Claiming him.

Refusing him.

With a ragged sigh, Edward clenched his hands and held his ground. His eyes remained closed, but his heart would record this defeat beneath Avice's mouth for the remainder of his life.

A worthy wager.

A worthy winning.

With a breathy sigh, Avice released him, pulling free of the lure of him. Leaving him with a slight dampness on his skin. Smiling, she let go of his shoulders, giving him leave to stand straight and tall, unreachable again. Yet she had left her mark. Not upon his skin, but upon his pride.

"The wager is met," Ulrich said. "And is it not the hour upon which our own wager will be played out?" he said, touching Juliane on the arm. A careless, careful touch. A touch of remembrance. A touch of claiming. A touch of promise.

Juliane ignored him and moved her arm away from his touch. "The wager is met," she said to her sister. "You played your part well, Edward. Our thanks we give to you."

Avice said nothing. She looked at Edward with knowing eyes, and smiled.

"You smile at me, sparrow?" Edward said to Avice, his hazel eyes hard as granite. "You have won nothing from me. Remember that. To keep your honor and your word intact, to fulfill *your* wager, I have played my part. Of losing, I have tasted none. Think on that as you smile, little sparrow; it is you who have lost, and your sister knew well what would be bitter gall for you to taste, marking your defeat. My skin under your lips. My scent in your nostrils. That is the mark of your loss. Smile on, Avice, and I shall smile with you for knowing that in me your loss was made flesh."

And with that, he turned and left them. Avice stared after him, her eyes glittering like winter ice, her hands clenched beneath the shadow of her bell-shaped sleeves.

Ulrich smiled and turned his face to the sky, giving her what courtesy he could in that he did not laugh out loud.

"You lost the wager," Juliane said to her sister, reaching out a hand to touch her sleeve. "You lost, yet you won something from him. You know you did. Do not let him deceive you into thinking you did not."

"I lost the wager," Avice said, turning to look at Juliane, "and you made certain the paying of my debt would scald. And so it has."

"You won something from him. Can you not see it? Why else should he hunt so hard for a weapon to wound you with?"

"'Twas you who gave him the weapon," Avice said, turning from her sister, pulling herself free of her touch and free of her company. Without another look, Avice walked up the steep incline that led to the tower of Stanora. There was no shade cast from that mighty tower. 'Twas close upon the hour of Sext.

"Was it so great a loss, then?" Ulrich asked.

He had moved to Juliane's side. She did not turn to face him. His presence she felt like a sparking brand, hot and red and smoking. Never had she felt such heat from any man. No man had the fire to break her ice into sheets of submission and compliance. Such fire none in all the world possessed; the very legend of her name declared it so.

Yet from him she felt the pull of fire. The lure of heat. The danger of passion's brand.

"To her, aye, it was," she answered, her gaze on Avice's retreating back.

"Ideal terms, then," he said.

"Aye," she said softly. Avice had disappeared into the black maw of Stanora's tower gate. Gone.

"You sorrow at her loss," he said, coming to stand in front of her, capturing her sight so that all the world suddenly narrowed to only him. His leather tunic was old and worn and smoothly shining. The blood from the wolves had left a splattering of darkest red upon the weathered brown. "Why, then, make the wager?"

"To win," she said, looking up into his eyes. She had no fear of him or of his heat. Let him see that in her eyes. Let him read that in her heart.

Ulrich grinned, his eyes slices of happy blue. "To win is worth anything."

"Are you asking or telling?" she said, matching his grin, showing him her lack of fear.

"Confiding," he said with a wink.

"We are sparring, my lord," she said, turning from him to walk the path that Avice had just trod. "We are not so intimate as to share confidences."

"Upon the hour of Sext, I will mark you for a liar."

"Upon the hour of Sext, you will mark me not at all."

"The very foundation upon which our wager is built. A mighty fortress it is becoming," he said, following her. "The hour of Sext has ne'er held such weight as now, to-day, with you."

"You are not a godly man, then?" she said.

"I am grown more godly by the hour," he said.

"A righteousness fueled by desperation?"

"Nay," he said, catching her by the hand, tracing the long line of fingertip to the sensitive curve of her thumb, "only hunger."

"Does God's holy writ speak of such hunger as yours,

my lord? I think not. 'Tis not righteousness you feel; you have misnamed it."

"And do God's chosen not hunger and thirst after righteousness? Am I not chosen?"

"Chosen? Not by me," she said, pulling her hand out of his and clenching her tingling flesh into a hard and resolute fist.

"And again we come to Sext," he said, lacing a finger into a strand of her hair, coiling it, tethering her, "when all things shall be shown and all choices revealed."

"You put much upon this," she said, watching him play with her hair, wondering why they were so alone in the middle of the day in the center of the bailey. Or was it just that she could see none but Ulrich? He filled her senses, leaving all else in hazy shadow. "'Tis but a kiss."

"But what a kiss," he said, laying his lips upon the hair he had tangled in his fingers, studying her face while he seduced her.

She kept her face composed and her eyes cool. She could feel nothing upon her hair. It was with the look of his seduction that he thought to bring her down.

"As to that, the hour of Sext will come and I will judge. But I will not lose to you."

Ulrich let her hair slip from his fingers, let it fall in slippery coils back to her shoulder, where it merged with all the rest, unmarked and undisturbed by his interference, unchanged by his touch.

"And I, lady, will not lose to you," he said with an easy smile.

Yet there was nothing easy about Ulrich of Caen. She could see that now.

Chapter Twelve

"Can she not see that there is nothing of ease in the man? He smiles, but there is no softness in him."

"I think she sees him very well," Avice answered her aunt.

Maud stood upon the battlements, watching Juliane at tender blows with the latest of her knights errant come to lay claim upon her.

"You are angered with her," Maud said, turning from her worried observation of Juliane to search the face of her niece. " 'Twas but a wager and a wagered kiss. 'Tis nothing to be—"

"I am not angry," Avice said stiffly.

"Oh," Maud said mildly, nodding, turning again to look down at Juliane. "It gives me joy to hear it."

"Aye, I can see that you are all thought, all concern for me," Avice said.

Maud shook her head and cast Avice a sidelong glance, as if she could not bear to take her gaze from Juliane, which, of a truth, she could not. "A pinprick to your pride only, Avice, if you would face the truth of it. You know 'tis so. Yet for Juliane, 'tis so much more."

"Aye, 'tis always so much more with Juliane."

"Avice, where is your heart?" Maud said, taking her hand and giving it a tug of mild reproof.

Bruised, Avice wanted to cry. Bruised and tender and near to breaking, she could have said, yet she held her tongue. Of what purpose to speak when all was ever and only of Juliane?

Juliane, the beauty. Juliane, the ice maid who could withstand the hottest pursuit, the warmest praise, the most ardent and chivalrous of men. Juliane, whom all men came to see and admire. Juliane, the legend.

Of Avice, whose eyes were the same blue, whose skin was as fair, whose hair was as lustrous, whose bosom was as high, none spoke. None came to win her. None came to praise and pet her. Of Avice, no songs were sung.

It did grow tiresome.

And that hulking, scowling, snapping Edward, who all could see was as churlish and ill-mannered as any bear, laughed at Juliane's bidding.

'Twas too much to be borne.

"Avice?" Maud said again, tugging on her hand.

"My heart," Avice said calmly, releasing her hand, "is exactly where it should be, Aunt."

"Well said," Maud replied, looking down into the bailey. "Father Matthew has come, taking Juliane with him into the chapel. It is well. I would not have Juliane spend unbroken time with Ulrich. He is too fast, too sure at this game."

That he was, thought Avice, smiling, her humor lifting. That he surely was.

"I would only ask that you search your heart, Juliane, and see where it dwells or would long to dwell in this life," the priest said softly.

"My heart dwells very firmly within my breast, Father," Juliane said pleasantly, her eyes pleasant, her manner pleasant, and her mood most pleasant now that Ulrich had been pleasantly dismissed. "Have no care for me."

"Yet I must have a care for all within my sphere, child; this you have known, as I have known you, from a child."

"Pray for me, then, Father, and you will do me good service. But of care have none, as I have none."

"We should all have a care, Juliane. The world is harsh, and life can be long and difficult."

"Yet I am safe within God's embrace, Father Matthew, my future assured," she said with a smile. "With your prayers to clothe me, what shall I fear?" she asked, blinking brightly her shining approval of him.

Of these conversations, this was not the first. He wanted her to enter the convent. She would not. Why he wanted it, she did not know. But she would not. To live within the cloister, bound and blinded, obedient to every voice and to the inflexibility of every rule? Nay, 'twas not a life she sought; she would not be pushed to it. Nay, nor lured either. But of lures, what could a priest hold out to her?

"Fear nothing," he said a bit stiffly. "Fear only the condition of your soul and your place in eternity."

"I do. As do all men. We are a fallen race, Father. I know my place in the ordering of the world, taught most well by you," Juliane said evenly.

"Then you know that you must marry, either man or God. A woman's place is as a wife."

"I will not marry."

"Then you fall out of the natural order of the world, child," he said. "What place for you then?"

"Maud did not marry," she said. Juliane had based much upon that truth. If Maud could carve herself a life without a husband to constrain her, then so could she. And with Maud's wise counsel, it would be done.

"She may still," Father Matthew said. "Her tale is not told complete, not as long as she lives upon this earth. A husband may come forth for her."

"At this hour?" Juliane said with a snort of disbelief. "She is too old to make a child. What purpose, then, to marry?"

"She is young enough still. I know of many women who bear the fruit of marriage when their hair is stone white."

"Then perhaps it is that I will marry when my hair is white, for surely, Father, I will not marry now," she said, her careful understanding of the world tilted by his declaration that Maud might yet marry.

"You are decided? You will not seek the abbey life?" he asked once more.

"Nay, Father, I will not," she said, making a statement of intent which he could not mistake.

"Then I will speak no more of it," he said, his smile fading.

"Yet let us speak of many other things, Father. I value your thoughts in all things, as is right," she said courteously.

"Would you know my thoughts regarding Ulrich of Caen?" he asked.

Juliane gave a delicate snort and shook her head. "There is no need for either of us to cast our thoughts in that direction. He is a man, like all the others before him and all others to come."

Father Matthew raised his brows. "So? Like all other men, is he? My eyes have deceived me, it seems, for I thought in him I saw something I had not yet seen. At least in men who come to test themselves against Juliane le Gel."

"What?" she asked, turning to search his familiar face. She had known this priest all her life and thought of him not unlike a cherished uncle. In fact, she preferred Father Matthew's gentle humor to her uncle Conor's brash ways. "What do you see in him?"

Father Matthew shook his head, the light from the distant wind hole turning his grayed hairs to beaten silver. "Can you not see it?"

"I see only his need to win and his arrogance that he will achieve a victory."

"And a fierceness of heart that springs from fierce love."

Juliane laughed and turned to walk out of the chapel. It was almost Sext. She would not be found here within when all came to make their prayers; she would not be named eager in Ulrich's eyes. She would meet the wager, but she would do so on slow feet.

"Aye, self-love. All men love themselves most well. It is their besetting sin," she said.

"Nay, Juliane, the sin that hounds a man through all his life is not the sin of love, but the sin of thinking himself equal to God, the sin of pride. This sin sprang forth in the Garden and lives on today, flourishing, flowering in the heart of man," he said. "This is the sin which must be rooted out and burned, before it destroys the very world."

"Do you yet speak of Ulrich?" she asked. Father Matthew had a most strange look about him, his face frozen into grim foreboding and determination. All this for an errant knight? Ulrich did not warrant such depth of consideration.

Father Matthew jerked his gaze back to hers, pulled from his spiritual discourse.

"Perhaps in part," he said, pulling forth a gentle smile,

"yet what I see in him is that he brings to you what no other man has brought."

"He brings no land, that is certain," she said with a wry shrug.

"Nay, Juliane, look beyond what the world lays value upon. A man is more than the measure of his worth in land or name. Ulrich brings a heart that can love. 'Tis no small thing."

"Small enough," she said. "Marriages are made between equal partners. Ulrich has nothing."

"Then you would prefer Nicholas of Nottingham? 'Tis your uncle's choice for you, and he presses most hard against your father to see it done."

"Prefer one man to another?" she said. "And one of Conor's choosing? I would make no such choice."

"Yet a choice must be made and soon, Juliane. Your father slows in his walk through life," Father Matthew said. "He must see you set upon your path before he passes out of earthly cares, his duty to you done."

"He has done well by me," she said. "I need no betrothal to confirm it."

"What of Conor? Will he say the same?"

"Conor has no charge over me. That care falls to my father, and my brother after him," she said, turning from him and from the dark foreboding of this conversation. "I must away for now. I have a wager soon to fulfill. With your blessing, Father," she said, dropping into a curtsey of submission, but walking away from him without his blessing or his leave.

"With my blessing, Juliane," he said to her back, watching as she moved through the cool dimness of the chapel, her will unchanged, as was her heart.

* * *

The chapel filled slowly with those souls who sought to pray away the hour of Sext. Juliane was of their number, of their rearward number, waiting in the shadows of the porch for Ulrich to pass within. She waited long. He did not come. The chapel filled, the noon hour song of prayer began, and he did not come.

Concerned she was not.

Curious, nay, not at all.

Let him be where he was, wheree'er that was, out of her sight, out of her thoughts, gone from all that touched her. He could touch her not.

It did not matter where he was during the prayer of Sext; let him only be in the stables for the meeting of their wager and he would be well met in that hour. In an instant, 'twould be over. He would speak softly, his eyes would shine, his mouth would turn up in a smile, and he would, for an instant, lay his lips upon her. Somewhere upon her.

It mattered not where upon her, and it mattered not how long he laid his moist mouth against her heated skin.

Nothing mattered but the winning of this wager, and the defeating of Ulrich, and the departing of Ulrich from Stanora. He would win nothing in Stanora.

Such were her thoughts as the congregation prayed around her. Their prayers, upon soft lips and from urgent hearts, flew upward into heaven. Her thoughts were anchored firmly on the earth, chained by will and passion to Ulrich.

If there was a winning in that for Ulrich, she closed her eyes to it, closed her eyes and pretended to pray.

* * *

She came to the stables with some slowness to her steps, dragging her toes over the dirt, surrounded by smells of straw and sunlight and horse. Good smells. Warm smells. The light was hot and direct, heating her head and shoulders like a brand; she hesitated upon reaching the dark, cool portal of the stables. Between hot light and shadow, she would choose light, if she could choose. Which she could not. The wager was for the stables, cool and dark, and so into the shadow she went.

He was waiting for her.

Tall amid the shadows, leaning against the worn wooden western wall, wreathed in darkness, he stood. The air was alive with sound: the stomp of hoof, the jingle of harness, the beating of her heart. Or so it seemed to her.

He stood so very still, so very shadowed. So very predatory. Like a wolf. And like a wolf, he watched her.

"You came," he said, not moving from his place at the wall.

"Did you doubt I would?" she said, clinging to the scrap of sunlight that skirted the doorway.

He shook his head slowly. "Nay, I did not doubt the word of Juliane le Gel in the matter of a wager."

The stalls were not full. There were perhaps three horses in the stalls, dozing, lazily munching straw, watching. She moved into the shadows and stood with Onyx at her side. Onyx's ears twitched in her direction, and Juliane smiled.

"Shall we, then, begin it?" she said.

"So that we may be the sooner done with it?" he asked, still unmoving from his post at the wall. His very stillness made her nerves jump like locusts in the grass. "Nay, I have waited too long for this to hurry through it."

"Too long? A few hours at most."

"Too long," he said softly, his words a growl of longing.

Nay, nay, not a growl, not a man who watched her with all the feral hunger of a wolf; only a man in need of winning a wager. That was all he was. That was all it ever was.

"You are impatient," she said with soft mockery, scolding him.

"Only for you," he answered, unabashed by her scolding, untouched by it.

"Pretty words," she said with a chill smile. "Yet are we not here for a kiss? A single kiss without the threat of blood to chill your ardor? Come, then, my lord, lay your mouth upon me. I will stand and take whatever is in you to deliver."

"So, you will stand while I come to you, a penitent seeking grace from a woman with a marble heart? Nay," he said softly, "I will not come. You shall come to me, Juliane. Come to me now," he quietly commanded.

"Is this part of our bargaining?"

"Must it be? Will you not come to me unless a wager is attached to the act? Must all be wagers and winning between us, Juliane? Can there be nothing of warmth and generosity?"

"In the winning of a wager?" she said stiffly. "Are you generous with your brother knights in the playing out of a wager, or is that only to be my gift to you, to ease your way to winning what I have determined you shall not win?"

"When I am certain of winning, then, yea, I am generous," he said. "Is it that you are uncertain of your victory in this, Juliane? Is it that you fear to draw close to me of your own will? Is there a falling in that, Lady Frost? Are you so easily tumbled that mere steps will see it done?"

He gloated. He prodded. He manipulated. All the things a man did to achieve his will by soft steps when blows and bluster would not serve. She knew all this. She knew the ways of a man. And still, he pricked her pride with his taunts. She felt her blood race at his dare, knowing that it was foolish to give him a single step of ground he had not fought for, yet knowing that she would meet his dare and walk to him, walk to him like a woman in love, running to the arms of her lover.

Yet mayhap she could turn even that to her advantage.

In every move of every game, there was always an advantage to be found and used, and no one was better at games than she.

"Watch and see," she said, her eyes smoldering with promise and with threat. Let him read that in her face and wonder. There was no fear in her. This wager had been won time and time and time upon time.

She stroked the black face of Onyx, making him wait for what she had promised. Waiting never suited a man; they were all quick hurry and blind need. She fondled Onyx's ear, running a hand down her sturdy neck, cooing meaningless words, ignoring Ulrich, feeding his impatience. Releasing the rope that bound Onyx into her stall, she patted, stroked, and caressed the beast until Onyx pushed her face into Juliane's chest, demanding more. With a final pat, she left her then, turning back to face Ulrich.

Who smiled, watching her. Who leaned with all the careless ease of a man with nothing to do but stand and watch a woman fondle a horse. Who waited softly, his temper unprovoked and untouched.

"I watch," he said. "What is it I will see? Will Juliane come to me of her own power? Will she lay herself under my touch? Will she submit her body to my will?" he breathed, the summer light golden at his feet, his blue eyes shining within the shadow.

"Your mouth upon me, that is all of touching you shall have," she reminded him, ignoring the bubbling race of her blood as she said it. "One kiss only shall you have of me."

"That is all I shall require," he replied.

If there was ominous promise in his voice, she pushed the threat from her.

And so she went to him, one step upon another. The distance was not so very great. Step after step she went to him while he waited, his arms crossed, his shoulders leaning back against the wood, his hips thrust forward, his eyes locked on to hers.

Too close—they were suddenly too close, the stables too small, the space too confined and hot and still to hold them both. That was the sudden knowledge that burst upon her as she left Onyx behind her and entered the heated radiance of Ulrich.

But she did not stop. She would not stop. This wager would be played out, and she would win.

She came within a handspan of him, pushing against the armor of his arrogance, pressing her own confidence and fearlessness into his heart like a talon. He straightened instantly, feeling the threat of her, and the tips of her breasts brushed against the fabric of his leather tunic, yet she held her ground and she held his stare in the grip of her own.

"Lady, I fear for you," he whispered, standing straight and tall before her, his breath covering her. "Make not so bold with me. I am no boy. If you offer, I will take."

"One kiss only may you take from me. One kiss I give you leave to have," she snarled softly, her eyes piercing his with the thrust of her pride. "Nothing more."

"I will hold to the wager," he said, looking down at her. "I will take nothing more."

He was tall and so very, very straight. As if the world had not pressed a weight of woe upon him. As if there were no earthly burden which he could not bear. As if heaven itself could shatter and fall and he would remain, tall and smiling and strong.

"Then take your kiss," she commanded, tossing aside the promise of his strength. He was a man; he had nothing to give her that she would ever want. "Take it and mark my silence. I will not moan in desire, and yet I will not resist. One kiss you shall have of me, but nothing more."

"Lady, if the kiss be right, I shall need nothing more."

And with those words, he moved.

Over the compressed pounding of her heart, he touched her.

In a single motion, his left arm swept around her waist, drawing her in, close, to press against his length. Too close. His arm was too long, entrapping her, making a cage of flesh from which she could not fly; these thoughts swam in her heart, muddying her mind, confusing her.

"Nay! There was nothing of embracing in our wager," she said, pushing him from her, her hands to his shoulders.

He let her open a space between their bodies. But he did not take his hand from her.

"Lady, my heart weeps for your loss that you have never known a kiss wrapped within an embrace. This is a kiss as I meant it. This is the kiss you shall take."

"This was no part of it," she said, holding him off, her elbows locked against the weight of him.

"It is now," he said softly, his voice a guttural growl that raised the hair on her arms.

Pulling her in to him again, against his heat, against the hard wall of his chest, he wrapped her to him, tying them together with his arms, forcing her head back, exposing her throat. She felt his breath upon her skin, the warm and moist mark of his mouth, hovering, caressing, yet touching not.

He did not kiss, he merely breathed his scent upon her. Marking her.

"Take your kiss and be done," she said, holding herself stiffly within his embrace.

"Be still and let me find my way upon your skin," he murmured against her, his mouth a tickle that burned upon her throat. "Be still and unresisting and you might yet win this wager."

"I will win. Take your kiss and find the truth of it," she said.

"Take my kiss and find me standing hard and fast, Lady Frost, for that is the wager beneath all wagers. I will stand."

"Against me," she breathed, closing her eyes against the feel of him.

"For you," he said softly. "Because of you."

Nay, nay, not because of her. He must fall. In his falling, all was won. All was hers if he would but fall, shriveled and cold and unmanned. That was all she wanted. That was all he must do.

His mouth lay upon her throat, nuzzling now, feeling his way along her skin as he held her to him. Her back arched, pressing her breasts against his chest, contrary to all will and wisdom. Contrary to all experience and history. Never had a man moved so resolutely and with such soft force against her will to chill him. Never had a man used her body as a weapon against her as deftly as Ulrich now did.

He touched his mouth to her, yet did not kiss. How that she could think of nothing now but his coming kiss? How that she yearned for his lips upon her, hard and strong and hot? How that she panted in curious longing for that which she most assuredly did not want? How that he had brought her to panting and longing and unwelcome heat?

For she was hot. She squirmed in his arms, the juncture of her thighs hot and swollen, twitching for touch, for heat, for some hard possession that she could not want. That she had never wanted before. Before Ulrich.

His mouth opened wider upon her skin. Now he would take his kiss, now upon her throat. She had thought he would claim her mouth for by such kisses men put much store and many women were won. Yet he hovered, skimming, teasing the tender skin of her throat. Her pulse jumped to meet the hot, soft promise of his mouth, and she arched her neck back, giving him his way. Showing him that she did not resist.

Nay, worse; showing him that she submitted to his mouth without restraint, without thought. All thoughts were of him and of this pulse beat he had fanned to life within her. The warmth of the stables, the soft hum of flies, the smells of animal and straw: all lashed within the golden moment of his mouth opening upon her skin, all lost within the pounding of her heart.

His arm pressed her to him, his hand broad and strong

upon her back. His mouth lowered, pressing, touching, consuming her throat with his breath and heat. His right hand snaked down her thigh, spanning it, caressing it, possessing, claiming, enticing. All the things a man was wont to do. All the things she despised. Until now.

"Now I shall mark you, a matching mark upon your neck to pair us," he said in soft threat.

Aye, threat. She heard it, yet could not make herself move from his arms, from his passion, and told herself that it was only the wager which kept her still and unresisting under his assault.

He slid his leg between her thighs, perilously, deliciously close to the ache and throb of her womanhood, pulling her into him. And then he set his mouth upon her.

At last.

A kiss so soft, so breathy and light and warm that she felt it to her feet. An entreaty. A promise. A foretaste. That was this wagered kiss and more.

She swallowed the sighing moan that floated in her heart, forcing herself to remember that to win was all. But it was hard remembering.

And Ulrich was still hard. She could feel him against her belly, hot and high and hard with passion unrestrained and unchallenged. How so? How that he was not falling in fear of her ice?

Ice? When all was fire and smoke, she could find no ice to call forth from her heart. She shimmered and swayed in the heat of him.

And then he kept his promise and opened his hot mouth upon her throat and bit into the soft skin of her neck. A gentle bite. A tasting. A meeting of pulse and tongue and teeth.

Wolf bite.

She swayed against him, clamping her teeth upon her cries, smothering breath with reason and the need to win. No cries. No resistance. But, God above, this was a test unlike any other she had faced.

He sucked her, biting, licking, kissing. Marking her. This would leave a bruise upon her throat for all to see and note and wonder upon. Had she won? Had he? The wager was to be marked by the bruising of her skin.

His hands tightened upon her, bringing her even more into the prison of his heat. His leg was hard between her soft thighs, and she yearned for hardness in that place, in whatever manner she could find it. He pulled her hard against him, lifting her onto his leg, urging her to ride him. And she did. She rubbed herself against his leg in frantic need while his mouth bit into her pulse, claiming her, mastering her. Defeating her.

She moaned. A half moan, choked back, swallowed, killed. Yet still, a cry of longing and passion and need.

He marked it well.

And did not stop.

Thank God, he did not stop. She wanted this, wanted him, wanted to taste him as he was tasting her, wanted her mouth to tangle with his in hot, wet battle, wanted Ulrich as she had wanted no man before.

A mighty push and they were disentangled. Onyx had her face against Ulrich's back, pushing him hard, her black eyes demanding that they part, that Juliane be freed from this wager and from Ulrich's arms.

Ulrich braced himself, protecting her with his body from a horse acting in odd aggression. He turned, taking her arm and leading her to stand with her back against the deeply shadowed wall of the stable, and then he faced the horse. Onyx eyed him coldly. Ulrich returned the look and then led the animal by the halter back to her stall, where he secured the rope that bound her there.

And with the doing, Ulrich turned and smiled. In victory, of course. She had cried out. She had lost the wager, though no eyes had seen it save Ulrich's and no ears but his had heard her cry. Still, she played each game with honor and she would not deny that he had won.

She braced herself to bear the weight of his victory and the pride of his boasting.

"They come to your aid, do they not?" he asked, walking toward her with the assurance of a conqueror. "The animals. You have trained them to protect you."

Chapter Thirteen

So that was how she did it. What man would not fall when attacked by claw and talon and teeth? Still, he had to smile. It was so very clever and had served her well, after all. But no longer. He had her measure now and had her cry upon his ears; he had won this wager and would only win with her. Juliane le Gel's legend was broken, and it was broken upon the skill of Ulrich of Caen.

He had good cause to smile.

She would make a wife. With her father's word, she would make a wife for him.

"I need no protection, nor aid," she said, trying to rip

NAME: _____

ADDRESS: _____

_____

_____

TELEPHONE: _____

E-MAIL: _____

_____ I want to pay by credit card.

__ Visa   __ MasterCard   __ Discover

Account Number: _____

Expiration date: _____

SIGNATURE: _____

Send this form, along with $2.00 shipping and handling for your FREE books, to:

Historical Romance Book Club
20 Academy Street
Norwalk, CT 06850-4032

*Or fax (must include credit card information!) to: 610.995.9274.
You can also sign up on the Web at www.dorchesterpub.com.*

Offer open to residents of the U.S. and Canada only. Canadian residents, please call 1.800.481.9191 for pricing information.

from him all his newfound knowledge of her. "I can repel where, when, and how I wish."

"Can you? Then what of this?" he asked, pulling down the edge of his tunic to show her the raw marks of her hawk upon his neck.

"Is it remarkable that my hawk finds blood where she may?"

"Do not deny your means, Juliane. I find no quarrel with them. Nay, I think you wise and resourceful."

"Do I care what you think?" she snapped, stepping away from him. "I care not. Think what you will. Say what you will. Only leave Stanora with this winning, for there shall be no other."

"Shall there not?" he said. "I think that I will have from you any winning I desire."

She laughed then softly, and her eyes shone in true amusement.

"Think you I have not been told that before? Think you that you are the first? In no way, and by no means is Ulrich of Caen the first to claim Juliane. Yet here I stand. Unclaimed. Unbound."

God above, she was cold. Cold and stiff and haughty. Where was the woman of moans and hot, wet passion? He had held her just a moment past, and yet 'twas as if she were the stuff of dreams and no fleshly woman at all. The woman who was Juliane le Gel stood before him now, her blue eyes cold with disdain, her spine stiff with arrogance. Yet he knew the truth, did he not? She was not as cold as she strove to seem.

Yet that knowledge, so recently found, slipped from him under the cold, hard, blue stare of her eyes. She made mock of all, including him. Especially him.

"What of your horse?" he said, holding himself rigid and feeling his smile drip away from him, pulse by pulse.

Juliane shrugged. "Am I a saint that I can command the very beasts of the earth to my will? You praise me, my lord, by setting such a high mark upon my skill and sanctity. I am no saint."

"That I well and truly believe," he said past the anger in his throat. She would not take this victory from him, souring it with her scorn. "A saint would have won the wager set between us. You did not. You cried out. A thing you swore never to do."

"Set me another wager and I will swear the same again."

"Nay," he said, advancing upon her, "no more wagers between us, lady. I will have you at my will, now and always."

"You speak bold for a knight errant. You have no claim upon me."

"By your father's word, and upon this wager, I will have."

"What have you set between you?" she snapped, her brows lowered in anger. Hot anger. Aye, he liked this angry heat better than chill disdain. He would take it, even fan it, to keep the frost at bay. "I am no pawn in a man's game."

"Lady," he breathed in a rough gasp, "you are what God has made you, and, by God, you shall be whate'er your father needs you to be."

"I am my father's to command. Not yours."

"And by your father's will, that may change within the hour."

She laughed then, a small, cold laugh that burned into his heart and all his plans.

"It will not. And if it shall," she said with a hard grin, staring up into his face with the ferocity of a falcon, "then I shall only need to call upon the very birds of the air and beasts of the wood to take me out of your grasp. I will not be taken by any man. Not even you, Ulrich. Not even for the price of a moan."

He towered over her, like a tower over the battle plain, yet she did not fear his anger or his will or even his passion, he realized. He had won the wager, he had made her moan in passion, he had held her in his hands and felt the wet heat of her desire upon his thigh, but he had won nothing. She stood and faced him as she had from the start. Smiling. Grim. Confident. As sure of her success as he was certain of her failure in this bout of hearts and minds and wills.

He was done with games. This was too vital. He needed this match too much to play at love with her, to play at seduction with her father's eye upon the outcome.

Twisting his hands into the long fall of her hair, he pulled her to him, holding her hard by the length of her hair bound about his fists. Her feet resisted; her hands upon his hands resisted; her eyes, as cold and hard as iron, resisted, fighting. Refusing.

But he had her in his hands. There was no escape from the tangle he had made. Jerking her to him so that she bumped into his chest, he lowered his mouth for a kiss as hard as her eyes. Hot, unrelenting, fighting against her will, pressing against her body, searching for the soft, dark glow of passion within her. It was there. He had touched it twice now and he could find it again. He would drag her to it again.

Her mouth was small and soft and wet and warm, and

he plunged inside her, making a space for himself where she did not want him. He could feel the fight rise up in her, the tightened breath, the stiffened back, the death of all softness which she called forth from somewhere in her heart.

Let her call. He would defeat her. She was a woman, and he knew well the many paths into a woman's passion, though never before had he been made to fight his way into a woman's heart. Nay, his history was all of soft speech and careful flattery. With Juliane, such methods were like mist, broken upon her stony heart.

"I will have moans from you, Juliane," he said against her mouth. "I will have all from you. Deny me not."

"I deny you all!"

He tightened his hold on her, uncaring if he wrenched the hair from her scalp, and plunged hard into her mouth. She knew what she was about. She had been kissed, and kissed hard, before. Even as she resisted, she showed her skill at love.

And his anger surged the higher that her father had been so loose in his keeping of her.

Yet had she not been married, even for the small space of two days? Had he thought that she had known no kiss, no touch, no passion in all her days? Nay, he had known it, yet now, with her body beneath his mouth and his hands, and yet her heart so far from falling into the net of passion he set for her, he wanted no other to have touched her. He wanted her only and always for himself. He wanted to be the one to claim her and his claiming to be complete.

He wanted all the things a man wants when he wants a woman.

All the things a man was denied when the woman he wanted was Juliane le Gel.

"Deny me, then," he said, lifting his mouth from hers, trailing his lips down the arch of her neck, which lifted for him, no matter her words. "Give me not moans. Give me only your mouth."

"My mouth pleases you not."

"Nay, your mouth pleases me well. 'Tis your words I can live without."

She turned into his mouth, seeking him, smiling, broken of her anger for the moment, giving him what he asked as they stood in the stables in the heat of a sunny day, the smells of fodder all about them. 'Twas fitting. She was like an animal—wild, untamed, willful. And he was like an animal when he was near her. He had never been like this before, so out of joint, so out of peace and plan. With her, all was need and hunger and desperation.

Yet he was equally desperate for his plan to be met. He could not forget the course of his dreams in the battle of Juliane.

"More," he breathed, still holding her hard by the hair. He did not trust her. "Give me more. A kiss I must not force from you. A kiss of your own devising."

He felt her grin under his mouth and then the prick of steel upon his groin. He opened a space between them and looked down. She had her dagger upon his manhood. He dwindled instantly, but kept hard hold of her hair, like twin ropes of gold wrapped about his hands.

"Does the kiss of steel suit, my lord?" she asked. "Release me or I will cut you where you stand."

Her eyes were cold, yet in the depths of blue he could see the spark of desire.

"A knife will not cut against our passion, lady," he said, holding fast, pulling her into his heat again.

"Will you stand against a knife, my lord? I think not."

"Look and see."

And she looked. And she saw that he was rising high and hot again, her knife a shadow weapon he wagered she would not wield.

"I will not fall to you, lady. This I promised you from the start," he said, staring into her eyes. Confusion and indecision mingled like murky clouds in the clear blue of her eyes. The knife wavered.

"And I promised that I would not fall to passion, to pledges of love, to promises made in heated stables by a knight who has much to gain by gaining me. Stand off, sir knight, else I will cut myself free of you," and so saying, she lifted the knife to her hair, slicing through the strands to free herself from his hold.

He fast released her and quickly took the knife from her hand. She did not yield without some temper, but he was a knight and she was a woman. He could and did disarm her at his will.

"Nay, that you must not do," he said. A thick strand she had already cut and he picked it from her hair and held it carefully in his hand. "Your hair is too lovely to be given up in battle. I release you. For now."

"You have won the wager," she said, holding her ground, not backing away from his nearness. She was bold, and that was honest praise. "What will you have of me?"

"You. I want you."

She was golden in the glow of hazy light, tall and strong and fierce and feminine. He wanted her as he had rarely wanted a woman, with every bone in his body.

But with this woman, there was also profit in the having of her.

"Have you not said that I am not my own to give? These terms will not hold."

Truly said. It was in her father's will to grant her to a man. And with this wager won, he stood in good way to be the man.

"Then tell me this truth and the terms are paid. You trained the animals in your keeping to keep you safe from passion, did you not? The hawk, the horse—'twas not by chance that they aided you."

"To give you the answer you want from me would be to confess to being a cheat. I do not cheat. There is no need," she said with brimming arrogance.

"Not only a cheat, but a liar," he answered with a lop-sided grin. A bold liar and an apt cheat; by the saints, there was much to like in Juliane of Stanora.

"If that be so, then we have much in common," she said with a slow grin, holding out her hand for her dagger.

He gave it to her freely. That battle was past. What new tactic would she use to thwart him?

By the saints, it would be something to see.

"Lady!" came a cry from without the stables. They both turned to face the sound. There was much desperation in it. "Lady! Your father has fallen ill; he sickens by the moment. Come!"

Without hesitation, they left their battle in the swirling dust of the stables and ran to the tower of Stanora.

"What has befallen?" Juliane asked as she hurried up the tower stairs. Avice had met her at the tower gate, a petite blade of sorrow swathed in pelisse and bliaut.

"His body failed him. He was carried to his chamber, and lies there still and unyielding, his face contorted. I know not more than that. Maud is with him now in his chamber," Avice said, sparing a glance for Ulrich.

Ulrich stayed within the great hall. The family of the lord of Stanora were what was needed now, not some guest of the house who was soon to be gone. The women of the house understood that, even if the men did not. Avice and Juliane told him all he needed to know of his place by ignoring him in total. They ran up the curving stairs, lifting their skirts in their hands.

The girls of the house, Christine, Marguerite, and Lunete, stood outside the door, whispering. Lunete was as white as new linen, her gray eyes watchful and huge. Juliane spared not a word for them but rushed past, through the door and into the lord's solar. The lord of Stanora lay upon his bed, his head propped high with pillows. His face was pallid, his skin covered in a sheen of sweat, his lips blue-tinged and parted, forcing air into his body. His manservant stood at his shoulder, holding a cup in his hands.

"Is that wine?" Juliane asked him. "Give it to him. 'Tis good for the blood."

"He refuses it, my lady," the man answered, his eyes darting and nervous. He did not want to be held to account if his lord died having refused the cup he bore.

"Drink, Father," Avice said, urging her father up by the strength of her arm behind his back. "Fortify yourself."

"The pain is past. I have ridden it down," he said softly, shaking his head slightly. Each word seemed to exhaust him past bearing.

"Fetch Father Matthew," Juliane said to the manservant, who quickly left the room, handing the cup to Juliane as he passed her.

"What would you have of me, Father?" Avice asked.

"Your prayers," he said in whisper, laying his full weight against her arm. She could not lift him without his aid. With a frown, she let him fall back upon the pillows. "Gather them, Juliane," he commanded. "It is my time."

Juliane looked hard into her father's face, her blue eyes fierce, and then she nodded. She would do as he asked. It would soothe him, if nothing else. She turned and left her father to Avice, passing Father Matthew in the doorway.

"His time is upon him. I go to begin it," she said.

Father Matthew nodded and entered the room. All was quiet within, the only sound being of Avice's whispered prayers on behalf of her father's soul.

It took only a week for them to come. Walter, Philip's only surviving son, came from his fostering at a gallop, his red hair a sweaty cap upon his fair head. He threw the reins of his horse to a groom, ran up the steps three at a time, and kept running until he reached his father's chamber.

It was not good.

The chamber was crowded with the men who formed the circle of Philip's life: his priest, his chief knight, his closest companions. All were arrayed within the chamber, all watching Philip take his leave of this life and prepare himself for the next. And now his son was come among them, his only son, to whom everything would fall as Philip made for heaven.

"Walter," Philip said from his bed, his skin of a shade to match the linens at his back.

Walter came and crouched by his father's side, taking his hand in his own. His father's skin was thin and dry, wasted of life like an autumn leaf.

"Father, what would you have of me? Your will is mine."

His father's eyes were so pale a blue now as to be like clearest glass, reflecting the hope of heaven and eternal peace like costly church glass, pale yet turned upon his son with all the fervor of last wishes.

"The cloths I brought with me from across the sea, you know of which I speak?" Walter nodded. "Let them be spread upon my body when I am laid in earth."

"Where, Father?"

"Fair son," Philip said with a smile, "next to my lady wife and I shall be content."

"It will be done," Walter answered.

"And as for you," Philip continued, his own life and death accounted for, "you shall have Stanora and Portesdone."

"Yea, Father," Walter answered. It was as it should be; he was the only son and inheritor of all his father's land. But what of his sisters?

"Avice is betrothed," Philip said, reminding the throng that stood about them, marking all, recording all in the event that any question was raised as to the lord of Stanora's disposition of his earthly goods. Death was a public event, and they watched to see how well and nobly Philip died. "See her married within the month of my death. I would have no disputes raised that she and you must face. Let all be cleanly done and well."

"She goes to Arthur of Clairvaux, that I know. All will be done as you have arranged."

"But there is Juliane," Philip said, his voice trailing off, his gaze drifting to the painted ceiling overhead.

Aye, Juliane, whom none would claim. What of her? There was small protection in this life for a woman not bound to a man. Walter would take her within his house, keeping her safe, but a woman without a man . . . it was too easy and too often that such women fell into dissolute lives. If any woman would push her way into dissolution, 'twas Juliane. She was too strong-headed, too reckless, to be well bound without strong masculine hands to hold her in check.

And there was Conor, whom Walter had no cause to trust.

"Bring Ulrich to me," Philip said, interrupting Walter's speculations.

"Ulrich?" Walter asked the room at large. He did not know the name.

"Ulrich of Caen," the priest said. "A knight errant come to Stanora a bare week ago. He is below or without, yet he is here. He remains within the shadow of Stanora."

"Fetch him, if you would," Walter said. He would not leave his father's side for an errand.

Father Matthew hesitated and then left the chamber with reserved dignity.

"You should not order him about," Philip said, squeezing his son's hand.

"I requested only," Walter said with a thin smile. This was old ground between them.

"As you will. I have no strength for this old battle."

"Your pardon, Father. I will not distress you again with battles won and lost between us."

"Say you now that you have lost this battle in the past? Or that it is I who have tallied a loss against my skill?"

"Peace, Father," Walter said, grinning through his tears. "All losses stand upon my name and none upon yours."

Into the chamber marked by manly death and manly tears came Ulrich. Walter took his measure. A tall man, wide in the shoulder, straight-limbed, with intense blue eyes and dark brown hair that swept his neck; a knight like most of them, loose upon the world, searching for a house and a name to bind them in place and give them purpose. What was it in this man that called to his father, and why was his name so close-linked with Juliane's?

The throng of men parted to let Ulrich pass in among them, a man among men; death was a time when men united, watching the passing of one of their number into paradise, yet Ulrich was a stranger to Stanora. What could the lord of Stanora have to say to him? Walter wondered. 'Twas a time of making things clear, of giving away all worldly possessions so as to be free to enter heaven as one had entered earth, clean and free of all encumbrances. What did Ulrich merit from his father?

Ulrich knelt at Philip's bedside, his head lowered in submission and expectation. Walter watched in curious perplexity.

"Tell me, then," Philip said.

"I fell not. Nor will I," Ulrich answered.

The priest cleared his throat in disapproval, but that was nothing. Father Matthew was wont to disapprove of the most innocuous events.

"And Juliane?"

"I won the wager, my lord."

"And then?"

"And then," Ulrich repeated, "nothing, my lord. All stands as it was."

"Your legacy. Tell me of it."

Ulrich lifted his head and looked hard into Philip's eyes. "I have no legacy. I am as I stand, my skill at arms the only merit upon which I stand. Or fall," he added in wry humor.

Walter lifted his brows in approval.

"Who is your father?" Philip asked weakly.

"He did not own me," Ulrich said simply without any rancor or self-pity.

"Yet who was he? I think I know and would only have you speak it out."

Ulrich stood and sighed audibly, his hands forming into fists at his sides.

"My father was Henry of England. I was born in Caen two months after his death. This my mother swore to me, and this her brothers swore was truth. I have no proof beyond the telling. I have no name beyond Caen."

"The king was past sixty when he died," Father Matthew said.

"I have no proof beyond the telling," Ulrich repeated without apology or excuse. Or denial.

"My eyes bear the proof," Philip said. "You have his look and something of his bearing. Little of his temper."

"How does this avail?" Walter asked his father. "To what purpose this knowledge, this man?"

"To this purpose," Philip answered. "He is for Juliane."

Chapter Fourteen

"Walter is come," Avice said.

Juliane spun about softly, careful of the birds of prey surrounding her. She had been spending much time in this warm darkness of late. Being a woman, she had no place beside her father in his journey toward death; that was for the men of his life. A man's life was surrounded by men; a woman's life was cloistered among the women. Except that Juliane had no deep fondness for a woman's life or a woman's company.

Walter was her younger brother by a year, yet a man by any measure and soon to be in charge of her. She did not relish it, nor did she dread it. She was fond of Walter; it was only that her father was an easier master than Walter, with his young pride and stern energy, would ever be. With Walter holding the keys to her confinement, her life would be confining indeed.

"But more," Avice said. "Ulrich has been called into the lord's solar."

"Why?"

"Can you not reason it out? Did he not win the wager? He did not fall to you, Sister. In your jousting, his lance did not fail him."

"He is no one," Juliane said, surely stating the obvious. "He has nothing beyond his sword and his horse and his arrogance. What match is that for me?"

"He has his sturdy lance," Avice said with a smile that

held some sympathy, if the soft light could show as much. "What more is needed to make a match with Juliane le Gel?"

And had Maud not counseled her that this was what she must beware of? This was where such legends as hers ended and where wagering led—to marriage to any man who could master his lance against her ice. Maud had feared this end, yet had she not held out the hope that Philip would never give her over into marriage? Had that not been the very foundation of their distant bargaining? So long ago now, more than five years past, yet did not all still hold together? Nothing had changed. The world was still as it was.

Even Avice did not know. Avice had been away at her fostering during the short days of Juliane's first marriage. Avice, like them all, knew only the legend of le Gel, believing it in full, seeing only the victory of The Frost over men who came to test themselves against her name. Wagering all to have her. Wagering as Ulrich had done, but unlike Ulrich in every other way.

Of the wager, of that golden time in the stables six days past, she refused to think. 'Twas like a dream, hazy and disremembered, the woman in the dream not her. Though the man in the dream remained Ulrich of Caen. Who was that woman who had fallen to smiles and touches and the hard grip of a man? Not Juliane of frost and ice and cold winds. She had no such melting in her. The verses of her legend sang as much.

Yet she had carried the mark of his kiss upon her throat for three days, giving weight to the illusion of dreams and the death of legend.

No man had ever before marked her so. No man had

bruised her skin and her resolve. And come too close to marking something upon her heart. There was no room for bruising in the meaningless courtly games of a meaningless love. And so, there was no room for Ulrich.

She had seen him in the days of her father's confinement. She had seen him in the hall and in the bailey and she had felt his eyes upon her, and even imagined that she felt some sorrow bleeding out from him over the lord of Stanora's coming death. But they had not spoken, and she had kept a wide distance between them. There was nothing to say. What had they ever had between them but the heat of their wagering? Now was not the time for wagers. And she was done with wagering against Ulrich of Caen. With him, the threat of loss was too great and too near. She guarded herself more closely than that.

"Our father would not pledge me to a knight with nothing, a knight he knows nothing of," Juliane said.

"Juliane," Avice said softly, wary of the birds surrounding them in quiet confinement, "you know he must see you settled before he dies. It is his duty. He cannot leave you alone in the world."

"There is Walter."

"And Walter has his own marriage contract to see fulfilled, his own life to set in motion as lord of Stanora. What place for you will he find? What place will there be for you?"

The same place as Maud's, companion to children yet unborn in her brother's house? So she had silently planned, and not found the planning too painful. To be in her brother's keeping for life. To be in her brother's *power* for life. That was more painful. A life could be a long travail, and Walter had little softness in him.

The church? She did not want a life of silence and prayer and meager crusts. She liked the meat of life too much, and the play. A cloistered life was all of duty and none of play. She would find no joy in it, that she knew.

To be her father's daughter, that was a life to be lived, yet without her father to author it, that life might be lost to her. Walter was not Philip. There would be little freedom with Walter as her master. And if Walter was in charge of her, he would hurry to find her a husband.

Yet did her father even now do differently? If Ulrich was his choice, it was a choice she could never accept. Ulrich had nothing, nothing but the power to seduce.

"Ulrich has nothing," she said, keeping to the shadows. Nothing but a cock that would not fall. Nothing but a heat that thawed her legend into mud.

"You do not know that. He could have more wealth than you know. All you know of him is his name."

"If a man has worth, he shouts it out. There is no mystery to it."

"Is Ulrich like other men?"

Yea. He was. Like all other men, full of pride and hot arrogance.

Nay. He was not. He was smiling and warm and unafraid of her. Of all the men who had come, each in his way had been afraid of her. Ulrich was curious, mayhap even intrigued. He was not afraid.

And he had won the wager. He had not fallen, even with a knife to his manhood. She had not thought it possible for a man to be so . . . stalwart. So hot. So vigorous.

"Let us see what he brings to this bargaining," Juliane said, pressing away a flush upon her throat at remembering the quiet confidence in his eyes, at remembering the feel of his mouth upon her skin, at remembering the thudding of her heart and the rush of heat to her loins.

"You go to see Father?"

"If he wills it."

And if he did not will it, she would see him anyway.

"He fails. By the day, he fails."

"And when he passes into paradise? Will you wait?"

"I will not wait. I begin it even now. Indeed, I began it long ago."

"How?"

"As he rids himself of all his worldly goods, preparing for his entrance into heaven's gate, some of his goods must find their way to the church. And if not to the church, then to Thomas who hides in France," Father Matthew said.

They stood in the orchard, sheltered by shade and hidden by leaf, but able to see all who came. Able to see that they stood alone and unheard.

" 'Tis treason to the king."

"My bonds are to God, who is above all earthly kings. 'Tis Henry who commits treason against the God of all by fighting for power with His archbishop. All power lies in God's hands, and by His mercy some is released to the kings of earth, for heaven's use and glory. That Henry has forgotten his place in the divine will of God is no fault of Thomas's."

"I do not argue it. I only see the need for caution."

"I follow God's path. I have no need for caution," the priest said.

"All men have need for caution, Father. Your life may rest on this."

"My life rests in God's mighty hand. I fear no man."

"Father?" Marguerite called from the steps into the church. "Father Matthew?"

Their talk died away, and Matthew walked quickly out of the orchard.

"Yea, child?"

"He asks for you, Father," she said, turning her dark eyes upon him in entreaty, not seeing the man who walked softly and in shadow to the orchard's edge, disappearing into the grim shadow of the wall. "Will you come?"

"Of course," Father Matthew answered with a smile. "I am ever in the way of doing God's will."

He left the orchard without looking back and followed Marguerite up the stairs and into the cool sanctuary of the tower gate.

"He has nothing. This cannot be God's will."

"He has what he needs to make this match. That is clear."

Walter ran a hand through his red hair. In appearance he was much like Juliane and perhaps in temperament as well, though he and Juliane both denied it vigorously. Avice had their mother's dark hair and more uncertain temper. Juliane's temper was always certain; 'twas her will that was a problem.

"He has a tale and nothing more."

"He has a tale he is reluctant to tell. That tells me more than I need to know," Philip said softly.

His color was fading, his features showing sharp, his breathing coming hard and thin; he would not last another week, if eyes could judge. Still, God could stay His hand and let Philip linger on this earth until the marriage of Juliane was set and settled. God willing, 'twould be so. Walter did not want to be the one to drag Juliane to the altar, and dragging it would take to get her there. If his father's will was followed, she would be married before he left this world for the next.

But still, Walter had his doubts. "He brings nothing," he said. "No land, no title, no influence. This does nothing for Juliane. She will never abide by this choice."

"She will," Philip said softly. "If I set her to it, she will. You must get Maud behind you in this," Philip said on a hiss of breath. "Bring my sister to me and I will see it done."

Maud? What part could his aunt play in this? She was a woman, and marriages were made between men.

"And what Ulrich lacks by an accident of timing in the matter of his birth, I will set to rights," Philip continued, pulling Walter's thoughts from Maud. "I was and am King Henry's man. King Henry the First shall be well served by me now in this raising of his son to a place deserving of his blood."

"He had many bastards, nigh beyond counting."

"And all provided for. He turned not from a one of them. Ulrich has his look and some shadow of his manner. Can any other man be better matched to my Juliane?"

There was that. Only a man of Henry's brood, blood, and bile seemed of the temper to take his sister and make her behave in the manner of a woman. If Ulrich had done that even in part without benefit of marriage, he could well be the man, the only man, fit for her.

"I will concede it," Walter said.

"Then set the wheels in motion, my son. My time is short, and I will not leave her without a home of her own and without the mantle of a man's honor to shield her from the storms of life."

"Aye, Father. I will begin it."

"Begin what?" Juliane asked from the doorway.

Walter stood and walked swiftly to her. He was the keeper of the lord of Stanora, monitoring all who entered the death chamber of his father. Death was a public event, but women were not in the public domain. Sheltered and sequestered they were supposed to be. How that Juliane did not understand that?

Worse, he suspected that she understood it very well and simply did not care. Finding a husband for such a one was a task most strenuous. Ulrich, close and ready, looked better by the hour.

"He tires. Leave him to his rest," Walter said, throwing an arm over the doorway, keeping her in the narrow gallery.

Juliane looked under Walter's arm. Her father did look weak and tired, pale and thin, his life drawing out like a fragile cord, frayed, and ready to break. She then cast a glance over her shoulder to the vast hall below. All eyes were turned up to watch the battle between brother and sister upon the wooden gallery, Ulrich's among them, blue and soft and curious. Compassionate. Avid. Of what concern to him that she speak to her father or not? He was a simple guest. Or so she prayed daily. He could be nothing more. He would be nothing more.

"I would only comfort him. He is my father, too, Walter. I want the joy of his company before he leaves us all," she said.

"Let her come," Philip said from the bed.

With some reluctance, Walter lowered his arm, and she

passed into the lord's solar and went to stand by her father's bed, away from the eyes in the hall. Walter stood in the doorway, listening. Let him listen, then. Let him learn the nature of her heart and the direction of her will.

"You look well and good," she said to her father.

He laughed, a gasp of air mixed with a smile, ending in a light cough. A dying laugh. A last laugh.

"Do not flatter now, Juliane. Your blunt speech is a treasure. Do not toss it from you for a dying man, which is what I am and how I look."

"You look good to me," she said, kissing his hand.

"Ah, that I will believe," he said softly. "But let us talk of more weighty things than my handsome face. You are to be married."

He delivered it like the blow it was, tempered by love, but a blow against her very life.

"To Ulrich?"

"Whom else?"

"He is a knight with nothing but a name."

"But what a name," Philip said with a lopsided grin and a slow wink. When she pulled her hand from his, he caught a fingertip and held on to her gently. "And would you truly not marry? What, then, Juliane? The cloister? Father Matthew would have it so."

"Nay. There is more to life than prayers."

"And so I told him you would answer. There are two paths open to you: church or marriage. Which will you choose, for choose you must."

"I would choose neither."

"So I have chosen for you," he said. "You bring Ulrich all a man would want in this life. He will take the gift of you and cherish you long. He will be thankful for the gift of Juliane."

"Is that how it is with a man? He cherishes the woman who gives him worth? Nay, I think that only resentment will grow from such a seed as that."

"You are wrong," he said softly, his eyes closing in exhaustion.

She could see that her father's impassioned plea had weakened him, leaving him breathless and tired. She would not for the world weaken him with argument. But she must protest the thought of wedding Ulrich.

"How can you give me up in marriage? This was not to be my path. Would you throw me to a beggar?" she asked.

"He is the man I have chosen for you."

He said it simply, his eyes on Walter at her back. In truth, he did not say much, but what weight beneath the words! She could barely stand against the force of it. Her father had given her much, and they would neither of them forget it. She loved him. She would do whate'er he asked, and he knew it well.

"Why?" she asked, looking down at him. He was not so weak that he could be pushed to something, anything, not of his will and wisdom. There must be some lure which Ulrich had thrown up to the sky to tempt her father to make this match. "Why this man of all who have come here, testing themselves against the tale of me?"

"He is Henry's son."

Henry's son. Not the Henry who sat now upon the throne, they were too close in age, but the first King Henry, who had cast his seed so often and so well. Ulrich was his blood. Or so her father believed. If Ulrich lied, he had chosen his lie well. There was none to prove or to disprove his claim, and what man would not wish for the blood of kings to run into his legacy?

"How do you know? He was not claimed."

"Henry's death came close upon Ulrich's birth. There was no chance of claiming."

"But much of lying. There is no proof he is a king's son."

"There is proof enough," Philip said, closing his eyes against all argument.

Proof enough for her father, who was counting down his hours and needed to see her wed before he passed into paradise. Proof enough for her? There was no such proof, and there would never be enough to satisfy her, even if the king himself claimed Ulrich as cousin.

"Even so, he has nothing."

"He has royal blood, and his blood stands hard for you. That should be enough for any maid. Or did he fall to you?"

"Nay," she said unwillingly. "He did not fall."

"Then it is done," Philip said.

And so it was done, unless Ulrich disavowed the match. Small chance of that; this was his path into wealth and power. He would not refuse. What man would?

What man would? Perhaps her brother. He could not want her cast to a knight errant with nothing but a legend of royalty and a knight's sword to mark him.

"Is it enough for Walter?" she asked, looking over her shoulder at her brother in the doorway. He had stood and heard all, as was proper, bearing witness to deathbed instructions and dispositions. All that was said here would be recorded and would come to pass.

Aye, he had heard all and found himself marveling at his father's wisdom and at God's timing. Juliane had grown even more rebellious and contrary since he last saw her five years past at her own wedding. What man could rule her but their father, who commanded her heart and her head both? If Ulrich had defeated any part of her fractious nature, then he was welcome to her, and Walter would only pray the deed well done and soon. His sister needed a man to guide her, and Walter had troubles of his own that did not include Juliane and her willfulness.

"It is enough for my lord father and so it is enough for me," Walter said, staring hard into his sister's eyes, forcing his will upon her. "You shall marry Ulrich of Caen without delay. Let us see this done before the day is spent."

"'Tis too fast!" she said, whirling to face him, leaving her father's touch. "The church will not consent without the banns!"

"Father Matthew will do as I tell him. This is my domain. All here shall be as I say it shall be," Walter said. "And it shall be today, Juliane. Prepare yourself as you will."

Chapter Fifteen

"She is yours, if you will have her."

Walter stood in the center of the hall, the fire an unnecessary blaze at his back. The day was hot even as the sun slid toward the treetops, slid down into darkness and Juliane still unwed. He would see it done, his duty to his father and his sister met this hour if he could, settling all before the dark closed in, ending the day.

Juliane stood at his side, stiff and cold, her face an icy mask of contempt and mute rebellion. He would brook no rebellion from her; she was in his keeping, passed from their father's hand into his, and he would do well by her, if she only had the wit to see it. She had grown too bold under their father's loose and indulgent grip.

There was a lesson in that, and he was certain of learning it; he would not hold his own wife in anything less than a firm hand of power. 'Twas what a woman needed, her nature leading her inexorably into sin and, worse, wantonness. His duty was to protect the women of his house, and, in spite of Juliane, that he would do. Delivering her into a strong hand was the surest course.

"I will have her," Ulrich said, looking straight into Walter's eyes. "Yet I bring nothing to the match but my name."

He was honest, and there was strong merit in that. And he was not afraid of Juliane and the tales of her. Another point in his favor.

"My father meets with his counselors and the scribes. Lands in St. Ives will be granted to you in fief. 'Tis the site of the herring fair, a rich property with rents paid at each fair. For the past three years, two fairs a year were hosted."

"You give this freely?" Ulrich asked, guessing it was from Walter's portion that Ulrich's gift was taken.

"For my father, yea, I give it freely. For my sister, I give it gladly."

"Then in your sister's name, I take it gratefully," Ulrich said.

"Take it in your own name at least," Juliane said. "There is none of me in this bargaining."

"Nay, you are wrong. 'Tis all of you," Walter said.

Ulrich said nothing, but his eyes shifted to Juliane.

"Then ask me what is my will in this matter of joining myself, my name, my lands to this nameless, landless knight," she said with stiff pride.

Again, Ulrich said nothing to this blow upon his honor, though his gaze fixed upon Juliane, his blue eyes cool and shuttered.

"He brings St. Ives to the match," Walter said. "A nice pairing to your dower lands in Stamford."

"He has St. Ives because you gave it to him!"

"And does it matter how a man comes into his land beyond that he earned it?" Walter countered. "Was not Stamford given to you?"

"It is mine by blood," she said, "and you know it well."

"By blood, I shall take St. Ives and make it mine," Ulrich said. "As I will make you mine, Juliane."

Aye, by her blood upon his cock he would own her. He used his words as a hammer against her pride and disdain. He would have her, no matter her pride or her ice. No matter the shame she cast upon them all by her public refusal of her father's will.

This was Juliane as he knew her, and still he would take her, without hesitation and without regret. He wanted her and he needed a wife. He needed land and the power of a name. If taking her would give him that, then he would take her with a will, getting from her what no woman had yet given him: land.

And make her like it, salving his own ragged pride in the doing.

Her aunt Maud appeared at her back, reaching out a hand to lead her niece away from further public disgrace. Or so Ulrich hoped.

"Come, child," Maud said. "Let them negotiate between them. This matter is done, for now."

For now? What meaning there? Ulrich wondered. This matter was done and set and would not be dissolved for Juliane's satisfaction. All that was left was the signing of the contracts. Pull a scribe into the room and he could be married within the hour.

And once married, then to bed. There was the crux of Maud's hope. Had not Juliane been married before? And had not that marriage gone foul? A woman's hope, to unman a man upon his wedding night, and this woman, this Juliane le Gel had done it once before. It would be once only, he vowed.

He was not to be unmanned by her, and they had enough history between them for her to know it.

Let her find the truth of it again. Let her find herself moaning in his grasp, his mouth hot upon her skin, his hands hard upon her, his cock raised to pierce her, rending her heart and her flesh in one stroke. He was the man who would remain a man with Lady Ice. He was the husband who would stick and stick it to her well.

He had not even the grace to squirm against his dark thoughts. He had sworn to leave off women. He had sworn off love play and courtly jousts of amorous words and the silent victories of stolen kisses. He had sworn to be a new man, better than before.

But then he had met Juliane. He had seen her, thrown words as hard and bright as new javelins at her heart, touched her, kissed her, and in all, he had fallen from his sworn oath. As he was falling now. But for such a cause as this, and with such a woman, were not all oaths cast adrift? He would not harm her—she was beyond that, her strength as full as any man's. He could not hurt her. He need not be wary and careful of her. She was a tested warrior in these things, and so he could look to his own needs, his own victory, knowing she would look to herself.

It would not be as it had been with Mariam. Juliane was nothing like her.

All this he thought as he watched Juliane leave the bright light of the hall for the narrow stair that would lead her to the gallery above him. All this he planned as he watched her skirts sway in the dim light of the gallery as she and Maud walked into the far chamber next to the rising stone of the tower gate. All this he hid from the eyes of her brother, who watched him as he watched the woman he would possess.

"Will this marriage stick?" Walter asked, mirroring his own thoughts.

"It will," Ulrich said. "There is no doubt of it."

"My father shares your mind on this," Walter said.

The hall was still full of folk; the girls of the fostering clustered near Avice, the men of his brotherhood arranged about the fire, and Squire William at his back. It was good that many ears could hear what was promised in this hour. There would be no turning back later. St. Ives had been given and received. Juliane had been given and received. All that remained was the paperwork, though unions had been severed by paper before. But not this time. He would not give her up. He had waited too long for this.

"Philip has good cause. I have a history with Juliane

which bears no clang of failure," he said, looking fully into Walter's face. "The marriage will hold. By my hands I will hold it fast."

Into his confidence strode a man, a bull of a man with auburn hair and ruddy skin and massive voice. Up the stairs he came, three at once, and at his heels followed a man of dark hair and eyes and smaller stature, though with the bearing of a knight. Into the hall they strode, and all eyes turned to face them.

"I am come! Where is my sister's husband? Where is Philip of Stanora?"

At Ulrich's side, Walter heaved a sigh.

"He is abed, Uncle Conor, and I will see if—"

"Then I am to him now, before he flies to heaven without my voice to follow him," Conor said, clasping Walter's hand in greeting as he passed him by, heading directly for the stairs that led up to the gallery.

Walter followed, leaving Ulrich and all the rest of them in the hall, the flickering fire quiet company in the utter silence that came rushing in after Conor's passing. The dark man lingered with them, his own silence a cloak he wore in comfort as all eyes within the hall turned to him.

"Show me the way out of this, Maud. I am entrapped and cannot see my way clear," Juliane said.

"It is a coil, that is true," Maud said, pacing her small chamber, circling the unlit fire at its heart. "Your father wants this badly. How you may refuse, disobeying him, I cannot see."

"You were full of wisdom before! You helped me then. Can you not help me now?"

Maud chewed her lip and shook her head. " 'Twas a

different game before, with a different man. Your father did not lie dying, his soul seeking to escape the bounds of earth. I dare not go against his will in this. I cannot help you. No one can. You must marry Ulrich."

"And have my legend stripped from me?" Juliane said, turning to face the wind hole and feel the air of freedom on her skin.

"I think he would take you despite your legend. He wants you desperately," Maud said from behind her.

"What care I what he wants? 'Tis my own wants that occupy me, and I do not want him," Juliane snapped.

Did none understand? With Ulrich, all was lost. He would rule her as he ruled his hawk, joyfully confident because the jesses were firmly in his grip. She could not live out her life constrained, tied to such a man.

She could not learn to love the man who kept her tied to his hand.

That was the depth of her fear, that she would learn to beggar freedom for the gift of Ulrich's smile, Ulrich's touch, Ulrich's passion. He could bring her to it. She would admit it to herself, now that all games were past her. Now that she was fighting for her very life, or the life she had worked to build. A life reflected in legend.

"You know the truth," Juliane said to her aunt. "You know how I have constructed my life, man upon man, building my legend with unwilling hands. All to stay free. All to live out my life as *I* have chosen. I cannot fight Ulrich. If he takes me, I will fall to him. You know this to be so. Can you give me no counsel, no plan, no escape?"

Maud looked at her, her blue eyes soft with regret and sympathy. "I have no counsel which will ease you, Juliane. There is no escape from this. Philip has determined it, and there is no freedom from his will."

Juliane took a heavy breath, the air forced painfully into her lungs. No escape. No escape. No escape beyond the bounds of her father's will. Why did he hurry now to cast a husband upon her? Did his death make such a difference, then?

She did not want a husband. Maud had shown her the wisdom of that choice in the tracks of her own life. Maud lived comfortably, without burdensome responsibility, without the hazards of childbearing, without the heavy companionship of a husband; Maud lived the ideal life.

Because Philip was the ideal brother?

She had not considered that. What would become of Maud now that Philip lay ready to depart this world? Would she remain under Walter's care? Only if Walter allowed it. Look how her own life was tossed into confusion because of her father's passing into eternity. Was Maud's fate any different?

Would Maud even have had the power to avoid marriage herself if her brother Philip had not by his very indulgence allowed it?

"Then this is the end of the legend of The Frost, Maud. I grieve to say it, yet it is so. Am I not to marry before the day is done?" Juliane asked.

"To marry is one thing. To stay married is another. Only foil his attempts at consummation and you may win free, God willing."

Juliane grinned in halfhearted humor. "He knows how I use the hawk."

"Does he?" Maud said, sitting on the edge of the bed.

"And who can fight a hawk? What he knows shall not help him in his battle to take and hold you."

"I think we are past the hawk," Juliane said, pacing the circle of the fire. It was not lit, for the day was warm, though the wind was rising, sliding into the stone-rimmed hole in the wall. "He stood to my knife."

"A knife?" Maud said, sitting forward, her eyes wide. "You held a knife to him?"

"Aye." She was not going to say *where* she had held the knife. Some things were beyond even Maud's counsel. "He did not fall."

"Fall? I am amazed that he did not strike you."

"He did not strike."

Nay, he had smiled, taunting her, pulling her close to show her the length and strength of his pulsing weapon, kissing her with gentle humor. Would a man with royal blood pumping through his heart react so? Henry the First was not a man known for his soft temperament. Ulrich acted nothing like what she knew of Henry. What did her father see that she did not?

"Perhaps because he knew your father's eye was upon him. Become his wife and he will strike you at will. He will have the right and the duty to keep you well in hand."

Aye, there was that. Claiming her as wife would give him all sorts of rights regarding her. Another reason to never wed. She would be her own and no man's.

Except that she was to be wed before Compline.

"There is nothing for it," Maud continued. "You must wed him. Your father is set upon it, and his will must be obeyed. He means only well for you, and you must see it done. But let it not be consummated. That is your weapon and the key to your freedom."

Let it not be consummated. How easily the words were spoken, yet how impossible the task. Win herself free of Ulrich's touch? She could not. Worse, she feared she lacked the will. He stirred fires in her that all the snow in England could not douse.

"What of *your* freedom, Maud?" she asked, turning aside the subject of consummation. "Will Walter let you stay as you are? You are young enough to marry. He may arrange it for you, thinking to do you a good service."

Maud slid down from the bed and crossed her arms over her chest as she, too, began to pace the room.

"Good service?" Maud mumbled. "I would run to the abbey and lock myself behind those doors before I ever took a man into me."

"The abbey? Truly?"

"Aye. I have no wish to be ruled by a man. Let me put myself under an abbess, if it comes to that. Though it may not. Your brother will have need of a woman in his house, even if he claims his betrothed before Christmas. She is only just come into her flux, according to the last report. She will need aid in managing Stanora. Who better than I, who knows Stanora so well?"

Likely true. Walter would welcome experienced hands to aid his young wife, and Maud's hands were experienced indeed.

But Juliane's thoughts were all of Ulrich. Did she want him or not? Did she seek the married state or not?

Did it matter in either event? She was to be married. The only question was whether she would *stay* married.

* * *

"Even if you marry her—"

"I *will* marry her," Ulrich interrupted.

"Even when you marry her," Roger amended, "can you *stay* married to her? Her first husband was in and out in a day."

"I can last more than a day," Ulrich said with a quick grin.

Roger chuckled and shook his head. They spoke in whispers, not wanting to be heard by anyone in the hall, particularly not by Nicholas, the dark and quiet knight so recently come into their midst. He had introduced himself as Nicholas of Nottingham and said little else after that. He had looked at the fire for a time and then set himself upon a bench and proceeded to sharpen his sword, ignoring them all. Hardly the best of manners, but Nottingham was hardly the best of towns.

"She does not want this," Roger said.

"I will teach her to want *me*. If she does not already do so," Ulrich said.

"You think she wants you?"

"I think," Ulrich said slowly, "I think she fears to want me, and by her fear, I have made good ground in winning her."

Roger shook his head. "That is too much thinking for my part. If that is how a woman's mind spins, 'tis no wonder they cannot be understood."

"I do not understand you," Conor said, leaning over his only sister's husband. His sister was long dead, but his duty to her children would never die. Such was the way of things in families. It would be the same for Walter, and was even now; he was responsible for his sisters and his sisters' offspring. The ties of a man to the women of his blood lasted beyond all else. "He is nothing, nothing but the promise of a name."

"And he is the only man who can stand against my Juliane's frost. That is something of great import," Philip said. "The decision has been made, recorded. I will not unmake it."

"And I will uphold it," Walter said at his uncle's back.

"There are others who would make a finer match for Juliane," Conor said, ignoring Walter. Philip was still the lord of Stanora and the one to whom all decisions would fall. "What of Nicholas of Nottingham?"

Philip shook his head on his pillow, too spent to speak. Which might work very well in Conor's favor.

"He has land and a name that goes back one hundred years. His land is old, and old is his hold on it. You need give him nothing. He can meet the worth of Juliane on his own merit. Tell me, what have you given to this knight to give him equal worth to Juliane?"

"St. Ives," Walter said.

"A rich holding lost to you to gain a man for her. Take Nicholas for her and you lose nothing," Conor said. He was still looking at Philip, but he was speaking to Walter, and all in that chamber knew it. "All is increased. Why should you rob your own son to enrich a knight errant? He alone gains by this. Is it not your duty to arrange a marriage which enriches all?"

"What do *you* gain?" Philip said, his blue eyes fierce for an instant before fading into exhaustion.

Conor smiled and laid a hand on Philip's shoulder, gone raw and thin in his wasting death. "What do you lose? St. Ives," he said, answering himself. " 'Tis too great a loss for Walter to be made to bear."

"I bear it willingly," Walter said, yet not quite so earnestly as he had before. "What does Nicholas bring?"

Conor turned to look at Walter. "A manor with forty hides of land north of the Trent River and a walled tower on the southern bank. The mill is his, and it is rich in fees."

Walter looked to his father, lying silent and still upon his deathbed. Conor watched him and waited.

"What is he waiting for?" William asked, eyeing Nicholas.

"What we all are waiting for," Edward answered. "For the matter of Ulrich and Juliane to be settled."

"It is settled," Ulrich said. "I am for her and she is mine."

"You say that because you do not know my uncle," Avice said, boldly joining the men in their circle of comradeship. Roger moved his body in such a way as to politely invite her in. Edward did not move at all, shutting her out.

She and Edward had not spoken since their wagered kiss, a condition she was most thankful for. She did not like him. She did not like his look or his manner or his nature. He was too quiet, and yet when he spoke, he said too much and all of it disagreeable. His eyes were too light. His humor was too caustic. He had the deportment of an ox, but without the usefulness.

She most determinedly did not like Edward.

That Edward seemed equally determined not to like her she found oddly gratifying. And so she found a perverse pleasure in invading his circle. She decided in that moment that she would make it a point to intrude upon him at every opportunity for as long as he remained in Stanora, which, God willing, would not be much longer.

"What of your uncle? He will abide by Lord Philip's wishes, as must we all," Ulrich said.

She felt a stab of pity for Ulrich in that instant; he was a stranger to them all and understood nothing of the currents of power and the weight of history that ran between Conor and Philip.

"Conor is my mother's brother, her elder brother, and he has an abiding interest in what happens in Stanora. He always has."

"And so he should, but the matter of a betrothal is the province of a father, not an uncle. Not when the father lives," Ulrich said.

"And so he comes now, when that tide is about to turn," Edward said, looking at Avice without his usual heat. Avice ignored him and answered Ulrich instead.

"He comes and brings a man with him, a man whose name Conor has whispered often into Juliane's ear," she said.

"Juliane does not decide upon her mate. That is the province of her father," Ulrich said, looking hard at Avice.

She truly did feel some pity for him. He was a landless knight of doubtful name; Juliane and her lands were surely his best hope.

"This I know, Ulrich," she said softly. "Yet ever and always do my father and my uncle strive against each other. It began when my mother married my father. Conor did not approve the match, but what could he do? The match was made, and he was powerless to prevent it. That my mother died with only three children to her credit he holds bitterly to my father's doing."

" 'Tis God's doing and nothing less," Roger said.

"So it is, yet Conor's will, a formidable thing, was thwarted in the matter of my mother. He had a betrothal of his own in mind, I think, one that would have allowed him to keep St. Ives, for it was through my mother that St. Ives came into Stanora's grasp."

"And it is with Juliane that it will pass out of all reach of Conor's grasp, once and for always," Ulrich finished. "St. Ives in now in my grasp, and I will not let it go."

"Do not let it go," Conor urged.

" 'Tis a rich holding and one my mother prized most high," Walter said.

The light was fading, softening, a gentle golden haze through which a thread of spider silk spanning the room glimmered like molten silver in the warm light. Philip watched them from the bed, his eyes alert, his mouth stilled as he listened to Conor spin a web of ambition around his son.

"Why should it go to this nameless knight when a baron of title stands ready to do his service to Juliane?"

"And will he stand to Juliane?" Walter asked, showing at least some resistance to the power of Conor's persuasion.

"What man would not? She is a woman of worth and beauty and piety. Any man would be glad of her. Any man could stand the test of her."

Which only showed how little Conor knew of Juliane and how little he believed the careful legend of her. Philip had known that Conor would interfere in her life, and in Avice's too, and he had acted accordingly.

He had moved carefully, protecting his daughters from any move Conor might make against them. From the start, he and Conor had been opposed, their battling crossing over into lives and fortunes and betrothals. Up until this very moment. Until he lay upon a bed, weak and sick and old, facing death. Even now Conor strove against him, seeking to defeat him, seeking to match Juliane to a man of *his* choosing, when it was a father's will which must be obeyed. As Juliane was set to obey his will. He had protected her well. Conor could not touch her now.

Yet now he watched Conor bargaining with his son for his beautiful Juliane. Thank God above that Avice was safe from him, her betrothal unbreakable, Arthur's worth unquestioned.

He would not allow Juliane to be bartered for St. Ives and for Nicholas, whom he knew to be a pawn of Conor's. Nay, Juliane would marry *his* choice for her, defeating Conor yet again. What meat it was to Philip to best Conor in this; it fed him. It fed him well to outplay the man who had sliced off his ear twenty years before.

"He seems very certain of it," Lunete said.

"He is certain. He will not let her go," William said.

"He may have no choice. The choice lies with Philip, not with him," Lunete said.

William shrugged and shook his head.

"What?" Lunete asked.

"He will not let her go," William repeated, his arsenal of arguments spent.

They stood on the broad stairs that led out of the hall,

sheltered by stone and shadow, unnoticed because they had determined to be so. They were small, still children, the world scarcely cast them a glance unless it had need of them. There was no need now; all was of Ulrich and Juliane and the steadfastness of Philip's pledge that Ulrich would have her.

"Does he love her?" Lunete asked, a woman's question.

William shrugged again, a man's response to a question he would rather not answer.

"Does he?" Lunete asked again.

"He wants her," William said.

"'Tis not the same as loving."

"For him, mayhap it is."

"Juliane will not see it so."

"Does anyone care how Juliane sees it?"

"I do," Lunete said. "Juliane does. Lord Philip does."

"Does he? That is good, then, because he is the one who chose Ulrich for her. If Philip stands by Ulrich, then Juliane must."

When William looked into her eyes, watchful and cautious, waiting for an answer, Lunete only shook her head. And shrugged.

"Why should I?" Philip asked from his bed.

"Because Nicholas is the better man, better in wealth and name, better for Juliane and for Stanora," Conor said.

"Better for you," Philip said.

"Nay, 'tis not so," Conor said.

"Hold!" Philip said, fighting the onslaught of Conor's words. "You dishonor yourself by bringing this to me now, as I prepare myself for paradise. Juliane is mine. Stanora is mine. St. Ives is mine. All I possess I must give before I depart this earth. I have given all, my duty done, my way assured. Juliane is for Ulrich. St. Ives is for Ulrich. Stanora is for Walter along with all the wealth and responsibility it encompasses. This matter is done. I will hear no more words on it."

Conor said no more, but Philip's vision was not so dim that he did not see Conor's glance at Walter and Walter's wavering determination.

"Bring the priest to me. I want them married here. Now," Philip said.

"Hold!" Conor said as the scribe rushed out to fetch Father Matthew. "To marry Juliane is not enough; that has been managed before. I would see it consummated. I would know that this mating will hold and bear fruit, in God's time."

"You had no doubts about that with Nicholas," Walter said.

"I know Nicholas. I do not know this Ulrich of bastardy," Conor said.

And he still did not know Juliane, Philip thought as the idea of public consummation of their vows rolled through him. Juliane would hate it, but she would bear it. Her core was tempered steel. She would not break even at this.

"Done," Philip said. "But I name the witnesses. Maud, for one."

"And I for the other," Conor said.

"And the priest for a third, in case there is dispute," Walter said.

"Done," Philip said.

Chapter Sixteen

They found her in Maud's chamber and ushered her across the gallery to her father's solar. Since two men-at-arms had found her and now flanked her, their callused hands on her elbows, it would seem that they expected some rebellion from her.

In that, she disappointed them.

She was not going to engage in a fruitless tussle upon the well-lit height of the gallery. Nay, her fighting would take place in private, as it had once before.

Her father lay quietly upon his bed, his body shrunken into the mattress, the linen sheet lying almost flat as it covered him. He looked almost shrouded, his death hovering, breathing cold against him, robbing him of the breath of life. All but his eyes; his eyes glowed like an old and steady fire, throbbing with life and purpose and will. She was comforted by those eyes.

Conor was in the chamber, as were Father Matthew, Walter, the scribe, even Baldric, the groom. Juliane raised her brows at Baldric in question; he shrugged in answer and pointed discreetly to her father. Philip wanted Baldric here? That meant only one thing, and it was no surprise to her.

"She is here," Conor said.

"Aye, I am, Father," she said. Conor would not speak for her, not with her own father.

Before another word could be said, there was a press

and movement of bodies at her back and Ulrich slid into the room. Nay, she was not surprised.

"It has been decided," Conor began.

"It has been decided," Walter said more loudly, grasping the reins of this announcement and pulling hard for control, "that Juliane be wed to Ulrich of Caen, though no more to be named of Caen, but of St. Ives. Let the marriage take place now. We begin with the signing of the contracts."

"Tell her the terms," Philip whispered.

Juliane kept her eyes on her father, trying to read his intention in that vivid blue, blue which shone more fiercely now than ever before, as if the very skies of heaven were reflected there.

"Juliane," Walter said, silencing Conor with a look. "Our lord and father would not leave you without the protection of a man's name and might when he passes out of this life. He would leave you within the grasp of a loving"—and here Walter looked briefly at Ulrich, who met his look—"protector."

"I do understand the concept, Walter," Juliane said curtly. "What are the terms?"

"Ulrich has been given St. Ives, which you know, but also, on your part, it has been suggested—"

"What?" she interrupted. Walter really could be so very long-winded at times.

"That the consummation be achieved under many eyes," Conor said with a slight smile of satisfaction. "With many witnesses to verify that this marriage is lawful and within the measure and meaning of church doctrine."

"Many?" she breathed. "Am I to be pierced for the amusement of all Stanora? Shall this breaching take place on a table in the hall? Shall bets be wagered on the cries ripped from me?"

She said all with calm calculation and cold precision. She was not ashamed, nor afraid. She was incensed, and a cold burning anger it was. This was Conor's doing; she could smell it.

"I can attest, without witnesses, that I am the man who can meet the measure and meaning of church doctrine on this," Ulrich said, his voice as brittle as an ancient sword. "No eyes need bear witness to our union. Our tongues will confess the truth of the act. Is that not so, Juliane?"

He challenged her not to lie, knowing in his arrogance and pride that he would not fall to her, that he would take her, marking her as his, placing her under the shadowy protection of his shadowy name. He had no name but the one she had provided him. She was bound to tell no truth to save him.

Yet was not saving *her* the issue? What man would mind an audience to any mating he might fall into? No man. Yet to spread her legs with so many watching . . . she would avoid it if she could. She would endure it if she must.

"This is beyond your authority," Conor said. "It is a condition of the marriage. Will you abide by Lord Philip's decision? That is the only question you must answer now."

"Tell me the terms," Juliane said, turning to Walter. "I would know all before Ulrich's word is taken on this."

"Not many eyes, Juliane," Walter said, turning his back to Conor. "Three pairs of eyes, and those all known well to you: Conor, Maud, and Father Matthew. The quiet privacy of your chamber, not the bustle of the hall at meal-time. The reason behind the act is the fear that this marriage will not be consummated and hence annulled, as happened once before. None here would leave you without a lawful husband; our father wants you well protected and is doing all in his power to see it so."

Aye, well protected. From Conor. Walter did not say the words, yet she could read them in his eyes. Conor was ever and always plotting something, his horse ever bringing him within Stanora's gates, his thoughts ever turned to opposing her father. Conor, who had his own plans for her, and for gain that had nothing to do with her safety or contentment. To thwart Conor was almost reason enough to acquiesce.

She could understand the choice of the witnesses. First, Conor, who wanted to prevent this marriage since he had not arranged it. She had seen Nicholas of Nottingham below in the hall as she had been escorted along the gallery. She knew that Nicholas was Conor's choice for her.

The second pair of eyes was for her benefit. Maud, whom she trusted, who had stood this test before with her, with her first husband. and by whose witness Juliane had been freed of that first, wrong mating.

The third witness was for balance. Conor might lie for himself, Maud might lie for her, but a priest would lie for no one. He would speak the truth, no matter where that truth would take them all.

Juliane nodded at her brother and then turned to look down at her father. He had been part of this arrangement, though she would wager high that he had not initiated this public breaching. That smelled of Conor. Yet what could he have done to prevent it? What could she do?

She might refuse the match before the mating. Her own voice carried no weight with these men, nor her wishes, but her father cared for her and would consider her wants and wishes. With Philip still living, she had a chance of escape.

She knew well what would happen during the breaching. She would fall to Ulrich.

"You want me wed," she said softly to her father, turning her back on all within that crowded chamber. "Is there not another you could name?"

Behind her all was still. She knew that Ulrich had heard her. She did not care. Let her father only name another man, a man far from Stanora, a man she could manage and defeat.

"I have chosen," Philip said softly. "Obey me, Juliane. I deserve no less from you."

"My lord," Father Matthew said into the awkward silence, "you will take nothing with you into paradise. All must be given so that you may pass out of this life as naked as when you came into it."

"I have given all," Philip said. "All my lands, my furs, my coats of scarlet and what coin I had, all given."

"There is Stamford," Matthew said, looking at Juliane as he said it.

"Stamford is mine!" she said.

"Stamford was your mother's, your father held that land in her name. Now it can pass to whomever he wills."

"Stamford was always meant for me. You know that," she said.

"God has greater need of it," Matthew said, saying it plain, staking what claim he could.

"Nay!" she said, turning to her brother. "You know Stamford has been mine from the start."

"We only have what we are given, Juliane," Walter said softly, seeing the wisdom of Matthew's idea.

"You press too hard," Philip said, trying to raise himself up and failing. "Stamford is given to the church. But I cannot leave her without a place of her own."

"She will have St. Ives if she takes Ulrich," Walter said.

"She will have nothing," Ulrich said to her brother, looking at her, his blue eyes hard and flickering like cold fire, "unless she comes to me, getting St. Ives in the bargain."

"If you will have her," Walter said.

"Without a name, I am not certain I want her," Ulrich said softly, torturing her, giving her bruises upon her pride to match his own.

"What of Nicholas?" Walter asked his uncle.

Conor shrugged, frowning. "Without Stamford he will refuse the match. There is nothing to be gained by it. Will you truly give Stamford to the church?" he asked Philip.

Philip looked at Ulrich and then at his son; he did not look at Juliane, for he knew what he would see there. But in Walter he saw careful wisdom, the shrewd manipulation and understanding of men that would be required of him as lord of Stanora. This was a good turning. It got Conor and his bruising will out of his gates. It got for Matthew what he most wanted: prosperous land for his bishop. It got for himself what he wanted: Juliane married and out of Conor's reach.

As for Ulrich, it was clear he wanted Juliane still, but he would make her clutch for him now, for had she not just been reduced to his place in the world? A place of no name and no land beyond what she could clasp to her breast in marriage. Aye, the tables would be turned most well. And it was only in this turning that Juliane would bend to marriage with any small measure of grace.

There could be no escape this time, for there would be no returning. If this marriage failed, all doors would be closed to her. Walter would not take her, that was clear. Conor would have no use for her. And he, Philip, would be dead, flown beyond all earthly cares. Ulrich was her only chance now.

She was no fool. She would take it.

"It is given. Let the monks of Crowland Abbey have it, and Father Matthew manage the transfer," Philip said, not giving Matthew what he wanted but giving him enough to keep him content, keeping to old bargains by a hairbreadth.

"You leave me with nothing?" Juliane asked him.

"I leave you with two good hands. Grab what you may hold," Philip answered.

"He has no name!" she said.

"My name is as good as yours, lady," Ulrich said. "Better, in fact, for I now have St. Ives and you have naught."

"You do not have St. Ives without me," she said.

"You ask me to take you, then? To make you mine? To put my name and my touch upon you?" he demanded, taunting her.

"Nay, I said nothing like," she said. "'Tis only that, even now and in all this negotiation, all springs from me. You are nothing, have nothing, without me."

"Is this true?" Ulrich asked Philip. "Without Juliane there is no St. Ives?"

"It is true. To get St. Ives you must take her to wife," Philip said, seeing clearly where this led and knowing it was the only way.

"Then to get St. Ives, which I want beyond all reasoning, I will take her," Ulrich said, smiling like a panting wolf.

"St. Ives was my sister's portion. It should return to me if there is no fruit from your union," Conor said. 'Twas a fair request.

Ulrich paused and looked down at the floor. He sighed and, looking up, said, "That I cannot do."

"Why 'cannot'? 'Tis a simple request," Conor said.

"Because I have a son of my loins and of my blood," Ulrich said. "St. Ives is for him."

"You will not satisfy your loins here. Juliane is given to Ulrich," Edward said.

Nicholas did not look up from the sharpening of his long sword. 'Twas a well-wrought sword with a smooth grip that spoke of frequent use. The scabbard was well-oiled leather, black and tooled in a scrolling pattern. The haft of the sword was set with an onyx eye that did not blink but, black and bottomless, saw all.

"Juliane may be given, but the giving may not take. Is that not the very fiber of her legend?" Nicholas said.

"It will take this time," Roger said.

They stood above Nicholas as he sat, these friends of Ulrich, trying to push him from Stanora. There was only one reason to want him to leave: They were afraid for him to stay. Whatever Juliane's fate, it was not yet set in stone. Only the bedding would see that done.

"Am I unwelcome here at the marriage feast?" Nicholas asked, looking up from his sword, his dark eyes taking their measure and marking the breadth of their courtesy.

"Nay, not unwelcome," Roger said. "'Tis only that you should know what befalls here and not set your eyes upon what is now beyond your grasp."

"'Tis for her father to say what is in or out of my grasp," Nicholas said. "I am here at the invitation of Conor, uncle to Juliane. I am no wanderer."

"Then be welcome in Stanora, as we have been made welcome," Edward said softly. "Only know, as we know, that there is no place for you or for us here. We are all wanderers who wander past Stanora's gate."

"I am no wanderer," Nicholas said again.

"Even Conor has no place here," Edward said. "He has only the place which he has been allowed by blood ties. Beyond that—"

"There is nothing more needed than a blood tie. Those ties do not die. Conor, and Conor's kin, will always be welcome in Stanora," Nicholas said.

"Are you kin to Conor?" Roger said. "There can be no match to Juliane if your blood runs with Conor's name upon it."

"I am no kin to Conor, nor to Juliane," Nicholas said. "I am a guest here only, as are you. I seek nothing here beyond the measure of hospitality due all travelers."

"And a bride?" Roger asked with a half smile.

Nicholas smiled slightly in return, easing the moment. "Are not all men in search of a bride?"

"Did he come here in search of a bride?" Marguerite asked.

Maud shrugged. "Who can say? He has one now, though, by the grace of God and the bounty of Philip."

"But will it last?" Marguerite asked.

"Will it last? The question is, will she marry him at all?" Christine said, twirling a long strand of her soft brown hair.

"She will do as she is commanded by her father," Maud said. "As do we all. Let no one say that Juliane is not a proper daughter. She serves her father well."

"Serves him well in what?" Christine asked. "Her life is spent in spurning suitors. What service in that?"

"Have you heard Lord Philip complain?" Maud asked. When general silence greeted her question, she said, "Then there is your answer. Her father is most pleased with her, and will continue to be pleased by her for however many hours God grants him life upon this earth."

"Then she is to marry Ulrich? That is certain?" Marguerite asked.

"Very certain," Maud said.

"Are you certain?" Lunete asked.

"Aye, I am," William answered.

They walked in a shuffling amble across the bailey, heading nowhere, in no hurry, eager only to talk and think and set all to rights within their childish heads.

"He marries her for her land, then," Lunete said.

"Why else to marry? He wants a place to call his own. What sin in that?"

"No sin. I only thought . . ."

"Aye?"

"I only thought that, being a knight of some name, he would have other choices."

"What is wrong with choosing Juliane?" William asked.

"Many would choose Juliane," she said. "It is only that

Juliane does not like being chosen. She will not like it that he has nothing to bring to the bargaining."

"He brings all he has."

"Aye, but a woman likes a high price set upon her. He has no coin, no land, no title with which to pay. How, then, can he attain her? Is her worth valued so low? That is what she will think."

"Is that what you think?" William asked.

Lunete shrugged. "I am betrothed. My husband is a man of much land in Dunvegan."

"Where is Dunvegan?"

"Far to the north of here and on the coast. 'Tis a good match. My father gains much by it—a good meadow and a mill."

"What of you? What do you gain?"

Lunete looked at William, at his black hair and clear gray eyes, at his quiet and careful posture, at his youth. Her betrothed, her husband in all but body, was a man fully thirty years of age.

"I gain a husband."

"So," Juliane said softly, looking at Ulrich. "So, I gain a husband with a living son. St. Ives is lost to my family forever. You bargain hard, my lord, yet I cannot say I am surprised by that."

"I did not set this bargain in motion, lady; that was done by others."

"Yet you ride this tide most gladly."

"That I do," he said, looking only at her, ignoring all others within the lord's solar.

He would say no more, not with so much resting upon this hour. There was much left to do, much left for him to achieve in Stanora. He could not let Juliane fill his thoughts. Not yet, though he felt the lure of her most strong.

There was more to this marriage than land. He did not expect her to see that; she was too full of her own defeat. Yet it was so. He wanted her for herself. He also needed a place to give him a name, a home, and a legacy for his son. He had to have that. It was at the heart of all he did. But still, there was Juliane. He wanted her.

And he wanted to protect her.

This public consummation—for it would be public with three pairs of eyes watching to see that he did not fall, watching to see that he slid full into her, watching to see that he pierced her to her blood—this he did not want for her. 'Twas much to ask her to endure, yet her father, and her uncle and brother, did ask it of her. Was there a way out?

There must be.

But first the matter of St. Ives must be settled.

"Will the matter stand?" he asked, turning again to Conor and then to Philip, still lord of this place and all within it. "St. Ives must stay mine and pass to my son. I can do him no less."

"And if your son dies?" Conor asked.

"If my son dies and there is no living child between Juliane and myself, then let St. Ives fall again to you," Ulrich said. "Does the bargain stand?" he asked Philip.

Ulrich stood to lose very little. His son would not die unless by God's express will, a thing which could not be run from, no matter where a man ran. He would keep to Juliane; that union would not fail. But if God closed her womb against his seed, there was nothing to be done about it. To bring a child into life and to maturity was God's doing, not his.

"It stands," Philip said, his eyes shining with hope. Ulrich meant to see that hope fulfilled. He would not let Juliane fall from his grasp. He would be the man her father hoped he would be.

"Draw up the contracts," Walter said. "They will be married before the setting of the sun."

"Aye, my lord," the clerk said, already writing frantically. Much had been decided in this chamber, and all of it must be recorded. There must be no disputes later.

"Such haste rarely reflects the Lord's will," Father Matthew said.

"It reflects my will, and that will have to be enough," Philip said. "You have your lands, Matthew. Take them and be glad."

"These lands are for God, for His use," Matthew said.

"And will enrich the coffers of the church," Walter said. "My father speaks rightly. Take what you have won and be glad of it. This marriage will seal all bargains. Let there be no delay."

"Are you content with that, Juliane?" Ulrich asked. She had been very quiet for very long now; much had been decided, and she had fought little. 'Twas not like what he knew of her, and he was wary.

"Content?" she said, looking at all within that chamber, at the men who had decided her life upon the urgency of her father's death, robbing her of the holding that should have been hers and giving her a man who brought nothing to enrich her. She looked at them all, her anger smoldering, ready to blaze forth with the proper fuel. "Aye, I am content. Only let this begin quickly. Let us proceed with all speed. The sooner begun, the sooner finished."

"This marriage will not be finished unless it is by death," Ulrich said.

"Then let it be so," she said, smiling at him most pleasantly.

Aye, he was wary.

Chapter Seventeen

They ate while the contracts were being drawn up. To proceed with the marriage without the signing of the contracts would have been pointless. Marriages were agreements, transfers of land and wealth. The marriage ceremony devised by the church fathers was the symbolic union of man to wife. The actual union was the signed and witnessed contract. She knew that. She was no such fool as to believe that any marriage was a union of souls bound until death parted them. If that were so, why were there contracts?

Nay, 'twas all of power and its transfer, and in her case, transferred away from her.

She had been a woman of means an hour ago. Now she was nothing, dependent upon her betrothed for home and name. If she were not so hungry, she just might gag up her meal, proving her anger by the act. But she was hungry and she was no fool. Her battle against Ulrich would come later, when they were bound, life to life, purse to purse, body to body. It was in the shelter of their marriage bed that she would stretch out her claws.

She would fight him. She could do naught else, though she knew she would lose.

That was foretold, no matter what the troubadours sang of her. A woman had just so many weapons with which to defeat a man, and hers had been spent upon the battle of Ulrich from the moment of his coming through Stanora's gates.

He was a mighty adversary.

He would make a very difficult husband.

This matter of the witnesses to the consummation was most inconvenient. How her father had been pressured into it, she did not understand. Certainly, if he were not battling death with both hands it would never have happened. At least Maud would be with her. Perhaps, between the two of them, something could be arranged. It was not beyond possibility.

"If you think to escape this, it is not possible," Ulrich said at her side. "You are mine now, and I will keep you."

She continued eating, not glancing at him. Nothing disturbed a man more than to be ignored.

"You were more amusing in our wagering," she said. "As a husband, you have little to offer."

"What I have to offer even you can see, Juliane. Look down and see what I bring you."

Of course he would offer *that*. When thwarted, what could a man do but dive deep into crudeness? She would not look down into his lap. She knew what she would see.

"Are you unusual in your offering?" she said, munching contentedly on a slice of pork. "All bear me the same gift. At least in the beginning. Whether your gift will survive the night is another matter."

"You know I will outlast any device of yours, lady. Even the wielding of a knife shall not deter me," he said.

He sounded angry. That was good.

He was too strong, this one; she could not yield to mercy or tenderness in her battle against him. She would not be married. She would not be stripped of all she owned to feed his greed. She would escape this trap somehow. Somehow. It would be done. It could always be done, if a woman used all her weapons. She had only to find another weapon.

Their marriage bed would be a battle plain.

"We shall see whose 'knife' falls first, my lord," she said, smiling at him as she wiped pork fat from the edge of her mouth with the back of her hand. It was a man's gesture, and she did it to goad him. She was no shrinking, shy, sweet damsel. Let him see the strength of her for what it was. In this game, she was his equal. It was only needful that he believe that. Perhaps it was the sureness of her legend that was her final weapon. How could he defeat what all others had fallen against? The power of belief was a strong weapon indeed. "My knife is ready to do battle. Is yours?"

His eyes glittered hard blue, like sapphires in a cold winter sky. He did not answer her, not in words. He took his thumb and rubbed it across her mouth. She could feel the smooth slide of animal grease upon her lips, and then he licked his thumb, smiling like a wolf before the bite.

She swallowed hard against his touch and the animal image of him. There were times when he surprised her, when the smiling knight of courtly fame disappeared into the mists and this raw, wolfish man arose in his place. This man she feared most. This man, this wolf of passion, would not play by any rules she knew in the games of courtly love and honeyed seduction.

This man would not turn or fall from any blade, but would impale himself upon it, smiling as he bled. And then grin hard, as he in turn impaled her upon his throbbing blade.

Aye, she could see it in his eyes. That was what he would do. And there would be no remorse in him and no mercy for her.

Ulrich pressed all this into her thoughts with the cold sparkle of his eyes, and then he took her hand from where it rested on the tabletop and guided it resolutely to his lap. He pressed her palm hard down upon him, down upon his jerking, hot knife, and then he grinned in cold supremacy.

"My knife is ready, eager to find blood and quench its thirst for passion and for flesh. Can you meet it, Juliane, or will you run, searching for escape? I tell you now, there is no escape for you. You are mine. Find what pleasure in it you can."

"There can be no pleasure for me in you, my Lord Nothing," she said, searching for anything to say which would put him off and cast him from her. She did not relish a fight she was not certain of winning.

"My Lord St. Ives, lady," he said. "If you would insult me, get the name right."

Her hand was still pressed hard against his passion, and, his smile fading like the sun at sunset, he rubbed her against him, forcing her to learn the length and breadth of him, holding her to his passion when she had none of her own. She would not win by falling into passion's maw.

The sensations that pricked along her spine and settled in her belly were revulsion and determination to escape this ill-gotten pairing, nothing more. Passion served her not; 'twas a man's game, and only a man could win it.

"If you seek release, pray do it yourself. Your hand will serve as well as mine. Better, for you know how to service yourself as I never will," she said, pulling her hand from his.

He yanked her hand back and pulled her to him, growling slightly deep in his throat. "Lady, you play with fire and will be consumed in an instant, burned beyond all reckoning. This game you cannot win. Leave off baiting me. I will not run from this or from you."

"I do not fear the fire."

"You will," he breathed in promise, pressing her hand down against his erection, which was still hot and throbbing and undaunted by her thrusts against his pride.

In truth, she had never battled so hard and won so little ground against a man. A shiver of fear slid over her skin, fear that he might be right, that there might be no escape from him, that he might take possession of her body and her lands, and that she would be helpless, tethered to his wrist like a hooded hawk for the rest of her days. And worse, that she would lose herself in him, losing all of Juliane in the hot nest of Ulrich's groin.

"You cannot make me what I am not," she said, hoping it was true, wanting to convince herself.

"I cannot, that is true," he said, raising her hand to his mouth for a light kiss. The tingle on the skin of her hand from the touch of his mouth was a light burning. She ignored it. "Yet I can call forth from you what is within. And that I will do."

That was exactly what she was afraid of.

"Now," he said, "drink, for this is our wedding feast, a time for celebration."

"I could argue that," she said, rubbing her hand where he had touched her, rubbing the feel of him from her.

"I know you could," he said, smiling lightly, "yet you will not."

"Do not think you know me."

"I know enough of you to know that you would not disgrace your father by ill manners and ill frowns. This battle is between us, lady. Let this company not partake of it. Whate'er passes between us here will find its way to your father's ears. 'Tis not good discourse for a man on his way to heaven."

It was most difficult to admit that he was right. And so she would not; she would only put a false smile upon her lips and cease her tussling with him. It would, of a truth, serve no purpose here. Let their battles be for later, when it counted.

"Mutton?" she asked, indicating the tray before them.

"Another name for me, lady?" he teased. "Nay, I would prefer more wine. Share my cup. Let us drink fully, for 'tis fine wine."

"You would have me drunk? Is that your method?" she asked before taking a healthy swallow of wine. It was good, smooth and dark and sweet.

"I use what methods are available to me, as does any good warrior."

"Then battle on, Lord Mutton. I will match you," she said, grinning.

"Then match for match, swallow for swallow, Lady Frost. Something must melt you, if I cannot," he said, laughing at her as he spoke.

"You cannot, nor can the wine."

It was only later, when she had swallowed much more wine, that she wondered if he had complimented her ability to resist him only to get her to drink more. But that thought, like all the others that swirled in her head, was lost almost before it was formed.

She rather suspected that she was drunk.

Not that that would help him.

Ulrich looked rather hazy, warm, and glowing. His skin was of a fine texture, smooth but for the shadow of his beard. His cheekbones were finely chiseled, as was his nose, straight and fine. He had a scar upon his forehead that only showed itself when his dark brown hair was pushed back, as it was now. He sat grinning at her, his smile wolfish, his hand upon his brow and his fingers lost in his hairline. Was his hair soft? It looked so. Soft and dark and deep, like untroubled sleep.

Errant thought. Everything about this man was troubled. And he was not soft, no matter how often he smiled. That had misled her at first, but now she knew him better. He was all hard purpose and hard doing. Only his eyes were soft. Soft blue, like summer, like a sunlit winter day, like still water, like December ice.

What?

Ice and summer? That did not mix.

She *was* drunk.

She took another swallow and smiled at him. She might be drunk, but he would not win. Whatever it was he was trying to win.

She seemed to have forgotten.

He took a swallow, his throat moving sensuously as the liquid slid down into him, dark and red and sweet. He wiped a drop from his lip with the pad of his thumb. He had done that to her not long ago. A strange sensation. She ought to have been repulsed.

She had not been repulsed.

She had been . . . interested.

"I match you, lady wife," he said. "Swallow for swallow, was it not decided? What shall I win if I win at this contest?"

"You have won me," she said softly. "Is that not enough for you?"

"Have I won you? I thought that was in dispute."

"It is," she said, nodding. Her head felt very loose upon her neck, pleasantly heavy. "Yet I had not thought it in you to challenge a lady to a drinking contest. Does not seem very rich in courtly valor to me."

"A strong opponent requires strong methods."

"The wine *is* strong."

"And sweet," he said, taking another swallow. "I have outdone you, Juliane. You are beaten by a swallow."

"I am not," she said, taking the cup from him with two hands, it was oddly heavy and awkward to her hands. She took a full mouthful and swished it in her mouth before swallowing. "There, you are defeated yet again."

"Until the next swallow," he said.

Was he closer of a sudden? It seemed so. Close and hot and smelling sweet. Nay, that was the wine, not this errant knight come clambering into her bed.

Nay, not her bed. Not yet. Not ever.

He would not have that of her, no matter the sweetness of his mouth.

Nay, nay, 'twas the wine that was sweet, not his mouth. Never his mouth.

"May I take your mouth in mine? I would test such sweetness for myself," he said.

What was this of sweet mouths? Had she said his mouth was sweet? There was too much of wine in her and not enough of discretion.

"Nay," she said, pulling herself up straight. She seemed to have been leaning heavily upon the table. "No kissing. This is all of drinking, and I mean to win, Ulrich. And no cheating on your part. I know how you play at games. If cheating will serve to win, then cheating you will do."

"I think you speak of yourself, lady wife," he said, taking another heavy swallow. When had a man's throat offered her such fascination? She could see his pulse pounding softly beneath the skin, could almost feel the heat of him rising out and grabbing her, pulling her into him, demanding that she kiss him there.

She bumped her head into something. 'Twas his shoulder. Pushing herself off, she said, "Forgive me. I lost my balance."

"Lean upon me at any time," he said, brushing a finger over her hair. It seemed strangely disordered. Perhaps he had done that, fussing with her as he was. "I believe you owe me another swallow. Unless you wish to cry off?"

"I will never cry off, and never to you," she said, pushing her hair out of her eyes. She could do that herself. She took another swallow and quickly followed it with a chunk of bread. A bit of bread would settle her eyes and bring all back into clarity.

She was becoming too easy in his company, and the pulsebeat in his throat was raw distraction.

He was doing that on purpose, she just knew it. It was only that she did not know how.

*   *   *

"He has managed to get her to drink herself into submission, though I cannot say I understand how he did it," Conor said in an undertone to Nicholas, who sat quietly by his side at this table of forced merriment.

Was there anyone in Stanora who wanted this marriage between Juliane and Ulrich? Aye, there was Philip, ever obstinate, ever contrary. But Philip was one foot into heaven. When he was fully there, it might be arranged for Walter to change his stand on the matter of Juliane and Ulrich.

But then it would be too late. Juliane would have been breached, her lands transferred to the church, and Ulrich in hard possession of St. Ives. It was too late now, but for the consummation.

All rested upon that.

Could Ulrich take her?

There should have been no doubt of it, except that it had been tried before unsuccessfully. Watching her now, soft with wine and swaying toward Ulrich, Conor thought that there was scant chance of failure. She would fall to Ulrich like a plum from a high branch.

Unless she fell to someone else first.

"He challenged her," Nicholas said softly, watching the couple at the high table, his dark eyes smoldering.

"He challenged her? That was not nobly done."

"But effective," Nicholas said with a crooked smile.

"You give her up too easily," Conor said, feeling his way with this man, like a spider crawling along a web, searching for breaks in the weaving with gentle legs.

"I never had her. What did I give up?" Nicholas said, turning his black eyes from Juliane to Conor. He did ever seem to watch Juliane. Perhaps that fire still smoldered after all, no matter his negligent ease in watching Juliane slip from his reaching hands.

"Neither does he have her. Not yet."

"The contracts are all but signed. Philip has made his will clear. 'Twas not my name he fastened upon hers."

"That could change."

"How? Did you not tell me that Stamford is lost to her? That her only chance of wealth is to take Ulrich and St. Ives? This game is done."

"If he does not breach her, all is off. The marriage undone."

Nicholas chuckled and looked again at the high table. Juliane was watching Ulrich speak, her eyes upon his mouth, her own mouth opened and her skin flushed red.

"He looks ready to breach her now, if he followed his wants. And hers. She will not stop him. He will not fall, not when she is so willing to fall before him," Nicholas said.

Conor considered Nicholas. He did not know him well, though they understood each other in part. How far Nicholas was prepared to go to achieve his ends, that he did not know. Yet the time for caution was running out. The contracts *were* all but signed, and Juliane *did* look all too ready to tumble into Ulrich's bed. It was act now or not at all, and Conor was not a man to turn from action, especially in regard to Philip.

"Not if she falls to you first," Conor said, his mouth hidden behind his cup.

Nicholas turned hard to look at him, his eyes black with tumbling shadows of consideration and doubt.

"You suggest that I steal her from under her husband's very eyes?"

"He is not her husband yet. Whoever takes her first takes her last. Contracts can be rewritten."

"This is not the way of honor," Nicholas said stiffly, holding Conor's gaze within his own.

"This has been done before. Time and again."

"That is no answer."

"Then what of this answer?" Conor said, his tone biting. "How do you think Philip came by my sister?"

The words fell from a height of surprise into sudden and thoughtful silence.

"He took her?" Nicholas said.

"He took her, his sister Maud aiding him most well with Emmelia, and then he was given her, and the riches of Stamford and St. Ives. I wanted St. Ives back and Stamford entrusted to the proper family."

"Away from Philip," Nicholas said, finishing the thought. "Yet Philip is dying. All now is loosed from his grasp."

"Yet not from his will. 'Tis his will in dispensing what he took by force that I fight now. Will you do what he has done and, by this equal measure, right things?"

"He has done me no wrong."

"Then you do not want Juliane?" Conor said, knowing the answer.

Nicholas turned again to look upon her. She glowed gold and white in the afternoon light in her bliaut of honey-eyed white and her snowy pelisse, a maid to make a man want and keep wanting, a maid to turn a man's thoughts from all but her. So it was for Nicholas. All men wanted

Juliane. Yet only one man could have her. She wore a large brooch of polished silver shaped like a bird in flight and adorned with warm amber and glimmering topaz; it suited her and seemed to speak to him. She was a bird about to be snared by another man, and Nicholas's hand was so close, so very close, to closing on her himself.

"Nay, I want her," Nicholas said in a hoarse undertone. "But what of Walter? Will he so quickly turn from his father's will and wish?"

"He will. He only wants Juliane settled into marriage. Does it matter the man?"

"What of St. Ives and of Stamford? Stamford is given, and St. Ives as well. What do I gain beyond Juliane in this taking?"

"Stamford is for the church and I will not fight that; that gift goes freely for good cause. But St. Ives I will not give so easily. St. Ives must return to me and mine. I will not see it go to this nameless knight with a legend for seduction. He fell well when he fell into Stanora and the legend of Juliane, yet this tale is not all told. Ulrich can fall out of fortune's path as easily as he fell into it. I will see him set upon another path, one of my devising, and then—"

"St. Ives falls free?" Nicholas asked, finishing the thought writ large within Conor's heart. "But only as far as my hand," he said, decided. "I want St. Ives. I will take Juliane."

"Done, if you but swear fealty to me. Take her and it is yours."

"Agreed. Yet what of Ulrich? How will you keep him from her?"

"I will take care of Ulrich," Conor said softly, his blue

eyes scanning the hall. "He has a son he must protect, does he not?"

William, standing behind Ulrich's seat, pouring wine and more wine, shifted his feet and quickly scanned the hall, which was still full of folk dawdling over their food. Ulrich and Juliane were drinking quite a bit of wine. William's arm was getting heavy and his shoulder sore from lifting the clay pitcher that held the wine. After the contracts had been written, signed, and witnessed, the wedding ceremony could proceed. And the drinking would stop.

That would be good. Juliane should stop drinking now. She could hardly keep her eyes open, and when they were open, they were looking almost sleepily at Ulrich. That was fine, William supposed. They were to be married. She should look at him with something other than disdain, which was her favored look for him. Ulrich deserved more than disdain. Ulrich was the best man William knew, and he deserved St. Ives.

He had worked long for land of his own, that was certain.

Ulrich said something softly to Juliane and she chuckled, ducking her chin down and casting her eyes up at him. She had lovely eyes, blue and long-lashed and merry. At least they were merry now. William had seen them when they had appeared quite cold and hard and determined. And haughty. Proud, too.

Mayhap even vain.

But she did not look like that now. She looked soft and relaxed and even pleased.

Ulrich signaled for another measure of wine.

William poured freely, thinking that if wine was the

cause of Juliane's improved temper, then Ulrich might well keep her swimming in wine. 'Twould be well done and worth any price.

"'Tis not well done of you," Maud said sharply. "I deserve better."

"Better than a fine man with a fine name?" Walter said. "I had thought it would please you, Maud, to be married at your age. You will finally have a man of your own. You might even have children. It has happened before. God may open your womb and bless you in such a way."

"'Tis no blessing to be forced into what you do not want."

"Then pray to want it and the blessing will be most readily found," Walter said tightly.

They sat side by side and spoke softly, pointedly ignoring the swift slide into drunkenness that was happening to their right. If the rose haze of wine would help Juliane endure the public spectacle of her bedding, they wished her happily into a fine drunk. In that they agreed. In that and nothing else.

"Does Philip know of your plan for me?" Maud asked. "We had a bargain between us that goes back years, to before you were born."

"He does not know and does not need to know," Walter said. "I am lord of Stanora upon his death. As to bargains, all bargains die with him. He is not stained by the breaking of it, and I am not bound to hold to ancient agreements. You *will* marry."

"You will have need of me here. Your bride does not know Stanora," Maud said.

"She will learn it. 'Tis her function and her place to

manage my holdings when I am gone from here. If she cannot manage Stanora, she is not yet fit for marriage."

"Then you may not marry soon."

"I will. She is ready. I will see to it. It is to your own life that you must now turn your thoughts. To bind yourself to Peter is a good match. He has never had a wife. He yearns for you most fully. What more does a bride wish of a man?"

"That he match my worth?"

"What worth is that, Maud?" Walter said coldly, looking down at her. He dwarfed her in size, for he was a big man and she was hardly taller than Lunete, though three times her age. "You have little to bring to any man, not even youth. In land, Peter cannot match you, but in worth? He has proven himself a man many times over. I do not cast you from me lightly. He is a good man," he said more softly, trying to mollify her. A wasted effort.

"Good for what? Without land a man has no worth."

"He will have your land and will hold it in your name until his death."

"You have done to me what you have done to Juliane. Is this how you rid yourself of the women of your house?"

"I give you in marriage. 'Tis your highest calling."

"Nay, there is another and one which I choose over any man. Give me leave to take the veil. I would enter the abbey, closeted from all men and their manipulations."

"What of Peter?"

Maud smiled without humor. "Give him to Juliane when she is through with Ulrich. She will manage him most well."

"You think she will defeat Ulrich in the marriage bed?" Walter said, his interest snagged against his will. Maud knew Juliane well. What did Maud know that he did not?

"I think that she will defeat him within and without it. This marriage will not stand," she said spitefully.

"Pray you are wrong, Maud," Walter said, suddenly disgusted with women in general. "Pray mightily as I direct you, for this is how it shall be. If Juliane fouls this marriage as she fouled the last one, then you *will* marry Peter. I will have one profitable marriage to mark my lordship of Stanora."

"Then if Juliane falls to him, you will allow me to enter the abbey? My future is dependent upon her skills in the conjugal bed?"

"Aye, you have it," Walter said, standing abruptly. "Pray according to your preference. I leave it up to you."

"I leave it up to you," Avice said.

"I will not take that wager," Edward said.

"Why? Because a woman offers it? You would take it from Roger," she said.

"I would not make this wager with anyone. 'Tis distasteful. There is nothing of honor or chivalry in it."

"Do not play the righteous man with me now, Edward. I know you better," she said with a calculating grin, leaning close to him as they sat side by side upon the bench of a lower table. This was great fun.

He hated her. He hated her look, her speech, her manner . . . and her wagering. It was the most glorious torture, and she did not even have to touch him.

Of course, touching him would only make the game more enjoyable. For her. He would likely start bleeding spontaneously from the nose in outrage.

Another reason to do it.

She bumped her shoulder against his arm and laid a

gentle finger upon the back of his hand; Edward stiffened and leaned away from her. But the bench was not that long. He would fall. Small pity. He had hairs on his hands, small and golden, like the tips of his hair and the sparks in his hazel eyes, golden sparks showered over him. Beautiful. Fascinating.

Gold was wasted on such a man.

"You will not take this wager because you fear to lose," she said with a smile.

Edward turned abruptly and faced her on the bench, his torso twisted so hard that she could make out the stretch of muscle and tendon lying just out of sight beneath his tunic. He was a powerfully built man. She did not like that about him.

"You make this wager because you know I will not take it. An empty challenge, Avice. What does it gain you?"

"I make no empty wagers."

His eyes were swimming with golden sparks, like shimmering metallic stars cast through burnished clouds. His lashes were dark and short and thick, dark like his brows, dark like his thoughts. Oh, aye, she could read his thoughts. He hated her.

"This one is empty," he said, "empty but for your desire to torment me. I understand you too well, Avice. You seek pain and desire in the path trod first by Juliane. Yet you will always run second to her, will you not?"

"I offered a wager. Nothing more. Either take it or not," she said, pulling away from him. She hated him. He was the worst man she had ever met.

"I offer you another wager," he said, swinging his leg over the bench so that he straddled it and fully faced her.

His legs were monstrous long. He was oafish in his construction. "Will you take it?"

"Will you speak it?" she snapped. "I take no wagers blind. I am no fool."

"Then here is the wager I offer you, though I hardly think you will take it, being as timid as you are and as contrary—"

"Am I to listen to insults for an hour? Is that the measure of this wager?" Avice interrupted, staring hard at him.

"Give Roger a kiss of your own making; make him believe it is a free gift of your doing and no part of any wager."

"That is the wager?" Avice said on a laugh. "A fine gift for Roger, but what is my gain in taking such a wager?"

"Do that and I will stand in this hall and declare you more desirable, more beautiful than Juliane. Your name will supplant hers. Your fame will grow in song and verse. I will tell such a tale of Avice that your name will outlive hers when tales of womanly beauty and power are told."

He understood her too well.

"Why?" she asked, studying his face. He looked most solemn, most serious.

"Must you know why? Is this not close upon what you want for yourself?"

"Why would you offer me a wager which I can easily win to give me something I—" She shrugged. She would not tell him she had wanted this in the quiet of the night. She would not admit that she envied her sister and her sister's legend. No man would have that confession from her.

"It is just a wager," Edward said. "Will you take it?"

To kiss Roger. Roger was a pleasant sort, well-featured and sturdily built. It would not be a burden to kiss Roger.

"When?" she asked.

"Now, or as soon as you can find him."

"Where?"

"On the mouth," he said slowly.

"Nay, I meant where. In the hall? The bailey? The stables?"

"Anywhere."

"Will you watch?" she asked, watching the flecks of gold in his eyes, the frown that wanted to turn into a scowl upon his brow.

"Do you want me to?"

"Will you watch?" she said again, studying him, learning best how to torment him.

"Aye," he said on a throaty growl.

Avice nodded and said, "Then follow me."

Chapter Eighteen

"You are in a hurry."

"Of course I am in a hurry. My father lies dying. I would be about other matters than the giving of a kiss in wager."

"Your father would not approve," Edward said.

"He would approve because I will win," Avice said. "Let it only be done quickly. I must attend my father, and then Juliane is to be married within the hour, if only that clerk would attend to his function. I have much to do today."

"He must believe the kiss to be freely given," Edward said, worried that with such preoccupations Avice would seem less than enthusiastic.

"Oh, he will," Avice said with a confident smile.

He hated her.

Why had he arranged for this? Did he not have better things to occupy his own time? Must he seek out the one person who prodded him with every breath she drew? Her dark hair was hanging loose down her back in small waves that swung to and fro with each determined step. She was tall for a woman, yet had the slenderness of a girl, though her bosom was full and deep. Her bliaut was too snug; he should not have been able to notice her bosom. She had probably sewn it so on purpose, to irritate and distract him. And it did distract him and irritate him.

He hated her, and not without cause.

"Have you seen Roger of Lincoln?" she asked Baldric, the groom.

"Nay, lady, not today," Baldric answered, eyeing Edward curiously. "You might ask Father Matthew, though. They spend some time together every day."

"Every day?" Avice said. "In confession?"

"Lady, I do not know," Baldric answered.

They stood on the high ground of the bailey, near the tower gate. Below them stretched the great expanse of the bailey, sloping down to the wall and chapel and armory and stables and kitchens. Roger could be anywhere. He would not have left the shelter of the wall. There was no reason, unless he went to hunt.

"Let us find his horse," Edward said to Avice. "If he is within Stanora's gate, we will know it by the presence of his horse."

"A small beginning," Avice said. "Stanora is large. We could lose an hour in the hunt for him."

"Lady, I cannot help you," Baldric said. "I must away. Does not Lady Juliane have need of me?"

"Only if she needs help in swallowing wine," Edward said.

Avice cast him a look of pure disgust and said to Baldric, "Go. She will need you. We will find Roger, wherever he may hide."

"I do not think he hides," Edward said as Baldric moved into the shadow of the tower gate and disappeared within it. "Especially when a kiss from your lips awaits him."

"Flattery?" Avice said with a sneer. "It does not become you. Stay your course, my lord. I need no false flattery from you to stay mine."

He hated her.

He hated flattery, and he had somehow found the words in his mouth and out before he had known what he was about. She mocked him more gently than he mocked himself.

"Lady, you speak true. I will attend," he said, taking her by the arm and propelling her toward the stables. "Let us get this done and behind us. First Roger, then the kiss."

"Then the payment you owe me," she said, looking up at him as he moved her along. Her eyes were the light blue of a clear spring sky, her lashes black and long, her brow and cheek softly freckled, as if gentleness had a place in her heart. How he hated her for that lie. She was all bite and tooth and snarl, her soul fed on vanity and deceit, her mouth full of venom.

How would he ever sing her praise if she should win this wager?

He had small cause to worry. She would not win. Roger was not the sort to take a kiss from a maid betrothed. For all his laughter, Roger was a very sober sort of knight.

It was well that Avice did not know that.

"Aye, then the payment. I will not refuse. I meet my wagers since I hold my honor dear. Have no fear of that," he said, burying his own sudden fear that, of all women, Avice might well be the one who could move Roger past his honor.

"I have good need of fear when men suddenly sprout words of honor over a simple wager," she said, dragging her heels. "Let go of me! I can find my way to the stables of Stanora without aid from an errant knight."

"Fine," he said, releasing her. They had reached the stables in any case.

"Fine," she repeated, straightening her sleeve where he had twisted it.

They marched into the stables side by side, each unwilling to give to the other the primacy of being in the lead. At least he knew that was true of himself. Why could she not deport herself as a woman ought? She was bold and arrogant and proud and impossible.

He hated her.

He hated her so much in that instant, with the sun lighting random strands in her dark hair to gleaming copper, with the light skimming her skin so that it glowed like pearl, with the air pushing her hair about her back in a caress of warmth, he thought he would die if he did not take her under his hands and break her into pieces.

And so he did.

Or tried to do.

He took her by the shoulders and pulled her to him,

wanting her to break, wanting to break her heart upon his hands, wanting to break her pride into shards that he could use to pierce her stony heart, wanting to crush her until every part of her was branded into his skin, obliterating her, owning her, destroying her, taking her.

But Avice was not a woman to be taken and destroyed. Avice would not break. Not even for him.

She pushed him from her, pulling his hands free of her, stepping back into the light and sound of the bailey.

"My wager is with Roger," she said. "There is none of you in this."

"Roger is not here," he said stiffly, like a man in a dream.

Of course Roger was not there. His horse was there. But Roger being there or not being there had nothing to do with his need to touch her and break something within her.

"My wager is with Roger," she said again, her breath shallow and her eyes wide and dark.

"Your wager is with me," he said softly. "You will act it out upon Roger."

"Roger is not here," she said on a breath.

"Nay, he is not."

"And if I act it out upon you, will the wager be met?" she asked, staring at his mouth.

He was a fool. He hated her. She hated him.

He wanted her mouth on him. He wanted it and her and he wanted her willingness, even if it was a lie. Even if it was all of wagering and none of winning hearts or breaking souls.

"It will be met," he said.

And at the words, she flew at him. He caught her up against him and it was like catching a storm of want and passion and fury. She wrapped herself around him, legs and arms, one hand gripping his hair and another clutching at his back. One leg she twined around his calf, the other stood on his foot, and she moaned against his mouth just before she opened wide and took him in.

She was fire. Blazing wet heat. Sweet breath. Sharp teeth. Wicked tongue. All set upon him, devouring him as he devoured her.

He was lost in her. Lost so deep that he forgot hate, forgot pride, forgot honor, forgot all in the long fall into her passion.

He grabbed her by her taunting fall of hair and pulled it, licking and biting his way into her mouth and down her neck and to her bosom. He wrapped his other arm about her, hard and low, grinding his hips against hers, pressing himself into her through the barriers of wool and chivalry. This was raw need. There was no chivalry left in him.

She did not fight him, though she pulled at his hair and tugged at his tunic, pulling at the throat of it, seeking his skin and kissing what she could reveal. When that did not satisfy her, she pulled at the hem and rolled it up his torso, exposing his belly and chest to her hands. She rubbed him, stroked him, fired him.

And he was fired. He pulled her legs apart and lifted her to straddle his thigh. She moaned and pulled his face back up to hers, laying her mouth upon his, opening herself to him and letting him dive deep into her. Taking her. Tasting her. Invading her.

She rubbed herself against the length of his thigh, twitching against him, running her hands over his chest, feeling the play of muscle and sinew and skin, marking him with her scent. Branding him with her memory.

He lifted her skirts, his hand reaching down and grabbing the hem. He had to feel her. He had to feel if she was hot and wet for him. He had to mark her as she was marking him.

To take her.

To destroy her.

To break her upon his passion until she was nothing but raw need and gasping heat.

With a hand, she stopped him.

With a moan, she slid down his thigh, away from him.

With a sigh, she left him, pushing back her hair with both hands, searching for a wall to lean against with unsteady hands.

Her eyes were black holes of want, her breath ragged, her bosom heaving. He reached out to her, taking a step to close the gap between them, to renew the heat he could feel coming from her. With a raised hand, she bade him stop.

He stopped and pushed the hair back from his eyes.

"No more," she said, panting.

"More," he insisted, though he kept the distance she requested. "There is more."

She shook her head and crossed her arms over her breasts. "Not for us."

"Just let me touch you."

"Nay. No more," she said, and it was a plea for mercy, not a demand.

He had her almost to the point of breaking. But she pled for mercy. He did not know how much mercy was in him.

"Avice," he said, hearing the breaking need in his own voice and uncaring that she had unmanned him.

"I am betrothed," she said, her voice shaking. "Would

you have me dishonor both him and myself? Of how
much more can we partake before honor breaks beneath
the weight of passion?"

"I do not know, nor do I care," he said. He did not know
himself. When had he ever thrown honor from him without thought?

Since all thoughts were of Avice.

"I care," she said. "I am betrothed," she said again.
"There is no unmaking it."

"So I am to be unmade."

"As am I," she said, staring into his eyes, her very soul
in the look she gave him.

It was that look he would take with him when he left
Stanora.

'Twould have to be enough.

"Come," he said, looking at the ground beneath her
feet. To look into her eyes would be to forget what shards
of honor remained to him and take her in the hay of the
stables. "Let me take you to your father. He has great need
of you now. I will steal no more time from you, Avice."

She hesitated, and then she walked out of the stable
and into the light. He followed, keeping careful distance
between them. With slow steps they walked up the hill to
the hall. All about them, people walked and talked and
worked. How strange that was, as if nothing at all had
occurred.

She was not as drunk as he thought she was, to judge by
the self-satisfied gleam in his eyes and the smirk on his
mouth. She could hold her wine as well as any man. And
had done so more than once.

It was only that, with the wine mingling so joyfully with her blood, she could admit that he was a very handsome man and might have a point or two that was deserving of praise. That did not mean she ought to marry him. That certainly did not mean she was going to let him bed her. No man would ever find his way between her thighs. She had to keep him out of her, away from her. She could not let him in. She could not. That had been decided long ago.

Juliane shook her head at the thought, frowning meaningfully at the tabletop.

"But what will you do to stop me?" Ulrich asked, his voice a whisper at her shoulder. "Your hawk is hooded, Juliane, and no horse could find his way up those twisting stairs to your chamber."

Had she spoken? She had not intended to. "You forget about the dogs," she said stiffly, looking him in the eyes. He had beautiful blue eyes and the straightest nose. His mouth was lovely as well. Not that any of it mattered. She could not want him, could not fall to passion and desire. In her falling, all would fall.

"The dogs?" Ulrich said, taking another small swallow of wine and passing the cup to her. She took her swallow and reached for the bread. The platter was empty. "How many dogs?"

"One will do," she said, eyeing him coldly, using her finest le Gel expression, whereupon he burst into laughter.

"You leave nothing to chance, do you?"

"I am a careful combatant," she said.

Too much wine. She must tell him nothing of the truth.

"I am glad," he said. "It is good for a damsel to be careful. Yet you have little need for caution now, with me. I am to be yours. I will defend you against all."

"I can defend myself," she said out of habit, looking down at his hands on the table.

He had wonderful hands, large and long-fingered and sprinkled with the lightest touch of downy hair near the wrist joint. A man's hands. Callused. Muscular. Many-veined. Her heart jumped awkwardly in her chest just from looking at his hands.

Best not to look at his hands, then.

"Yet there is no need to defend yourself against me," he said softly, taking her hand and lifting it to his mouth, whereupon he kissed the inside of her wrist with re-strained hunger. A shock of heat and longing slid through her veins. "You need only give yourself to me, Juliane. Think only on that," he breathed against her skin, his eyes gazing into hers.

"I will not fall to you," she said, the only thing she re-membered in the heat of his eyes and the soft melting of his mouth upon her.

He nibbled his way up the inside of her arm, and she did nothing to stop him. There was a fire in her belly and in her brain, and she could not see her way out of the throbbing heat of him. She could not fight this, not all alone. Where was Baldric? Where was Morgause?

"Then fall with me," he said. "There is no loss in that. A double fall, where two become one and fall together. A single falling to mark us. A fall to bind us. A fall to melt our hearts until they are forged into a single beating." He took her hand and placed the palm upon his neck, over the pounding of his pulse and the thick muscle where neck met shoulder. His skin was hot and smooth. She wanted to lay her mouth there and taste him, feel the blood rush under his skin and against her lips. "Come, fall with me, Juliane. I will hold you in this falling, sheltering you, protecting you."

"Taking me, having me," she whispered, staring at his mouth.

"Aye," he answered in shared whisper. "But taking only what you will freely give. Give yourself to me, Juliane. I will cherish thee."

"Juliane?"

Into the misty haze of desire, her uncle called. Conor's voice broke the weaving spell of passion and wine and Ulrich's promise; Juliane shook herself free of it and looked to where Conor stood at the entrance to the stair.

"Juliane," Conor repeated. "The contracts are complete, awaiting only Ulrich's signature. Your father awaits. 'Tis time to be married."

'Twas quickly done. Ulrich signed the marriage contract, gaining both Juliane and St. Ives in an instant. Avice and Maud stood at her back, Walter at her side, all looking appropriately grim. She could hardly fault them. Father Matthew gave a shortened and hurried version of the ceremony binding them in God's sight. Her father smiled and nodded his blessing. She did not nod in return.

'Twas done. She was married. Again. 'Twas only lacking the consummation of their vows to make all binding. She had faced this moment before. She had been less afraid then than she was now.

Then, she had not faced Ulrich in the marriage bed. He would not fall to her.

She knew that now.

Another way must then be found, if she still wanted to find a way out of this unequal bonding. She was not as certain as she had been. What did she gain by refusing him? What did she lose by taking him in? Her father had thrown her into Ulrich's bed, her aunt had shrugged and turned away from all useful counsel—why should she not tumble with Ulrich, sharing the fall he had promised her?

She *must* be drunk.

"'Tis done, Father," she said, leaning down to him, throwing off thoughts of Ulrich. "I am married to the man of your choosing."

The chamber slowly cleared of folk. It was considerate of them to give her time with Philip before she must leave to face the public bedding he had forced upon her.

"Let him be of your choosing," Philip said weakly. He was all bone now, skin hanging loose upon a dry frame. "Do not fight him, Juliane. Let him find his way into you, making you safe."

He spoke in riddles now. Was he confused in his mind, caught between two worlds and unable to see either one clearly?

"I did not choose him," she said. "I would not have done so. How can I do what must be done? How can I hold to our bargain when all the world looks on? Do you not care that all will fall at this?" she said over buried tears of frustration and confusion.

"Juliane," Philip whispered hoarsely, searching for her hand upon the sheets. "Fight him not. The world is harsh. Conor would have unmade you."

This made little sense. Conor was harsh and too often in their way, yet he was her uncle and loved her, just as her father loved her. The two men were of a mind on that, though on nothing else. 'Twas the bond of Emmelia which bound them to each other, a bond of love for the same woman, her own mother, dead now ten years and more.

"I am strong enough to make my way in the world. You made me so when you built my legend," she said. "I rested well within its walls. Why break all for Ulrich?"

"I made you to assuage my guilt," he said, his eyes closing. "My guilt weighs upon you."

All was folly now. He was speaking in senseless riddles, like a man in a dream, speaking out against imaginary foes.

"Father," she said, leaning down to him, holding his face between her hands, "you have no cause for guilt. You are clean of all sin. Go to heaven with light steps, running to paradise."

"Come," Father Matthew said, laying a hand upon her shoulder and turning her from her father's bed. "Let us celebrate your marriage in the chapel, where it is fitting. 'Tis time for Vespers."

"Aye, I will come," she said, allowing the priest to lead her. She turned to look once more upon her father's face before she left his chamber, but he was looking at the wall, hiding his face from her.

"Ulrich has gone on at Conor's bidding. He had some question about Ulrich's son and he would not rest until he had his answers," the priest said.

"That sounds like Conor," she said as they went down the curving stair to the great hall below. The hall was deserted, the tables put up against the wall, the fire banked and low in the center of the room. "What is there to know of Ulrich's son?" she asked. It could never matter to her.

Ulrich would not stay her husband, his child would not be her child.

"I know not. Ulrich is not eager to speak of him, except to secure his legacy in St. Ives."

"That sounds like Ulrich," she said ruefully. If Ulrich was not trying to best her at a wager or seduce her into submission, of what did he speak? Nothing. She had never known a man who said so little of himself. He clearly had much to hide.

"Father? A word?" Roger said from a far corner of the hall.

Juliane had not seen Roger for an hour, which was odd. He was most often in the center of all activity. Of course, for the past hour she had had little thought for any but Ulrich and her next sip of wine. Who had won that wager? She had lost count. Had he relented or had she?

"Aye, a word only. Vespers awaits us all," Father Matthew said. "If I may leave you, Juliane? I will come anon."

Juliane nodded and smiled absently, her mind still on the wine wager. She should never have taken that wager. Had she not decided never to wager against him again?

She made her way slowly, for of a truth, she was loose-limbed from the wine, carefully descending the broad stone stairs that led to the tower gate. 'Twas dim going, but she had run this course in the dark since childhood.

It was in the center of the dark tower gate that she stumbled and reached out a hand to steady herself against the gray stone wall. And met human flesh instead. Most odd.

"May I assist, Juliane?"

What voice was this? She did not know this man, this voice, this scent. He was new to her, though not unwelcome.

"With thanks," she said, letting him take her by the hand. "Does assistance have a name?"

"Nicholas," he breathed.

Ah, small wonder that she could not clearly see him. Nicholas of Nottingham was dark of hair and eye and wore a black tunic and a cloak of oaken brown. He would disappear like shadow in such dim light as this. And so he had.

"You do not attend Vespers?" she asked.

"As you do not," he said, and she could hear him smile.

They went down the steps slowly; she could have gone faster, but he held her back in the shadows, his cloak sweeping down and brushing against her hand.

"I go now," she said, "and should hurry. I am a bride, you see, and must not cause tongues to wag over my delay."

"I think you like tongues to wag over you very well," he said. "And not because of delay. There are other things said of Juliane le Gel. Truths I would test."

"Did you not hear? I am a bride this very hour," she said, smiling.

This game was old and she played it well. Of fear, she had none.

They were at the outer door of the tower gate and the light was again upon them; a soft light it was, as the day was waning, soft and low and golden with haze and dust. She looked well in such a light and knew it. Let Nicholas look his fill. Such an old game. She knew every move, every word that would be played out. She was very, very good at this game.

Suddenly she was very, very weary of it. On and on she had played it, man upon man, until her legend filled the air, blocking out the sun, keeping her wrapped hard in the chill of her name, forced to play the game again, and yet again, man after man, year after year.

Definitely drunk, to think such thoughts. She threw them from her, rags that had no worth and no use. She was Juliane and she played the game well.

"Then let me kiss the bride of the hour," he said.

Conor had spoken true of him when he had tried to turn her heart toward Nicholas of Nottingham. He was a handsome man, dark of hair and eye, tall and lithe, his smile a weapon against a lady's heart. 'Twas a shame she had no heart for him to pierce. She was stone. Ice. Beyond his touch, or touching, beyond his grasp. She was Juliane le Gel—did he not understand that most basic truth? That most ancient lie?

"So sweetly asked," she said, "so sweetly must be granted. Take a kiss of me, I give it freely. But take no more."

"I take only what is given, lady. I leave it to you to ask for more."

Juliane grinned and then laughed and then her laughing stopped. Nicholas wrapped her hard within his arms and pulled her into him for more than a simple kiss of chivalry and meaningless flirtation.

He was hard against her, his mouth a hammer that beat against her lips, his hands clenching into her clothes. A most unwelcome, hot, invasive kiss. All wrong, it was. No fire did he arouse, but smoke, choking and gagging her. No fire, but dry terror to be so wrapped in someone else's flame.

'Twas not Ulrich's kiss.

"More?" he asked, lifting his lips from hers.

Arrogant oaf. Where was Morgause when she was so sorely needed?

"More than enough, my lord. Release me. This game is done," she said, pushing against his chest.

"I would never release you, Juliane. I would have you for a wife."

"I am a wife already. Did we not discuss this?" she said, trying to wrench herself free of him. He was like a viper, all coils, wrapping wild and holding fast. God above, she was weary of this game.

"I believe you did," said a voice from the sunshine of the bailey. Ulrich. "*My* wife, in fact," he said, coming into the thin shadow of the tower gate with Baldric at his back. "Release her," Ulrich said softly, though there was nothing soft in his look. He looked ready to kill.

Nicholas stepped back, releasing Juliane, and considered his opponent.

"Your pardon. I partook too freely of the wine and lost myself in the legend of her name. She is beautiful. You would do well to keep close guard of her virtue," Nicholas said.

"Her virtue is assured," Ulrich said, "by my own hand or by her own. My lady can defend herself, though I am here to do that glad service should she have need of me."

But she could not defend herself well, could she? Nay, she stumbled from more than the wine. She was so very tired of hiding, of running from a truth that could not be told.

"Defend herself? Why should she, with a husband at her front? 'Tis a man's duty and right," Nicholas said.

"You have said it well. She *is* my wife. It is my right

and joyous duty to defend her. Stand off, though by her look, she will bite you before I can draw steel. My lady sees to herself right well," Ulrich said with a cold smile that did not touch his eyes.

"Your wife? Not quite yet," Nicholas said stiffly. "Another has failed before you."

"You speak of yourself," Ulrich said. "I do not have to fight her for her kisses. Nay, to me she gives them freely."

She had never heard a lie more sweetly told. She could almost love Ulrich at that moment.

The wine had truly taken her past all reason.

Nicholas ground his teeth until they squeaked, but he held his tongue. He had no ground on which to stand. Ulrich was her husband and could have killed him with impunity for both his actions and his words. That he did not . . . that he did not . . .

Why did he not?

Did he value her so little, then? Now he had St. Ives, what need had he of her?

Did she want him, then, to bed her? Did she want his rescue, his sweet defense of her? Did she want him to want her more than he wanted her land?

She had no answer that would give her rest. She could not have him, could not want his wanting, could not rest in his care. Ulrich was beyond her reach and must remain so, as all men must remain so. She was le Gel, and there was no place for a man in her legend. And her legend must stand or all would fall.

Her thoughts were like smoke, heavy and murky and slow. She was losing her way; struggling between want and need. She wanted Ulrich, but she needed her freedom, and the only way to keep it was to defend her legend. Where was the winning in that? How was she to win at marriage with a man she was coming to love?

Love? Nay, there could be no love. She had spurned love to live in legend.

Such thoughts, such regrets, were born in wine. She would never again try to drink a man into submission.

"I am to church," she said into the stiff silence of the pair. "Fight this to the death if it please you. I will arrange for a lovely burial, trust me in that," she said with a falsely sweet smile for her husband. Nicholas could go bury himself.

"I am to church with you, lady, my arm to support, my sword to protect," Ulrich said, looking hard at Nicholas.

Nicholas returned the look measure for measure.

Juliane sighed in exhaustion and then groaned when the light of the westering sun hit her squarely in the eyes. She put up a hand as a shield, but it was too late. Her head burst upon her shoulders and her eyes were put out by burning knives.

She bent down and threw up her dinner in the dirt.

At her side, Ulrich said, "This is a legend I had not heard of you, lady. I think a new verse must be composed. Something about mutton in a wine-red stew."

She hit him, her elbow to his chest, and then threw up again. Ulrich held her hair back with a single hand and hummed contentedly, stroking her back through her heaving.

"If Nicholas had kissed me, I would toss up my dinner as well," he said when she had achieved a respite and was gulping in air.

That he should make her laugh while vomiting up her food was surely cause for annulment. She would talk to Father Matthew about it when she could raise her head again.

Chapter Nineteen

Roger and Father Matthew stood by the wellhead in the far corner of the great hall. It was a dark spot and quiet now that the meal was past. The broad stairs leading to the tower gate were across the wide hall from them, and they could hear the subdued voice of Juliane and the rumbling answer of a male voice within that sheltered place. Ulrich, each man surmised. Who else on the day of her marriage?

"He gave up Stamford," Roger said.

"Aye, but not to me," Father Matthew said. "He gave it to Crowland Abbey. Those rents Thomas will never see."

"I fear you are right, Father," Roger said. "By the king's law, he can lay claim to no rents in England now."

"The king's law," Father Matthew said, each word a stone of outrage. "The king is not above God, nor is his law. Thomas is God's man on earth, and no man of God shall ever bow to any but God. This must be put to rights. Thomas must return to England."

"And so the struggle continues," Roger said. "I come not to argue it out with you. I come only to find where your loyalties lie . . . and to get what coin I may for the purse of the just."

"I cannot give what is not mine to give."

"Is there no way to get Stamford under your hand?"

"Nay. The will is set and the ink dried. Stamford is given and not to me. I did what I could. At least it will go to serve God and not man's greed."

But it would also not aid Thomas of London in his holy battle with King Henry. Roger kept that thought to himself and merely nodded at this priest who would not give what was not his.

Father Matthew hurried into the chapel, late for Vespers. None there seemed to care. If any in that solemn and holy chamber had a thought for prayer, Ulrich would have been most surprised. Nay, all thought was devoted to the coming consummation of his marriage upon the bridal bed.

He was not looking forward to it.

All the carefully won effects of their wine wager were undone, vomited up in the portal of the tower gate. Juliane was sober again, disagreeably sober, and frowning up at Father Matthew. Ulrich had hoped to give her the haze of drunkenness to blunt the coming trial. The only thing blunted now was her good humor, and she had little of that to spare.

Nay, he was being ungenerous. She was awash in good humor, particularly at his expense, and he could not seem to fault her for it. Never had he jousted so willingly and so enthusiastically with a woman. She never cried "foul," and she never pretended offense. He enjoyed her fully, and that was something of a surprise.

He had played at the joust of seduction since his first chin hairs sprouted, and he had loved the game. He loved the smiling warfare, the twisting of words to suit his amorous purpose, the stolen kisses that were not stolen at all. He had excelled at the game from the start. He had made a name for himself, a name for courtly courtesy and ardent flattery and for the sweet winning of a lady's heart. 'Twas a noble game, smiled upon and encouraged by

Eleanor, queen of England and lady of Aquitaine, and he performed in this ritual of hearts with ease.

He had nothing else to sell. He was proficient in arms, but so were all knights. He had sold his sword and his loyalty to many a baron and even a count, but he had been cast loose when money, that merchants' disease, ran thin or when favor ran out. Hard living, to be so free.

But no more. He had his place. He was not free upon the earth, like an eagle searching for hare and finding only mice. He was Ulrich of St. Ives, and he would give his child a place and a name. This would last. This would be where he would plant his feet and find his footing. St. Ives and Juliane. St. Ives because of Juliane.

For that alone he would cherish her.

For that alone he would protect her.

But it was sweet rejoicing that he found so much joy in her. That, he had not planned for.

It was also clear that she had not planned for him. What maid would? He brought nothing to her but a smile and a sword, and she had been awash in those since her breasts sprouted from her ribs, if he could judge. And he could. He was well versed in women and their attributes and saw the wealth of Juliane beyond the worth of Stamford, lost to her now by her father's hand. Juliane had a firm grasp of her own worth, rare in a woman not a queen, and resented him for tumbling her value in the eyes of the world. For so it would be. She married beneath her station, if not her blood.

He was proclaimed Henry's son.

That Philip believed his lineage had been unexpected, but not unwelcome. To be the bastard son of a dead king was honor small enough and worth nothing in coin. But his parentage mattered little now. He had the only thing he had ever sought: a wife and land. His son's place was secure.

"You seem quite pleased with yourself."

Ulrich looked down at the top of Juliane's blond head. "I am."

"You should be. You have what all men want. Me."

"I know," he said, grinning.

"You think you will keep me," she said, snorting delicately and derisively.

"Yea, I think I will keep you," he said softly, running a fingertip down her spine.

She swatted at his hand. "One other believed the same. You are not the first," she said with some satisfaction.

He pulled her hair lightly and whispered, "You are not my first either."

She glared at him and used her pointy elbow to prod him in the ribs. He grabbed her by both arms and held her elbows well behind her back. And smiled up at Father Matthew, who was watching them with a frown.

"You are angry," he said. "You thought you were the first to capture my eyes and then my heart. I have been long out in the world, lady wife. I have fallen many times for a lovely face and form, for a sweet mouth and honeyed discourse. You do outshine them all," he said playfully, "but you are not my first."

" 'Twas my land you fell for," she said, trying to discreetly pull her arms back to her sides.

"That, too," he agreed with an innocent smile.

"And all for your son. I am bartered for a boy," she said. "A bastard."

"Aye," he said softly, looking up at Father Matthew, "he

is a bastard, yet he is mine, my son, and I will give him better than was given me. He shall have a home, Juliane. Think on that. If you take no pleasure in giving me a name, think of how you give a small boy a home."

"Yet mine is lost to me by this giving," she said, looking up at him. "All of me is lost in this giving."

He could feel her eyes upon him and he looked down at her. Her blue eyes were sparkling bright with unshed tears, her face held stiff against pain and loss. He knew the look and would not be the author of such pain. But he could do nothing to counter this sorrow. He could not give up the land to assuage Juliane. He had to give his son a legacy and a place upon the earth. He could not give him less, not when the prize was won and in his hand.

"St. Ives will be your home, and mine. Can you not accept the gift? Take me and my son and the holding of St. Ives. Give us a home, Juliane, for I have wandered the world all my life, searching for the haven of you. Let me find my rest in you and the bounty of St. Ives."

He spoke from his heart, all chivalry and courtly manner abandoned in favor of blunt need and open pleading. He wanted her, for she was home and rest. He needed her.

"I will not submit to you, Ulrich," she said, her eyes shimmering and her look uneasy. "I cannot give up without a fight. It is not in me to do so, no matter your needs."

"This I know, Juliane le Gel. Fight on if you must, yet when this fight is done and past, will you be a good wife to me? Will you submit to loss with grace?"

Juliane smiled crookedly and said, "How can I answer you, Lord Mutton, when I have never lost? I do not know the manner of my losing. I pray to God I never shall partake of that knowing."

"Fair enough," he said, smiling down at her. She was a fair adversary, and there was much joy in fighting on level ground. She was a beauty, in truth, in body and in spirit, well deserving of her legend and her name. He would not tarnish her for all the holdings in England. "I shall win you in this wager, our final wager. I shall lay you down and you shall fall to me. Your virgin's blood is mine, Juliane," he said in soft promise.

"It will not be," she vowed solemnly.

Looking down at her, at the blond, shimmering fire of her, he said, "It must and will be, lady. Be sure of that."

"Oh, I am sure of many things, my lord," she said, all vulnerability sheathed again behind her cool allure.

"Then let the final wager begin, lady. The hour of Vespers is drawing to a close. It is time for our vows to be made full."

"It is time, past time," Conor said. "Our plans must be set and our action swift now. Nothing can stop this false marriage but the consummation, and I do not want to lay my hopes and plans upon the rising and falling of that knight's cock."

"I am with you, step for step. Let it begin now. I am ready," Nicholas said.

He had not been so keen until his thwarted kiss with hot Juliane and the double dose of insult he had taken from that errant knight who had smiled his way into land and title. Nay, now he was in it to the full. He wanted Juliane and he meant to have her. And it would be the sweeter for the sharp knife of lost winnings that he would hold to Ulrich's throat. To lose Juliane was hard.

"You are in this with me? Step for step?" Conor asked.

" 'Tis for my house and my sister's name that I act. You have no such cause in this fight."

In his sister's name? Nay, this was all for Conor and the feeding of his pride and vengeance. Of his sister, there was only rancid memory, the foundation upon which his war was built. Nicholas knew enough of Conor to see that truth. But why argue it? They were allies now, allies in the taking of Juliane.

Had Philip's bond with Maud in the taking of Emmelia been any different? There were none living who cared.

"I have my name, which I prize as highly as you do your own. I want Juliane and I am worthy of her; an equal pairing we would make between us. I will not take insult from a nameless knight and not rise up to fight against it. That is my cause. It is enough."

"Aye, it is enough," Conor said, looking at him in hard appraisal.

Nicholas met the look and waited. In this pairing, they must trust each other well or all would fall apart.

"For my part, I must be swift," Nicholas said. "I must take her now, before he can lift her skirts and find her blood. Keep him from her for a time, as they leave the chapel and all is confusion. I will take her off, away from here, and make her mine."

"Of her seizing, I have no doubt, but are you certain you can find her blood and mark her? This is the crux upon which the whole matter falls, the taking of Juliane and the legendary failure of men to do so."

"Have no doubts, as I have none. I have tasted her mouth. I will taste the rest," Nicholas said. "What of the son of Ulrich? St. Ives may still be lost to you unless Ulrich can be dissuaded from giving chase."

"I know who is the son," Conor said, "and I will make a threat against him that no father could ignore."

"Who is the son of Ulrich? Is he here in Stanora? That was careless reckoning on Ulrich's part, to have the key to all his hopes lying about for any to grab and hold against his plans."

"Aye, he is here," Conor said. " 'Tis yon boy of raven hair. William, he is called."

"But all are going to watch. That is most unfair," Lunete whispered to William as Father Matthew raised his voice to be heard above the muted conversations swirling below him.

"Only three," William said. "And 'twas her father's will and wish, none of Ulrich's. He should not be held to account."

"I do not hold him to account, but it is most unfair. I would not like it. I would not do it."

"What would you do to stop it?"

"I do not know, but . . . something," Lunete said, her fair cheeks turning pink at the thought.

"Will Juliane do something?"

"I do not know that I should tell you. You are with *him*."

"Aye, he is my lord, the knight I serve, but," he said, chewing his lip in thought, "but I will not betray you, if what you say does not betray my lord."

"Non-binding trust," Lunete said. "How much weight will that hold, I wonder?"

"I give you what I can, Lunete," he whispered, watching Father Matthew and the agitation in his eyes. The chapel was most loud today, and not with the holy strains of Latin. "Can I do more? I cannot betray my lord."

"Nay," she sighed. "You cannot. I will not ask it."

They said nothing for a time, watching Father Matthew with bright eyes and still lips, their thoughts far from Vespers and heavenly prospects. The coming battle between Juliane and Ulrich consumed the thoughts of all within that chapel at that hour. Surely God, knowing the frailty of the human heart, would forgive?

"So," William whispered, "will Juliane do something to fight this? Will she break against her father's will?"

"She will not go down quietly, I can promise you that."

"But she will go down?"

Lunete chewed her bottom lip and shook her head. "I was not here before, for that first marriage that fell to ruin for lack of virgin's blood, but I know her legend is built on foundations firm. I cannot see how he will defeat her."

"Let her only submit to him and Ulrich will do his part as a man. The marriage will stand. Ulrich will have his portion, and he will be content for once. 'Tis all he wants, this land, this place for himself."

"What of Juliane and what she wants? Is it only the weight of her land that makes him want her? That is what will keep her fighting. Do you not see it?"

"I see only that Ulrich should have what he has worked so hard to get. She loses nothing. 'Tis only that she gains a husband."

"Then what matter the name of her husband? Why should she take Ulrich without a fight to mark the union?"

"Because Ulrich is a better man than most. He is a worthy knight, equally full of valor and of heart, his smile as swift as his sword. Would not a woman welcome such a man?"

"You talk as if you know him well. How long have you been in his service?"

"I have known him all my life," William said. "I know him well and love him better."

Lunete sighed heavily and said, "I do not think Juliane will ever say as much about him."

"I have heard nothing about him that gives me pause. He is a knight like any other," Nicholas said. "Good fortune only has made him husband to le Gel."

"Worry not as to that. Take Juliane, make her yours. The marriage will follow upon your taking, as it did for Philip. But take her—that is the point upon which success lies. Without her blood upon you, all falls to dust, our plans unmade."

"Worry not as to that," Nicholas said with a hiss of anger. "I am no such man as to be unmade by a maid. I do not know how she came by her legend, but I will strip it from her. Once free of Stanora, she is mine upon that hour."

Conor considered his sudden ally in this game of gain and revenge. Nicholas was strong and sure, and sometimes that was enough to see a deed done. Would that it be so even now.

He wanted this. He wanted to defeat Philip in the making of this marriage as Philip had defeated him in the making of Juliane's first marriage. He had been the one to forge the betrothal; it had been his man who had been forced from the marriage bed, his cock useless and soft, the legend of Juliane taking flight upon the death of that bond he had arranged with such care.

Philip had had some hand in that death, though he

could not see how. It was only that he knew Philip and knew there was no boundary beyond which he would not pass to see hurt brought to Conor. And so it was the same for Conor unto Philip. This battle, begun in Emmelia, would play itself out beyond their deaths.

Yet in this battling, he had no wish to cause hurt to Juliane. He could not see that the changing of one man for another of greater name and worth would harm her. Nay, for at least Nicholas's worth was as great as hers, and that would please her vanity.

But if Nicholas should fail in the matter of her breaching, then all would fail. He had no heart to take the boy William without the assurance of victory in the winning of St. Ives unto himself. And so the two of them stood in uneasy rest upon the competence of the other. For his part, he thought the taking of Juliane to be the harder test. To make off with an untried bastard youth was an easy matter.

"Now listen well," Conor said in an undertone. "When the chapel empties, I will speak with Ulrich, taking him from her side. In that moment, lure Juliane to you by whatever means you may. Take her from Stanora and get her far from here. Do what must be done and do it quick."

"What of Ulrich? He will follow. He will fight. He will not let her slip with such ease into another man's grasp."

"He will," Conor said with confidence. "I will give him something else to do. I will take William upon that moment. Given the choice, whom will he follow? His bride untouched or his son beloved?"

It did not require an answer. There was no man upon the earth who valued his wife above his son. Of wives, there were plenty. Of sons, those who lived were few. A man loved his son above all others upon the earth. Ulrich would follow, seeking William. Juliane would be left on her own with Nicholas. There would be none to save her.

Chapter Twenty

"Has he sealed the bond? I am losing this battle. Death rides me hard and I am weary."

Walter, ever at his father's side, took Philip's hand and kissed it. "Vespers is almost done. They will go to their chamber anon and Ulrich, as you trust him, will do his part. The marriage will be set and sealed. You will have no cares left to you, Father, and can fly to heaven without worry."

"I cannot leave her so," Philip said, as if Walter had not spoken. "Ulrich must take her, binding her to him. I cannot leave her to Conor's grasp."

"And you do not," Walter assured. "She is well set. Ulrich is close upon the binding of their vows."

"Close upon," Philip muttered. "Close upon. Much can befall a maid at such a time."

"But will not. She is safe within Stanora's walls, her body bound to a man of your choosing. Nothing can befall her."

Philip closed his watery eyes, so pale a blue now as to be almost silver. "Anything can befall her."

"What is amiss?" Walter asked. "What hounds you, Father?"

"Conor is ever at my throat, biting, seeking blood."

"Aye, he is most troublesome, is my uncle."

"But he was not always so."

"Nay? What changed him?"

Philip opened his eyes and pierced his son with a silver-white stare. "I changed him."

Walter looked down at his father, so weak and thin now, once so strong and broad and fit. What deathbed confession was upon his lips? What memory did he purge even as he flew past heaven's gate?

"How?" Walter asked, holding tight onto his father's hand, holding him fast against the call of heaven.

"I took Emmelia and made her mine. She was betrothed to another. I wanted her. I wanted Stamford and St. Ives."

"You took her?" Walter asked, his voice hoarse in disbelief. This put a different spin upon everything he had ever known of his parents, of his whole world. "You stole her from her lawful betrothed and from her father's hall?"

"By giving Stamford to the abbey," Philip continued over Walter's questions, "I thought to pay that debt. Many prayers will that buy me."

"What of Conor?"

"Conor," he said scornfully. "Your mother learned contentment. I gave her Stanora, did I not? A rich prize. She held it dear. Our marriage pleased God, for did we not have three children grow to maturity? God forgave me. Conor did not. Conor will do anything to avenge himself upon me."

"But not upon Juliane," Walter said.

"Even upon Juliane," Philip breathed out through cracked lips. "He made Juliane's first marriage, with your mother's blessing, for did she not want all wounds healed between our houses? I agreed. I let him make his match, but when your mother died, the betrothal contract scalded in my hand."

"What did you do?" Walter demanded, his voice rising. "What *could* you have done? All know what befell that night. All know that Juliane was wed and that her husband could not rise."

"Aye, all know it," Philip said. "I made certain of that."

Raw understanding broke into Walter's thoughts, changing the very order of the world.

"'Twas all a lie," Walter said softly as he worked it through in his mind. "Her husband *did* breach her, the marriage was valid, yet you would not have it so, and so the lie of Juliane was born. Maud served as witness, party to the deception, but what was it you offered Juliane so that she would toss that worthy man from her? And what did you offer the man, he who would have a name for falling when he had not fallen at all?"

Philip said nothing. He held Walter's gaze, but he also held his tongue.

"Speak out!" Walter said. "I must know what went before so that I can preserve what I may of Stanora's name."

"Juliane was given her freedom," Philip said.

"Freedom? Freedom from what? To do what?"

"Freedom to never marry. Freedom to live her life as she would. And the glory of a legend to mark her place in the world."

"And she agreed to that," Walter said, running a hand through his hair. "Aye, she would, with Maud ever in her ear and with her own youth to misguide her."

"She has been well content!" Philip said stiffly, flicking spittle into the air.

Walter ignored that defense and asked, "What of the man? What of him?"

"What of him? Do you even remember his name?"

Almost he remembered it, but it trailed away like a dim shape in the mist, lost without being grasped.

"None remember him," Philip said. "It was my promise to him, and I have kept it. Of Juliane and her victory over her husband's cock, all remember. Of her fallen husband, none. I paid him well and set in motion the beginnings of a new betrothal with a fine damsel. He is well content. I did no harm."

Did no harm. Did no harm, except that he had broken a binding betrothal for little cause other than his own pride. No harm, except that now Juliane, by Philip's word, was in the path of harm from Conor, in some way. How? He could not see it, his mind did not turn into these twisted paths that his father and his uncle roamed at will.

Walter pushed his confusion to the back of his thoughts and forced himself to think of why his father spoke of these old wounds now. Of how an uncle could wound a father through his daughter.

And then he knew.

"Conor will take Juliane. He will not allow this marriage you have arranged to stand without a tempest to mark it," Walter said, rising to his feet, releasing his father's hand. "Only the consummation stands in his path, and he to witness it."

"Guard my will in this," Philip said from his bed. "Keep her far from Conor and his Nicholas until Ulrich is in her, hard and fast within her."

Walter turned back to face his father from the door. "Nicholas? But Nicholas is here. He came with Conor."

Philip tried to raise himself, the veins in his neck standing out like roots, his blood pulsing hard and thick. "You kept this from me? This man is nothing but Conor's pawn. He will do what I did long years past. He will steal Juliane from here, thwarting my will and my choice."

"And why was Ulrich your choice?" Walter asked harshly. "Nicholas of Nottingham *is* the better match, if not for your stubborn war with my uncle."

"Ulrich is my choice because he was here when I fell into this wasting death," Philip said without emotion and without remorse. "Any man is better than the one Conor would thrust upon my will."

"Because it thwarts Conor's will yet again? What else does Ulrich bring besides the bruising of Conor's pride? What else, Father? *Nothing.* Again, it is a woman caught between your will and his."

Philip's eyes blazed white in his sharp-featured face. "Why else does Conor fight this bond but that he seeks to wound me? What has changed between us? Nothing. Nothing, and so I say, find Juliane and protect her. I am still lord here, and my will must surmount."

"So you say," Walter said, thinking of all the lies that lived within Stanora by this man's will.

"Obey my will."

Walter bowed stiffly and said, "I always have."

But he did not say he always would.

Nicholas pushed into the church as she was pushing out. She had no wish to see him. Why did he not leave Stanora now that Stanora's legend was beyond his grasp? All other men before him had. What else was there for a suitor but the testing of his skill against the legend of The Frost?

When that was done, the game played out, all hours slipped again into their proper uses. She hawked and hunted and played at chess and rode a fine horse beneath the wide sky—all without thought of men. All without thought of future. Her future was secured, set, and sealed. A future of no husband and no child; that had been the price of the bargain, and she had met it well.

Why had her father broken their bargain?

Why did he cast her into this marriage when it would break all to shards?

She had to find a plan of escape, a way out of this bedding her father had arranged. If she did not, the lie they had spun dark years ago would be revealed.

She looked again at Nicholas. Perhaps he had a purpose yet. Perhaps she could use him to work her way free. St. Ives was rich, but even a land-poor knight would not tolerate the loss of his good name with his fellow knights. A wife unmanageable was a wife unpalatable.

She looked at Nicholas. And smiled.

Ulrich was not behind her, as he had been. She saw that Conor had pulled him off and was talking softly to him, yet with an urgency that was usual for Conor. A most urgent and intense man was her uncle, and inclined to bluster into trouble for its own sake. But if Conor kept Ulrich at his side, could she not use that to her own good?

She must find a way out of the consummation. She would not lose, not at this. It was almost certain that Ulrich would not fall. His ardor was too hot, his confidence too high, his enjoyment of their battles too keen. Aye, that was what was sinking her chances in this game of bodies and of words. He had no fear of her. He enjoyed her barbs and bristles, reveling in jousting with her, smiling at her jabs and laughing at her insults.

Was there ever such a knight?

She credited him too high. A knight who was hungry for land and place would endure much. Let there be no soft wrapping around the hard force of his ambition. He cherished her because he cherished what he could have by winning her.

'Twas the way of the world. She did not despise him for playing so well within the rules. 'Twas only that she would not.

He had called it right. She would lie and cheat to win because to win was all that mattered. Her father had taught her that.

The only rule was winning, and the only measure was success. And if success grew cold and dark, shadows within empy shadows, what could she do against it? She was caught within the jaws of a lie, a distant bargaining she must keep, for if she listened to her heart, if she let herself melt into the heat of Ulrich, then he would know her for what she was: a liar and a cheat. Her legend nothing but a lie. Juliane nothing but a lie draped in the cloak of ancient deceit. Ancient, for this lie had wrapped itself around her heart for years, and there was no escaping it now. Not now, not ever. What man would want her if he knew the truth?

Ulrich would hate her if he knew the truth.

She would rather live without him than live within the borders of his hate.

"Do you go to your chamber now?" Avice asked from behind her. The press of bodies was all about them. Avice was pushed hard against her back, though her words were spoken softly. "I will attend, if you like."

"Nay. I am not going to run up the winding stair, pretending willingness," Juliane said, eyeing Nicholas. "I would rather fight this battle in a chamber without a bed to mark it."

"'Tis late for that," Avice said.

"But not too late. Until his cock drips upon the sheets, I can still work myself free of him."

"Do you still want this fight, or is it only that you cannot bear to lose?"

Juliane looked askance at her sister. "Are you so fond of losing, then?"

"Nay, but not all things may be won," Avice said softly.

Juliane stopped and stared at her sister. "What have you lost that you say so?" When Avice said nothing but only met her stare with a stony look, Juliane suddenly knew and said, "Edward. What has he won from you?"

"A kiss," Avice said, dropping her gaze to the stone slabs beneath their feet.

"A kiss? What sort of kiss to leave you so changed?"

"A simple kiss," Avice said stiffly.

"Simple?" Juliane snorted. "Not to leave you so. I know something of kisses, more than you, and this kiss robbed you, Avice. You are not as you were, and he has made you so, with much rejoicing on his part, I am certain."

"Certain, are you? Look at him and tell me the same," Avice snapped, jerking her head in the direction of Edward.

He stood beneath the rood, rooted there, by the look of him, his glowing eyes of hazel dimmed by sorrow and anger and loss, his mouth a frown of confusion, his shoulders stiff under a load of pain. Or so he looked.

Romantic rubbish, a vision fit for a troubadour, but not for Juliane. She was too experienced at deceiving to be so deceived.

"What was the wager?" Juliane asked.

"A kiss, given willingly by me, and then he would sing my name throughout the land, praising me. As you are praised, Juliane."

"Why this wager, Avice? What did you gain that has any meaning?" Juliane asked softly, taking Avice by the hand and stroking her sister's fingers with her thumb. So innocent she was. So young to desire the power of legend, not knowing that legends had weight and form and made demands of their own.

"A name, Juliane," Avice said, tears rising swift and strong. "A name which all men speak and a legend to follow me into heaven."

"In heaven we are free of legends," Juliane said gently. "'Tis only on earth that we must bear the weight of them."

"You bear no weight, Juliane," Avice said, blinking away her tears. "Your legend is a golden shield, shining bright and strong for all to see."

"Aye," Juliane said, taking Avice into a soft hug and whispering in her ear, "a shield. To keep all away. Look not for legend. It is an empty chalice."

"Empty? That is not so. Your legend fills your life, making you great."

"Great? Because troubadours in search of food and a roof sing of me? Because men come to test their mettle against a living legend of frost? What greatness there, Avice? Men come, but not for *me*; they come to make their own legend by killing mine. If any man came for me, then that would be something of which to sing. But they do not," she whispered. "I stand alone. Ever alone, with only my legend to cloak me. And I, even I, grow cold with such a thin cloak to shield me from the world."

"Yet what of Ulrich? If you do not fight him, he can be yours. You need not be alone."

Juliane looked to where Ulrich stood, tall and fierce and clean; would that she could let herself fall to him, fall into him, safe and warm in a cold world ruled by battle and by victory. But she could not. She could not. She was trapped within the lie.

"I have my legend," she said, tears filling the corners of her eyes as she pulled her gaze from Ulrich to face her sister. "I must be true to it."

"I love you," Avice answered, smiling through her tears, "but I do not understand you."

"I love you in return," Juliane said, taking Avice in her arms for a soft embrace, "and understanding is not required for love." They stood so, letting the chapel empty some, letting some measure of peace and healing fill them. "Tell me: Did you win the wager?"

Avice pulled back and smiled crookedly through her drying tears. "Aye. I won."

"Of course you won," Juliane said. "Now tell me how the winning stripped your heart and left you empty of all but loss."

"Lady," Nicholas said, intruding with ease upon them. Such was it with men; they ever believed themselves to be welcome. "May I have a word?"

"Only one?" Juliane asked, and then remembered that she might find some purpose for this forward man and quickly cloaked her sarcasm in a smile designed to blind. "Of a certainty, my lord. As many words as you wish."

"Lady," he said, "I make ready to leave. Will you walk with me, bidding me farewell?"

He was leaving? She must use him now or use him not at all.

"Aye, I will," she answered, "though I wonder that my husband will not beat me for such converse with a man he has good cause not to trust."

Nicholas grinned and said, "Lady, I do not believe it is in any man to beat Juliane le Gel for any cause. I think Ulrich knows well just what he has won in winning you."

Juliane raised her brows in some surprise and smiled back at him, thinking hard. What did he want? Why else did a man offer praise but that he wanted some thing of a woman, some dark and self-serving thing.

"Avice?" Christine interjected. "Edward wants a word. Will you go to him?"

"He begs a word," Juliane said, smiling at her sister. "A victory most profound, Avice."

"Aye, I will," Avice said. "My lord?" she said in parting to Nicholas, who bowed upon her leaving.

"And now we are alone," Nicholas said.

"In a chapel full of folk," she answered with a tilt of her head.

"I would have more solitude than this. If you will agree."

"I will agree, with my groom at my back," she said. She was no fool. Nicholas had proved himself by that forced kiss; she would not trust to chivalry with him. Let Baldric prove his function, that of protecting her from rough knights angered by defeat. "I will walk with you to the stables, if my husband agrees. I wonder if he will. He has no cause to trust you."

"Yet he has no cause to distrust you," Nicholas said.

"Not yet," she answered, laying out her lure for him to consider.

If Nicholas made another move upon her, and she received it well, would Ulrich discard her? It was not likely. Broken fidelity was a matter between men; women, the object of the game, played the smallest part of all. Yet what else to do? She could not be Ulrich's wife upon Ulrich's bed; her path had been decided long before the coming of Ulrich to Stanora's gates.

Hard loss, to lose such a man and in such a way. But she could see no other path than the one before her, Nicholas at its gate, urging her to enter and leave all doubt behind. And so she went, decided. There was no turning from this path. She had made her choice long years ago, though she had not seen this bleak end.

"Not yet? You entice me, lady," he said.

"Have I?" she said with a slow smile, taking the first steps in breaking her bond with Ulrich. "Does my husband watch, and does he know that you are enticed by his wife of an hour?"

"Your lord and master is well engaged," Nicholas said, indicating Ulrich with a flick of his head. It was true. Conor still had Ulrich by the shoulder, filling his ear with nothing that would aid her, that was certain. "He has no eyes for you. Not such as I have."

"Then let us walk, my lord," she said with a soft smile, casting Ulrich away with hands that trembled just a little.

Casting dreams aside because of a bargain made when she was as young and naive as Avice was now.

Baldric appeared from out of the shadows of the chapel and walked without a word to a spot behind her back. Without a word, though he looked most troubled and unsettled. So troubled that she gave him a questioning look.

He scowled and pointed back to the chapel, back to where her husband stood, back to what could only be the place of her dishonor and defeat. She could not go back.

"You are content in your marriage?" Nicholas asked, taking her arm in his hand.

"Content?" she said. "I spoke my vows by my father's will. What other answer must I give?"

"You are dutiful," he said, looking down at her. His eyes were very dark and very deep, his lashes long. A wide scar marked his temple and slid into his hair, leaving a narrow strip of shining scalp. "In all the tales of you, none mentions your gentle submission. A careless omission."

"Perhaps because women are always to be gently submissive. What power in that tale?" she said. "The troubadours would starve if they sang of the mundane."

"You are far from mundane. You are celestial, Juliane. A woman who deserves the very stars. A woman who sings out—"

"I am a woman very much of the earth," she said, interrupting him. If he did not do *something* that would scald Ulrich before he left, what good did he do her? She must break free and Nicholas must play his part. "I have no need of stars."

Baldric mumbled something at her back and she turned

to him, frowning. He stopped mumbling, but he did not stop scowling.

They had almost reached the stables; the bailey was quiet, the summer twilight softly growing by pink and purple bands of cloud.

"Would you ride with me then, Lady of Earth?" Nicholas said. "Would you ride with me down the plain until the track enters the wood? I would keep your company as long as I may, stealing from Ulrich what I might."

Ride off through the gates of Stanora with another man within the hour of exchanging marriage vows? Aye, that might do it, might break Ulrich's pride and free her from his grasp. And from his heat.

"'Tis a soft twilight," she said, smiling up at dark Nicholas. "I would enjoy a ride across the plain of Stanora. But only to the wood," she teased, "for I must guard my heart and my good name."

"Lady, your name is safe within my care," he said, teasing her in return.

Baldric coughed loudly and then spat, drawing her attention most well.

"Aye?" she said, turning to Baldric.

"Ulrich awaits, lady," Baldric said. "You should stay here, within the walls."

"Your lady does not answer to you," Nicholas said, his dark eyes glowing with sudden anger. A most changeable man, his temper uncertain. Best get this done and quickly.

"And well he knows it," Juliane said, taking Baldric by his stout arm and leading him into the shelter of the stables. Once Nicholas had been left without, she whispered, "Get Frost for me. I will need a mount that will run upon my whim. I have a plan in play. Do not thwart me,

Baldric. Only stay the course a bit more, and all will be accomplished to my will."

"And what of your father's will? Nicholas is of Conor, and Philip does not hold with anything of Conor," Baldric answered.

"My will ever circles upon my father's wish," she said. "I do nothing I have not done a thousand times before."

"You were not married to Ulrich before," Baldric said.

Juliane looked at him with a reluctant smile and shook her head in gentle admonition. "Just get the horse."

"Aye, I will," he said, jerking a thumb at a stableboy, directing him with a grunt and a gesture. "One for you and one for me. I will not leave you in his dark care," he said with a jerking of his head to where Nicholas stood. "He is no good knight to take a lady off on her wedding day."

"Then I am no good bride," she said with a grin. "And so I would be found."

"You play at things that are games no longer, lady," he said, his brown eyes solemn and large. "Ulrich is a good man. All would be right with him. But for this."

"I am who I am," she said, shaking off his words and his solemnity. "I will not turn from it now. There is no turning, Baldric, even if I so chose. This path was set long past, and the walls that keep me in are very high, beyond escape."

"Let Ulrich decide it," he said. "Give him a chance."

"Nay, for once he knows the truth, he will hate me. And I will lose all," she said.

"I would away," Nicholas said, holding the bridle of his mount. "Are you ready, Juliane?"

"Aye," she called out, looking sadly into Baldric's eyes, "I am ready. Let us depart."

Baldric, grumbling and shaking his head in mumbled warning, lifted her onto her saddle. She arranged her bridal skirts while he mounted his mare, and then they joined Nicholas, her smile as carefully arranged as her clothes.

They passed through the bailey in quiet talk, passed through the gates, passed out of the town that hugged the gates, passed over the plain, soft gold and tawny in the warm and slanting light, and when they were upon the track that would wind into the wood, Nicholas pulled free his sword and, turning his horse most gracefully, sliced Baldric free of life. Baldric fell from his saddle, a spray of blood following him down, his head hitting first, then his body and then his legs and feet. So slowly he seemed to fall. So gently he fell to earth, falling into death and the glory of heaven. So quietly, so silently, so unlike grumbling, mumbling Baldric that she almost could not believe he was fallen.

Yet he was gone, and she was alone with Nicholas, her uncle's pawn, wearing the manner of a knight. She was a simple piece upon a chessboard, about to be taken up and out.

"You are in Stanora often, then?" Ulrich asked.

"Often enough," Conor answered, "I am an uncle of the most devoted sort."

"That is clear. I have never known an uncle to take so much interest in the marriage arrangements of his niece with a father living," Ulrich said softly, smiling.

"A father living," Conor repeated. "It could be better said, 'a father dying.'"

"All men die, yet their wills and dispensations are ever

honored. Will this marriage be honored, Conor?" Ulrich asked.

"By me, certainly," Conor answered readily. "I plunge no sword into a fight not my own."

"We speak of fights now?" Ulrich said with a smile. "I am a laggard, thinking only of my bride in this hour. I fear I fail to follow your thinking. Will there be a fight for Juliane? I cannot see whence it would come."

Conor shrugged and smiled. "Not all fights announce themselves with trumpet blast."

"That is so. That is the province of the tournament. You have played within those boundaries?"

"Aye," Conor said. "Often and well."

"You must travel frequently to the Continent, to the lands bordering the realm of King Louis, is that not so?" Ulrich asked.

"As do all who compete," Conor said, his expression closed.

"Was there not one such tournament just last month, at Joigny, which lies close upon Ile-de-France? I think I am right when I say I saw your name upon the lists."

"There are many tournaments in Caen, a place well fixed to your name," Conor said in counterpoint.

"So there are," Ulrich said slowly. "Yet I thought we spoke of your love of tourney and your need to travel out of England to see your love requited."

"A man will travel far to see his love and to taste of her," Conor said. "You must know that, being a knight with a name for loving."

Ulrich grinned and looked about the chapel. Juliane he did not see. And suspected Conor was the cause. Yet this jousting was outside his need for Juliane. This was of the king, and the very purpose of Ulrich's coming to Stanora. An unknown traitor to the king, a man in tryst with King Louis and, by that bond, with Thomas Becket of London, had some tie to Stanora. Ulrich had sniffed that out and so had come, thinking to find in Lord Philip the man he sought. Yet here stood Conor.

"A knight is called to have a name for loving, is he not? By fighting, we are made. By loving, we are made great. Or so I have always believed."

"A belief that has served you well. You have won a fair wife with the skill."

"So I have," Ulrich said softly, "and so I mean to keep her."

"As do all men who take a wife," Conor said.

"You have a wife?"

"Not yet. The betrothal is in negotiation."

"A taxing time," Ulrich said. "I commiserate with you. Her name?"

"There is nothing set," Conor said.

"I know how that is," Ulrich said with an easy grin, calming Conor by his ease. "Until all is signed, all may fail."

"That is so," Conor said with what appeared to be grim pleasure.

"I heard of a maid," Ulrich said in casual contemplation, "whose father was in the midst of arrangements for her. What *was* her name? A most beautiful name, I do remember that much."

"Compared to Juliane, what woman can compare?" Conor said, trying to lead him off. Failing to lead him off the topic of this girl.

"None," Ulrich said. "'Tis only the name I seek, not

the lady herself. That lady is bound for you, if God and good bargaining wills it. Ah, now I do recall it," he said, piercing Conor with his gaze, measuring the sweat that beaded upon his brow. "Adela. Adela du Perche."

Conor, his fair skin and ruddy coloring betraying him, flushed. Snared by a name. Adela du Perche and her father, the count du Perche, were bound to Louis of Ile-de-France, not Henry of England and Anjou.

Chapter Twenty-one

"What did you tell Juliane?" Edward asked her.

"I told her of our kiss," Avice said, looking about the chapel and not at Edward. If she looked at him when their bodies were so close, the heat of him drawing her in, she would attack him, as she had in the stable.

"Why would you tell her that?" Edward said, his voice going hard. "Unless you meant to proclaim your win to her."

Avice looked up at him now. He was killing all desire in her and leaving her only with the taste for vengeance in her mouth. How was it that this man could so quickly drive her heart before him? She had hated him from the first. He was arrogant and haughty and he had hated her. A most apt reason to dislike a man.

"I *did* win," she said.

Edward growled and took her by the arm. She shook him free and smoothed the wool of her sleeve, eyeing him coolly as she did so.

"Do not say you do not remember it, my lord."

"Oh, aye," he said, his voice pitched low and harsh, "I do remember it. A most willing kiss. But why, Avice? Why kiss me with such hot willingness? No such fire was required of you."

Of course he would remind her of that. She had won. He looked to find some flaw in it. And he had struck dead upon it.

Why such heat?

Because he caused a fire to burn in her that anger only fanned. Because his eyes were ever upon her and no man before had ever looked away from Juliane to look at Avice. Because she glowed like a brand whene'er he spoke to her, aye, even now, and it did not seem to matter if his words were hard or soft, cold or hot; she burned. She was no Juliane, a woman of ice and frost. She was all fire and smoke and pulsing heat, and all Edward had to do to start the blaze in her was to say her name.

"I am all fire, Edward," she said, matching the tone of his voice, wanting him to somehow choke on the smoky fire of her. "Tell me, did I burn you?"

"Aye, you did. But I did not burn alone, lady. You singed me with your passion."

If he meant it as insult, she rejected his intent. Let Juliane be ice; Avice would be smoke. Let Edward build her legend upon that fact. And if he remembered her for the rest of his days on earth, she would . . . she would . . . only thank God, since she would carry the memory of Edward into paradise.

She swallowed against rising tenderness and the threat of tears. There was only one way this game could be played out. She had a betrothed, chosen by her father and his, the contracts signed. She would travel to Arthur upon Lammas, the final day of summer, and there would become his wife as fully in body as she was now by law. She was fifteen, ripe for bedding and ready for wifery. Edward had no place in her future or her life, unless that place be in song and memory. 'Twould have to be enough. There was nothing more.

"Will you make certain that is voiced in your song?" she said with a false smile of victory. "I rather like the image: Avice of fire, the lady who singes the unwary with her smoky passion. A nice complement to Juliane and all the words of ice and snow which are chained to her name. I would compete, you know, and does not fire defeat ice at every turn?"

He would hate·her doubly now, which would only serve him well in future days. She understood the hurt and rage and confusion in his hazel eyes, for did not her own eyes mirror his? He would forget the passion and the need in that kiss of theirs and remember only his anger. He would forget even his defeat in the fire of his fury against her pride and haughtiness, which was good.

"Aye, Avice," Edward said, holding himself away from her. He probably wanted to strike her, she thought. "Aye, I will sing of your fire and passion. Your legend will live through me until my breath is gone."

And so it would. He knew what she did. They had nothing between them, no betrothal, no bond beyond desire. She threw him from her, casting him down so that he would not hope, so that he would not believe there had ever been more between them than a wager. But he was a man, well versed in desire and passion, unlike the innocent Avice. She lied to give him armor to defeat the pain of losing her, she whom he had never had hope of having.

If he had not loved her before, he would have loved her now for her valiant fight to give him a reason to hate her.

"And when your breath dies?" she asked softly, her arms folded around herself. "Will the legend of Avice die as well? A poor legend, to only live for the life of one man."

"Nay, it will not die," he whispered, staring down at her. Ever would he remember the look of her in that moment, the soft melting of her eyes, the trembling of her pale lips, the hunger in her gaze. A thousand years in heaven and he would know her still. "Your legend will live beyond me, beyond you, beyond our time. The legend of Avice and the fire of her love will outlast the foundation of the earth."

" 'Twas not love," she said, and he could see the choking swallow she made. " 'Twas the meeting of a wager in the fire of passion. Tell only that. There is nothing more than that."

" 'Twas not love. Never love," he said, nodding in agreement, loving her more with every breath he drew. "I will tell it true."

The chapel was still pressed hard with people. Most had come to take a long look at Ulrich, this man who would try to claim Juliane in his bed. Another had tried, failed, and been cast out of her life. Who would not want to see the next man, a poor man with no mighty alliances, no great wealth, no rich lands, who would attempt the taking of Juliane? Many wagers would be cast upon the air, wagers measuring his fitness, the duration of his claim, his ultimate failure or victory in the bedding of The Frost of Stanora.

If it were not ill-mannered, Ulrich might have placed a wager of his own. For victory, most certainly. Conor still spoke and Ulrich made his murmured responses; he had found what he had come to Stanora to find. The traitor to Henry's will stood before him. Ulrich had been given no charge to kill him, that was for the king to decide. His duty was to find and report, and that he would do once he left Stanora. Having found his man, he was now bored with this talk, eager to lay his hands upon his wife. Ulrich stifled his frustration and kept silent, though his gaze scanned the chapel for a glimpse of his bride. He did not see her.

He did not think it in her to hide. Certainly she would never run. Not Juliane. She was too sure of victory, too keen to pit her skills against his. Female pride would devour her in the end, but his would not be the mouth to tell her that.

She might be in the mews, making talon plans with her hawk. That would be like her and was a proven course in defeating amorous men. He had the scar to prove it.

There would be no hawks allowed within their chamber. He might have the wind holes barred as a precaution. He did not favor another scar upon a more vulnerable region of his body.

"I think you hear me not," Conor said, and Ulrich jerked his attention back to Juliane's maternal uncle.

Ulrich smiled and shrugged. "I beg your mercy. I am full of thoughts of my bride. A common failing, I would wager."

"Yea, you wager much," Conor said with a matching smile. Both their smiles were brightly false. "And often, it is said. It seems you have some skill and better fortune in your wagering."

"No more than any other man."

"Does any other man have Juliane? Nay, I think you wager very well. But if a man cannot hold his winnings close upon him, then all wagering is for naught."

He heard the threat. There was no mistaking it. There was also no answer for it. A fight with Juliane's blood kin was not a fight he would take unless pressed beyond all bearing.

"True words," Ulrich said easily. "I have seen it often and have learned from watching. I do not wager over-much and keep my winnings close."

"Yet I do not see Juliane," Conor said, looking out over the mob in the chapel.

"Nor do I," Ulrich said, "and so I will take my leave of you. I am a laggard bridegroom to lose his bride so quick. I must mend that. I would not be found wanting by any."

A warning was there, if Conor had the wit to hear it. Ulrich would not bark, hackles raised, teeth bared; he was a man who would bite when the need was in front of him. But, until the need for teeth grinding against bone, he would smile and hold his sword close upon his hip. A careful man was Ulrich. Experience in the wide world had shown him that wisdom. A man without a house and name to back him did not seek out enemies, but an enemy made was an enemy destroyed. With no one to watch his back, he could allow none to skulk behind him. And if that enemy was Conor, then Juliane must learn to live without an uncle, and the king to live without a live traitor to condemn.

From what he had seen of Conor's welcome in Stanora, he did not think many here would miss him.

"I think you are missing yet another," Conor said. "Where is your young squire?"

And why would Conor note anything at all about William? This did not bear a pleasing scent; nay, all was foul. He did not even need to look about him. William, ever at his back, always within call, was gone. Far from him. He could feel it.

Ulrich bared his sword in a single smooth arc and held the blade to Conor's chin. Conor, to judge by his look, had not expected such a quick answer to his query.

"Where is he?" Ulrich breathed. "Tell me and you may yet live."

Nay, he was not a man to growl in warning when a bite to the throat would serve him best.

"I do not have him," Conor said, stepping back across the chapel stones. Ulrich followed and pierced his skin with the tip of his blade. The blood rose up in shining drops, red and bright.

"Where?" Ulrich whispered.

"You would not—"

"Where?" Ulrich asked again, pressing the point hard, catching Conor's jawbone against the warm steel. The blood ran down in a delicate stream of red, twisting over the contours of Conor's throat, slipping over skin made smooth with sudden sweat.

"Where?" William asked. "Where are we going?"

"Away from here. 'Tis not a good time to be in Stanora."

William looked up at Roger, his expression both curious and trusting. Roger was well loved by Ulrich. This hasty departure must be by Ulrich's command.

"Why not? Because of the marriage?"

"Aye," Roger answered the boy, who sat on a small horse behind his own mount, the reins of both held within his fist. "Much has changed with this marriage."

"But Ulrich wanted it to change. I can still serve him," William said.

"Aye, but not for a time. Let him find his way with his wife; then you may serve him as he wills. For now, I could well use a squire well trained in his duties. Will you serve me for a time? I will be an easy master."

"I am sworn to Ulrich. I cannot serve another without breaking my bonds to him."

"'Tis only for a time," Roger said lightly, keeping his eyes upon the horizon. The wood was deep and the light slanting and dimming as the day fell into evening. The call of the owl could be heard in the dark depths of the wood and beyond it, the careful steps of deer in deep leaves. The gray walls of Stanora were not far behind them; all creatures must step with care until Stanora and all her swords were far removed. "Your honor is not broken upon this, William."

His horse trod carefully, the track through the wood scarcely used, to judge by the heavy and unbroken fall of last year's leaves which blanketed the path. The sunlight was greenish in the shade, and every breath of the horses seemed to echo into the shadows.

"For how long?" William asked.

Roger looked back at him, at the small dark-haired boy who looked at him with such trust and confusion, and smiled. "Not long."

"But where? Where are we going?"

Roger did not have a ready answer for that question and so he said nothing at all.

"*Where?*" Walter shouted, his voice bounding off the vaulted wooden roof of the chapel.

Conor, his uncle, only shook his head, his blue eyes stony with defiance. And victory. It would be a brief victory, Walter vowed. He would see him dead for this, though Ulrich looked ready to do the task for him.

For such a smiling knight, Ulrich acted quickly and without paralyzing deliberation. Good traits in an ally, and they were allies now. Marriage and the threat of harm to Juliane had accomplished that.

"Why?" Ulrich asked.

Conor smiled. This was a question he seemed willing to answer most readily.

"To repay an old debt," Conor said.

"What debt?" Ulrich asked, his hand turning the sword so that the blade slid with hungry energy over Conor's throat.

"Between myself and Philip," Conor said. "A betrothal gone foul. A point of honor between his house and mine."

"Between your pride and his," Walter said. "And Juliane caught in the crushing maw of it. What honor in that?"

"She will not be harmed. She will find her life as the lady of Nottingham most fair, most honorable," Conor said.

"Nicholas," Ulrich said on a hiss of breath.

"Nicholas," Juliane said on a ragged breath, pushing her hair back from her eyes, "this avails you naught. I will not submit to you."

"Lady," he breathed softly, "you will."

With casual ease, Nicholas swung his arm down and struck Juliane across the face with the flat of his hand. A pounding, raw sting. The taste of blood on her tongue. A careful swallow. A cold look to show that she was not afraid, that she would not submit, that she would not be fractured into compliance by his blows.

Yet she would.

She had no armor against this; all her allies were flown, her time-won confidence shattered. Baldric was dead, Philip dying. Walter was just as content to have one man take her as another, as long as she was out of his house. Ulrich . . .

Ulrich.

Would he come? Would he even know to come? Would he come for St. Ives if not for her?

Would any come for her?

She knew what Nicholas wanted. He wanted what all men wanted when they came to Juliane le Gel. He wanted her blood upon his cock. He wanted to pierce her of pride and rip the ice from her name.

He wanted to defeat her.

But she would not be defeated. She could not be. She could never be. And so the game had been played for five years. She was the queen upon the chessboard who could not and must not be taken else all would be lost.

Her father would be proved for a liar; a man who broke contracts and lived without honor.

Her aunt proved for a liar; a woman who watched a mating and declared the man unfit, destroying a marriage and a man by deceit.

And Juliane proved for a liar and a cheat; a woman who betrayed her husband of an hour to gain the gift of legend.

An empty gift it had become.

At the game of love, with the protection of Stanora surrounding her, she had become a master. She parleyed, she jousted, she flirted, she teased, and she won. She won, and it was all of winning, was it not? So her father had taught her. To be certain, winning was better than losing, but the taste of winning had soured as the years passed. The same game. The same men wearing the same look and bearing the same pride. The same, the same, yet she herself changing and no one to see it because all wanted to see the legend of Stanora, not the woman Juliane. Because who wanted a woman when there was a legend to be had?

Nicholas swung his fist again. A blow to her belly, stripping her of air and leaving only pain. Yet the pain seemed to wane with each blow. Her body was learning the gift of pain. Her hopes of rescue learning to die quietly. Her legend learning to fall.

Nicholas wanted what they all wanted: to push his way into her, owning her by the act.

Yet if he did . . . if he did, he would know the truth, and no man could know the truth. For no other reason had she relinquished Ulrich.

She was trapped within a lie and there was no way out.

"Where has he taken Juliane?" Walter demanded.

"And William? Where is the boy?" Ulrich snarled.

Conor looked at his nephew as if he had not a care in the world, though his blood seeped out from under Ulrich's blade. A threat only. Who would harm him here?

He was blood kin, and no hand in Stanora could touch him.

"He takes Juliane and will make her his own," Conor said. "Nicholas is a good match for her, and no one is harmed by her taking but this nameless knight."

"I am nameless no more," Ulrich said in a hiss of fury, "and I act in the center of the lord of Stanora's will. There is nothing of you in this, Conor. You reach outside your walls to manage another man's fief. 'Tis an act without honor."

"This goes beyond you and my father, Conor," Walter said. "I will not see my sister used in this way. Where are they?"

"And where is William, and what part is he to play in this battle of wounded pride?" Ulrich said.

"A simple part, but of so great a weight that all must bow before it," Conor said, his blue eyes shining with spiteful victory. "Two are missing from Stanora. Who will be saved? Save Juliane, if you can, and the boy dies. Your boy. Your son and heir. The thing you sought, the wealth of St. Ives, will be lost because you could not save him. Or will you save your son and let Juliane fall onto the point of another man's prick? She will be lost to you, as will St. Ives. Either way, you lose St. Ives. I will not see that land fall into your grasp, you who are nothing and who bring nothing to the family of my name and blood."

"What of *my* blood? You speak of my sister!" Walter shouted. "Tell *me* where she is before she falls into this trap. You are her blood kin, yet you cast her into dishonor."

"She is a woman," Conor said coldly. "She falls where and how she must."

"You took neither of them," Ulrich said softly, his

blade held steady and firm against the skin of his enemy, his will as steady as his steel. "Nicholas took Juliane. Who took William?"

"Your trusted friend, who cannot be trusted much," Conor gloated. "Roger."

"Roger?" Ulrich said, his brows raised. "You trusted Roger to betray me? Why?" Ulrich spoke calmly, as if nothing at all rested upon the answer. As if time had ceased to pass. As if they shared a cup of cordial wine and not the threat of red violence.

"You know him not," Conor said, pulling again away from the blade but escaping the point of it not at all. Ulrich, for all his ease of manner, kept him beneath his steel and coaxed Conor's blood out of him, drop by drop. A steady stream it was, thin but bright, soaking softly into the neck of his tunic. "He plots with Stanora's priest to get Stanora's wealth for the use of Thomas Becket."

"Stanora's priest runs false to England's king? Does treachery know no bounds?" Walter cried, his fair complexion red with anger and outrage.

"'Tis not treachery," Ulrich said, "not on Roger's part. His heart has bound his honor to the church. There is no fault in that. But enough of this," he said. "Where is Juliane?"

Conor shrugged. "The deed is past the doing now. Nicholas was well taken by her charm and beauty. That matter is done. There will be no undoing of it. He took her somewhere near the abbey of Thorney. I know not where. His goal is Nottingham, where he will make her his wife."

"Except that she is mine," Ulrich said.

"Not now." Conor grinned.

"Now and always," Ulrich answered him, his own grin thin and cold. He turned to Walter and said, "I am your man by the giving of St. Ives, my oath given to you. Give me leave to kill him. He is deserving of it."

Walter and even Conor started at that cold request.

"He is my uncle," Walter said. "I cannot grant that request, though he does deserve it."

"You know nothing of blood ties," Conor snarled at Ulrich. "Never would any of my kin lay hand to me or I to them. Your bastardy shows strong in such words."

Ulrich ignored Conor and said to Walter, "What of Juliane and your bond to her?"

"She is past saving now," Walter said, "her future hard in the hands of Nottingham. Think of your son. He may yet be saved."

Ulrich looked hard into Walter's eyes. "William is not my son."

"What?" Conor spat out, jolted from the comfort of arrogance for the first time in an hour. "He *is* your son. There can be no other."

"He is the son of William le Brouillard of Greneforde, given into my keeping for a time, as my son was left in Greneforde. My son, a bastard like his father, is a babe of toddling steps. Nay, the boy you took and thought to kill is the son of William, close upon the king and his counselors. A mighty enemy you have made should any harm befall his son. Though no harm will, not by Roger's hand."

"A fine enemy you have made for Stanora, Conor!" Walter roared.

"He is loose in the manner of choosing allies," Ulrich

said. "But I am not. Roger will not betray me and not with the blood of a child."

"He *is* your son! You lie to protect him!" Conor said, his throat gone hoarse with fear and doubt.

"Protect him? How does my speaking the truth protect him?" Ulrich asked, pressing his blade against the older man's throat. Conor's pulse jumped as he tried to slip from beneath the press of steel, but there was no escape from Ulrich's judgment. "Give me leave to kill him," he pleaded with Walter.

It was clear that Walter wanted to, yet Conor was blood kin and he could not betray him unto death.

"I cannot."

"Then do not," Ulrich said, swinging his blade sharply up with the words and slicing Conor's head nearly off his body. He fell in a bloody mass, his head hanging on by the bony ridge of his spine. Ulrich knew he had lost all by his act. He did not care. He had killed the very man King Henry had sent him to find. He had betrayed his lord by defying Walter's will. He had lost St. Ives.

But he would not lose Juliane. All was cast down for the hope of having her. All was lost to save her, and it was sound bargaining. She was a woman worth having. She was a woman who merited the price of a life, a holding, a king's anger. For Juliane he would risk all, lose all. For Juliane he would abandon everything but the need to have her for his own.

"You have lost St. Ives by that," Walter said when the shock of seeing his uncle killed before his eyes had cleared.

Ulrich stood upon the stones, the blood from his kill

dripping upon them, splattering all about him with sticky blood. He looked up at Walter, his blue eyes alight with a fire of passion and raw fierceness, like the eyes of a wolf before he sinks his mouth into the warm blood of a kill.

"Keep it, then," he said, turning from Walter with the swiftness of a hungry hunter. "'Tis Juliane I will not lose."

Chapter Twenty-two

Help did not come.

Ulrich did not come.

Thrust by thrust, Nicholas claimed his prize.

He lay between her legs, grunting like a boar, bruising her with his force and with his cold and battering seduction. Yet she endured. He rammed his way into her, stretching her wide, holding her knees up with his hands, ignoring her as she pushed against his shoulders.

He did not release her. Nay, he kept defeating her with every thrust, cold and deep and hard within her womb, casting her into ice more surely than any legend could.

Ulrich did not come.

Her legend was shattered. The very reason she had run from Ulrich and from marriage had been nullified upon the straw of an abandoned shed. She had refused Ulrich for no cause now. Nicholas and all the world would know the depth of her lie. She had lost Ulrich, and it was hard losing.

Even if he came, he would not want her now.

No man would want her now. The legend of Juliane was lost. Nicholas, far from falling, had risen hard and pulsing when he had seen her spread before him in the hay like a royal banquet.

Her legend was made a lie.

Her legend had ever been a lie.

"You are mine now," Nicholas said, his voice a rasping breath against her ear.

He had stopped his grinding thrusts into her. God be praised for even small mercies. She was covered in bruises, bleeding from the mouth, and her back felt broken into eight small pieces. Of her tears, seeping out in gentle drops from the corners of her eyes, she would not think. She would not honor them with acknowledgment.

She had been taken, beaten. She could not bear a life of this. Nay, she would not go to that without a fight. One more fight. One more, if she could summon the courage. There was still a fight left in her, some small remnant of heart and will that kept her chin up and her gaze frosty when her very bones shouted that she was lost. Lost and unfound. Lost and unsought.

Ulrich had not come.

That loss, that pain, was almost worse than the stinging ache that bled throughout her womb. She had been used hard. Ulrich would not want her now, even if he came. But he had not.

Walter would not object. Her future was secured in the hands of a man of means and title. What else mattered in the workings of this world? A marriage was made, the contracts could come later. None cared that her life would be bound by misery with Nicholas in her bed.

None cared and none came.

Tears flooded up, closing off her throat and blinding her eyes. Nay, nay, that was no way to face a final battle. She knew what form the fight would take. For this very reason she had been bound to refuse all men, for if she wed, if she was taken upon the marriage bed, then a man might know the lie that had shaped the life of Juliane.

As now Nicholas knew.

Upon that point, she would need to skewer Nicholas. This would be her final battle against a man and his pride. Kill her he might well do, only let her, please, God, let her fight stoutly and with honor. Let her name stand for more than deceit.

"You are mine," he said, his dark eyes glowing with conquest and the joy of victory.

"Am I?" she said, squirming beneath him, wanting the protection of her skirts about her.

He grabbed her fist and crushed it in his hand. She flinched but did not cry out. She had learned to live with pain since knowing Nicholas.

"Why fight on?" he said, releasing her hand slowly as he slipped from her, leaving her wet and sticky and smelling of him. She pushed her skirts down, masking the smell. "You belong to me. No man will have you now."

"I am still married to Ulrich, unless you have forgot," she said, trying to squeeze out from under him, wanting him away from her.

"I have not forgot, but that is legal wrangling, soon made right when you are fat with my child in you."

"Such poetry," she said, spitting into the hay and leaving a bloody mark.

Nicholas did not seem to hear her. He was looking at his cock. And now the game began in earnest.

"Where is your blood? Where is the mark that I have taken you and been your first?"

"Look upon my face," she said, slowly standing. Every joint ached. "You will see blood enough."

He grabbed her by the back of her hair and pulled her face down to his cock. "Look! There is no stain upon me. You were no virgin!"

"Did I ever say I was?" she asked, looking up at him from her forced obeisance.

He shoved her then with a roar of frustration, and she fell back against the wall, stumbling on a buried rake. A poor weapon against a knight, yet it might slow her death. She would not be taken without some blood of his to mark her fight.

The high, long cry of a hawk came from the sky, piercing and wild, and her soul lifted to hear it. She knew that cry. 'Twas Morgause.

And then the sound of horses, and the answering call of Nicholas's mount, and Juliane knew she was not as lost as she had been.

Nicholas heard the same and grabbed up his sword. He would have grabbed Juliane to him, but she scrambled back, tripping on the hidden rake again and snatching it up to hold him off.

Ulrich had come.

"Say nothing," Nicholas whispered to her as he looked between the wide cracks in the planking.

Say nothing? She would scream out her need though he kill her for it. Ulrich had come. He had come after all.

"Stanora," she called out through cracked lips. "Mercy and aid. Stanora, to me."

Her eyes stayed on Nicholas as she said it, knowing he would take some action against her if he could. He moved toward her with speed and put his hand over her mouth and much of her nose. She could not breathe and began to fight and gag for air.

"Mercy is upon you," she heard over the roaring in her ears. Nicholas's hand dropped away from her to grab up his sword.

Ulrich stood in the low doorway, filling it. Behind him stood Edward, but her eyes were all for Ulrich. He had come.

He had come too late.

"You have used my wife most hard," Ulrich said softly, his eyes a flame of vengeance that warmed her. She began to shake, her teeth to chatter. "You will die for it," he said and licked his lips in predatory hunger.

"I used her as she demanded," Nicholas said, holding his sword at the ready. "I took her and made her mine. She will be my wife now, if I still choose to keep her. She was no virgin. She had known a man before me, making a lie of her legend."

Ulrich looked at her, and, trembling in relief and fear, she tried to return his look, but gave way before the questions in his eyes. She could not bear to watch as realization sparked to life. She had been no virgin. Nicholas had no cause to lie. Where, then, the lie?

Where else but between Juliane's thighs and upon Juliane's lips?

Ulrich had not touched her. She was legendary for not having been touched. Yet here was Nicholas, proudly crowing of his rape and declaring her to have been used before he fought his way into her. What was Ulrich to think?

What could he think?

That she had known a man before, before Ulrich and before Nicholas.

And what was it but the truth?

All she ever had to offer a man was a lie with the gloss of legend to cover it.

Did Ulrich see that now? Did Ulrich see the lady behind the false legend she had made for herself? A legend built solidly upon a lie, a legend to give her power and renown. A lie to set her free. A lie to please her father. A lie that trapped her within a legend she had come to hate.

The legend of Juliane. Without it, she would have been like any other woman, a pawn in the game of power with no power of her own. Without it, she was nothing. With it, she could win at every game. So her father had promised her, and so it had been.

Did Ulrich see that now? Broken, her beauty beaten into bruises, she was defenseless. Would he let her fall to Nicholas? Did he want her now that her legend was a wisp of nothing churned into the mud?

Ulrich searched her eyes, and she could not shelter herself from the blazing heat of his look. In truth, she did not want to. Let him see her as she was in truth. Let him cast aside the legend built around her name and see only Juliane. The Juliane she had been before the lie of legend.

He saw the lie of legend, saw what it was she had done, though why she had done it he could not answer.

That first marriage had been true. It had not broken upon her chill. She had not defeated a man with ice and frost, beating back his seduction with her cold blue eyes. She was a woman, and if a man wanted to find his way into her, he would find his way. She had no power beyond her tears to stop him, and few men were stopped by tears when lust was hard upon them.

So it had been with him when he had taken gentle, trusting Mariam.

He had not beaten her, not with his fists as Nicholas had done to his golden Juliane, but he had beaten against her chastity with words of soft seduction, urging her to give him what he wanted, what every man wanted of every woman. And she had. With her blushes and shy smiles, her ragged breath heated by desire, her eyes smoldering in passion and in need, he had found his way into her, her virginity his prize.

He'd had no intention of hurting her. It had been a game played out upon a wager. A game of seduction, and for his prize in prizing from her that which could never be replaced, he had won himself a dagger most fine.

Fine winning. Aye, he had been well received by his fellow knights with much laughter and drinking as they celebrated his victory over a naive girl. Aye, such chivalry, such honor among brothers in arms. Just a game, it was. Just a simple wager which he, to add luster to his legend, had to win. And so he had.

And so Mariam, dark of hair and eye, living with her family on the Street of the Tent Makers in Antioch, had swelled with child. His child. His son had been born and cast to him, and Mariam put to death for so dishonoring her Saracen kin.

Put to death.

Killed in final payment of a drunken wager.

Yet his name, his legend for seduction, had risen to the stars. Legends were ever built upon pain and deceit. It was even so with Juliane.

Juliane. Nicholas had beaten his way into her. There was no other way into her; Ulrich understood that now. For her legend would be broken upon the man who found his way inside her.

Let legends die; 'twas Juliane who mattered. He would not cast her away. She was more to him than a name, more to him than land, more to him even than life. She was Juliane, and he wanted nothing more.

"Known a man before? And am I not the man?" Ulrich said, staring hard at her. "Why else would her father have gifted me with such a prize? I bring nothing to her, yet she took me in and gave me all. And I made her mine. For she is mine," he said softly, still holding her gaze within his own, "and ever will be."

"*You* took her? You stole her virginity?" Nicholas asked, his eyes bulging.

"Nay, you fool," Juliane said, still locked in Ulrich's gaze. "I gave it to him. He is the man who melted ice. Ulrich is the one who broke the legend of Juliane le Gel. Let the world know it."

They smiled at each other at this telling of the last lie, the lie that would end the game. For them, there was no more need of lies.

"Yet first, a killing," Ulrich said with a feral smile, turning to face Nicholas.

And with the words, he struck. Nicholas, ready, met his blow, steel ringing against steel as the sun fled the sky.

The dusk was long and warm, the sun throwing up rosy banners of light like trails of blood.

She pressed herself against the wooden walls and watched them fight. Ulrich was quick and cautious, like a wolf eyeing a buck. The wolf had teeth, the buck antlers to be wary of, yet it was the wolf hunting the buck. Nicholas was being hunted. There was no other way to describe it. Recognizing that fact, Nicholas began to panic, just as the buck will panic when set upon by snarling wolves. Edward slid into the shed and stood in front of her, his shield up to protect them both. He said no word, but by his look, he was waiting for the wolf to bring down his prey.

With a baring of his teeth, Ulrich struck a slicing blow across Nicholas's midriff, exposing muscle and blood and the pale yellow ripple of shielding fat. Nicholas fell back a step, his hand to his belly, his eyes narrowed in bewildered surprise.

"You fight? You, who are all of smiles?" he said.

"It does not take frowning to kill a man," Ulrich said, holding his sword up and ready, as Nicholas held his. "I like to kill. It brings me pleasure. Especially now. With you," he said softly.

"I am not yet killed. Nor will be," Nicholas said, lurching forward.

Nicholas was a fair hand with a blade and strong, even with a wound to distract him, yet Ulrich was quicker and more cunning, waiting for Nicholas to bleed away more and more of his strength while he kept his careful distance. Nicholas, with time running out for him and Ulrich yet unmarked, lunged in for a blow that made Juliane gasp and close her eyes, sure that Ulrich would be cleaved in twain. But when she opened them, they battled on, Ulrich unharmed, his blue eyes steadily upon his prey, his nerve unshattered. Nicholas had expended much in that last lunge and faltered now in his steps.

It was enough. Ulrich sliced again, a handbreadth higher upon Nicholas's chest, and laid open the flesh to the cage of bone that entrapped his heart. Nicholas looked down at his dual wounds. Fatal if not tended right soon.

Fatal, then, for none here would aid him.

"Now you are killed," Ulrich said.

"I am not," Nicholas said, falling to his knees and dropping his sword, his hands clasping and trying to hold himself together, to repair what was past repair.

"You are," Ulrich said with a snarl.

"Then finish it," Nicholas said, holding his head up for the blow as one knight of valor to another, demanding a quick end.

"I have finished it," Ulrich said. "My part of it. It is my will that you bleed out your life in this dark hole to which you dragged my wife. That you lie beaten, bleeding, dying, and knowing it. That you know you can do nothing to stop it. That you suffer the fate you pressed on her. That you die without hope, without help, without—"

"Enough, Ulrich," Juliane said, laying a hand upon his arm. He was shaking as much as she. "Enough. It is enough."

"Not enough," he murmured, touching her face, skimming over her bruises with a fingertip dipped in tenderness. "Never enough."

"At least have me shriven," Nicholas said, interrupting them. "Have me buried with my father's people."

"You shall be attended," Ulrich said, not looking at him. "Would you kill him, Juliane? I give him to you."

Her heart stopped to match her breathing. Kill him? Kill Nicholas? To be given his living body upon which to feed her revenge?

A tempting thought, a thought which hovered. A chance to hurt as she had been hurt. A chance to kill.

'Twas not a new thought. She had dreamed of it while he pummeled her and forced her legs apart. Death would have been most sweetly visited upon Nicholas then. But now? When cold reason ruled more fiercely than the hot need to survive?

To kill a man?

Could she do it?

Should she do it?

"I do not know if I can," she said.

"You would let me die by a woman's hand?" Nicholas gasped out, his hands clasping what could not be contained. The dirt around him was muddy with blood. He would die like an animal.

"She has earned this chance at you and I am honored to give it to her." Ulrich said, looking down at Nicholas. "Take his life, Juliane. Let justice come from your hand."

She could almost, almost love him, this man who made death a gift, who thought to give her a power that women were denied. This man, this Ulrich. She could almost, almost love him.

And so she did.

Why had all been of winning and losing in her mind? Why had she not seen that loving was the greatest gain of all, though hearts were lost as souls were merged into a oneness that defied cold logic? Her legend was lost, proved a lie, yet Ulrich stood tall beneath the falling of it, the broken truth not enough to make him turn from her.

When she had forged her bargain with her father, she had not known that there was no freedom within a lie. She had believed him when he told her of the joy of power, the luster of legend, the prize of freedom. But she had not been free. Nay, she had been required to play and play again within the bounds of her legend, held there by the lie of cold invincibility. Held off from warmth and passion and easy laughter, held hard to the illusion of her legend, forced to play a part that no longer fit her heart.

Her only power had been in denial and scorn. 'Twas no power that had any merit. She knew that now, long years past the moment of decision.

"Juliane?" Ulrich said, offering his dagger. "Either you kill him or we leave him here to die."

"Kill me, then," Nicholas said, looking up at her. "Do not leave me so. Have the mercy to kill me if he will not. To die so, to inch toward death, my body rotting before my soul has flown . . . do not leave me to that, no matter your vengeance."

"For mercy, then, and not for vengeance," she said, taking the dagger.

For mercy it would be, and so she would be quick, no doubt or delay to prolong it. Crouching down upon the bloody mud, she sliced his throat. He did not hinder her. This was quick death and painless, and he wanted it. A long slide of the dagger, the skin peeling back, red and torn, and then his life draining from him as his soul broke free of earth.

So it was that Nicholas of Nottingham met his end. So it was that Juliane sent him into eternity.

* * *

Ulrich set her carefully upon her horse and took the reins and led her out of that darkened yard where her life had crumbled under another man's foot. With Ulrich nigh and the threat of Nicholas behind her, she felt herself fading into exhaustion and despair. There was no one left to fight and no one to be strong for, and so the tears that had teased her eyes came surging forth from deep within her heart and bled down her cheeks and into her silently crying mouth.

She wept.

She wept and could not find the will to stop.

And then her horse stopped and Ulrich's arms were about her, lifting her down, holding her up, embracing, supporting, comforting. And still she wept. And wept. Too weak to hold him. Too weak to speak. Too weak to fight even once more.

"Forgive me, Juliane," he said. "Pray, forgive."

"I thought you would not come, yet all I could do was pray that you would come," she said through teary hiccups.

"I came as soon as I could learn from Conor where you had been taken. Ever will I come for you. Ever will I protect you. But pray forgive me, Juliane," he said in a rush of words blended with kisses upon her hair. "I was too slow and I was too loose in my grip on you. I should have protected you better. It is no worthy man who lets his wife be taken from beneath his hand."

"Wait," she said, shaking her head against his chest. "Wait, I cannot . . . Conor? Conor was in this?"

"Aye, and he is killed for it."

"By your hand?"

"Aye. And I have lost St. Ives in the killing."

"Lost St. Ives? We have lost St. Ives?" she said, shaking her head clear of foggy exhaustion and trying to make sense of this. "How? This is too much telling. I cannot follow it."

Ulrich sighed and pressed her head back onto his chest, hiding her from all the world and the growing dark and sounds of night.

"Know this only for now. I came for you, Juliane. I will always and ever come for you."

"But St. Ives lost," she said, breathing in the scent of him. He smelled like musk and the night itself, wild and dark. "You came for me with St. Ives already lost?"

"I lost St. Ives, yet I grieve not," he said, rubbing his hands down the length of her back to bring her ease. "By killing Conor without Walter's sanction, I lost the right to St. Ives for defying my liege lord. I did not care. I *do* not care. In my heart all that signified was you, and William, for he was taken too, to split my search and weaken my will to fight."

"William? Why William?" she asked, her voice sleepy.

She could not keep her eyes open and her joints felt like melting tallow. Yet there was something she should note about St. Ives. If only she could think clearly. But she could not. All she wanted was to tumble into Ulrich and into sleep.

He had come for her, and there was no St. Ives to propel him.

"Conor thought William was my son."

"William? He is no son of yours."

"Think you not? Why not?"

"He is nothing like you."

"Nay? I think him most handsome, most agreeable, and most able. For a boy of eight."

"Aye," she said, smiling against the wool of his tunic. "Nothing like you."

"Come, then," he said, and she could hear the smile in his voice. "You are in your strength now. I take you to Thorney Abbey."

"I want to go home," she said, her voice weak and tremulous. Her strength was gone from her, lost, as all was lost. "And what of my legend and the lie that was its seed? Does it not—"

"To Thorney Abbey, where all questions and all fears will wait until you are yourself again."

"I am myself," she grumbled, feeling nothing like herself at all. She wept on, her tears flowing like salt rain, in direct opposition to her will. She could not stop.

"If you are Juliane, then I am Lunete," he said with a laugh that seemed to light her up inside, as if all the darkness of the day had not passed over her and through her. As if she was as she had been. As if there had been no Nicholas. "Come to the abbey. I will attend," he said lightly and then, with a note of heavy sorrow, he said, "You are safe now, Juliane. I will not leave you."

And on that promise, she tumbled softly into sleep.

Chapter Twenty-three

She awoke in an abbey bed. She knew it instantly by its hardness and lack of good blankets. And then knew with the next thought that she was safe. She snuggled fitfully under the thin blanket and sighed. Safe. Of Nicholas she had many thoughts, many dark memories, but of fear she was free. Nicholas was dead.

Ulrich came in with Morgause on his arm.

"Ah, you awaken," he said.

"I have," she said, sitting up and pushing her hair back from her face, wincing at a tender bruise upon her cheek. "He left his mark, did he not?"

"Only if you allow it," Ulrich said, sitting on a stool at her side. "All warriors bear their scars and bruises. You are in good company," he said softly, taking her hand in his.

"You are very tender," she said, unable to look at him. "I do not think most men would be so, in such a time, for such a cause."

Ulrich chuckled and shook his head. "You are most stubborn, not to see that I am unlike any other man you have ever known."

"Nay," she said, smiling with him, and then her smile fell from her, "I am not stubborn. 'Tis so. You are not like anyone." And then she whispered, dropping her gaze to her knees, "I do not know what to say to you of a sudden. I am ashamed."

"You deserve no shame," he said. "Nicholas did all—"

"Nay," she interrupted. "Nay, let me speak of it, and if it breaks all bonds between us, then let them break, only let me speak. I have hidden for so long. I would not hide from you."

"These bonds will not break," he whispered, running his hand down her arm and over her fingers. "Speak, so that I may prove it upon my honor."

"You know the legend was a lie," she said, looking at his hand upon hers.

"Was it?" he said softly. "The legend spoke of Juliane, her beauty golden and hot, her manner the chill of frost. Men came to her, bewitched, and she cast them down from her, broken upon their pride. Where is the lie in that?"

"Let us not play at this," she said, pulling her hand from his, crossing her arms over her chest. She had slept in her clothes. Why had he not disrobed her? "I am trying to tell you something; I want you to understand . . . what I do not understand myself," she said, shaking her head in confusion. "I do not know how I came to this."

"You lived within a lie, Juliane," he said. "Truth is the door to freedom from the shackles of deceit. Tell your truths, and I will tell you mine."

"Truth, then," she said, sitting up straight, bracing herself. "I did not want that first marriage. When a way of escape was opened to me, I took it."

"And who opened the way to you?" he asked, holding her gaze, blue eyes meeting blue.

"Maud, I think," she said, remembering. "She lived a life of freedom from the bonds of marriage. Why not I? And it was so simple," she said, smiling in fresh pain, "so simple. All we had to do was lie, a small lie to set myself free."

"What of your father? Did he take no part in setting this in motion?"

"Nay," she said, frowning, "he had his part. He knew. He was not pleased with the betrothal either."

"There are other ways to break a betrothal."

"True, yet," she said, her brow furrowed as she struggled to remember, "yet this way seemed good to him. It gave me power, did it not? A name. A legend."

"A legend you guarded very well," he said.

"And could not let fall because all would have fallen with it," she said, touching his hand again, looking into his eyes. "So I had to refuse all who came to test The Frost."

"For if a man found his way past your frost, then all lies would be revealed," he finished, holding her hand in his.

"You understand," she breathed. "Can you forgive? I am not the woman you came to find."

"I came to test a legend, which I did," he said. "Of the woman behind that legend . . ."

"What?" she asked, leaning forward, pulling her hand from his and laying it upon his face. "Without St. Ives, am I cast off?"

He shook his head and took her hand in his and kissed the palm.

"I made that choice when I killed Conor, and I will not repent of it all the days of my life. Nay, Juliane, think not that. Think not that I would ever turn from you. I know how legends gather life; I have a legend of my own, do I not?" He grinned, but his grin fell from him like autumn leaves in an icy wind. "I have a legend for seduction, and in feeding it, I have gained a son and killed his mother. I know the dust from which legends form."

"Never will I believe that Ulrich of the Sweet Mouth would kill a woman, certainly not the mother of his child. Women die in childbed every day. 'Tis not your—"

"Hold, Juliane," he said, rising from his stool, removing himself from her touch. "You have it wrong. Let me tell it as it is. Judge you if I am a man deserving of his 'legend.' She was young and innocent, and for the price of a wager, I took her body and planted my seed within her. *For a wager,*" he spat out in disgust. "And when the child was born, her parents had her stoned to death, the price for chastity lost in that realm. And so my legend stood the taller. Had I not taken the untakable? Had I not proved my worth by such a deed? Am I not a man?"

She had risen from her bed and crossed to where he stood. He faced her, his beautiful eyes filled with rage and shame and emptiness. She did not touch him, but stood to face him, woman to man, warrior to warrior, legend to legend.

"You think that by your wagering you brought Nicholas to me? That you have been the cause of . . . all of *this*?" she said, sweeping her arms to encompass the chamber, and then wincing. Her ribs were on fire with pain.

"Juliane," he answered her. "I *am* Nicholas."

She understood him not at all.

"Not true," she said, taking him by the arms, holding him fast for her scolding, as if all could be made right with words.

"Not true?" he snapped. "Nicholas took you to take St. Ives. He took you, his body to yours, to win you and the riches of your land. Have I not done the same? Was it not in my thoughts to use you so? I *am* the same!"

"You are not," she said softly. "You would not have forced yourself upon me."

He looked down at her, at her golden softness, at the purple bruising on her cheek, at the dried blood upon her lips, and marveled at her naive heart. He looked at her, at the legendary Juliane who glowed like a promise of dawn, at the woman who inspired song and upon whom a legend had been built.

He had not come to Stanora to find love, yet he had been found by it, drawn in and held fast.

But he would not lie to her. There had been enough of lies.

"Would I not?" he said. "Are you so certain, then, for I am not. Would I not have taken you by force, by guile, by false charm, to seal the bonds of our vow? Would I not have taken you before the eyes of others, shaming you to claim you, having you by any means? Would I not have done anything to get St. Ives?"

"Yet you lost St. Ives for my sake," she said, her eyes flooding with tears. "Does that not prove what you would or would not do? 'Tis proof enough for me."

"But not for me. I know my heart," he said, turning from her.

"And think the worst," she said, grabbing his arm and forcing him to face her. "Praise God we are not judged for what we *might* do, but for what we have done. That is enough to bear, is it not? St. Ives is gone, but you are here. What more is there?" she said, a single tear breaking free to slide over her swollen cheek and past her battered mouth.

"Lady," he said, tearing his heart from out of her hands, "what has changed? Nothing."

"*All* has changed. The legend is broken and I with it, and I care not. My only care is for you. You love me, is that not so?"

"I love you," he whispered. "That is so, yet it can change nothing. Can you not see it, Juliane? Your legend breaks, and your father's honor upon it, only if we tell the tale of its breaking. St. Ives is lost to us both, back in Walter's keeping. Where should we live? I am a knight errant; I roam the earth, circling it, circling, ever searching for a place to pledge myself, a hall in which to rest, a lord whom I may serve. What place for you in that? A knight without land cannot take a wife. You know it," he said, his voice breaking as he turned from her face, once so hopeful and now filled with grief. "This has ever been so. We cannot change the ordering of the world."

"But we are married, our bodies and our lives conjoined," she said, coming to stand before him, the small wind hole at her back, her golden hair lit to fire by the morning light. "'Tis done and cannot be undone."

"Cannot be undone?" He smiled sadly. "You know better than any how false those words are. Our marriage is easily broken upon this point: We have not consummated."

"But we will. Even now, here is the bed. I am willing," she said, taking his hand.

"But I am not," he said stiffly. "I will not lead you by my passion into a life that is no life. Can you live upon the back of a horse, by the scant heat of a woodland fire in a pelting rain or by the grace of some small lord to sleep upon the rushes of his hall? Answer not that you would, for I would not allow it."

"We are married still. 'Tis a legal union," she said, her own anger rising.

"Without the consummation it is not," he returned. "And with Juliane as bride, will any man doubt that I could not pierce her? Your legend will secure your freedom, lady, as it ever has. Nay, stand off, Juliane. I have won this battle. This marriage will not last out the day. I will free you. I will see you safe within Stanora's arms."

"But not within your own," she said tightly.

"Not for all the world, and that is all I have—all the world in which to roam and no small place to lay my head," he said, stepping to the door, eager to leave her and the angry entreaty of her eyes. "We depart when you have your strength. I will ride with you as far as Stanora."

"I have my strength now," she said. "Let us depart within the hour."

He nodded in acquiescence and left softly, his booted feet marking his disappearance from her life by shallow echoes down the long, stone abbey gallery.

She had her strength well enough, enough to fight him, though she could not see how. Yet. But there was a niggling in her thoughts, trying for coherence and failing, whispering that there was some flaw in his reasoning.

She would find it.

Some parts of her legend were well founded in truth. Her skill and appetite for victory were two of them.

They arrived in Stanora early in the evening, just as the sun melted beyond the trees. Her father was dead. She knew it the moment they passed through the gates and into the bailey.

It was a blessing. He had suffered, hating his weakness, and now he was free of it. He was also free from harm, his honor safely stored in heaven when the news of her lie became known. And it would become known. She would not let Ulrich ride from her life as simply as he seemed to think. Nay, there was fight in her and the hunger to win. That Ulrich was the prize only made the game more vital.

She would not lose him.

She loved him. What more was there?

Walter met them at the stables, his expression going grim and hard when he caught sight of her face.

"Who did this to you?" he asked.

"Who do you think?" she snapped, her temper torn past repairing.

Walter, all of eighteen years and little acquainted with thinking, thought hard and looked at Ulrich.

"She is marked by Conor's pawn. I would not use her so," Ulrich said, coming to Juliane's side to help her dismount. An embarrassment she could not avoid; her body was a mass of aches and sharp pains. She was certain that if she jumped down off her horse, her legs would shatter.

"Then Nicholas is dead?" Walter said.

"Aye," she said, turning from the warmth of Ulrich's arms to face Walter. "Killed by my hand. His body taken by the brothers at Thorney. They will see him to Nottingham in due time."

"By *your* hand?" Walter said. "Then he paid dear for his hard hand with you. He did not succeed in Conor's quest, then?"

Juliane looked at Ulrich while he looked upon the ground at Walter's feet, his silence an invitation for her to speak. Would she lie? Would she say that Nicholas had not touched her? Would she keep the legend alive and herself safe within it?

There was no safety in a lie, and she tired of this legend that kept her solitary. She would not live a lie again.

"He beat his way into me, if that is what you are asking," she said, looking at Ulrich as she said it. "The Frost has fallen, the legend of her broken."

"The legend of le Gel lives," Ulrich said, returning her look with hard purpose. "The bruises that she wears bear the marks of her battle against the passion of a man who failed in his pursuit of her. He beat her for his failure. That is all. She did not fall. She never shall."

"I will not tumble into deceit again," she said. "Would you push me to it, my lord? You, who knows as well as I the pain of living within the shadow of legend? I *did* fall to Nicholas. He *did* fight his hard way into me."

"A rare stand," Walter said into the hot and steady battle of their words. "A man who declares a wife untouched, and a woman who declares herself most defiled. What does Edward have to say?"

Both Ulrich and Juliane looked to Edward, their bodies stilled as they awaited his response.

"I will say what I know for truth and what cannot be disputed: Nicholas is dead," Edward answered.

"True," Walter said. "There is no turning from that. You know of Conor's death and by whose hand?" he asked Juliane.

"Aye, and 'twas well done. You see what Nicholas, by Conor's whim, has done to me," she said. "Why did you rob my lord and husband of St. Ives for it? 'Twas poorly done and shows little love for me."

"There is much you do not understand of matters between Conor and Philip," Walter said stiffly, "but what you certainly must concede is that I cannot endorse a killing between my sister's husband and my uncle. That way I will not follow, breaking all tradition within Stanora by the doing. All feuds must die."

"My lord," Ulrich said over Juliane's gathered breath, cutting her off before she could begin to scour her brother with her tongue, "I understand your reasoning and do not argue with it. I only add one thought: I am not Juliane's husband, by the very terms of the contract. There has been no consummation. And there will be none," he said for her ears, yet again.

By Saint Basilissa, he was stubborn. But she could match him in this, as in all else.

Yet his words struck some chord, some chime of clarity and resonance. What had he said? "By the very terms of the contract"?

"Brother," she said with a grinning foretaste of victory. Ulrich, knowing her so well, frowned to see her so. "My husband has said it. The contract terms have *not* been met. By my father's will, this marriage between us, though endorsed by God through his blessed priest and though the contracts be signed and sealed, this marriage is not binding until our union is consummated in the public eye."

"Aye?" Walter asked. Ulrich still frowned.

"Well, then, how could Ulrich have lost St. Ives by your word and will? He may have sworn fealty to you, yet his vows, by the very contract they rest upon, will not be in force until he takes possession of *me*. St. Ives will not become his until *I* am his. You could not take from him what was still resting in your hand."

Now even Walter frowned. Ulrich was past frowning; he looked ready to kill her for her cleverness. Edward, though, he smiled full enough and nodded his appreciation.

"This makes strange sense to me," Walter said.

"And why should it not?" she said. "I but repeat the terms of the contract. Did you think I would forget such a detail as a bedding before the eyes of many?"

"I will not bed you," Ulrich said. "We have agreed on this."

"I agreed to nothing," she said. "Not even the terms of the contract, yet I play within its bounds. Can you not match me?" she taunted, her smile sharp as a blade.

"You turn this into wagering?" he snarled. "After what we have shared, one to another?"

"Nay," she said, softening her smile, "no wager. A simple challenge, my lord. I *will* bed you, making the contract complete."

Ulrich surged toward her, his face a brand of anguish and anger. She held her ground. Of all men, this was the one she trusted. Never would he hurt her. By the saints, he was determined not even to bed her.

"Juliane," he hissed, his face hard above hers, his voice lowered, though she was certain Walter and Edward and even the stable grooms heard him most well. This would make fine telling by some fire some day. "In order for the contract to be fulfilled, you must be pierced before many eyes. I will not subject you to that. You have endured enough."

"I will endure worse if you leave me," she said. "Can you not see that? Do you see nothing beyond your need to protect me? I need no protection from you, Ulrich. I want none."

"But this public bedding," he said, dropping his gaze, shaking his head. "'Tis too much. I swore when I saw you, when I saw what Nicholas had done to you, I swore that I would take a higher path. I will not use you so. I will not take a woman for what I can gain. There is no honor in it, and too often my choices have been empty of honor."

"This was not your choice," she said, laying her hands upon his hair, feeling the shape of his scalp with her fingertips. "I do not hold you responsible for it. Let us only do this thing and all is behind us."

"I will not," he said. "'Tis not for me I say it, but for you. I do not think you know how bruising this will be. There must be no more bruises for Juliane."

"And so you leave me? Is that to be a mercy upon me?"

"I give you what mercy I can. I can do no more."

War, then. He would not see reason. He thought her too fragile, too frail to see it done. With one last act he could cure all, yet he turned from it, thinking to spare her. She was stronger than he knew. It was only that she could not and would not live without him. Well, if it be war between them, then she would win it.

"You can do no more," she repeated, releasing him, stepping away from his scent and his heat, preparing herself for battle. "Then stand fast, my lord. I shall do all. I shall take *you* and put my mark upon you."

"What say you?" Walter said.

"I said that I would take Ulrich, his body into mine, sealing all vows, all contracts, and all bargains."

"Lady," Ulrich snarled, "you will *not.*"

"My lord," she said with a pleasant and determined smile, "I *will.*"

"You cannot see this done. 'Tis not possible. I am unwilling. I will not succumb to you."

Juliane could not stop herself. She laughed.

"Oh, I think we both know that you will. I will have my way with you, my lord. Adjust yourself to it. Will you or nil you, you shall be mine."

It was then that Edward joined her in laughter.

Chapter Twenty-four

Walter, by a sharp look, kept everyone at bay. They walked alone through the bailey and the tower gate, up the broad steps, and into the wide and welcoming hall. Ulrich and Juliane walked side by side, with Walter just behind them. A fitting entrance for two combatants. Maud, Avice, Christine, Marguerite, and pale Lunete stood upon the gallery, their bodies pressed to the rail, watching. Wondering. Waiting.

"I will not do this," Ulrich said to her in an undertone.

"You must. It is in the terms of the contract. You signed it, sealing us both into this effort," she whispered. "Do not fear. I will not hurt you."

He growled like a wolf beyond the reach of fire, hidden in the dark, for the hall was dark now, lit only by the central fire which burned low on such a hot night as this. The torches had not yet been lit. All was shadow in twilight, his blue eyes burning like twin lights of cold flame in impotent anger.

She felt like laughing. This was a new game to her, and yet she knew that she would win it.

"You mock me," he breathed harshly. "Unwise, lady. You do not know what I may do. You have never battled in this game before. Have a care lest you be burned."

"Burned by you?" she said, raising her voice as they climbed the stair to the gallery, twisting in the dark as they wound upward into stone. "I welcome it. Do your worst, my lord. I shall not be burned." And then she stopped and Ulrich bumped against her back, his hands coming forward to rest upon her waist and hips, seeking balance and steeling her against a backward fall. "Unless it be the burning of lust," she said, loud enough for Walter at Ulrich's back to hear. "Did not Saint Paul say it best? ' 'Tis better to marry than to burn.' Let us burn together."

"Let us not burn at all," he said, pushing her from under his hands.

She laughed then, a long, low, seductive laugh meant to mock and entice.

"Would you have lies of me? Have not we two always and only burned together? Have you not always risen high for me? What may be done to cast you down? I tried, my lord; I tried most diligently to make you fall. Yet you did not. Think you that you can fall now, when I am so very set to make you rise, hot and hard and pulsing for the taste of me?"

"God above," he growled. "Cease!"

"That I will not do," she said with a smile as they left the stair. "Now, Brother, where shall this consummation occur? And who shall be our witnesses?"

"I, for one," Walter said. "I trust no eyes but my own in this battle of wills upon the bed furs. Would you name a witness of your own, Ulrich?"

"Aye, I name Edward."

"And I name Avice," she said.

"Avice?" Walter said. "She is too innocent for such things."

"She is to be wed within the month," Juliane answered. "Let her learn now what she will face."

"Only if she will agree to it," Walter said. "Her eyes are too young for such a thing."

"Yet not too young to marry?" Juliane said. "Brother, you must get your thinking ordered aright. Can she be too young to see and yet not too young to perform?"

"Your sharp tongue will earn you a slap from me, Juliane," Walter said as they entered her small chamber. "I would not add to your cuts, but when provoked—"

"You shall do nothing," Ulrich said, his words cast from him like heavy stone. "She is not for you to touch."

Nay, she was all for Ulrich's hand. And now he remembered it. This battle was going most exceedingly well.

Edward and Avice came together, their looks carefully guarded. When Edward agreed to act as witness, Avice quickly echoed her agreement, almost as if they were in a competition of sorts. Most strange.

Also strange was the prospect of seducing Ulrich with three pairs of eyes watching. There were three tall candles in the chamber, pushing all safe shadow to the corners and holding it there with a hot hand.

"It is as I said," Ulrich said to her, the other three in the chamber hearing him easily. "This cannot and should not be done."

"Am I not worth such effort?" she asked, trying to keep her eyes on only him, pushing the sound of breathing and the creak of shifted weight from her. Let there be only Ulrich. Let there be no other.

"I would do anything but shame you, and this is shame upon you, Juliane," he said. "I would cut out my heart and give it to you, but I will not do this. 'Twould be a wound from which there could be no healing."

"I do not want your heart," she said over a tender sigh

from Avice. "I want your life, Ulrich. Nothing else will do. Nothing else will satisfy. Nothing but your life lived out in time with mine. Do not leave me, Ulrich. Take me and make me yours." And when he shook his head in slow refusal, she added, "Then I ask that you do not bump against my bruises when I take you and make you mine. I am very stiff and sore. Be gentle in your fight against me, I pray you."

He stared at her for a moment and then he grinned. He laughed. A great, rolling laugh that drove down all his defenses and made him easy in her company.

She was winning this battle most handily.

"You are managing me well, I think, lady. Too well. I had forgot, looking at your bruised eyes and swollen lip, that you play hard and play only to win."

"I use what weapons I can," she said with a grin. "You are an able adversary."

"I thank you," he said, bowing slightly.

"If you could manage to hurry," Walter said. "I have other things I must see done as lord of Stanora."

"*So* inconsiderate of us, Walter. I will try not to keep you long," Juliane snapped.

"Lady," Ulrich said, taking her hands to lock them gently within his own, "look not at him but at me. I am your adversary in this chamber of stone and light. Do you not see that I cannot do this thing? The echo of the other is heard too loud within my heart."

"That echo lies," she said, looking up into his eyes. "I am none of her, and there will be no wounding in this."

"Juliane, can you not see that from the start I wagered against you because I saw none of her in you. I saw strength and valor and an arrogance that matched my own. I played hard. I did not protect you as a man must protect a maid, she being the weaker vessel, to quote Saint Paul yet again this night. And look what my carelessness has wrought. Again. Another woman taking blows I could have prevented. I will do no more. I will not add this blow upon the others. I would only protect you, and so, I will not take you."

"I am not she," Juliane said softly, pulling him into her embrace, holding him against her heart. "She did not fight for you. I will. I may be bleeding, but *I am not broken.* Fall against me and find the truth of it. The only breaking in me is if you ride away from me, throwing stones against my heart until it can no longer beat. But until my heart is dead," she whispered hoarsely, tears gathering at the edges of her eyes, "I will love you and I will fight for you."

He grabbed her to him and held her hard against his body, his face buried in her hair, his hands lost in the folds of her bliaut. He murmured something, his voice a plea.

"Now," she said into the sweet heat of his scent, "will you lie on the bed or must I knock you down?"

"Lady," he said, leaning away from her, his grin wobbly with emotion, "you speak fierce, yet let us play this out slowly. I will withdraw at a word from you."

"I do not know the word for withdrawal. I am ever forward," she said, leaning up to kiss him on the chin. His scent was like wine to her, heady and spicy sweet.

"Aye, you *are* ever forward," he said, kissing her softly on the mouth. Then he stepped free of her and let his cloak fall to the bed.

He lifted off his tunic next, and she could do nothing but watch, and try to control the hard hammering of her blood. He stood in his mail, glimmering gray and silver against the yellow light. Edward came forward silently from out of the shadows and lifted his mail from him, a heavy piece of work. The mail in his hands, Edward drifted back into shadow, the chink of metal marking his passage.

Ulrich stood in the light of flame wearing gambeson and leggings, the leather marled by sweat and the strong scent of him. His dark hair hung down over his forehead and about his shoulders, curled with moisture, wet with heat. Blue eyes, piercing, molten, studied her. He did not take his eyes from her as piece by piece he stripped himself bare.

She could not look away. Not even when he stood naked before her eyes, his shaft lifted high and hard. Unfallen.

From the watchers she heard Walter's grunt of satisfaction and Avice's gasp.

"Look at me, Juliane," Ulrich said. "Think only of me."

To look at him, at the hard, naked force of him, at the long expanse of muscle, at the jagged scar that marked his left shoulder and the puckered scar that ripped through the muscle of his right thigh, would be no hardship. Yet was not Avice looking also?

A quick shift of her eyes confirmed it. Avice, her eyes wide and hungry, was looking hard.

"Put out the candles," Edward said. "Leave only the smallest light that we may see the marriage done. This chamber is like as to the noonday sun."

"Aye, put them out. I would not have you see my lady," Ulrich said, "nor what she is prepared to endure."

Edward squashed the wicks with the palm of his hand, leaving only a single candle, which flickered fitfully, cast-

ing twisting shadows and contorted light. Ulrich stood
with the candle at his back. He stood in silhouette, a dark
force of animal hunger that reached out to her like the lick
of a wolf before the bite.

"You look fierce of a sudden," she said. "Are you trying to frighten me from this fight, my lord? Nothing in
you can ever cause me fear. I will not run. Not from
you."

"Then I will have my taste of you," he said, his voice
heavy and dark.

He leapt upon her, his fists tangled in her hair, and lowered his mouth to hers.

She met him open-mouthed, ready for his heat and his
rage and his passion, welcoming him into her, devouring
him with her mouth. Losing herself in desire. His tongue
raged within her, licking, snarling, tasting.

She could not get enough of the scent of him, of his
heat and power and hunger.

She wanted this, wanted him, wanted the feel of his
hard body against hers, the scent of his skin mingling
with her own, the hot wet of his mouth on her. Marking
her. Claiming her.

If he thought to make her fear, he had badly misjudged.

He pushed her to the soft edge of the bed, the eyes of
their witnesses behind her, hidden in shadow, though she
could feel them and hear their quickened breathing. She
fell upon the bed, the mattress sinking down under her
weight, her legs hanging over the side. He fell atop her, his
weight a welcome heaviness, his heat branding her. She
slid her arms around his neck and lifted her throat for his
touch. He did not disappoint. His mouth nipped down from
her lips to her jaw to her throat, and there he bit her, a sharp

nip of ownership and dominance that caused a shiver to roll within her belly.

His hand slid up her thigh, dragging the heavy shield of her bliaut and pelisse with it, touching her skin, his hand splayed out to hold her thigh in his open hand, his mouth moving down her throat and over her shoulder, ripping the seams of her clothing with teeth and hand, exposing her right breast to the light. To him. To his mouth. To his hand. To his teeth.

"Are you not afraid?" he breathed against her nipple.

"Only that you may stop," she sighed, closing her eyes to the chamber and her thoughts to those who watched.

"Can you bear this? This public consumption? For I would eat you raw, lady, leaving not even bone. I want to be in you, surrounded by you, a wild devouring that will leave nothing behind but sweat and pants of pleasure. Can you bear it? Tell me now, Juliane. I am losing the will to stop with every beat of your heart."

"Let my heart then speak for me, Ulrich," she said, gasping beneath his hands. "Lose your will and lose your way in me, for I can stand up to anything you may attempt. Have I not always proclaimed it?"

"Then, by your word and upon your strength, this marriage will go forth," he said. "I will see it done so that none may say that Ulrich fell to Juliane."

His fingers stroked between her thighs, those wet folds that throbbed with hot need. She wanted him. She could think only of the need he must quench, the hunger he must fill with his body and his touch and his sweat.

He was covered in a mist of sweat, his back arched above hers, his chest glistening. The scent of sex permeated the very air. She soared upon it, drunk on the smell, ravenous for more.

He plunged his fingers into her and she jerked with pleasure. One finger. Two. Three. She could feel him stretch her, but there was no need. She was wet for him, wide and hungry and pulsing with empty want and desperate need as she had never been for Nicholas.

Nay, an errant thought. There was no space for Nicholas here. Not now. Her thoughts were only for Ulrich.

His manhood, hot and hard, pressed against her, seeking entrance as his mouth opened wide upon her own, his tongue delving deep, learning the taste and shape of her, sucking out her very breath so that their scents were merged, so that she could not breathe.

Nicholas.

Nay, Ulrich.

Cold panic ran through her blood, rushing her heart to frantic beats of terror. She could not do this. Not now. Not yet.

As the tip of him, hot and moist, touched the opening of her womb, all passion died before the living memory of Nicholas and his cold, hard push into her.

She bucked beneath him, Nicholas or Ulrich, it did not matter, she had to throw him off. She had to get free of this. She pulled his hair and kicked out with her feet, breaking free.

Winning free.

"You are free, Juliane," he said, rolling off her, his hand gentle on her trembling thigh. "I release you," he said quietly, his blue eyes moist as he looked down at her.

Released? She did not want to be released from Ulrich.

She wanted Ulrich more than life, yet . . . yet she could not lie beneath him and let him plunge into her.

"I have fallen," Ulrich said to the witnesses. She heard a sniff of tears from Avice. "The marriage is broken. Her legend stands."

"Nay!" Juliane cried, her tears breaking free of her will and tumbling down her cheeks. "I want no legend which is not bound to Ulrich's life. This is not over."

"What is not over, my love?" he said, standing naked and unashamed, his cock falling softly to lie upon his thigh. "I am broken upon your legend, as must all men be. 'Tis foretold, is it not?"

"He cannot win," Avice said softly from her corner. "You defeat them all. 'Tis a fact well known."

"My father believed in you," Walter said. "He misjudged. As did I."

"Nay," Juliane said, lifting herself from the bed and turning to face the witnesses. "I know my legend best of all, and I can break it."

"None can break you, Juliane," Avice said. "Is it not now proved?"

Juliane would not lose him. Not now. Not because of a lie she had been too foolish to refuse. She had thought that being untouchable, unconquerable, would be only to her gain, that she would soar upon the air of freedom with the wings of legend to lift her. All false. She had been untouched in solitary seclusion, living out her legend upon a lonely plain of empty song. As to freedom, she had less than any woman, for all her choices were made before they had been birthed. She was le Gel, destined to drive all men from her, destined to live out her life alone, living only in legend upon a stranger's lips. Living a lie.

But no more.

She loved, and she would not have love die to feed the fires of legend. She loved, and she would fight to keep Ulrich to the end of her days.

"It is not proved," she said, thinking fast and hard. "It is only proved that none shall *take* Juliane le Gel, but she may be *given*, and so I do. I give myself to Ulrich, taking from him what I would take from no other man."

"What is this?" Walter said. "Giving, yet not taking? These are words, when actions are all that are needed now. He must pierce you. That is all. He has not. There is nothing more. The marriage is broken."

"Watch yet and see if I lie," she said. "I will take this man who is bound to me by oaths and vows and I will make him mine. Can I not see it done, my lord?" she said, turning to face Ulrich.

He stood in silence and considered her. He was beautiful beyond the words to tell of it. Tall and broad of shoulder, long of limb, his throat a cord of muscle, and his eyes the blue of fire. And he was hers, if she could only reach out to take him. If he would only help her see it done.

"Lady," he said softly, his eyes smiling, "I know you can. See it done. Prove it upon my body."

"My lord," she said, smiling, a tear breaking free to fall in a silver arc to the floor, "I shall."

The chamber was still of all but the twirl of smoke from the flame. Ulrich came forward, took her in his arms, and held her fast. She slid her hands down his body, soaking up his heat and the hard feel of muscle beneath her hands. Her clothing hung about her loosely, the right shoulder ripped from her in their earlier frenzy. She let it hang, a single breast exposed, but she would bare no other part of herself to this crowd. She would have Ulrich in *her* fashion and her time. She would take him on her terms, and Walter would accept them.

"Why?" he whispered, shielding her from their eyes with the width of his back. "Why fight so hard for this? I would release you, freeing you, at a word."

"Because I want you," she said, holding him by the back of the neck, nuzzling her face into his throat. "Why else?"

"That is all?" he murmured, laying a hand upon her breast in gentle supplication. "You have wanted me from the start."

She chuckled softly. Ulrich ever and always made her laugh. There was none of Nicholas in this. She slipped her hands down along the lean edge of his hips, muscled and covered in a sparse coating of hair, and then up again to cup his buttocks in her hands. He was softly furred, like a wolf.

"As you wanted me," she said, stroking his buttocks and the small of his back.

"And always will," he said, letting her touch him. Letting her find her way with him. Letting her find her power again.

"I shall prove that upon your body, my lord. A new legend shall be born this night," she said, pulling his hips against her own with gentle urging, finding safety in control. He was high and hard again, though his back was to their witnesses. "Will you show them that you are not fallen?"

"Lady, I will do whatever serves you best," he said. "Ask and it shall be done."

She turned him with soft hands upon his shoulders, letting their eyes see the high profile of his manhood in the fiery light.

"He is risen and shall not fall," she said.

"Let him pierce you and all will be settled," Walter said. "Can you not hurry? I grow desperate for a long draught of wine."

Avice made a squeaking sound of assent. Edward, looking askance at Avice, grumbled.

"I think you like having Avice here," Juliane said, sliding into humor, her fears fading at the soft smile in Ulrich's eyes. There was nothing of Nicholas here; he had never made her feel like this, like flying into laughter, lost in the sun upon a mountaintop.

"*I* did not choose her," he said as her hands came softly down to stroke his length. His voice ended on a groaning grunt.

"Shall I take you now?" she breathed against his chest, caressing herself against his skin. "Shall I release Walter to his wine?"

"Release me, lady," he said, running his hands down her back, pulling her hard against his cock. "What care I for Walter and his thirst? I have my own needs calling loudly to my ears."

"I am certain you do," she said, laughing and throwing her arms about him, nuzzling him with laughter and with smiles.

"Then take me, Juliane," he said, suddenly serious. "For I am yours and ever will be."

"You were slow to learn it," she said, lifting her face to him. "I did despair of you for a moment. I will confess it."

She opened her mouth to his, wanting the taste of him on her tongue. Their kiss was long and deep and full of groaning need. When he lifted his mouth from hers, she sought him out, like a blind chick seeking food, and so she felt. Blind with need and hunger for him. Wanting all he was and all he had to give her.

She pushed him to the floor, upon a wolf pelt near the darkened hearth, and straddled him, lifting her skirts to cover him. Walter, Edward, and Avice came forward and leaned over the bed, watching all, their eyes wide, caught by the sight of Juliane lowering herself upon the shaft of her husband. Though they could only guess. They could not see. Unless they could judge by the sigh upon her lips or the look of rapturous surrender upon her face.

And she had surrendered. Surrendered to passion and to love. Surrendered all false dreams of power. Nay, she had it wrong still. She simply surrendered to Ulrich. An easy falling, after all.

He gripped her about the waist and lowered her onto his shaft. She slipped easily down upon his length, taking him into her, letting him fill her up, pushing all remnants of Nicholas from her. There had been no Nicholas. There had ever and only been just this.

He held her fast, thrusting up into her, pulling her hips down hard against his thrusts. Her head fell forward, her mouth upon his throat, sucking hard at his pulsing vein. Wanting the taste of him in her mouth. Wanting to absorb him into her skin, to take him in, all in. To possess him as he possessed her.

He came fast and hard, as did she. A blinding fall from the sky that left her gasping. A hammering, throbbing fall. An invisible clutching at her heart. A binding of souls that would stand until they stood before the very judgment seat of Christ at the falling of the world.

They fell against each other, into each other, merging, blending, becoming one in heart and will and body. Healed of past wounds and old aches. Finding love. Finding each other in a dark, cold world.

"Is it done, then?" Walter asked, his voice a rasp, his face flushed.

"Aye," Ulrich gasped, his hands deep within her hair, mapping her skull, stroking her nape.

"More than your word is needed," Walter said.

"Then look, Brother, and see," Juliane said, lifting her skirts to her waist.

She was impaled upon the length of Ulrich, her thighs clasping his hips, his shaft lost in the golden tangle of her curls, gleaming wet in the timid light of a faltering candle.

"He has done it," Avice said in wonder, looking hard into their faces. "I did not think he could."

"He has done what any man could do," Edward said, taking her by the elbow and pulling her back into shadow.

"Yet Juliane is not any woman," Walter said. "Let there be no doubt."

"As you say," Ulrich said. "Let there be no doubt, now or ever."

And so saying, he lifted Juliane from him, and he was shown to be still firm and long, though not so long as he had been. He had been taken by Juliane and had stood the test of it.

"You did not fall," Walter said to Ulrich. "The marriage stands. St. Ives is yours in fief, my sister yours in all."

Edward ushered the others from the chamber before Juliane could bite out a retort. Of course Walter would see it that way, but was it not so that Juliane had taken Ulrich, making him her own?

"You have won," Ulrich said, standing and raising her to her feet, distracting her from Walter. "I did not think you had it in you."

"You did not think it in me to win?" she asked, looking him over well and proper. He was a most wonderful-looking man.

He turned her and began unlacing her, stripping her efficiently. In moments, she was as naked as he. And just as unashamed. Though when he looked at her, his face grew hard with stony anger. She looked down and saw what he saw. She was covered in bruises. Her ribs were gripped by bands of purple, her shoulders dark red with bruises in the blurry shape of fingers, and she knew her face was a mass of red. Her eyes were swollen and her vision blurred, the result of Nicholas's brutality. But did Ulrich find her so awful to look upon?

"If I had seen this, you would never have seduced me. Did I hurt you?"

"Nay, nothing you have done has ever hurt me. Can you not see that, or do you only see that the wife you have claimed is not beautiful?"

"Not beautiful?" he said, running his hand lightly across her skin, as if he would heal her with his touch. "You are more beautiful to me now than you ever were."

She melted into his embrace, twining her fingers in his dark hair, smiling as he lifted her and settled her upon their bed.

"You love me," she said, grinning up at him.

He lifted the blankets and climbed in beside her. She kicked her left foot free of covering and laughed up at him as he braced his head upon his hand and looked down at her.

"You do love me," she said again. "Come, tell me that you do."

"I love you," he said with a smile, leaning down to nip her throat and trail his mouth to her ear, licking her. "But only as much as you love me," he whispered.

She shivered and pulled him against her, reveling in the feel of his skin against hers, the smooth glide of bodies in a soft bed.

"Oh, I think you love me more than I love you," she teased, grinning as she kissed her way across his muscled chest. "I am so very lovable, after all. You loved me from the first look. Admit it."

"The first look? Lady, you are not so powerful as you think. 'Twas your hawk that had me entranced. Never have I seen such a fine, mettlesome bird," he said, lying on his back and crossing his hands beneath his head, letting her have her way with him.

"Liar," she breathed against him, her tongue flicking his navel. His stomach muscles tightened into ridges and he swallowed an audible moan. "You were lost in a mist of love from our first shared words. I could read it in your eyes. 'Tis no use denying it."

"I think you must speak of yourself, lady," he said, crossing his legs, the image of a man in repose. "You have loved me long, and fought against the power of it. 'Tis time for you to rest in love, to give in to its call, to admit how deep and strong your love for me does flow. I await, at my ease."

"At your ease?" she said, lifting herself up from him, letting her hair tickle his torso. "No man is at his ease with Juliane le Gel."

"But that name no longer suits, my love," he said, sitting up and dragging her into his arms, where she went most contentedly. "A new name must be found for you."

"I will not be called Lady Mutton. Lord Mutton suits you well enough, but for me—"

"Trust me as you love me," he whispered, stroking her hair, kissing her on the sensitive corners of her mouth. "This name you will enjoy."

"You must think I love you very much," she said, raking her fingernails down his belly.

"Only as much as I love you," he said, catching her hand in his own and holding her still against him.

"That much?" she said, grinning.

"That much," he said, his grin a perfect match to her own.

A perfect pairing they made together, and it was only to be expected that they knew it.

Below, the watchers in the vast hall of Stanora observed with open mouths as first Edward, then Avice, and finally Walter left Juliane's chamber, closing the door firmly behind them.

"What do you think happened? Is it over?" Christine said to the hall at large.

"It is over, whatever happened," Marguerite said. "I do not think we should be standing here gaping. 'Tis not proper deportment."

"Go on, then. I will tell you later what occurred," Christine said.

"He has won her," Maud said softly.

"What? How can you tell?" Marguerite asked.

"Look at their faces," Maud answered. "They did not expect this."

"Look at Edward's face," Lunete said. "*He* expected it."

"Aye, 'tis so," Maud said on a sigh. It was over and she had not played Juliane false. She was free to enter the abbey and would not be handed over in marriage. She sat down suddenly with the relief of it.

"I wonder how Juliane's face will look," Christine said.

"Not disappointed," came a voice from across the hall. "You can wager any and all on that."

They turned. They knew that voice well. 'Twas Roger, with William at his side, and at his back a tall, handsome man of dark and curling hair who carried in his arms a toddling boy of sultry beauty.

Lunete ran across the wide hall to William and took his hands within her own. "You are returned! I was afraid . . ." she stammered, blushing. "I thought never to see you again."

"I only went to find my father," William said, "and so I have. This is he, William le Brouillard of Greneforde, and about his neck, the son of Ulrich, young Olivier."

"But it was thought," Maud said, after the ladies had bowed their welcome to Lord William, "that Roger was in league with Conor, that Squire William's very life was forfeit."

"It was thought?" Roger said in outrage. "I will wager all I own that Ulrich did not think it."

"Nay, he did not," Lunete said, releasing William's hands and looking up at Lord William. Who had not heard of him? The folds of his scarlet cloak flowed about him like streams of silken water, his raw masculine beauty of such strength as to rob a soul of breath.

"Where is Ulrich?" William le Brouillard asked, clasping the squirming boy about the waist and holding him like a bundle beneath his mighty arm. "And where is Walter of Stanora? I have words to speak to both of them."

"I am Walter," Walter said, coming from out of the dark tunnel of the stair, Edward and Avice trailing behind him as they entered the open hall. A fire had been lit, and all within were cast in glowing shades of yellow and gold as the fire took breath and soared upward. "Who wishes words with me?"

"William le Brouillard of Greneforde," William said stiffly. "My son had hard welcome here and would have met a death most foul if not for poor choosing in accomplices."

"Lord William," Walter said, trying to control his flush of embarrassment before this older, more warlike man, "that was not of my doing and done when my father still ruled Stanora. None here would harm your son."

"Yet it was not my son who was the intended target," William said. "'Twas the boy here in my arms, who struggles even now to find his father's embrace. Where is Conor, the author of the act? I would have my pleasure of him."

"Dead," Walter said with some apparent gladness that he could say it. This man was formidable. "Killed by Ulrich's hand for daring so."

William grunted and nodded in what appeared to be disappointment. He set Olivier down on the floor, whereupon the boy tried to find his feet by holding fast to Lord William's knees and wobbling ferociously.

"And where is Ulrich?" Lord William asked.

"Upon his marriage bed, I would wager, my lord, and finding good pleasure there," Roger answered softly.

"Is that so?" William asked Walter. "He is wed?"

"Aye, and to my sister," Walter answered readily and with great gladness in the face of such stern justice. "They even now consummate their vows."

"You gave him to your sister, he who had killed your uncle?" William said. "Strong doing. That took some mettle upon your part. And who is your sister? She is worthy of him? For I hold Ulrich in no small measure. He is like a son to me, and so my son was entrusted well into his care, and his son into mine. A tangled and strong bond we have forged between us. I would have him well served in the matter of his marriage."

"My sister is Juliane le Gel. You may have heard of her," Walter said with some pride of his own. Greneforde was not the only holding that had its share of legends.

"He took le Gel?" William said, his gray eyes wide with surprise and then with mirth. He burst out laughing, knocking Olivier from his wobbly perch. The child then crawled on both hands, one knee, and one foot toward the beckoning fire. "That is good taking. If any man could, it would be Ulrich. They are truly wed?" he asked, chuckling hard.

"Aye, well and truly," Walter answered.

"Then I have no quarrel here," William said as his son scooped Olivier up and away from the fire, to the boy's vast and noisy disapproval. "Conor is dead and Ulrich well rewarded for his valor. Am I a welcome guest within Stanora, Lord Walter? Or would you toss me from your hall?" William asked, as if any man could toss him anywhere.

"You are very welcome in my hall," Walter said with some dignity now that the matter of vengeance had passed.

With both dignity and good humor, William walked at Walter's side to the high table, which had been hurriedly prepared while they wrangled and now was being spread with cloths of sparkling white and jugs of wine, platters of cheese, and trenchers of bread. For William le Brouillard's welcome, there would be no stinting.

"But I thought you were in league with Conor," Marguerite whispered to Roger.

"Nay, and Ulrich would put no faith upon such thought," Roger answered. "We are bound by chosen brotherhood, bastards finding family in each other. My honor and my heart lie always with him and for him, as with Edward. We are bound by love, though we do not often speak of it. Still, 'tis the foundation of our lives, and nothing may break it."

"How did you fare with the good priest of Stanora?" Edward said, coming into their circle of conversation.

"Well," Roger answered him. "All is well there, as it should be."

He would say nothing more now, but they would speak of it in the privacy of their ride from Stanora, when they could talk freely of the duty set upon them by the king. Of traitors to King Henry they'd been sent to flush from cover. Of Stanora's priest, who in heart sided with Becket but who in practice would not step outside the law. All was well in Stanora, and Matthew could keep his quiet place there. Hearts would not be judged when acts did not follow.

"But what happened between Juliane and Ulrich while I was off?" Roger said. "I think I must have missed good wagering there. They are wed, truly and in all?"

"Aye, most truly," Edward said.

"I wish I had seen that," Roger said with a gleam in his eye.

"Nay, 'twas not meant for seeing," Edward said, whereupon Roger lifted his head like a hound who has caught the scent.

"You *saw*! You saw it done!"

Edward turned and looked at Avice, who turned and looked at the fire. Maud had drifted off, a serene smile on her face. Young William and Lunete chased after Olivier in his scrambling dance toward the ever beguiling fire. Marguerite looked down at her hem, a look of reserved dignity painted most determinedly upon her milk-white face, while Christine smiled and coughed and looked all about the hall, upon everything but Roger's face.

"What happened?" Roger begged. "Were any wagers won?"

"'Twas not a thing for wagering," Edward said.

"Not a thing for wagering?" Roger said. "*Anything* may be wagered. 'Tis the meat of life."

"Yet not this," Edward said, leaving the branding heat of the fire, his hair caught in sparks of gold, his eyes gleaming golden in the dim light before he disappeared in purple shadow within the wide hall.

Avice turned again to watch him leave, and then, turning, left the fire to circle wide the place where Edward was, leaving him to his shadows as she found her own to hide herself within.

Roger watched her, watched Edward, watched their careful distance and felt the ripples of heat that authored it. And then he said, his eyes alight, "Then who will take up another wager with me, since the matter of Juliane and Ulrich is done?"

"What wager?" Christine asked, looking at him directly again.

"A wager concerning Avice and her betrothed."

"Arthur?" Marguerite said. "What wager in that? They are to speak their vows within the month."

"Shall we wager on it?" Roger said, grinning.

The Legend

And so it was that he came to her, bearing a legend of his own, burnished bright and hard through years of telling.

Tremble she did not, for was she not the Lady of the Frost? No man could warm her, and so she stood well within her tale, secure in the foretelling of her victory. He would fall, as did they all, and so she would remain, standing firm and hard and cold as men fell against her, frozen by her name.

They came together, the two of them, each certain of the winning. Each striving in confident ease to protect the gloss of legend.

Yet one must fall.

Yet one must ever fall.

And so it was that they strove together upon a summer's heat, her hawk upon her arm, his hand upon his shield. Many battles they endured, hawk finding blood, warrior melting ice, until upon the Eve of Lammas all battling did cease.

Of what occurred they never told and banned all telling. Of legends they had swallowed full and would suffer them no more.

Yet of such a pair, could legends ever die?

And so it was that this tale was born upon the death of tales.

And so it is that he is known as being leashed by love as she is warmed by wolf.

He wears a braided chain of her golden hair clasped tight about his throat, a heavy length of hair she once did cut to prize herself from his hand in one of their battles rare.

Yet she is marked and branded by much the same as he, for she wears a dark blue cloak banded wide with a black wolf pelt, a killing she did see. Warmed by wolf, she says, and smiles when she does speak.

And so she calls him Lord Wolf and he names her Lady Hawk for the bird she never is without. And he is Wolf, for ever does he run beside her in wild defense of her. They are a pair to match their tale, though they would hear no telling.

And so I close my teeth against my tongue, stilling all fair tales. I would not wound this pair, the joining of hawk to wolf, a pair most rightly made.

Yet might I tell a tale of the sister of The Frost, she who is called The Flame? She has a long tale of her own and does not ban its telling.

She was set upon her marriage path, her name not yet smoke, yet a man of golden sparks did capture her heart setting them both to fire.

She never followed that path to her betrothed, finding joy in flame.

Yet not that tale? Then let me find another. For what is an autumn night without a tale to mark it?

CLAUDIA DAIN
DEE DAVIS
EVELYN ROGERS

SILENT NIGHT

Snow falls, but this is no ordinary white Christmas. There's no festive cheer, no carolers, no mistletoe. Three women are running for their lives: a college student home on break, the wife of a murdered DEA agent, a Denver widow. They're frightened and alone.

And Lindsay Gray, Jenny Fitzgerald and Tessa Hampton *are* in peril. A desperate snowmobile chase through the forest; a raspy, anonymous telephone call; a bloody stranger by the side of the road—every step seems to lead farther from safety . . . but toward what? Who waits in the darkness? Friends? Lovers? And on a cold, silent night, when do you call for help?
